maya

माया

A Novel

C. W. Huntington, Jr.

Wisdom

Wisdom Publications
199 Elm Street
Somerville, MA 02144 USA
www.wisdompubs.org

Library of Congress Cataloging-in-Publication Data
Huntington, C. W.
 Maya : a novel / C. W. Huntington.
   pages ; cm
 ISBN 1-61429-198-5 (softcover)
 1. Fulbright scholars—Fiction. 2. American—India—Fiction. 3. India—History—20th century—Fiction. I. Title.
 PS3608.U594968M39 2015
 813'.6—dc23

                          2014044814

ISBN 978-1-61429-198-5   ebook ISBN 978-1-61429-215-9

19 18 17 16 15
5 4 3 2 1

Cover design by Phil Pascuzzo.
Interior design by Gopa&Ted2. Set in Janson Text LT Std 10/13.78.
Author photos courtesy of Samuel L. Huntington.

For Liz

Māyā, (f.) art, wisdom, extraordinary or supernatural
power, illusion, unreality, deception, fraud,
trick, sorcery, witchcraft, magic.
—MONIER-WILLIAMS,
Sanskrit-English Dictionary

What prevents you from knowing yourself as all
and beyond all is the mind based on memory.
It has power over you as long as you trust it.
—NISARGADATTA MAHARAJ

PROLOGUE

BEGINNING SOMETIME after 1962, when Allen Ginsberg made his legendary pilgrimage to India, the city of Banaras became the home for a sizeable community of expatriates bound together not only by their shared fascination with South Asian culture but also by the fact that they represented an alien presence in a society that had historically reacted to outsiders with distinct ambiguity. It was, in many ways, a magical time, the temporary conjunction of unstable forces. In 1984, after the assassination of his mother, Rajiv Gandhi enacted much stricter visa regulations, ostensibly in an attempt to regulate the entry of foreigners supporting Sikh terrorists in the Punjab. Since then, the Westerner in India is much more likely to be either a tourist or a professional whose time there is precisely circumscribed, either in its duration or its purpose.

Things have changed a great deal since the days when young people from Europe and North America journeyed overland on the Magic Bus through Baghdad, Tehran, and Kabul, eventually settling in the mountains outside Manali or Dharamsala, or among the twisting alleyways of Banaras, where we could live out solipsistic fantasies of worldly or spiritual power without any fear of being ridiculed or called to account for ourselves by family and friends left behind.

I have never understood whether we remained in India during those years because we were afflicted with the spiritual malaise of our own time and place, or if our unquenchable thirst for South Asian philosophy, religion, music, and art were engendered by the force of the local environment. Whatever the case, expatriates living in Banaras during the sixties and seventies were *mlecchas*, foreigners occupying the no man's land that was neither Western in any recognizable form nor truly Asian. We took possession of India's ancient culture and made it our own, as if by right of birth. At the same time, Indian family life, her feudal politics, and above all the complex hierarchy of social relationships known as caste, were for us so remote as to be virtually nonexistent.

No one, however, could avoid the omnipresent poverty. One had, at the very least, to chew and swallow one's chapati in company with the shrunken frames and hollow eyes of human beings and animals that roamed the Holy City like a silent army of hungry ghosts. One was compelled to bear witness. How each of us accomplished this disheartening task was, in some sense, a matter of style.

The joys of everyday life are not easily dismissed, even though they come bracketed in sorrow. And yet, the constant vacillation between pain and pleasure can wear thin. At one time or another everyone dreams of escape. This is the record of such a dream.

1

I WOKE TO THE TOUCH of her fingers moving up the inside of my thigh. She was leaning over me, the sheets thrown back, one arm tucked under my shoulder, her breasts resting heavily against my bare chest. For a moment I thought it was Judith. Then I turned—drifted really, still half asleep, my eyes closed—and pulled her closer, not caring. I felt her lips brush my ear, her breath, her mouth pressed against mine, the long muscle of her tongue . . .

What the fuck am I doing?

But it was obviously too late for such a question.

And anyway, I already knew the answer, only too well: *You wanted out. That's why you didn't care then—not enough, anyway—and that's why you're here, now, alone.*

I leaned over and pressed my forehead against the oval glass, straining to see, my eyes burning from lack of sleep. Shadowy wisps of gray streaked by the window against a background of formless light. My jaw swiveled side to side and I felt my ears pop. The metal body of the Boeing 747 shuddered, rolling the sweep of its wings ever so slightly, first one way, then the other, as Pan Am flight 101 from Chicago, via London and Tehran, descended on the Indo-Gangetic plain through a dense morning fog. The haze lifted only moments before the plane's wheels squealed against the concrete runway. We taxied to a stop a good hundred yards from the main terminal.

In those days at Palam Airport in New Delhi, no enclosed walkways connected aircraft to the terminal; passengers had to disembark down a flight of stairs directly onto the tarmac. While I waited, packed into the aisle with what seemed like one enormous extended Indian family, everyone wrestling with their carry-on luggage and yelling to each other in Hindi, the door of the plane was ceremoniously unbolted and drawn back like an iron gate opening directly onto the vast temple of South Asia. An invisible, viscous odor poured into the cabin, enveloping me in its spell: sandalwood and shit, mango, jasmine, and diesel exhaust, valerian and turmeric and smoking patties of dried cow dung, chili and asafetida, tamarind, musk, saffron and coriander, burning tires and burning human flesh and hair, cumin seeds sizzling in mustard oil, rotting vegetables and dried urine, ginger and anise and holy basil—leaves of Tulsi—sacred to the great god Vishnu. This potent, beatific fragrance was the traveler's first encounter with the subcontinent, one that lodged itself in my memory with a peculiar force. To this day, I have only to open any old edition of a Sanskrit text published in India, bury my nose deep among the pages, and I am poised, all over again, at the doorway of Pan Am flight 101, about to step down the stairs.

I landed in the early morning of June 26, 1975, approximately six hours before Prime Minister Indira Gandhi's terse announcement was broadcast to the nation over All India Radio: "The president has declared a state of emergency. There is no need to panic." By the time I got through airport customs, the police had already been deployed throughout New Delhi and across the country, making precautionary arrests of Gandhi's political opponents, many of them future leaders of the Janata Party, whom she had labeled "dupes of foreign governments and ideas hostile to India."

The Fulbright office dispatched a wonderfully round, black Ambassador car to meet me at the airport and bring me to the Lodi Hotel, where I checked in and went straight to my room. The heavy drapes were drawn and an air-conditioner droned in the darkness. Everything smelled vaguely of mildew. A bucket and tap in the bathroom sat next to the twin-footpads of the Indian toilet. I ladled cold water over my naked body with a plastic cup, toweled myself dry, and collapsed onto the bed. I vaguely recall ordering some food that was brought to the room, but my next distinct memory is waking to a ringing phone and the almost unintelligible Indian accent of the desk clerk asking me to hold for a call.

Indira Gandhi was deeply paranoid of the CIA, and it was not the ideal moment for an American scholar to arrive in India. No one knew what was coming next. The Fulbright people took all of this very seriously; they wanted me away from the capital, where I might inadvertently get swept up in the erupting protests. I had planned to spend my first few months studying Hindi with a tutor at Delhi University, but arrangements had been hastily made to shift my operations to the Central Hindi Institute in Agra—the Kendriya Hindi Sansthan—an arm of the Ministry of Education intended "to facilitate such courses as are conducive to the development and propagation of Hindi as an all-India language as envisaged in article 351 of the constitution." There I would attend classes with non-Hindi speaking students from various locales around India and a handful of other foreigners. The person on the phone said they would send a car within the hour.

"Please wait near the front of the hotel, Mr. Harrington."

Less than twenty-four hours in India, and things had already taken on a life of their own.

I quickly rinsed off again, got dressed, and ate a small breakfast—an omelet, toast and jam, and a pot of tea delivered to my room on a silver tray by a waiter in a knee-length white linen tunic, scarlet sash, and turban. Moments later I was outside the hotel lobby, cowering in a patch of shade, waiting for the car to arrive. The heat was suffocating, the air so dry it was impossible to sweat. High overhead, iridescent, jet-black birds circled and dipped against a cloudless sky, calling out to each other in a desolate, throaty snarl that struck me as utterly foreign until I realized, with a start, that it was nothing but a flock of crows.

2

MAHMUD, MY CHAUFFEUR for the trip from Delhi to Agra, was a polite young Muslim who spoke no English. Though I had memorized a great deal of Hindi grammar and vocabulary in my classes at Chicago, I could barely manage to get a word out of my mouth. For the first hour or so, the two of us struggled to communicate in a variety of creative ways until we gave up and I retreated into a corner of the Ambassador's back seat, peering out the window as rural India presented itself to me for the first time. On either side of the road, hard red earth dotted by scrub brush and gnarly, parched trees stretched to the horizon. Now and again we passed a cluster of earthen houses hunkered down around a single ancient tree, where oxen and water buffalo rested in the shade. A woman in a sari moved languidly along the narrow pathway that led to an open well, a polished brass vessel balanced on her head.

About halfway to Agra we stopped briefly in the small town of Hodal. While Mahmud bought chai, I sat on a wooden bench under a great banyan tree with roots dropping all around me like stalactites. He returned with a steaming clay cup the size of a shot glass, smelling of cardamom and black pepper, and offered it to me with a smile and one of his narrow, hand-rolled cigarettes. I don't smoke, but I accepted his gift. As we sat together in silence, puffing on our bidis and sipping tea, a camel plodded along the road slowly lifting and dropping its spongy feet. On its back rested a colossal burden of emerald sugarcane stalks. A man wearing only a loincloth straddled the beast's neck. He waved to us from his perch.

We entered Agra in the early evening and the city of the Taj crowded around us, engulfing the Ambassador in a tumult of bicycles and rickshaws. Monkeys ran like squirrels along the edge of the rooftops. Humpbacked cows wandered everywhere, grazing on refuse.

Until that moment, all I had known about Agra came from history books. Tucked in the backseat, examining the details of life outside the car, I felt the pages of those books filling in the unseen dimensions of the street around us. Sikandar Lodi, one of the sultans of Delhi, founded the city in 1506, but its ancient past is, as they say, shrouded in the mists of time. The Lodi dynasty was conquered by Babur in 1526, and from then on Agra was governed by a succession of Mughal rulers, the most famous of which is Shah Jahan. In the middle of the seventeenth century, he built the Taj Mahal as a tomb for his beloved wife, who had died giving birth to their fourteenth child. As the shah grieved, artisans were recruited from Bukhara, Syria, and Persia. Marble was quarried in Rajasthan, turquoise transported from Tibet, crystal from China. From Sri Lanka came sapphire, from Afghanistan lapis lazuli, carnelian from Arabia. Over a thousand elephants and twenty times that many workers contributed their labor to the construction of the Taj—a monument to matrimonial devotion, and a monumental reproach to those of us who have not loved so well.

For a short time, Agra was the capital of what was likely the greatest empire of its day. Then the center of political power shifted north, and the city began its inevitable descent into obscurity. It took centuries, though, to make the transformation from a cultural metropolis to the hard-edged working-class city it was when our car, horn blaring, pushed its way into the narrow streets through a haze of exhaust and of smoke from the smoldering dung over which the city's denizens were preparing their evening meals.

Our path eventually led to an obviously affluent neighborhood. Rows of one-story stucco houses lined the unpaved street where pigs and feral dogs scavenged among heaps of garbage. Mahmud stopped the car in front of a brick wall bristling with the jagged edges of broken bottles that had been upended and driven, neck down, into a layer of mortar. He took my bag from the trunk and walked with me through an ornate iron gate into a small courtyard. We said goodbye to each other—Mahmud bowed slightly and saluted, then turned and walked back through the gate. I watched him start the car and drive away.

The Fulbright office had arranged for accommodations with two other students from the institute: Ajay, a government employee from Madras, and Alain, a postdoc from the Sorbonne doing research in Political Science. There was a chaukidar—a sort of guard—who appeared to come with the house. He dressed in wrinkled khaki and passed most of every day lounging by the gate, sipping chai and smoking. One morning on my way out to class I found him on his hands and knees, just outside our front door, carefully spreading a spoonful of sugar on the porch. When I asked him, summoning my best Hindi, what he was doing, he told me he was feeding the ants. It apparently had something to do with a vow he had made to a local deity.

A few days after my arrival I met Mickey, a twenty-two-year-old from South Boston. Raised Catholic, he had taken robes in Thailand and lived as a Buddhist monk before drifting to India, where he'd been for almost two years now. I was on my way to purchase an aerogramme, and there he was, just outside the post office, fiddling with the rusty lock on his bike. Lanky and muscular, with tawny, short hair, his clear blue eyes the color of the Indian sky. He looked up at me and dusted off his hands. "Hey man, you got a bidi?" Just as if we were old friends. His white kurta-pajama gleamed in the morning sunlight, its creases neatly pressed.

I was attracted to Mickey immediately. He appeared totally self-contained, profoundly comfortable in India. His Hindi was fluent, and he seemed to be expert in living on almost nothing. We hit it off right away, in part because of a shared interest in meditation. He had a room on the second floor of a crumbling red sandstone building, the men's dormitory for Agra College, where he was studying Mughal miniature painting and vocal music. My memories of his room are infested with the whining of mosquitoes that feasted with impunity on our sweating bodies as we sat motionless, legs crossed, on the floor. Everything Mick owned fit neatly on one shelf of his almari, and those belongings included neither a mosquito net nor a fan. It irritated me that he appeared so oblivious to the insects and the heat.

One evening, he managed to fall asleep with his legs wrapped in a full lotus posture. Who knows how long he was sitting there, silently dozing, before gradually folding, little by little, until he toppled forward, his forehead descending in a graceful arc directly onto the point crowning the brass Buddha in his makeshift altar. My attention was so intently focused on the mosquitoes that I literally bounced in terror at his cry. For days afterward he had an ugly wound just over his third eye.

I had some idea that to do anything to escape the droves of mosquitoes would amount to an admission of weakness. If Mick could deal with the discomfort, so could I. Having only been in India a short time, I was just beginning to discover the limits of my willingness to do without the amenities of life in the West. For a middle-class American graduate student who had become rather proud of his sparse material existence, life in India presented a series of increasingly uncomfortable challenges.

Mickey's Theravadin monkishness set a high bar, but it was nothing compared to the gentle fanaticism of my Marxist housemate, Alain. He shunned cold drinks of all kinds, including the fresh lime sodas that I craved. Not only this, he shrugged off, as an unnecessary luxury, the ubiquitous boiled mixture of tea leaves, milk, and sugar consumed by everyone from Indira Gandhi to the leprous beggar who sipped his chai from a dented bowl clamped between two stumps.

I could not see the point in denying myself these cheap and delicious treats that seemed an essential element of life in India. Nor, in the context of Agra and its poverty, could I take such things for granted. I learned how to savor a two-rupee soda, to give myself over to the luxury of the refrigerated bottle as it rested against my lips, the icy bubbles foaming over my tongue, chilling my teeth and throat, sending up lime-flavored balloons of carbonated air from a thoroughly bourgeois stomach with no greater concern than its own sensual pleasure.

This troubled me. I had come to India not only to do research for my dissertation but also on a sort of ill-defined spiritual quest, which I equated, in part, with the ancient path of renunciation traversed by the Buddha and other great Indian saints and yogis. I wanted to strip off everything inessential until I reached the core, to discover my true self by peeling away, like the layers of an onion, everything I did not really need: *Not me, not mine.*

As it turned out, the discomforts and difficulties involved in just getting through each stifling day in Agra were my salvation. They absorbed my attention, diverting it from another, more fundamental problem. A loss I had not anticipated. A loss I could not affirm. Originally this journey to India was to have been an adventure shared with my wife, Judith. In the weeks preceding my departure things had not gone as planned. Things had not gone well at all. What had happened? How could two people fail so miserably to nourish their hearts' desire? How could we have hurt each other so badly? I asked myself these questions frequently during those first days and weeks in Agra, when the borderline between reality and dream began to erode.

Reality: Judith had never really wanted to come on this trip.

She was an artist, a sculptor whose stylish metal contraptions were built from the detritus of American industry, most of it scavenged from junk-yards around Chicago. She worked out of a warehouse filled with tanks of oxyacetylene and propane, hoses and torches and grinders and impact wrenches, an arsenal of demolition equipment and a one-ton chain-fall hoist she used to move stuff around. What was she supposed to do in India without the tools of her trade? To make matters worse, she'd have to pay rent on the studio the whole time we were gone.

Once I received the Fulbright she had grudgingly acquiesced, step by step, as the signs of our imminent departure accumulated. In the beginning I might have returned the fellowship had she asked me to, though in all likelihood I would have been incapable of doing this without becoming so bitter it would have destroyed the marriage. One always wonders how much of oneself can be given over to a relationship before there is no self left to relate. No doubt Judith was wrestling with some variation of this same conundrum.

Reality: I fucked up.

Or I should perhaps say that I established an unfortunate precedent when, a month before we were scheduled to leave for India, I allowed our friend, with whom we shared a large apartment on East 53rd Street, to slide into bed beside me. This friend of ours was the quintessential earth mother who loved gardening and baking bread. She was a woman who identified strongly, as I discovered, with her sensual appetites. While Judith socialized over brunch, I lay back and let her work me with her hands like a lump of warm dough, rising at her touch.

Reality: I confessed to Judith, naively assuming that our marriage would survive a single indiscretion. Hadn't we talked endlessly about free love? Wasn't *everyone* talking endlessly about free love?

Judith freaked out. Our friend's husband—a graduate student writing his dissertation in economics—moved out. That left just the three of us. The weeks that followed were what you might call tense. Judith and I argued constantly.

The whole thing climaxed at a party I threw for graduate school friends and faculty. I knew I was in for trouble when Judith started drinking early. Jack Daniels on ice. No water. By the time the guests arrived, she was plastered. One of her friends brought along a joint of Thai stick, which didn't help.

I was in the kitchen talking with Abe Sellars, my academic advisor, when someone came in and told me I might want to go outside and see if

Judith was okay. *Outside??* I bolted downstairs, through the small lobby, and out the front door. When I caught up with her, she was standing in the middle of the street in her party dress, consumed with rage, her eyes blazing in the head lights of passing cars. "Fuck her again!" she shrieked, loud enough for the entire neighborhood to hear. "She wants you! She needs you! She's waiting for you up there, right now, in our bed!"

Among the guests who viewed this spectacle from the box seat of our balcony, I noted Sellars up there sipping his scotch, gazing down like some Olympian deity on me and my sorry life.

Reality: Despite all of this I was nevertheless caught by surprise when, only a few days before our scheduled departure, Judith went off to her studio to work late and didn't return until the next morning, at which time she announced that she hadn't really been working at all. She had spent the night with Bruce Wilkins. Wilkins was a friend of hers who played drums in a proto-metal band called the Roto-Rockers. A guy I barely knew, apart from the few times Judith and I had gone to hear him play at a bar. She had, furthermore, decided she was not going to India with me. She would come along later. On her own. When will you come? I asked. Later, was all she would say, when I've had time to think.

Dream: That she would write telling me to meet her at the airport in Delhi.

Reality and dream: The interminable nights when I would drift in and out of consciousness, waking in a soggy pool of sweat overwhelmed with the sheer strangeness of being in bed alone, of having lost this woman without whom, I now saw, I could not survive.

Yes, I wanted to learn to do without, to escape the confines of my life in Chicago, and god knows I had imagined often enough what it would be like to be on my own again, free to pursue my spiritual aspirations. But no matter how much I tortured both of us with such fantasies, losing Judith wasn't part of the master plan. I reached out in my sleep for the familiar curves of her body. Or was I actually awake in the alien heat, listening to the demented braying of some wretched, brutalized donkey? The threshold between sleep and waking was easily dissolved by a thousand unfamiliar sounds, or by the absence of sound, as when the electricity failed and the ceiling fan coasted to a stop, the reassuring chop of the blades giving way to a dreadful silence that would pry its way into my dreams, rousing me with a start.

If the loneliness in my room was unbearable, the black expanse of the

South Asian night was worse. Just outside the iron bars of my open window lay the tangled alleyways of Agra, a world that belonged, after dark, to the same disease-ridden dogs that cowered during the daylight hours, avoiding all human contact. Out in the shadows they fought each other and copulated and filled the air with their hungry, mournful cries.

Following hours of semiconscious torment, I would fall into a heavy, narcotic sleep that inevitably gave way to the first dim light of day and the rhythmic crunching of termites. The frame and legs of my charpoy were perforated with their holes. My initial sensation every morning was of an invisible weight of damp air and misery pressing my body down into the ropes that crisscrossed the bed. The small space inside the mosquito net smelled of hemp, cotton, and wood. In those first moments of consciousness, I succumbed all over again to the pull of debilitating sadness, a manic exchange of voices, an argument I could not win . . .

> *Judith is gone.*
> *Be still.*
> *You did it.*
> *Be*
> *still.*
> *You pushed her away.*
> *I loved her.*
> *You feared her.*
> *You wanted out.*
> *I wanted only . . .*
> *What?*
> *I wanted . . .*
> *What did you want?*
> *. . . to find*
> *myself.*
> *So find yourself,*
> *you*
> *stupid*
> *son of a bitch.*

I was caught off guard by the intensity of my reaction to the sudden collapse of our marriage, dismayed at the realization of how deeply my identity was bound up in our relationship. I had imagined myself to be much stronger than I obviously was, much more independent. But now the voices in my head showed me otherwise. They bled into a compulsive undertone that lacked any center of gravity, revealing only this one great discovery: without Judith I was lost.

Every morning I had to command myself to sit up under the net, cross my legs, and attend to the cycle of respiration that carried me through the next hour and into another day. I talked myself down, felt my lungs expand and compress. The minutes dragged on until, eventually, I found some degree of stillness suspended on an anxious tightrope of breath.

As morning crept into afternoon, afternoon to evening, all over again the pain crystallized into images of our final days together. I rehearsed every detail of those last few weeks, the arguments and accusations, angry words driven into each other's hearts like the shards of glass embedded on the wall outside my room. I wanted to believe she would come. I fought to convince myself that I did not need her to come. I willed myself to forget. I waited, every day, for letters that did not arrive. I had no idea that mail often took two weeks or more to make the trip from Agra to the States, and at least two more to return. As far as I knew there was no international phone service of any kind in Agra, a city where it was hard enough to find a refrigerator.

Passing through the tunnel of my loss, I emerged in a world far removed from anything I had encountered in my previous life. One after another, habitual patterns of thinking—of believing—gave way under a barrage of sensations, a reality so starkly foreign, so saturated with extremes of beauty and horror, that it simply could not be reconciled with memory or expectation. The effort to escape my anguish pushed me ever deeper into the texture of unfamiliar sounds and colors and smells. Driven by my need to forget the past, I threw myself into experiences that were only slightly less disturbing than the images I longed to repress. My white skin, my wealth, the very fact of my existence in this place was reflected back to me in a mirror of incomprehensible poverty and disease. Sensing my weakness, the beggars engulfed me, shoving battered tin bowls up toward my face. I flung coins into their outstretched hands until my pockets were empty, then retreated to the safety of my room and hid behind the bars that covered my window.

There were two men who passed by my house every evening just at dusk. One of them, a leper whose hands and feet had rotted away, rode on a crude wooden cart—really nothing more than a few boards strung together over four pitted iron wheels. He lurched past my window swaddled in grimy rags, propped upright and pushed along on his miserable journey by another emaciated man only slightly less disfigured. The fellow on the cart sang the same enchanting bhajan every evening, so predictable that I waited for his voice as a signal to close my books and prepare for meditation. The melody could be heard from some distance off, weaving through the streets above the laughter of children playing, the cries of vendors peddling samosas and chutney and chai, the voices of goats and cows and water buffalo, the shrill whistle of a steam locomotive. It was a love song to God, a song so sublimely beautiful that, sitting at my desk, listening, for those few moments every day I could almost imagine a way out of my pain.

3

THERE IS A PASSAGE in the Pali suttas, among the earliest of Buddhist scriptures, where the Buddha observes that in direct, first-person experience—which is all we ever really have—"mind" and "matter" are inseparable:

> Within this fathom-long body, O monks, equipped with thought and the other senses and sense objects, I declare to you is the world, the origin of the world, and also the cessation of the world.

This may seem like an abstruse philosophical claim, but it's quite obviously true. Looking back, for example, I can see that in Agra a corner was irrevocably turned. Like the young prince Siddhartha, I found myself outside the palace, in a new body and a new world, where nothing was quite the same as it had been and everything was unsettling.

It was during those first weeks after my arrival in India that I began the task of acclimating myself to an unceasing parade of discomforts and petty inconveniences. I learned to appreciate electricity when it was available and to stay calm when the ceiling fan died, leaving me drenched in sweat that ran down my face and fell in salty drops onto my books and papers. I conditioned myself to approach the tap with no fixed expectation, to store buckets of water for bathing, to lay in a supply of candles, to apply extra glue on my aerogrammes and postage stamps, to ask directions from several different people and to believe nothing they said. I practiced striking the spindly Indian matches at a particular angle so they wouldn't snap in my fingers. I struggled to cultivate equanimity while jockeying for a place in the unruly crowd at the post office, at the train and bus stations, at the bank.

Any counter, every public office or shop, was always crowded, no matter what time of day I arrived. I recall one occasion when, after patiently allowing myself to be elbowed, squeezed, stepped on, pressed, and shoved for an hour while waiting to buy a train ticket, my "turn" finally arrived. As I approached the window the clerk informed me, in the most offhand manner, that I needed to go to window number 5, immediately adjacent to his own, where I would have to pick up a form that he himself was not authorized to issue and, bearing that form, return to him, at which time he could sell me the ticket. This meant at least another hour in the train station. When he finished speaking I struggled to find a Hindi vocabulary sufficient to express the profundity of my disbelief.

"Aap ne kyaa kahaa? What did you say?"

But he was no longer looking at me. He appeared to have forgotten me entirely. He turned to receive a glass of chai handed to him by the friend operating window number 5. From where I was standing I could easily see what looked like a stack of blank forms just out of his reach, to the left of the agent who handed him the glass. I forged another sentence in Hindi, carefully crafting the delicate syntax and a tricky use of the causative form of the verb, rehearsing it once in my mind before attempting to speak.

"Can't you have *him* give you a form?"

He sipped at his glass of chai, then set it down in a space painstakingly cleared at the side of a stack of battered ledgers. He examined the book in front of him. He rearranged the narrow vertical columns of tickets that lined a wooden dispenser. Eventually he glanced up and seemed to be surprised to discover me still out there, clutching with both hands at the bars that separated us.

"My dear sir . . ." The English words were brimming with wearied condescension, as if they were heavy objects that had to be carefully hoisted up from somewhere far below. "What is the problem? I am not making the rules. You will please collect necessary form and return to this window. If you are having some problem, please . . . you go and fill out complaint form at window number 8."

"Why isn't it posted?" I gave up and spoke English, no longer willing to struggle with Hindi. My voice shook. I was straining to be polite. "I waited over an hour to get here. Please, just this once, have your friend there give you the form." I was pleading, shameless, and prepared to do anything to get that form. "*Please* . . ."

He was immersed once again in the same enormous record book. I did not exist.

The man is a total asshole. I hate him.

I told myself to be patient. I reined in my anger and extracted myself from the rabble that had all the while been smashing me against the stone counter. Resigned to the worst, I shuffled over and inserted my body into the morass of other bodies pressing around window 5. After what seemed like forever I returned with the required form and endured the same process of fighting and shoving. At last I found myself once again at window 4, just in time to see the ticket seller slam a *Closed* sign in my face, turn his back, and walk away. The window was shut down—for an hour, for the rest of the day, perhaps for all eternity. One could not know. In India, as I was discovering, some things simply cannot be known.

I slammed my palms against the bars in a display of impotent rage, aware now that I was drawing undue attention to myself, aware that I, the foreigner, appeared to have lost my mind while everyone else around me remained strangely unaffected.

There was much to learn in this India, a place altogether unlike the intensely philosophical India so familiar to me from reading Sanskrit texts in seminars at Chicago, or the India captured in the serene black-and-white photos of temples in Heinrich Zimmer's *Art of Indian Asia*, a book I owned and loved.

Among the people I met during those first few weeks in Agra, I remember one of my teachers in particular. Ashok Mishra, an instructor in modern Hindi literature, befriended me early on. In his midthirties, he was frail and meticulously groomed, with a closely trimmed black beard. As a graduate student, Ashok had studied for a year at Oxford, and it had completely destroyed him; he was obsessed with only one thing—his longing to return to England.

He had a goddess for a wife and a little boy who looked like a miniature prince from the pages of the *Arabian Nights*. Evidently neither his wife nor the child brought him any happiness. On the occasions of my evening visits, the two of them, mother and child, sat side by side in silence, observing us from across the narrow room with liquid brown eyes while Ashok and I conversed in English and listened to the old jazz albums that he had carried back with him from England. His bitterness seemed to have infected the whole family. No one spoke but Ashok, and the topic to which he invariably returned was his abject hatred of Agra. "This city is a shithole, Mr. Stanley. A place fit only for pigs and cows." Every other word that left his lips was an expletive hurled at the injustice of a destiny that had condemned him to live in this filthy backwater town from which he would never, ever escape.

I later came to see that there were, at that time, many such people in India—people whose lives had been stunted through contact with the West. For some it was enough simply to hear about the affluence of Europe or America to be forever enchanted by its lure, or perhaps to enter this fantastic realm through the occasional Hollywood film that played at the Bhagavan Talkies, a cinema in the neighborhood of Dayalbagh, not far from where I lived. As a foreigner I could not easily avoid these wounded spirits, for they were fatally attracted to Westerners and seemed to love nothing more than to pass time in our company lamenting India's backwardness.

While my host ranted, I sat mired in my own private hell of loneliness, marveling at the perfection of his wife's skin, the very color of our chai. I longed to reach out and touch the soft contours of her sari where it fell over her breasts, across the gentle curve of her naked stomach, and down around her hips to the delicate silver ankle bracelets that jingled, faintly, as she nervously shifted her bare feet. What joy such a body could give and receive! Truly this man had been cursed. He could find no place of rest in the life he had been given. We talked about a lot of things: music, literature, film. But more than anything else it was this terrible defect that rent Ashok's soul, this brokenness he carried within, that we shared.

And then there was Penny. Miss Penelope Ainsworth. I met her through Mickey. Penny was doing research for her dissertation at Oxford, working on a project dealing with the ancient sandstone sculptures of Mathura. She had a slim, boyish figure, ivory skin, and pale green eyes. She kept her chestnut brown hair tied back in a single thick braid, in the style of Indian women. I only saw her a few times in Agra, but she was always dressed in either salwar kameez or sari—never in Western clothing. Like Mick, Penny spoke fluent Hindi and appeared to be entirely at ease in India, despite the fact that she was, very obviously, both a woman and a foreigner and therefore subject to a certain amount of routine harassment from men. Still, it was as if she were surrounded by a protective force-field that held them at bay. She was beautiful and, in her profound self-confidence, unapproachable. The three of us—Penny, Mick, and I—went out to dinner once or twice at the Kwality Restaurant, not far from the Taj Mahal. That was about it. Except for the bus trip to Mathura.

Sometime in late September Penny invited Mick and me to travel with her to the government museum in Mathura, a few hours from Agra. She had an appointment with the director, a Mr. Bhattacharya.

After browsing the collection for a while, Mick and I left her in the director's office and went outside for chai at a little kiosk nearby. It was a gorgeous, late summer afternoon. The sky was clear, and I was feeling uncharacteristically at ease, relaxing with my tea under a vast pipal tree. Mick had just lit up a bidi when Penny came striding purposefully out the museum door and across the yard to where we sat. Her eyes were blazing. She refused to speak other than to rouse us and demand that we all leave immediately.

On the bus back to Agra, we got the short version of what had happened. Apparently, the whole time she was explaining her research to Mr. Bhattacharya, he had been sitting behind his big desk surreptitiously jerking off. She hadn't noticed at first, until he sort of got carried away and started jiggling up and down in his chair. Eventually it became a joke between the three of us, but at the time she was understandably furious.

On top of everything else I was dealing with in Agra, health problems made it even more difficult to focus on my academic work. My body was under constant siege. Not long after the trip to Mathura, my stomach began to rumble, then to boil and churn. I quickly learned how to balance myself while squatting over the Indian toilet, how to wash myself with the fingers of my left hand. Cup by cup I emptied the buckets of water that had been set aside for bathing as I hovered over the porcelain hole, five or six times a day, massaging my sore anus. I became a connoisseur of shit, bending down and scrutinizing each gelatinous mess for signs of possible intestinal disorder.

A few weeks of this sort of thing and my appetite faded, then virtually disappeared. I realized one afternoon that I had been surviving for days on a diet of nothing but Milk Bikis and chai. My throat was raw, my head ached, and some obscure valve in my nose broke, discharging a flow of mucus that would not stop. I purchased several handkerchiefs at the bazaar but eventually gave in and attempted to master the local custom in such matters:

Step 1: Tip the head forward, making certain that the nostrils are extended well out beyond the legs and feet. This is the tricky part, the part that requires repeated practice.

Step 2: Use the fingers of the right hand to plug first one nostril, then the other, all the while forcefully ejecting wads of snot onto the ground.

Step 3: Once the nose is emptied in this fashion, the fingers may then be wiped clean on any convenient vertical surface.

I forced myself to eat bananas and yogurt, then rice and lentils. My intestines gradually settled down, and after what seemed an eternity, the cold faded away. I adapted to living with a sort of chronic fatigue punctuated by sporadic episodes of severe diarrhea. These improvements left me time and energy to worry about other sorts of health issues.

The monsoon in India is a hothouse for every imaginable fungus. Sometime in August, a few months after my arrival in Agra, I began to constantly scratch my armpits. I scraped at the skin behind each knee and discreetly clawed at my inflamed scrotum. Under constant siege by armies of microscopic warriors, I retaliated with every available weapon, smearing myself with Ayurvedic creams and homeopathic ointments, downing pills and capsules for giardia and a host of other infestations. I still remember the first time I had to choke down those immense pink wheels of Flagyl. I studied the warning on the foil package carefully: "Metronidazole has been shown to be carcinogenic in mice and rats. Unnecessary use of the drug should be avoided."

Unnecessary use?

What did it mean that I should be forced to decide between having my guts overrun with worms and poisoning myself with a known carcinogen?

The circumstances of my new life in India were so novel that it often seemed as if every sensation had become a source of anxiety or, occasionally, of sheer wonder. Perhaps it was simply that I had never before been so conscious of my body, of the curious throbbing of my heart or the rush of blood pulsating through arteries and veins. One afternoon I was quietly studying Hindi grammar, absorbed for a few blissful minutes in the words on the page, when I become aware of the singular pressure of the chair under my thighs, lifting me up, holding me there, ever so gently. The smooth, tubular surface of the pencil thrust itself against my fingers, pushing back, asserting its own will. The virtually inaudible scratch of an ant's tiny feet moving across my papers inserted itself into my awareness with a compelling urgency. I sat absolutely still, listening intently. In all of this, it was as if there were something essential I did not understand, something I perhaps did not want to understand, calling out for my attention.

Focusing on sensations came naturally, in any case, since my daily sessions of meditation provided a laboratory setting for the meticulous, detached observation of my inner life and its workings. Back in Chicago— years before coming to India—I had taught myself to meditate following the instructions in Phillip Kapleau's *Three Pillars of Zen*. I got Judith interested, and for a time the two of us attended early-morning sittings at a local zendo. The sparse, samurai world of Zen didn't suit her style though, and before long she lost interest. After she left, I too quit sitting at the zendo, but I kept up my practice. No way was I going to stop. After years of searching, it felt like I was finally pointed in the right direction. I found I preferred sitting alone.

What captivated me about meditation from the very start was something both entirely simple and utterly profound. Until I began sitting, it had never occurred to me that one could learn, with practice, to distinguish between attention, or awareness, and its objects. But just this is the central and most basic technique of meditation in all the yogic traditions of India, first described some 2,500 years ago in the Upanishads. In those ancient texts, the meditator is instructed to observe literally every element of experience from afar, to simply bear witness to anything and everything that arises and passes away before the mind's eye. That's it. Just sit there, without moving, and watch, allowing the focal point of identity to shift from the *contents* of awareness—thoughts, feelings, and sensations—to awareness itself, where all trace of agency dissolves and the burden of personality can be set aside.

Although I worked to cultivate equanimity around my various infirmities and trials of these first few months, the effort to step back from the tumult of thoughts and emotions was like trying to paddle a canoe upriver against a swift current. My loss was too deep, the images of Judith too powerful to repress. And India itself was overwhelming.

In the Pāli scriptures the Buddha is reported to have asked his disciples,

> What, monks, do you think is more—the water in the four great
> oceans or the tears that you have shed while roving, wandering,

lamenting, and weeping on this long way because you received
what you feared and were denied what you wanted so badly?

There were plenty of reasons to shed tears in Agra. Every day as I
bicycled to and from the institute, I encountered myriad forms of human
and animal suffering. The sick and dying wandered aimlessly through the
streets, or lay where they had fallen—wasted, half-naked human bodies
twisted into an astonishing variety of deformities, noses rotted away, faces
bubbling with raw pustules. But it wasn't just the omnipresent disease
and poverty that was so disturbing. There was a kind of violence here that
was unlike anything I had ever encountered. Indian society incorporated
forms of casual brutality that I found unimaginable.

I remember one morning I passed a group of boys entertaining themselves by throwing rocks at a puppy. They had formed a wide circle around
the little dog to prevent it from escaping. Every time one of the missiles
found its target, the animal would let out a pitiful, anguished yelp, and
the children would cheer and laugh. This was taking place in the middle
of a crowded street, and no one—not the shop owners, the pedestrians,
the cop on the corner, the men sitting in the nearby chai stall, or even the
wandering holy men—seemed to care or, for that matter, to even notice.
On another occasion I came across a similar scene, only this time it was a
single boy dressed in his school uniform—navy blue shorts, white cotton
shirt, and a clip-on tie, a little knapsack full of books. He was standing in
a street not far from where I lived, flinging chunks of broken concrete at
a sow who lay in a nearby ditch nursing her brood of tiny piglets. I came
up behind him, indignant, yelling in Hindi, angrily commanding him to
stop. I was only a few feet away when he turned around, confronting me
with a distorted reflection of my own blanched, implacable face. I had
never before seen an Indian albino, and the torrent of my pious wrath
instantly collapsed into silence. His orange hair had obviously been dyed
with henna, but his eyebrows were pure white. He squinted at me, a jagged wedge of concrete still clutched in one hand, his eyes glowing with
pride and arrogance. After a few seconds he turned back to his game as if
I didn't exist.

One afternoon at the institute, during our lunch break, I read an article
in the *Times of India* about a bus that had struck and killed a child. The
accident happened in a rural area just east of Agra. Villagers broke into the
bus and hauled the driver out, chopped off both his hands, and left him

to bleed to death in a ditch. No arrests were made. The story was buried somewhere in the back pages of the paper, along with accounts of bride burnings and small-time political scandals.

Before coming to India, as an adult I had rarely cried; but here in Agra, cloistered in my room among the dictionaries and grammars, where no one could see, I wept. And yet despite the obvious suffering everywhere around me, I cannot say that my tears fell for these others. Like the disciples of the Buddha, I was only truly sorry for myself. Hemmed in on every side by a multitude of living beings, I was entirely alone. No doubt losing Judith had made things worse, but I now saw that I had been living this way since long before coming to India. My life was built around an endless, exhausting battle to get and keep what I wanted and to avoid or destroy everything that threatened my perceived self-interest. Only in my most distant childhood memories was there a suggestion that things might once have been different.

In an old copy of one of Edward Conze's books, dating from my early years as a graduate student in Chicago, the following sentence is underscored: "Fear of loneliness is the icy core of much that passes as human warmth." The margin bears a single line, scrawled in my own nearly illegible hand: "I am incapable of love." Granted, there was more than a touch of melodrama here, but it is nevertheless true that I had tormented myself—and Judith—with such thoughts throughout the years we were together. The voices in my head were right: our marriage had been deeply wounded by my constant probing into the selfish motivations behind what, in my view, only passed for love. In Chicago this may have been little more than an adolescent failure—itself just another self-centered game. But in Agra my loneliness was no longer an existentialist affectation; the game lost any charm it may once have possessed.

Judith had abruptly disappeared from my life along with every other familiar landmark by which I might have navigated such a loss. And in my cultural and social isolation I could not avoid facing the truth: just as Judith had existed primarily as a reflection of my hunger for company, so it was clear to me now that all these human and animal others served merely as so many reference points for my own anxiety and fear. It was all about *me*. I cared for them only to the extent that their anguish was a source of pain for *me*. In this peculiar sense their suffering was not really theirs at all; it was mine, and in my present situation I could no longer pretend otherwise. In Agra it became obvious, for the first time, that some essential cog in the great, hidden machinery of the soul had long ago jammed, leaving me imprisoned in a fortress of solitude.

I recently discovered, in a box of old papers and notebooks from graduate school, a journal I kept during these first few months in India. The box had been stowed up in the attic behind a rack of old clothes. I had no idea the journal still existed; I quit using it a year or so after arriving in India and hadn't given it a thought since then. Leafing through those pages, reading words I'd written so long ago, I came across something that stopped me cold. It's the account of a dream—a dream I would never have remembered had I not found it recorded in this old journal. But I remember it now. Vividly. And now I see how everything that came after—the whole story I'm about to tell, in all its detail—must somehow have been leading inexorably to this dream, to this moment of remembering, where the beginning and the end come together.

Here is the entry dated October 20, 1975:

> It's Navratri and the entire city has gone mad with worship of Durga. Mick and I were out late last night wandering around, and when I got back it took forever to get to sleep. And then, early this morning, I had a bizarre, disturbing dream. Only it didn't feel like a dream. It felt like a memory—the memory of something that had happened long ago, something I had forgotten or repressed. Something I didn't want to remember.
>
> I was underground in a shadowy chamber—a cave, I think— and there were packing crates and stacks of old books everywhere. Just in front of me a small, luminous globe seemed to float in space, radiating white light. Below it the floor fell away steeply into pitch darkness, and from somewhere down in the darkness a faint sound drifted up. At first I thought it was the grunting and squealing of pigs, or women crying, but then I realized it was laughter—a man laughing crazily.
>
> In my arms I held a dead child. It was the albino boy I saw in the street a few days ago. Only it was me: The dead child in my arms was both him and me. One side of the boy's face was crushed, the bones shattered. His eyes were transparent, like two windows opening onto infinite, empty space. I desperately wanted to get rid of the corpse—to drop it over the edge and

let it tumble down through the darkness, all the way down to the laughing man—but the dream was like one of those dreams where you're stuck on the railroad tracks and you hear the train coming and you can't make your feet move, no matter how hard you try. I could not make myself let go of the boy. I just stood there, vainly commanding my fingers to loosen their grip . . . until, at some point, I realized that I was awake—or so it seemed—lying in bed with my eyes wide open.

I have no idea when I woke up. I only know that when I realized I was awake, it was dawn, and a hint of light was visible through the bars on my window. Somewhere in the distance a dog was barking. I found myself in a world of exquisite stillness. A world that seemed to glow with the simple wonder of being. It was as if I had stumbled upon some hidden, magical quality of things. I wanted to lie there quietly forever, to lose myself in love of this world, but the perfection was heartbreaking, the stillness too much like loss. I couldn't bear it. I needed to get away.

I tried to sit up and discovered—to my horror—that my body was paralyzed. The intricate mesh of the mosquito net closed in around me like a tomb. It was as if the dream wouldn't end, as if I were trapped between waking and sleep, or between two selves: one of them alive but impotent, the other dead and suffused with power. I was truly scared. My heart thudded against my ribs as if it would explode. At last—was it only a few seconds?—the alarm clock rang and my body convulsed and jolted upright in terror at the sound of the bell. I nearly tore the mosquito net apart flailing out to turn it off. The sheets were soaked in sweat.

After that I was afraid to lie down again, so I just sat in bed waiting for the light, enveloped in the spell of the dream, my fingers opening and closing, the muscles in my hands flexing and relaxing, learning to let go.

4

For the next several days the world shimmered with an ambiguous aura, a strange mixture of dread and unfulfilled promise. Absorbed with the exigencies of my life in India, my memory of the dream gradually faded, though its emotional overtones lingered. Near the end of October I received word from the Fulbright director, Mr. Akaljeet Singh, that I was permitted to return to Delhi. Shortly thereafter Mahmud arrived in the black Ambassador, and I said goodbye to Agra.

By the time I returned to New Delhi, it seemed to me that the capital had more or less reconciled itself to the demands of Indira's Emergency, though there had apparently been some problems with the newspapers during the first few months. Certain highhanded editors, accustomed as they were to a democratic press, thought it necessary to publish articles critical of Mrs. Gandhi's administration. Prior to publication such articles had fallen under the watchful eye of V. C. Shukla, head of the Ministry of Information and Broadcasting, forcing him to intervene. The censored material was then replaced in the following day's papers by so many column inches of blank space—a clever trick not at all appreciated by Mr. Shukla. When this practice was forbidden as well, the *Times of India* took to substituting for the censored words famous quotations from the writings of Tagore, Gandhi, and other freedom fighters critical of the British Raj. This, too, triggered an equally vigorous response from people on Mr. Shukla's staff, who were quick to see the thinly veiled allusions. After that such games were largely finished. A provisional calm now prevailed in the capital. For the moment, people appeared willing to accept the relative order that came with the Emergency, especially after the nearly constant turmoil of protest marches, strikes, and open battles with the police that had preceded it.

Meanwhile, the seasons were changing, banks of dark monsoon clouds giving way to the crisp, sunlit skies of winter. Overnight the temperature dropped and the air became clear and cool. Suddenly everyone who could afford to wrapped themselves up against the morning chill. Wealthy Hindu ladies from Defense Colony and Haus Khas dug into their winter wardrobes and came up with luxurious salwar kameez of raw silk and intricately embroidered Kashmiri shawls. Their husbands could be seen every morning standing like big, lost boys in the drive or on the veranda in garish synthetic bathrobes that hung heavily around their ankles. They hovered there in patches of bright sunlight, a bit edgy, toes tapping ever so slightly, smoking cigarettes and drinking chai, calculating the expense of a young daughter's dowry. Drivers of the motor rickshaws flying along the crowded thoroughfares near Lodi Colony and South Extension were bundled in scotch-plaid blankets that flapped in the wind like woolen wings. Even the cows were draped in cleverly tailored burlap sacks that allowed space for their floppy humps to protrude.

Wrapped in my own gray woolen shawl—a luxury I had purchased just before leaving Agra—I settled down to the task of creating a life for myself in Delhi. I found a small room in Lajpat Nagar and soon fell into a routine. A few afternoons a week I was obliged to attend classes and seminars at the university. This meant a long bus ride, but there was no choice, since my involvement at the institution provided the official justification for my visa. The monotonous lectures were delivered in Hindi, which was useful for learning the language; still, these interminable hours at the university stamped my speech with a haughty, Sanskritic flavor it has borne ever since. It was only later on in Banaras, under Mickey's patient tutelage, that I learned to wield a repertoire of Bhojpuri maledictions so foul I was scared to use them in public.

I have many poignant memories of those months in Delhi. There were long bike rides through the city at all times of the day and night, trips to the bookshops in Connaught Circle, and outings to Lodi Gardens for afternoon walks among the tombs of the last Delhi sultanate, Turkish Muslims who once ruled all of northern India. There were, as well, excursions into the crowded bazaar around Jamma Masjid, the neighborhood of the great red mosque, where bearded Muslim traders hawked everything from auto parts and used clothing to spices, perfumes, and meticulously worked silver jewelry. I fondly recall several performances of Beethoven and Bach at Max Mueller Bhavan, an organization promoting appreciation of German culture. On one occasion, by exploiting my Fulbright connections, I got myself invited to a piano concert at the Italian embassy. Arriving in the dusk of early evening, as always on my black Atlas bicycle,

I peddled through the imposing wrought-iron gates and up the softly lit circular drive, where New Delhi's elite patrons of the arts moved in a stately procession of polished Mercedes-Benzes.

My education in the eccentricities of contemporary Indian society continued. I remember one afternoon in particular, shortly after making the move from Agra, when I was riding my bicycle through the orderly streets of an affluent neighborhood south of India Gate, only minutes away from the grandeur of the houses of parliament. On either side, I passed the homes of some of India's wealthiest, most respected citizens, the heads of major multinational corporations, retired admirals, MP's, and other high officials in the federal government. These are the people who even now shape India's future relations with the international community, the politicians who will decide whether or not to engage Pakistan militarily, the scientists and high-level bureaucrats who plan and operate India's vast economy. Every house was surrounded by a steep wall and watched over by a chaukidar who stood guard just outside the gate.

I was coasting along taking all of this in when the distorted squelch of a loudspeaker caught my attention. I followed the sound, riding my bicycle down a few streets to a spacious public courtyard, where several hundred people had gathered under a gaily colored tent. I peddled closer, hopped off, and walked my bike up to where I could peer inside. This was definitely not a wedding. Only women were in attendance, the plump wives of India's economic elite and their svelte, unmarried daughters, all of them thoroughly captivated, so far as I could make out, by two men who looked down on the audience from an elevated stage at the far end of the tent. One of the two was an old fellow with a marvelous, bushy beard. He was sitting quietly, legs folded, eyes down, as if meditating. The second man stood in front of him addressing the group through a microphone. Neither of them wore any clothing whatsoever. The one at the mike was handsome in a movie star sort of way. He was holding forth on the subtleties of Digambara Jainism, an ancient religious sect that dates from the time of the Buddha. The Jain path to liberation is a form of complete renunciation that culminates in death by starvation.

I was certainly no naked saint, but a heartfelt disgust with my own impurity was nevertheless driving me deeper into a self-styled asceticism. The Fulbright grant made me wealthy by Indian standards, yet amid such widespread poverty I refused to live anywhere near the level I could afford. I sought out the grimiest dhabas, public eating places distinguished by a row of massive aluminum cooking pots lined up out front on a masonry stove. While I sat over my dinner—a few peas and a chunk of potato submerged in mustard oil and chilies—cockroaches scurried around my rubber sandals. The spices had tears streaming from my eyes. My sinuses poured. All around me Sikh mechanics and taxi drivers dismembered plates of scarlet chicken, the grease in their moustaches and beards glistening under the glare of neon tubes. A gold embossed picture of Guru Nanak blazed down from where it hung on the wall over the wooden cash box, illuminating us with his blessing.

After one of these meals I was stricken with food poisoning and spent the night dry-heaving over a plastic bucket, my body straining to turn itself inside out. For the next two days I was repulsed by the thought of food, yet I felt strangely cleansed—spiritually pure—a sensation that almost compensated for the ordeal. Nevertheless, within a few days I was my old self again, foaming at the mouth to do something—anything—to purge myself of an indelible stain that seemed to taint my very being.

One evening I fell into a horrific brawl with my landlord, who was apparently trying to cheat me out of a month's rent. The ferocity of my rage at this old man caught us both by surprise. All it took was a few lost rupees to set me off. What other ugly emotions were there, just under the surface, waiting to erupt?

November arrived and I was besieged by sentimental memories of Thanksgivings past. Of course the holiday did not exist in India, but I resolved to mark its passing with a thirty-six-hour fast. On the morning after the fast, I awoke ravenous and went directly to a shop and purchased five pieces of pista barfi. But after one or two timid bites I was overcome with self-loathing and ended by dumping the sweets into the hands of a beggar child who had trailed me as far as the threshold of the store. Later that night I crouched over my desk, lonely and exhausted. I wrote in my journal, "I'm tired of being selfish, tired of being greedy and hateful. Hollow as a cracked shell yet soaked with desire."

From time to time some tiny, pleasant episode would distract my attention—the sight of a small girl with jasmine flowers tied in her hair, a kind word from a shop owner—and for a moment or an hour the world would appear innocent and hopeful, as if to be sentient, to wake up in the morning embodied and self-aware, was not such a painful thing after all. But always, before long, I felt the earth crest under my feet and the path begin its descent. Being less than fully healthy most of the time—and indisputably mortal—I could not rid myself of the conviction that my self-absorption was more than psychological. I felt as if somewhere in the raw, wet darkness of my body the hard seed of a tumor had quietly sprouted.

I clung to my academic work, which meant that I was constantly reading. There was the library at Delhi University, of course, and the big American Library near Connaught Place, where I often went to browse. But there were also lots of cheap bookstores in the markets of New Delhi. The only thing I spent money on was books. My favorite place for this was Motilal Banarsidass, in Jawahar Nagar, not far from the university. I spent many afternoons, after class was dismissed, foraging through those dimly lit, chaotic aisles stacked with books on every aspect of Indian culture. I read voraciously, books on religion, books on mysticism, logic, mythology, psychology, and philosophy.

All the while I continued to research the early history of Vedanta—a Hindu philosophy that was to have been the foundation for my dissertation. I found Sanskrit, the ancient language of India, mesmerizing. Its phonetic structure, its ability to form compounds of truly extravagant length, its complex grammar—eight cases, six types of aorist, singular, dual, and plural forms in every declension and conjugation. The undisputed queen of Indo-European languages. And then there is the inconceivable wealth of vocabulary, developed over the more than three thousand years when this language was the primary vehicle for South Asia's intellectual and artistic culture. Reading the Upanishads, the Brahma Sutras, or some other classical text in the original Sanskrit meant that I was engaging with the actual words of Indian philosophers, poets, mystics, and yogis who were otherwise lost in time. To study their writing like this was to gain privileged access to a way of understanding—to an entire world, really— inconceivably remote from my own.

I should acknowledge that this trip to India was made against the express wishes of my graduate advisor. He considered it unnecessary. In his own words, "Going to India is a waste of time." And I suppose he should know. Abraham Bentley Sellars was an internationally renowned historian of religion who occupied an endowed chair at the University of Chicago. Sellars was the author of countless articles and three books on the history of religion in India that were widely acknowledged as both learned and original. Every bit of this dazzling work had been done in the library, or right in his office in Swift Hall. That is to say, Abe Sellars had never himself set foot in India, and he had no desire to do so. His interest in Indian culture was strictly professional. He delighted in exposing the delusion and outright hypocrisy that—in his view—lay behind ancient Hindu ritual practices and, one gathers, behind the entire ancient Indian religious world. He had built his substantial reputation brick by brick, demonstrating in considerable detail how—through a meticulous historical analysis—humanity's deepest spiritual impulses could be adequately understood in terms of competition for power and wealth. Abe Sellars was a man of formidable intelligence, but he was cursed by a sort of reverse Midas touch: In the brilliant light of his intellect, everything could be explained and everything turned to dust. I had come to India, against his advice, to see if I could find here something important, something alive, something not even Abraham Sellars could kill.

Late one afternoon I took a break from my reading and made my daily ride over to the Fulbright office to check the mail for a letter from Judith. I removed a stack of envelopes from the "H" box and took them over to the couch, where I could sit down and sort through the pile—a task that didn't take long. I was about to run them by one or two more times, just in case, when I felt someone's eyes on me. I looked up and saw a woman standing across the room obviously waiting to get my attention. I had been peripherally aware of her conversation with the secretary. She had arrived in India a couple days before and was in the process of straightening out the formalities of securing a research visa. She wore tortoise shell glasses and a printed cotton dress, one of those Indian imports found in stores with names like "The Middle Kingdom," that had about it a crumpled, detached air. Her short, frowzy hair appeared not to have been given much creative attention since sometime before the preliminary exams and dissertation, years ago. Then again the style may have been calculated to give an impression that this hair adorned a head with better things to think about than how it looked in a mirror.

Few places are more convivial than the Fulbright lounge, where one can be assured of coming across an intrepid academic type anxious to recount, with a vaguely jaded air, the latest adventure in Rajasthan or Kashmir, or to whine on interminably about the exorbitant cost of housing and domestic help in New Delhi. Even more likely is the possibility of spending an hour being assailed with every last detail of some obscure research project. All of this can be entertaining in its own way if you're in the right frame of mind. It is a ritual act, one that every academic engages in, a sign of membership in the guild, curiously reassuring even when the conversation is excruciatingly pedantic.

I nodded in her direction and offered a faint smile.

She walked over to where I sat and extended a hand, which received a cursory shake. "Hi. Mind if I sit down?"

I motioned to the space on the couch next to where I had stacked the mail.

"Margaret Billings. Columbia. I'm working on medieval inscriptions." She leaned back into the soft couch, eased one leg confidently over the other, rearranged her dress and began rummaging through a purse the size of a small suitcase. "I know they're in here somewhere . . . ah, *la voilà*!" She took out a package of Dunhills, flipped back the lid, and offered me one.

"No thanks."

"So you don't smoke?"

"Nope."

"Well good for you. I wish I didn't." She gazed wistfully at the box in her hand. "These are duty free. I picked up four cartons at Heathrow, but when they're gone . . . oh, the hell with it. I've been through it before. I suppose I'll survive. But those Indian cigarettes . . . my god. Believe me, you have no idea." She lit up and took a long drag.

I began to rifle through the letters again.

"What a pain."

I held a finger in the stack and looked up. "What?"

"Oh, you know." She sighed. "All the shit they put us through: half a dozen pictures, forms, and stamps, one office after another. I've got to go over to foreigner's registration at Hans Bhavan this afternoon, then who knows where else before I'm finished. I'll tell you one thing, though . . ." She leaned forward conspiratorially and lowered her voice. "These Fulbright people don't know their head from their ass when it comes to getting a research visa taken care of. The truth is they're totally dependent on the American Institute. If the director over there hadn't agreed to help me out, I'd still be waiting in some god-forsaken office at Hans Bhavan next month. He's sending a man here right now to escort me through."

"Very nice," I said. "I had a friend with an AIIS grant a few years back. I know what you're saying. They know how to work the system."

"If you ever need help you certainly know where to go." She puffed on her cigarette and exhaled slowly. "I guess I'm happy to be back again. A little less pressure would be okay by me, though. I'm under the gun. My research has to be finished in time to present at the AAR conference in San Francisco next fall. I'm chairing a panel on Gupta rock inscriptions. My paper will deal with the Girnir material. The archives here in Delhi are packed with photographs and rubbings that no one has even looked at. Frank Davis—at Chicago, you know?" She glanced at me just long enough to take in my nod.

Bonding, I thought to myself. But it felt all right to belong, to be accepted as a colleague of sorts, even in this trivial way.

"Well," she continued, "he published his last paper in *The Journal of Asian Studies* without even a footnote acknowledging this stuff exists. Can you believe it?"

She broke here for another drag, evidently expecting that all of this should make a deep impression on me.

"He went into detailed speculation on the local city administration of the Gupta, all of it based on a single inscription. Nothing but formal panegyric."

"His paper?" I realized my attention had lapsed. I must have missed something.

She looked at me as though she were beginning to suspect that I might not be able to hold up my end here after all. "No, not his paper. The inscription. The inscription at Girnir praises a man named Chakrapalita, apparently the son of a provincial governor Parnadatta."

"Right," I said. "The inscription is a formal panegyric. I see."

"The point is," she continued, hesitating slightly to catch my eye, "Davis has built his entire case on a single inscription that he misunderstood, for God's sake. Typical, isn't it? Like everybody else there he's only interested in weaving together a good story. No concern with putting some solid research under his speculation. Things have got to change, that's for sure. These Chicago people have had their way long enough. Don't you agree?" She stopped talking and waited for confirmation. Her tone had become slightly indignant, but I couldn't be sure whether it was directed toward Frank Davis or me.

"I, uh . . ."

"Oh shit," she said. "You're from Chicago, aren't you?"

"Yeah, I guess I am. But I don't work much with Frank Davis. I took a few classes with him, that's all. He's around the department." I paused. "And he's on my dissertation committee."

"Look, I'm sorry."

"Don't worry about it." I tried to seem reassuring. "The truth is, if you want to know, I sort of wish he weren't on my committee." This seemed to make her feel better.

We sat there on the couch for a minute or two without saying anything more, then it occurred to her to ask me what I was doing in India. I explained that I was here to pull together research for my dissertation on an aspect of Shankara's work, though I had to admit that the project was not as well defined as I would have liked. She chain-smoked Dunhills while I talked a little about my struggle to find the right text, one that I felt comfortable working on. After listening to me babble for five or ten minutes she finally interrupted.

"Stanley," she said, "do you mind if I ask you something?" I shrugged. "Why are you putting so much energy into finding 'the right text'?"

I considered this for a moment and got nowhere. "Maybe I don't understand your question. I mean, shouldn't I look around and find a project that seems significant somehow . . . to me, at least?"

"Not necessarily." She put on a no-nonsense, let's-talk-business sort of expression. "Wouldn't it be wiser just to pick something you know you can finish? I'll give you a clue." She bent ever so slightly in my direction as though she were going to let me in on a well-kept secret. "Nobody's going to read that thesis. What you want to do is to come up with a topic that you can squeeze a few articles out of. Get them written and published. Then show up at the conferences and do some glad-handing. Get yourself known." Her voice had gradually taken on a tone poised somewhere between matriarchal concern and condescension. "The last thing you want to do is spend too much time over here. Sure it's fun. And important. You want to visit and get a sense for where the material comes from. But unless you're doing art history or some kind of modern culture studies, you're basically wasting your time in India."

"Excuse me," I said. She stopped talking and looked in my direction, smoke curling up from her fingertips. "You asked me your question, right? So do you mind if I ask you something?"

"No. Go ahead."

"If what you say is true, then why are *you* here?"

She smiled. "*Touché*! But I told you already. There are things at the archives I need. Let's face it, though. No one's fooled. Very little real work gets done in India. If you can manage to collect a few documents, use the grant money to buy some books . . . take a break. Do some shopping. But listen, I'm telling you the truth. It's not smart to stay too long when you don't have a tenured position back home. Jobs in South Asian studies don't exactly grow on trees. You want to get what you need and get back to the States, where you're in touch. Were you at last year's AAR conference?"

I stared at her blankly.

"There was a panel on Vedanta. You should have been there. You should have presented."

"I didn't make it."

"So you weren't there." She raised her eyebrows. "Why not?"

For a moment I considered being completely honest, trying to explain to her that I had trouble with the institutional, *professional* side of academics. That I wasn't exactly looking for a career. But I knew damn well she would not be interested in my personal history. Why should I even try to explain myself to her? Fortunately, I didn't have to. Not immediately, at least, since she excused herself to go the bathroom, leaving me alone for a few minutes with my thoughts.

It pissed me off that this woman was lecturing me so sanctimoniously. She was nothing but a clone of my fucking advisor. Everything she said amounted to no more than a single piece of advice: Give up even thinking about anything but money and job and status. Academic success was all that counted.

I thought back to the beginning, to Hesse and Watts, Kerouac, Gary Snyder . . . then Suzuki, Conze . . . to how I first taught myself to meditate by following *The Three Pillars of Zen*. I actually considered telling her about how I had never been the same since dropping acid, how, deep into a hallucinatory journey, it hit me with the force of a powerful realization that what we call "reality" is simply a matter of perception. She would never understand how little her world mattered to me. That I was looking for something far more important, I was looking for . . . for what? For myself . . .

Myself?

The word stuck in my throat. In that instant everything I had gone through during the past few months came crashing down around me like a mud hut in the monsoon rain of rural Bihar. Talk about bullshit. What did all my pretentious so-called spirituality really amount to? The more

I thought about it, the more juvenile and self-serving it sounded. Me, me, me. All those years wrapped up so proudly in *my* spiritual search, *my* studies, *my* meditation practice, *my* need to be left alone. And now I had left my wife and come halfway around the world to be . . . what? Alone?

Sitting here reflecting on the same advice I had always rejected so scornfully, it suddenly appeared entirely possible that this righteous contempt I nurtured for graduate students and faculty who fretted over publications and career was simply a romantic, adolescent pose. The whole grand, mystical story I'd been telling myself for years about who I was and what I was doing—a story brimming with ambition, resentment, and pride—was nothing more than a kind of elaborate, self-absorbed fantasy. Now what the *fuck* was I supposed to say to this woman? If only I could have laughed. Instead I pulled my lips together tightly in a forced grin and did my best to look nonchalant as she walked back across the room and sat down again on the couch. The way she looked at me, she obviously expected a reply to her question, which had been left hanging in the air.

"Dr. Billings, I don't know why I didn't go to the AAR meeting. I never go to conferences. And my advisor is constantly telling me the same things you just said." I wanted to vomit. I must have gone pale or something. I could see that she was studying my face now, as though I had suddenly begun to morph into a werewolf.

"Are you all right?"

"Yeah, I'm fine. My stomach has been rebelling lately. I'm okay."

"You want a drink of water or something?"

"No, really. I'm fine." I coughed self-consciously.

I could see her struggling to pick up the thread. "Well, anyway, the main thing is to get published, go to the conferences, and meet the right people. That's the way it works. That's how you get a job."

"Is that what you did?"

"If I hadn't I wouldn't be here now, that's for sure. I was presenting sections of my dissertation at conferences as fast as they were written," she said. "Kept my eyes open for positions I could apply for. I must have sent out at least fifty letters while I was writing. God, I was all over the place, that's for sure."

"What did you write on?" I asked.

"Gupta administrative policy."

"And how did you come up with that topic?"

"Just like I told you. I sat down and did some serious thinking. Weighed my interests against what I knew I could finish. And what I could extract some good articles from, of course."

"And you got what you wanted? It paid off?"

"Yes, it did." She dusted a few stray ashes off her lap. "It paid off. If things work out, I've got a good shot at tenure. Well," she looked up, "I've got a driver waiting outside. I better get going." She stood, straightened her dress, and casually slung the long strap of her purse over one shoulder. "It was nice talking."

I waited until I was sure she was gone, then slunk out the door and pedaled back to my room, with no letter from Judith and lost in a dark cloud of unknowing. I no longer had any idea what I had hoped for out of grad school, or from marriage—or from anything, for that matter.

Maybe you've seen someone do that stunt with a tablecloth, the one where the cloth is yanked out from under a vase so quickly that the vase stays right where it is without falling. If you think about it, there must be a moment—not more than a fraction of a second—when the vase hovers just over the table, poised for the fall that will determine whether or not the trick is a success. I felt just like that fragile piece of china suspended in midair, waiting to see where—or how—I would land.

5

I CONTINUED TO PLUG AWAY at my research and to attend lectures at Delhi University. But what I best remember about this time were the regular meetings, three evenings each week, with Shri Anantacharya Swami, my first Sanskrit teacher in India. I had been looking for a more traditional arrangement—something outside the context of the university—and the Fulbright staff helped me find this lovely man.

Several years before we met, Shri Anantacharya had accepted a respectable position in the federal bureaucracy and moved, along with his wife and ten children, from their home in Madras to what was for them the alien society of northern India. He was a gracious host, an articulate, highly educated scholar who had, before turning to government work, published several studies of Sanskrit drama and poetry. The move north was simply another step away from his old life as a Sanskrit pundit. What was most important now was to see that his children did not lose touch with their roots.

Through the years he had preserved his love of the traditional literature despite the financial demands that made it necessary for him to sit in front of an anonymous desk, day after day, surrounded by stacks of forms and rows of other desks, peons scurrying back and forth on pointless errands, fans turning slowly over the whole unhappy collection of broken-down file cabinets, murky glasses of chai, and drawer upon drawer overflowing with the ubiquitous rubber stamp. All the while Shri Anantacharya recited to himself verses from the Sanskrit classics he had memorized as a child.

One evening a week or so after the encounter with Margaret Billings, when my Sanskrit lesson was finished, I fell into a long conversation with my teacher's eldest son, Krishna. Anantacharya had excused himself and retired to a back room, leaving the two of us to finish our chai and namkin. As it so happened, arrangements were being made for Krishna's upcoming wedding. He was to be married to a woman whom he had never met, a woman selected for him by his parents.

Before coming to India I had known about arranged marriages, but I had not realized how common this practice is, or precisely what it means that the vast majority of Hindu weddings are engineered by the parents of the bride and groom. A desirable candidate is located—in the old days by consultation with village elders, more recently through an ad in the personal section of the newspaper. Once an initial contact is established, background checks are then made through a discreet process of inquiry. At some point an astrologer is consulted in order to compare the charts of the prospective bride and groom and to assess their chances for a success-ful marriage. Finally, if everything appears to be in order, all four parents hammer out the contractual details of dowry, wedding expenses, and any other potential transfers of material wealth.

"So it is," Krishna assured me in his polished South Indian English, "that we shall have the greatest possible opportunity for a happy life together."

He was astounded at the willingness of Westerners to plunge into mar-riage simply on the strength of feelings, feelings that were little more than sublimated lust. How could we possibly be so foolhardy as to hope to support the responsibility for our future together—for our children and ourselves—on such an unstable foundation? Where did we derive such unwarranted confidence in our emotions? The ultimate proof of our immaturity in this matter, the kernel of ignorance that lay at the center of it all, was our peculiar conviction that love was possible outside of mar-riage. Here Krishna's voice became resolute.

"Outside of marriage there is only passion, and passion is not to be mistaken for love. Love is built on commitment to one's dharma—one's sacred duty—and not on personal desire. One's dharma is much greater than the personal desires of a man and a woman. The circumstances of life determine to whom we must surrender." His eyes dropped for a moment; his voice softened. "But the person to whom we surrender is only of sec-ondary importance, for in truth, we are surrendering to our dharma."

I mulled this over.

"Mr. Stanley," he began again, "why do you suppose we Hindus marry?"

"Sons?" I suggested hesitantly, then quickly retracted my answer. "Children, I mean."

"Besides that." He smiled. "What other reason could there be, for the man and the woman?"

Once again I deliberated for a time and finally admitted I was stumped.

"Marriage," he said, without the slightest trace of condescension, and with a confidence that I would have given anything to share, "is the seed of love, and the soil where that seed can plant its roots. Only then will it come to flower in children." On this point he was adamant. "Without the *saptapadi*, the seven steps, love is impossible. Each of these steps is a vow, and these vows are the foundation of love, not only between a man and a woman, but between man and God as well. One needn't follow the Hindu system, but there must be a vow. And once made, it can never be broken. I think that Americans find this very difficult to understand and accept."

I knew I should just be quiet and listen, but I had to ask. "And what if one is miserable after taking those seven steps? After making the marriage vows? What happens then? Are a Hindu husband and wife always happy together? Do they never argue? Do they never fight and abuse each other? Do they never, ever regret these vows?"

Krishna reflected for a moment before answering. "It is a risk."

"But we're human," I insisted. I was determined to press my case. "We can never know what will happen, even tomorrow. What good is it to pretend otherwise?"

"There is no question of pretending," he replied. "One resolves to act then lives on the strength of that resolution. It may fail—one may fail to fulfill one's dharma—but there is no other path to love. There is no mystery, Mr. Stanley. Love is not about getting what we want. Love is about how we live with what we are given."

This was not the sort of thing I wanted to hear.

A handful of letters had come from Judith since my return to Delhi. She wrote of her job as a secretary in some god-forsaken office. She sent a sketch, with a description attached, of a piece she was struggling to complete—an intricate maze of gears and sprockets sprouting like tulips from the carcass of a wrecked car. She was still at it, poking around scrap-metal yards in her rusted Toyota pickup, scavenging bits of jetsam for her creations. But lately she had achieved some recognition. She wrote that her work had been included in a show and a few pieces had attracted the attention of a prominent critic. For years I had watched this process from a distance, secretly envious of her dedication to the task, her relentless labor to give birth to these brutal iron children, blue and orange sparks from the acetylene torch crackling off her welder's mask as she hunched over her work like some crazy shaman rescuing yet another lost soul from the land of the dead. Her letters described the life she was living without me. Our separation was becoming a given, though neither of us knew what the future would bring.

Sometime in November, weeks after I had begun to anticipate such a letter and even to shape my response, she wrote of a "tired anger." She would not be coming to India. I immediately sat down and composed a dramatic pledge of eternal, undying love. I did my best to convince her that this separation was itself an element of our relationship. "We have to see that what is happening now belongs to our marriage just as much as the time we spent together." In some perverse way, I actually believed this. A few days later I wrote to her that my letters were like the pieces of a jigsaw puzzle. "You need to assemble them, if you can, into some larger picture, in order to understand me as I am now, as I've become." But I knew that the metaphor was inadequate; it disguised the tenuous complexity of our situation, for both of us were changing far too quickly to communicate through the mail. The feel of the envelope as it slid from my fingers signaled the first leg of a long journey that could only end in loss.

One day not long after Thanksgiving, I went out and got my hair cut short. Back in my room I looked in the mirror and was shocked with the sudden recognition of my unconscious motivation, the pitiful, childish defiance that lay behind my trip to the barber. Years before, Judith and I had argued absurdly over the length of my hair. She wanted me to let it grow long, down over my shoulders; I wanted it short. In the end I had provoked her by asserting my right to decide for myself how I should look. The result was my "prisoner of war" haircut, as she called it. She could barely wait for it to grow long again. "Only God could love you for yourself," she said afterward, quoting Yeats, "and not your yellow hair."

Undeniably, I had learned something from Judith's example. She encouraged me to go through the motions and repeat my lines. But I was never convincing in the role of husband. My love was stained with the conviction that all of it was nothing more than a peculiar form of living theater. And still, it was true: Judith made me yearn to love. I longed to commit to her, and to the world, in her superbly romantic way, but always I failed. I dismembered her warm, human affection and replaced it with sadness and pain and fear.

And now, in India, everywhere I looked I gathered more evidence that there truly was something wrong with the world, something fundamentally amiss. Life was a continually deferred promise of happiness, a lie that no one dared expose simply because the alternative seemed worse.

It was early December, as I recall, and I was browsing the stacks at the American Library when I stumbled upon Ernest Becker's *The Denial of Death*; it had only recently been published. Leafing through the pages, my eye fell on the following passage:

> What are we to make of a creation in which the routine activity is for organisms to be tearing others apart with teeth of all types—biting, grinding flesh, plant stalks, bones between molars, pushing the pulp greedily down the gullet with delight, incorporating its essence into one's own organization, and then excreting with foul stench and gasses the residue. Everyone reaching out to incorporate others who are edible to him. The mosquitoes bloating themselves on blood, the maggots, the killer bees attacking with a fury and a demonism, sharks continuing to tear and swallow while their own innards are being torn out—not to mention the daily dismemberment and slaughter in "natural" accidents of all types: an earthquake buries alive 70 thousand bodies in Peru, automobiles make a pyramid heap of over 50 thousand a year in the U.S. alone, a tidal wave washes over a quarter of a million in the Indian Ocean. Creation is a nightmare spectacular taking place on a planet that has been soaked for hundreds of millions of years in the blood of all its creatures. The soberest conclusion that we could make about what has actually been taking place on the planet for about three billions years is that it is being turned into a vast pit of fertilizer.

As a child growing up in the American Midwest, the woods and streams and fields had always been, for me, a place of comfort. At an age when my friends were staying after school to play team sports, I treasured the solitude and silence of the small, forested area near my suburban home. I couldn't comprehend why anyone would want to stay at school longer than necessary when he was free to roam outdoors, away from teachers and coaches and all the exhausting social games. The smell of damp earth in the early spring, the crackling of leaves under my feet in late October: this was my refuge.

As an undergraduate I hiked and backpacked in the Smokey Mountains, the Adirondacks, and the Rockies. Later on, after Judith and I were married, we went together on camping expeditions. All my life I had turned to nature in order to escape the drudgery and nonsense of human society. It had never occurred to me that nature could be viewed as a "nightmare spectacular." Becker's words opened up a new and unsettling perspective.

I passed the remainder of that afternoon and the next few days moving from one troubling book to another, from one bibliography to the next, following a trail of words that led like breadcrumbs ever deeper into the dark recesses of the natural world. I read of murder and cannibalism among lions, hyenas, and a seemingly endless number of other vertebrate species, many of which routinely organize in warring packs, maiming and killing their enemy's young and battling each other to the death. But what I found most distressing were the unspeakable horrors of the insect world. There was Fabre's Sphinx Wasp, capable of performing "the most delicate and exacting nerve operation on its grasshopper prey," immobilizing the insect's legs so that it can be sealed up alive in a darkened chamber with an egg deposited on its stomach. The egg releases a tiny larva, which begins, shortly after birth, to feed on the paralyzed grasshopper, chewing methodically into the living body of its host, avoiding essential organs, preserving the life of its benefactor for as long as possible. Ammophila wasps substitute a caterpillar for the grasshopper, leaving several eggs instead of one, so that the soft, living body of their victim writhes and squirms as it is eaten alive.

This was a natural world far removed from the bucolic scenery of my childhood experience. But as an adult, how could I have remained so terribly naïve? It now seemed to me that I had been living, all these years, in a Disney film, some fantastically romanticized world that had nothing at all to do with the merciless truths of nature. It was all there in the title of Becker's book: *Denial of Death*. Why had no one ever pointed this out to me until now? Why had no one forced me to look?

There is a Sanskrit phrase describing the teaching of the Buddha as *yatha bhutam darshanam*, "seeing things as they are." In Chicago I had studied Buddhism in the context of my graduate work in Indian religion and philosophy; but early on I had decided to specialize in the Hindu philosophy of Vedanta. Chicago was now far away; decisions I had made there no longer seemed quite so important. After reading Becker I decided to take another look at what we had learned in those classes and seminars on Buddhism. I began by reviewing the basic doctrines in the Pali canon. Pali is the classical language of Theravada Buddhism, the form of Buddhism practiced in Thailand, where Mickey had lived as a monk. This was where I turned for a fresh look at the most fundamental of all Buddhist teachings, the so-called four noble truths.

According to the first of the four truths, every dimension of our present experience is infected with a kind of existential dis-ease called, in Pali, *dukkha*. Dukkha is the gut-level understanding that things are not in our control, and the anxiety that accompanies this understanding. Dukkha is most apparent at times of sickness and physical pain, or when confronting the infirmities of old age. But it is also present in the inevitable force of change and loss, in the shadow of death that falls over all our earthly joys. In order to enjoy our lives we repress any disturbing thoughts—including the thought that this present sense of well-being cannot last. However, some 2,400 years before Freud, the Buddha taught that while disturbing thoughts may be successfully repressed, the effects of repression boil up unpredictably, giving shape to all manner of perverse desires and fears. Even the best of times—what we call "happiness"—when viewed through the lens of this first Buddhist truth, are seen to be permeated by a chronic, inescapable unrest.

The second noble truth teaches that dukkha originates in *tanha*: an insatiable thirst. The commentaries make it clear that the word "thirst" has two primary connotations, craving and clinging: "Craving is the aspiring to an object that one has not yet reached, like a thief stretching out his hand in the dark; clinging is the grasping of an object that one has already obtained, like the thief clasping tightly the object of his desire." Reflecting on these words, I looked back over all the years I had spent reaching out for one thing after another—clothes, cars, status, sex, knowledge—only to see the anticipated pleasure slip through my fingers.

To have and to hold, till death do us part.

And what does the thief want *now?* What is the rarefied object of his present desire?

The third noble truth—that the flames of this chronic malaise might once and forever be extinguished, not at death but here in this life—was a proposition truly beyond reckoning. Rifling through the Pali canon I discovered that the Buddha was reluctant to speak on the topic of nirvana, and when he did it was always through the media of poetry, parable, and metaphor:

> Certain recluses and brahmans have abused me with ground-
> less, empty lies. They claim that I have led people astray with

these words: "When one reaches nirvana, called the beautiful, and abides therein, at that time he regards the whole world as ugly." But I never taught such a thing. This is what I say: "When one reaches nirvana, called the beautiful, then he knows for the first time what beauty is."

Robert Frost wrote somewhere that there are no two things as important to us in life and in art as being threatened and being saved. And it was right around this time in December, absorbed in Becker's grim visions of nature and the teachings of the Buddha, that something did change. I would not call it nirvana, nor was I saved. But something changed.

Since coming to India I had been increasingly troubled by a peculiar feeling—for lack of a better word—that I could not escape from myself. This feeling was epitomized in the dream where I stood, paralyzed, wanting desperately to get rid of the dead child in my arms. I recalled the dream one morning while laboring to unravel a particularly convoluted Sanskrit compound. I had by then entirely forgotten it and had in fact wanted to forget. But now, from wherever lost dreams are hidden, the memory of that dream returned along with the recognition that this urge to escape from myself was nothing new. Since long before Judith and I were married, I had fantasized about being someone other than who I was, someone wiser and more compassionate.

But who is this person who so craves to be someone else?

Dominated by this longing to be someone more spiritual, I had never thought to ask myself this simple question. Not, Who do I wish to be? But rather, Who am I? I had never really looked at myself without blinders or filters, prejudices or fantasies. To *see* myself as I was, however, I needed to *accept* myself as I was, for the two were, in practice, no different.

I looked down at the dead child in my arms, no longer anxious to push him away, and as I watched he gradually came to life. He was, in a sense, resurrected from the shadows of night into the light of day, moving with me from one kind of dream to another, until all that remained of the unsettling image from Agra was his fair complexion. It was still me, but in this new vision I appeared to myself in the guise of Pierrot, the sorrowful, whiteface clown, pining away for his lost love, peddling his black Atlas bicycle along a tightrope stretched high in the air, his bland features branded with a greasepaint frown: pitiful and absurd, and in constant danger of falling from his lofty perch.

It was not a particularly agreeable self-image, but it was entertaining in its fashion, and not altogether without romantic appeal. The character of Pierrot is, after all, an icon with a long pedigree: painted by Watteau, Fragonard, Chagall, Modigliani, Picasso, given breath and movement in Deburau's mime, literary subject of Janin and Gautier, bourgeois citizen of post-revolutionary France, devotee of Schopenhauer, disillusioned hero of the Symbolists. Watching the clown perform—going about my daily business with classes, dealing with people at the Fulbright office—I began to come to terms with my role. Little by little the desire to be someone else no longer monopolized my attention, for my attention was now drawn of its own accord to the sheer spectacle of this tragic, alienated naïf who took himself and his troubles so very seriously, doing his clever tricks so far up there above the ground.

Sitting alone in my room, a barrage of new questions pressed in. Where had this clown come from? Did he have any other life, before his life on the wire? Who was he when the costume was removed? Who was he at night, all by himself in the dressing room, seated without his makeup in front of the brightly lit mirror?

Who was he, really?

I resolved to see clearly who was incapable of love, who was lonely and filled with contempt, who was so dreadfully fragile, so eager for attention.

All my life I had been told a story about myself—I had told myself a story—which, until now, I had never thought to question. In this story I was unique, with a special destiny all my own. I was defined by my capacity to evaluate opportunities, to make judgments on the basis of those evaluations, and taking into account such judgments, to make decisions and take appropriate action. It was moreover essential that I perform all these tasks correctly, for as the protagonist in my own story, I was defined not only by my choices but also by the necessity to endure their consequences—consequences that would cascade down upon me with the passing of time. The personality had to be groomed with the utmost care. Being somebody is, undeniably, a very serious business.

And now I began to suspect that this story was, if not exactly wrong, somehow incomplete and therefore deeply misleading. What is consistently left out in the telling is the part about how this unique individual with the power to shape his fate inevitably serves as the pivot point around which the entire mechanism of suffering turns. Every action, every word, every thought that revolves outward from this center sows the seeds of pain in myriad forms. To be somebody—trapped in character—is to live an unending drama that is at once joyful and heartbreaking, beguiling and perilous, but above all, false. For the ego is, ultimately, nothing but a sad clown, a performer condemned to discover his own selfish desires and fears everywhere reflected in an endless hall of mirrors we call "the world."

6

I MADE PLANS to travel to Banaras over Christmas. Not that Christmas meant anything one way or the other in India. In Hindi it's called *Bardha Din*, or "Big Day"—as when a waiter said to me one afternoon, while depositing a stainless steel saucer on my table:

"*Aap kaa Bardha Din aanay wala hai na, sahab?*"

He stood there smiling cheerily, a damp rag slung over one arm. Waiting, I suppose, for some response. I stared at the contents of the saucer, a mound of sliced red onions encircled by a small wreath of green chilies.

"Isn't your Big Day coming soon?"

Right.

Christmas just seemed like a good time to get out of town, and the holy city of Banaras seemed like a good place to go. I had a contact there, a fellow named Ed Rivers. We met at that party where Judith freaked out under the watchful eye of my doctoral advisor. At the time Ed had been in Chicago visiting a mutual friend and this friend had brought him along to our apartment. He and I barely exchanged a word the entire evening, but Ed made a strong impression on me. He was fresh off the plane from India, and I could smell it on his clothes.

As far as I was concerned, he might as well have been a visitor from Neptune sitting there in our Hyde Park apartment. He probably felt like one. This was a period when every male in the country under age thirty had shoulder-length hair either tied back in a ponytail or else left wild, flying in the wind. There was no other option. We dressed identically in ripped bell-bottom jeans, blue work shirts, and heavy construction boots. But here sat this placid man with short, neatly combed hair glistening with intensely aromatic oil. His manicured mustache extended out in two points that appeared to be *waxed*. And he was wearing tight polyester pants and blue rubber flip-flops. I don't think he spoke more than three sentences all evening. He just settled into Judith's big wingback chair and sat there, silently smoking dope and twirling the ends of his mustache, nodding and smiling like he was viewing a mildly entertaining documentary film on social customs among the people of the Amazon rainforest. Early in the evening we talked briefly about India, but as the night unraveled, I pretty much had my hands full.

Still, the image of Ed Rivers, so far removed from the mad disarray of my life . . . it stayed with me. All I really knew about him was that he was a musician who had been living in Banaras for almost ten years, but when the Fulbright came through, I got his address from our common friend. In early December, when I began making travel plans to Banaras, I decided to write to Ed and ask if I might come for a visit. A week later I received a pale blue Inland Letter containing an invitation to stay at his place in the Shivala neighborhood.

It was appropriate that this first pilgrimage to the holy city came when I had just begun to contemplate the significance of being threatened and being saved, of death and resurrection, for Banaras is traditionally known both as the Great Cremation Ground and the Forest of Bliss.

The first epithet goes back to a collection of tales preserved in the Puranas, where the story is told of a minor deity who conspired to enhance his prestige by hosting a grand Vedic sacrifice in the holy city. He invited more or less everyone in the universe of any mythological stature except Lord Shiva, the Great Destroyer. Shiva had been intentionally left off the guest list because of his notoriously erratic behavior. This was to be a genteel affair, not the sort of gathering where one wants a known miscreant tricked out in leopard skin and dreadlocks, stoned off his ass, just waiting for the chance to hit on every goddess in the place and finish off the evening with his infamous dance of cosmic annihilation. Such is Shiva's reputation. Unfortunately, when word got around that he hadn't been invited, it caused a stir. A Vedic sage named Dadhichi stood up and publicly denounced the whole business, declaring that without Lord Shiva, the sacrificial arena was nothing more than a polluted cremation ground.

In the *Kashi Khanda*, a medieval chronicle, we are told that Banaras is the "graveyard of the cosmos" because even the most exalted deities come there to die at the end of the Kali Yuga, when Shiva crushes the world under his dancing feet.

People say that in Banaras death is welcomed as a long-awaited guest. Death in Banaras is the end of rebirth, and so it is also the end of re-death. In Banaras, the texts say, the mighty tree of samsara, which grows from the seed of desire, is cut down with the axe of death and grows no more. Shops in the old city behind Chowk do a brisk trade providing bamboo biers for carrying the dead. Corpses routinely float through the crowded bazaars of the city, born aloft on the shoulders of village men who carry their deceased relatives from far away to be cremated here on the banks of the Ganges. It's not uncommon to see such a litter with its macabre cargo strapped disconcertingly upright into a rickshaw, wheeling its way to the cremation ghats, or to catch a glimpse of somebody's grandmother strapped flat across the roof of the family Ambassador like a freshly cut Christmas tree.

In Banaras, only the flames of the funeral pyres never die. The cremation fires are the many mouths of Agni, oldest of the gods. Agni devours our offerings and cleanses this moribund flesh, unleashing the soul from its bondage to the wheel of samsara.

Banaras is not only the Great Cremation Ground but also the Forest of Bliss. And Lord Shiva is not only the Great Destroyer, the supreme yogi unmatched in his ascetic fervor; he is also the greatest of lovers, unmatched in the enormity of his sexual passion. In what may be Shiva's earliest surviving representation, a terracotta relief excavated along the banks of the Indus River, we see a male figure seated in the classic lotus posture, legs crossed, deep in meditation, a massive erection rising to his navel. My lingam is everywhere, Shiva proclaims in the *Kashi Rahasya*, like sprouts rising up in ecstasy.

In Sanskrit the lingam is the male organ, and when Lord Shiva boasts that his lingam is everywhere in Banaras, he is not exaggerating. The city is littered with stone units. There's a hard-on in the inner sanctum of his temples, a love pump tucked under every other tree or standing proudly outside the neighborhood chai stall. Pricks, dicks, schlongs, and dongs of various sizes are exhibited on street corners or poking up along the river, each one inserted into a stylized vagina—*yoni*, in Sanskrit—that strongly suggests at least one way of understanding the reference to "ecstasy." There are thousands of them in Banaras, an estimated total of some 30 million such lingams in India.

In classical Indian epistemology the word *lingam* also refers to the characteristic mark or sign of any object, evidence that a thing is what it is: smoke is the lingam of fire. For me Banaras was precisely that. Everything I had heard about Shiva's city seemed to confirm my experience and stamp it with the imprimatur of truth. In Banaras, apparent dichotomies are immediately resolved, the relative and the absolute merge, sex and death, the sensual and the spiritual—*bhoga* and *yoga*—flow together like two mighty rivers joining in one great, swift current that bears on its shoulders all the joys, and all the sorrows, of this earthly life.

7

WHEN I STEPPED OUT onto the platform in Banaras, Ed's hair, his moustache, and his tight synthetic pants were everywhere.

My rickshaw departed from the station, bumping along the streets through markets where cows feasted on vegetable refuse, while troops of monkeys, fuzzy orange acrobats, swung through a tangled maze of electrical wires. It was early morning. Here and there men dressed in brightly patterned lungis stood idly massaging their gums with twigs from the neem plant. The smell of chai and incense and hot vegetable puri seemed to emanate from the earth itself. Razorback hogs and furless, skeletal dogs skirmished over heaps of garbage. Untouchable sweepers, their heads wound in grimy scarves that left no more than a thin slit through which they glared out at the world, waved their straw brooms in wide arcs, as if they were sorcerers who had conjured up this fantastic scene and could just as easily cause it to vanish.

I carried with me Ed's hand-drawn map showing the way to his flat. He lived not far from Shivala crossing, on the second floor of a three-story gray stucco building. The rickshaw stopped just across from Agrawal Radio, at the entrance to a narrow cul-de-sac that led to Ed's house. Nearby a woman crouched at the knotted foot of pipal tree, holding what looked like a brass teapot cast in the shape of a cow's head. She poured water into one palm and shook it over a smooth upright stone smeared black with sandalwood paste. On its surface two points of vermillion marked the eyes through which some primordial spirit, revered in this way for countless centuries, looked out from a deep silence upon our mortal labors.

The entrance to Ed's lane was marked by a granite bench with ornate, ponderous arms carved into the shapes of stems and leaves. A cow tied at one end fed placidly from a concrete urn, her long eyelashes flecked with straw. On occasion, over the years, I have chanced to pass by that bench, and every time I succumb all over again to the curious mixture of excitement and peace that I felt standing there on that first morning with Ed River's map clutched in my hand.

I paid the rickshaw-wala the fare we had agreed on at the station, and ignoring his appeal for more, stepped cautiously around a pile of fresh manure and walked down the lane to Ed's door. I knocked, tentatively at first. Then, finding no response, I rapped a bit more loudly. From inside I could hear the delicate beat of tabla, a complex rhythmical cycle that flows like blood through the heart of every Indian musician. And then, the unmistakable slap of bare feet. A chain inside rattled, the wooden panels were pulled back, and I was confronted by a stout Indian woman in a muslin sari drawn up to just below her knees and tucked in at the waist. She looked me over for a moment before speaking in a matter of fact tone: "*Aaiyay.*"

I stepped inside and she announced my arrival by hollering up the stairs, her voice loud against the concrete walls: "*Dilli say aap kaa dost aa-gayaa hai!*" With one hand she motioned for me to come inside, then closed the doors with a clatter and climbed up the cramped steps. I kicked off my shoes and followed along.

The second floor rooms were set back from a walkway circling the periphery of an indoor courtyard that rose upward through the center of the building, allowing fresh air and light to enter. A large extended family occupied the bottom level; the clanging of pots and the sound of wet laundry slapping against the floor echoed up from below. My guide led me to a small room that adjoined the kitchen. This would be my quarters for the next few days. It was no more than a concrete cell, a monastic cave with a single small window opening onto a dimly lit alleyway. The air inside was damp and chilly. The only furnishings were a low wooden table, a single chair, and a rope charpoy like the one I had slept on in Agra. A plastic knob by the door controlled the bare electric bulb that dangled over our heads.

I unpacked my bag and had just finished arranging my Sanskrit and Pali books on the table when Ed walked in. He was accompanied by a man about my age with shaggy blond hair and brown eyes. Both he and Ed wore checkered lungis.

"Hey, Stanley." He clapped me on one shoulder. "Welcome to Kashi. How was the trip?" He gestured in the direction of the other man. "This is Richard."

Richard flashed me a smile that made him appear both naïve and trustworthy. He had the kind of face you'd like to point to casually, from across a room, and say, *that's my friend*. We exchanged greetings in the Indian fashion, palms raised together at the chest.

"Ed's told me all 'bout you, mahn. You being a Sanskrit scholar an all." He ducked his chin just a touch. "Very cool."

The British accent was unmistakable.

"Richard's a sitar-wala. We share the rent." Ed looked around as if he were unsure what to say now that the initial greetings were over. "Okay, then . . . how about we go up top where it's warm."

He turned and led the way up another flight of stairs that opened onto a flat roof.

It was exceedingly pleasant on the roof, a large open area with views of the city in every direction. We sat together on a cotton dhari, soaking up the bright winter sunlight. The same woman who had answered the door soon reappeared bearing a stainless steel platter on which she had arranged three clay cups of yogurt, a small bunch of bananas, and three glasses of milky chai. Over the next few days I discovered that this woman did everything but clean the floors—an unacceptable task for someone not born a sweeper. For that they hired a boy who came every morning for half an hour and waddled around like a duck, squatting on his haunches and waving a damp cloth over the floor.

Ed and Richard did pretty much nothing other than practice their instruments and go to lessons. They had been living like this for some eight years, immersed in a world of music and friends and conversation, a world where time was measured only by glasses of chai, all-night concerts, and the slow revolution of seasons. In March, when cool winter days edged toward the intolerable heat of summer, they packed up their instruments and retreated to a hill station somewhere in Himachal Pradesh, returning to the plains in August with the monsoon rains.

Despite its obvious appeal, this privileged life was—by European or American standards—an austere, ascetic existence. They owned nothing but their instruments and a few pieces of clothing, ate simple vegetarian food prepared over a single-burner kerosene stove, and slept on straw mats rolled out on the floor. Hiring a cook actually saved them money, since—as an Indian woman—she could purchase food in the bazaar at a fraction of what they would have paid if they did the shopping themselves.

There was something else, however, about the way they lived, something not to be accounted for through any financial calculations.

Though they practiced their instruments for hours every morning and went for lessons with their teachers in the afternoon, both Ed and Richard seemed to take it for granted that all of this considerable effort was heading precisely nowhere. So far as I could tell, neither one of them hoped to gain any public recognition as a performer, nor did they appear to entertain any ambitions toward making a living from their music. Studying sitar or tabla was an act sufficient unto the moment. Like Lord Krishna's childhood play in Vrindavan, their constant practice was a form of *leela*, an activity entirely devoid of purpose. Their life here was nothing more than an unchanging present—an illusion of time shaped by the repetition of complex patterns of sound that returned full circle, ending exactly where they had begun.

This way of living was inconceivably remote from the world I had known back in Chicago, where graduate students and faculty were consumed in an unending struggle to prove their worth, to get the right job and hold on to it, to succeed. Observing Ed and Richard, everything I had done back there seemed to draw meaning only with reference to a future that never arrived. As a friend at the university once put it, "At this place you're only as good as your next book."

During our conversation on the roof Ed and Richard became engrossed in a heated exchange concerning a movie they had recently seen at the Lalita Cinema. The disagreement had to do with the film's musical score: was the raga pure Bhairav or a form of Kalingada? The technicalities of classical Indian melodic structure were beyond me. I listened for a while, then took my chai and walked to the balustrade, where I could look out over the city. The sky was a spotless aquamarine. Laundry hung drying on every rooftop, saris rippling on the lines like brightly colored sails unfurled to the winter sun. Tiny kites swooped high overhead, sharp points of red and yellow and green twisting and diving. Not far off a temple bell tolled for morning puja.

From the perspective of my old life in Chicago, it looked like Ed and Richard had simply given up—collapsed into some kind of passive disengagement from the world. But this was clearly not Chicago, and from where I was standing at that moment, it seemed very much as if they had discovered here a freedom I had never before imagined possible. Agra had been an exotic hell realm. Delhi was too big, dominated by politics and industry. But that morning when I saw Banaras stretched out before me in a maze of crooked alleyways and broken-down temples and palaces, the ancient Indian center of literature and drama, music and philosophy and religion, I knew beyond doubt that this was what I had come halfway around the world to find. I was home.

After breakfast I left Ed and Richard to their practice and struck out on foot to explore the neighborhood. I had no map and no clear idea where I was going; I knew only that I must see the sacred Ganges; I must receive Ganga darshan. Unlike Delhi, there were no sidewalks in Banaras, no motor rickshaws, and very few cars—none at all in the inner city, where most of the streets were too narrow to accommodate their passing. People got around on foot, or by bicycle or rickshaw, or perched atop the occasional horse-drawn carriage.

The great, fluid body of the goddess was not far away. I could feel her power just as you can feel the power of the ocean reaching out and pulling you toward her long before the blue expanse of waves rises into view. Passing through Shivala intersection, I wound my way back along the constricted lanes and through the busy market south of Bengali Tola to where I emerged on Raj Ghat, high above the river. A vast, turbulent plain of water opened out before me: calm, almost motionless near the bank, farther out a slowly churning mass of liquid brown that surged north under Malaviya Bridge toward Calcutta and the Bay of Bengal. In the distance the far shore was white sand bordered by jungle, the gray trunks of palm rising up into a tangle of broad green leaves. A single stray dog prowled the water's edge. The village of Ramnagar was barely visible in the upriver mist; silhouettes of shops crouched low along the crenellated walls of the maharaja's palace. The sun was a medallion of yellow fire rising in the eastern sky. To my left and right the ghats followed the river's curve in a steep crescent of stairs ascending from the shoreline up into weathered stone buildings punctuated by tunnels and gates and high, arched doorways, portals leading back into the city's shadowy interior.

Directly in front of me the stairs led down to a flat, open area where cows and goats roamed freely. Nearby, a glossy black water buffalo the size of a small truck stood placidly chewing a garland of marigolds, one cheerless eye turned in my direction. A string of blossoms dangled from her chin; the petals came loose and rained down in orange flakes of light. Monkeys and stray dogs scavenged for food amid the continuous coming and going of the city's human population, here to offer themselves to the goddess Ganga-ji and to Surya the sun.

The air was chilly, and the water must have been frigid, but still the river near the steps was crowded. I watched one enfeebled woman leaning into the arms of a younger man, the corner of her sari pulled to cover her head and face. The man helped her into the water to where she now stood waist deep, palms together in prayer. People ascended the stairs carrying pots filled with water for morning puja, a time when their household deities would be awakened, bathed, and dressed. I stepped carefully down the broad stone stairs and walked south along the river.

Even before I saw the flames at Harishchandra Ghat, I was assailed by the acrid stench of burning human hair and flesh. This is where the journey ends. This is the ultimate destination of every pilgrim. The place of crossing over.

Things are not in my control.

I drew closer, unsure of the rules. At what I hoped was a discrete distance, I paused and watched. In all, there were three fires. A corpse lay near the water, still lashed to its bier and covered with a shroud of fine saffron-colored cotton trimmed in gold. The fabric was soaked from ritual immersion in the Ganga, and I could clearly make out the shape of the body beneath.

I came of age in the 1950s, absorbed in my parents' *Life's Picture History of World War II*, turning from one glossy black-and-white photograph to the next, in thrall to the parade of mutilated human forms: bodies starved, bodies frozen, bodies gunned down and stacked in ditches along either side of the highways leading out of Paris. Later, in college, along with everyone else, I watched the Vietnam War on television. This was to have been my war; I escaped only through the luck of the draw—a draft number high enough that I was never called. For me, it was another war in pictures. All those pictures of death. Until this moment, though, the only actual human corpse I had ever seen was my grandfather's. He died when I was in first grade.

I remember the unsettling silence of the funeral home, the rubber soles of my Keds brushing against the deep pile of the carpet, my mother's hand holding mine as we approached the casket. I was just tall enough to look over the edge. Inside was a gentle, familiar face, eyes closed, asleep in a wash of creamy satin. I was profoundly confused. I could not believe what the adults seemed to be saying, that this man I knew so well had simply vanished from my life. Was he not still here with us, sleeping? Would he not awaken, when he was rested, and invite me to sit and watch, once again, as he employed his old pocket knife to remove the peel from an apple in one long, winding strip of red and white? "You get a wish," he always told me, "if the peel doesn't break."

Shall I wish—on an apple peel, or a monkey's paw—that we might live forever?

I was a small child, struggling to understand. I could not see, then, that any effort to understand death is futile because death is nothing that can be grasped and held. Death is a blunt, unadorned absence, a black hole at the center of thought into which our hopes and dreams pour like light from distant stars.

There were no caskets here at Harishchandra Ghat, no stiff carpeting, no funerary bouquets. Only sand and water and fire.

As I watched, several men trudged up and down the stairs, each of them shouldering a load of split logs held firmly against his back by a woven strap that ran underneath the wood and up around his forehead. They were barefoot, dressed only in shorts and frayed t-shirts impregnated with soot. Their skinny legs were taut with muscle. Just above me, two men labored at splitting the knotted root of a mango tree. One of them held a wedge while the other swung an iron hammer that fell with a heavy, repetitive *thunk*. In the midst of this activity the bodies of the dead reclined on their fiery beds, smoke billowing up around them and spreading out over the river in a dense haze.

My eyes stung as I leaned forward, straining to see through air rippling with heat. Hidden in among the flames of the nearest pyre I could make out the contours of a human leg, the foot jutting out at an odd angle. Flesh bubbled and peeled away from the calf like blackened strips of bark. A man stepped forward from among the small group of mourners and approached the end of the fire farthest from where I stood. He gripped a stiff bamboo rod tightly in both hands. He paused and bent forward, staring intently into the flames. After a moment he seemed to find what he was looking for. He straightened up and planted his feet firmly in the sand. And then in a single motion he cocked back his arms and thrust the rod forward like a lance, plunging its tip directly into the crown of the skull, shattering bone, freeing consciousness from the burning rags of desire.

8

Back in Delhi, I dreamed of returning to Banaras and settling in there. I imagined myself living like Ed and Richard, meditating and reading Sanskrit in my own room overlooking the Ganges. But these fantasies were soon interrupted by plans that had been made weeks before, through the mail, to telephone Judith. We had agreed on two possible dates. My journal shows pages of contradictory notes on what I wanted to say to her, all of them infused with my apprehension at the prospect of talking again after being separated for so many months.

Telephoning from India to the States was an ordeal. The call had to be booked for a particular time at least twenty-four hours in advance. As the designated hour approached I peddled through the purple dusk of early evening to the Fulbright office. Ambassador taxis crawled through the smog like beetles, finding their way among a riotous swarm of bicycles and motor scooters. I glided past four barefoot men hauling a cargo of long, rusty iron rods loaded precariously across a wooden cart, the ends extending so far out in front and back that they sagged almost to the pavement. On Ashoka Road, just north of India Gate, I came upon a Tata truck collapsed in the middle of traffic; its rear axle lay shattered under a towering cargo of sugarcane stalks. One of its tires had spun off the road, and someone had set the rubber on fire. Dense plumes of smoke billowed up from orange flames. A group of men, heads wrapped in woolen scarves, stood around it warming themselves, drinking chai and laughing.

When I arrived at the Fulbright offices, I found Mahmud sitting on a cane stool outside the front gate, doing service as night guard. He saw me coming and stood up and offered an abbreviated military salute as I pulled my bike inside the yard. The lounge was completely deserted at this hour, the staff gone home to their suppers. I sat down on the vinyl couch next to the phone, where a single lamp had been left on, and waited for the operator to call.

When Judith's phone rang in Chicago, it would be midmorning on

Saturday. I wondered if Bruce would be there, the two of them in bed together, curled up on the black satin sheets I had given Judith for her birthday the previous year. He might even answer the phone. What will I say? How can I possibly deal with that?

Fuck him, I thought to myself. *If she can't answer the goddamn phone when she's known for a month exactly when it's going to ring, then fuck them both.*

I sat on the couch growing ever more nervous and impatient, my palms sweating, when all of a sudden the phone went off. I took a deep breath and lifted the receiver. The lilting accent of an Indian operator crackled somewhere off in the distance.

"Mr. Stanley Harrington, please."

"Yes." I cleared my throat. "This is Stanley Harrington."

"Your call to the United States has gone through. Please hold the line."

From far, far away I could hear the sound of Judith's phone ringing. And ringing. Either she wasn't home or she wasn't answering. I let it continue until the operator finally came back on the line and suggested that I book another call for later. Judith and I had agreed that if, for any reason, the first call didn't work out, we'd try again on Sunday evening.

I got through the night, somehow, and the next day, only to find myself waiting all over again by the phone. This time the moment the bell sounded I pounced on it, wrenched the receiver from its cradle and jammed it to my ear. When the call went through I began counting the rings: *One. Two. Three.* There was a distant click followed by a moment of silence. And then I heard the faint sound of a woman's voice, tentative, almost frightened, but unmistakably Judith.

"Hello?" Electrons collided with each other, pushed their way through the line, snapped, and buzzed as if exerting stupendous effort. "Stanley?"

"Judith?"

"Stanley?" More fuzz, then a rasping sound, like a file being dragged over the edge of a tin can. I thought of the old police radios on Dragnet. "Oh, Stanley, is it really you?"

"What?"

"Is it you, Stanley?"

"I can barely hear you!"

"What?"

"I SAID . . ." by now I was practically yelling into the receiver, "I CAN BARELY HEAR YOU!" Mahmud stuck his head in the door, saw I was on the phone, and abruptly returned to his post.

This incoherent exchange went on for a minute or so until we adjusted to the poor connection.

"I'm so sorry, Stanley."

"Sorry?" I could tell she wasn't faking it. "For what?"

"Yesterday, when you called. I was helping Marsha and Phil move up to their new place in Evanston—Phil got a job at Northwestern, a one-year contract or something. They were supposed to drive me back Saturday morning . . ."

"They have a car?"

"They had to buy one, I guess, when he got the job. But the stupid thing wouldn't start. Because of the cold. At least that's what Phil said. He had to walk to a Kmart and get some jumping cables, and it took, like, *forever*. I'm sorry. Really."

I swallowed. "It's okay."

I wished her a happy twenty-sixth birthday. She thanked me. The line sputtered and popped. We both started to speak at once, then retreated into an awkward silence, each waiting for the other to try again. Even under the best of circumstances, it's not easy to hold an intimate conversation on the phone, without body language and eye contact, and this was far from the best of circumstances. An odd whining noise rose to a crescendo and then trailed off into the void.

"Stanley, I got a letter from Beth." Beth was a good friend of ours, and I'd written to her several times. "She says you might be staying on in India."

"She does?" I managed to sound astonished.

"Longer than the time you were supposed to, I mean."

"She told you that?"

"But is it true? Are you thinking about not coming back this spring?"

I should not have written to Beth about my thoughts of staying on. But it was too late to think about that now. I couldn't tell whether Judith sounded simply hurt, or incredulous, or both. Her voice was so small, so distant.

"It's a different world here," I stammered. "It's been hard, you know, just getting used to everything."

"What do you mean?"

The line crackled and popped.

"Judith?" More static. "Are you still there?"

"Yes, I'm here. Can you hear me now?"

"Yes, I can hear you."

"I said," she repeated, "what do you mean?"

I hesitated. "I don't know what I mean . . . I mean it's strange. By the time you adapt to life here . . . something inside you has changed. You're utterly miserable, but you don't want to leave after working so hard to get *used* to being miserable." I pretended to laugh, but what came up was more like a snort.

"You don't want to come back home?"

I couldn't think of how to respond to this, and for a while neither of us spoke. I listened to the static while precious seconds dropped like tiny sparks into the night air. At last her voice emerged from the steady hum of electrical silence.

"Do you like it there?"

"I don't know, Judith."

This time she faked the laugh. "You don't seem to know much of anything."

"Yeah, I guess I do . . . I mean, yes. I suppose I do like it here. Somehow."

No response to that. Instead, she told me about a friend of ours who had recently moved to Chicago. They had gone to lunch together just the day before in an Indian restaurant not far from where he lived. She told me everything she had ordered: "some kind of mushy spinach and cheese, and tea with about a ton of sugar."

"But it was good," she added, in a faintly apologetic tone.

She talked about her job. I told her I was changing the focus of my research from Vedanta to Mahayana Buddhism. We exchanged this sort of disjointed information for another few minutes, punctuated by cries of "Hello? Hello? Are you there?" while I strained to take hold of the familiar sound of her voice as if it were something tangible, something I could touch and smell and taste.

In the end it was me who couldn't go on.

"It's hard to say goodbye," she said. "Oh Stanley, I wanted this to work." She was crying.

"Judith . . . I love you."

"Do you? Do you really love me, Stanley?"

"Yes, of course." *Of course?* What a totally stupid thing to say.

"Please write," she said. "The letters help."

"I will. I promise."

"Soon, okay?"

"I'll do it tonight. I . . ." But there was nothing left to say. "Goodbye, Judith."

"Goodbye, Stanley."

I let the receiver fall from my ear, then realized she was still on the line and snatched it back up just in time to hear a soft, feminine voice disappearing into the ionic haze.

". . . you so much."

"Judith?" I pushed the receiver so tightly against my ear that it hurt. She was gone.

9

SHORTLY AFTER MY PHONE encounter with Judith, there was a cocktail party at the Fulbright office, a reception honoring Frank Davis—the epigraphist who had been tagged for death by Margaret Billings. Since Davis was on my dissertation committee, I reluctantly decided to go over and mingle. Ever since my conversation with Margaret, I had more or less avoided the office. I never had been comfortable there, but lately it had gotten worse. I felt like an imposter, as though I might be exposed at any moment and arrested for impersonating a legitimate fellow.

It was almost nine when I arrived. The guard let me through the gate and I walked unobtrusively into the lounge, where the party was already well underway. There must have been forty or fifty people in all, mostly other American scholars, either new arrivals in India or those stationed in Delhi. Their Indian colleagues and research associates were scattered here and there among the group, several of them poised uncomfortably at the periphery of small circles of men and women who were talking and laughing loudly. It was evident that people were drinking hard. Waiters dressed in regal white coats festooned with rows of brass buttons circulated through the room bearing silver trays stacked with pakoras, samosas, and other South Asian hors d'oeuvres. Under one of the festive red turbans I recognized Mahmud. He looked my way and nodded a silent, formal greeting.

The typewriter had been removed from a table near the kitchen and replaced with various bottles of duty-free liquor and an assortment of Indian beer. Another of the regular office staff had been pressed into service behind the bar. Next to him stood the director, a distinguished Sikh in his late fifties, short, with the obligatory upper-class Indian paunch and a friendly smile full of white teeth. He was wearing an emerald green turban that perfectly matched his silk tie, a white linen shirt, and a conservative brown suit with barely perceptible, green pinstripes. As I approached the bar he extended his right hand, which carried with it two heavy gold rings, one set with a diamond, the other with a row of pink rubies.

"Good evening, Mr. Harrington. How are you this evening?"

"Fine, Mr. Singh."

He shook my hand, a bit limply, then withdrew his fingers and dangled them over the bottles. The rings glowed softly, reflecting the tiered flames of a brass butter-lamp that burned at the end of the table. "What will you have to drink?"

I studied the labels on the beer. The choice was between Rosy Pelican, He-Man 9000, and Tipsy. "Any of these will be fine."

"Balaram!" He turned to the bartender and spoke to him quickly in Hindi.

I accepted the glass, thanked Balaram, and nodded to Mr. Singh, who was already setting off to take care of some other business in the kitchen.

"Now what?" I wondered. I suddenly imagined myself, as if from across the room, dressed in white pantaloons and a loose white satin blouse with large buttons, my face painted with a frown.

I moved away from the table and surveyed the crowd. Three people were standing off to my right near a bookshelf displaying publications of past Fulbright scholars. I heard a familiar nasal voice and recognized Margaret just as she looked my direction and smiled, motioning me to come over.

"Stanley, how nice to see you here." She gave me a knowing look. Before I could respond she turned to face an elderly gentleman wearing a baggy tweed coat and a pair of scuffed hush puppies. He had a drink in one hand, a pipe in the other. "Stanley, this is John McIntyre, from Harvard. He's been gathering material for a study of early Buddhist logic. John, Stanley Harrington. Chicago. Quite an authority on Vedanta." Once again she caught my eye with a portentous glance.

"Glad to meet you, Stanley." He glanced at his hands, both of which were occupied, then shrugged and smiled.

"Good evening," I said.

"And of course you and Frank are old friends," Margaret continued, directing my attention to the man on her left. I hadn't noticed until that moment who it was standing right across from me.

"Good to see you here, Stanley." He gripped my hand and pumped it up and down a few times. "How's the research going? We haven't heard a thing from you."

"Professor Davis," I said, as enthusiastically as I could manage. "Hello. Welcome to Delhi." He was a tall man with fleshy lips and heavy, sagging jowls. His hairline had retreated over the years, surrendering a pale, liver-spotted forehead to a pair of glasses with square plastic frames. His nose hung from the bridge like a rubber carrot.

"Stanley, Abe tells me you haven't written to him. Not once since you left. That's no way to treat your advisor!" He chuckled and glanced over at Margaret, who responded with a tight smile. "He told me to look you up, see if you hadn't perhaps run off to the Himalayas to meditate in a cave or something." Once again he turned to Margaret and laughed, as if meditating in a cave were the most preposterous thing in the world.

It was true, I hadn't written a word to my advisor. "I guess I've been so busy I, uh, let it slide." *Frank, you and I both know that the bastard wouldn't care if he never heard from me again. He's far too busy with more important matters.*

"Well then, tell us what you're up to with your work on Shankara."

"Actually," I said, before realizing my mistake, "I've recently changed the area of my research. That is, I'm sort of shifting the focus of my concern, you might say."

The carrot twitched. He reached up and adjusted his glasses with the tip of one finger, pushing them back in place. "How so?"

"I've gotten much more interested in Buddhism."

"Isn't that a bit like switching horses in midstream?" He frowned. "I believe you were awarded the Fulbright on the basis of the proposal approved by the members of your dissertation committee."

Professor McIntyre had perked up at the reference to Buddhism and was about to say something when Margaret chimed in and cut him off. She had obviously been following this exchange with growing concern. "This *is* news, Stanley." Somehow she managed to pack a staggering amount of disapproval into the single syllable *is*. "How intriguing. This must have happened sometime after we talked?"

"It had been coming for a while before then. But yes, I made the decision not long after our conversation." Poor Margaret. This odd maternal affection I inspired in her was obviously hurt by my apparent disregard for the advice she had given me.

McIntyre drained off a bit of something that looked like a Manhattan and pulled on his pipe, letting the smoke roll out one corner of his mouth. "What exactly are you reading?"

"Nothing in particular yet." Out of the corner of my eye I could see Margaret's look of disbelief. I fully expected her to reach over any second and prod me. "I've been going over a lot of Pali sources, reviewing the grammar, trying to rebuild some fluency. I spent a couple of semesters with the language a year ago."

"The Pali canon?" McIntyre looked surprised. "That material has been pretty much raked over, hasn't it? What do you hope to find?"

"It seemed like a good place to start, that's all. I want to go back and take another look at all the basic texts," I said, aware that I was beginning to sound defensive.

Once again McIntyre was about to respond when he was interrupted, this time by Frank Davis. "Your advisor will most certainly be interested in all this," he said with a vaguely sardonic air of authority. "Perhaps you ought to drop him a card when you make up your mind."

Margaret looked distinctly uneasy. She was unquestionably perturbed with me for letting things get out of hand like this. I could tell that she was busy cooking up some scheme to bail me out. "John doesn't live very far from you, Stanley." She turned and addressed Professor McIntyre, rather presumptuously, it seemed to me. "Aren't you over in Lajpat Nagar, John?"

It was impossible to tell if he even noticed Margaret's tone. He was simply pleased that the conversation had finally turned his way. "Not far from the market," he announced proudly. "'A' Block. One thirty-seven."

"You wouldn't mind giving Stanley a little guidance on this, would you?

"Not at all. He could drop by anytime." Having said this much, he pulled his shoulders back just a touch and puffed contentedly at his pipe, then swiveled about to face me. "By all means, Stanley. Do come and visit. I would love to bat around some ideas I've had on Dignaga's *Pramana-samucchaya*. I've come to believe lately that Hattori might be a little off base here and there."

"You should get together with John and talk." Margaret impaled me with her gaze, then took a drag on her cigarette and withdrew it from her lips slowly. I noticed that it was an Indian brand. The Dunhills must have run out sooner than she had expected. Meanwhile, McIntyre, who interpreted her remark as an invitation to proceed, launched into a monologue on the intricacies of Dignaga's critique of Sankhya theories of perception.

Medieval Indian Buddhist epistemology is an amazingly boring subject to all but a small club of intellectuals who have for some unknown reason staked it out as their territory, but the monotonous drone of McIntyre's voice took the heat off me, and I was more than happy to stand there and swill my beer while he held the floor. In fact I was deriving some real pleasure from watching Margaret and Frank Davis suffer, when just about this time Mahmud approached with a tray of hors d'oeuvres.

While the others gathered around the food, I chanced to look over his shoulder and spot an attractive young woman standing alone near the bar. It was Penelope Ainsworth—the art historian from Agra. I was surprised to see her here. I had no idea she was in town. She was wearing a sapphire-blue sari that cascaded to the floor in a stream of elegant folds. A thin gold chain hung from her neck and trailed down over her angular collarbones. I watched as she examined the bottles and made her choice, directing Balaram to pour her an immense scotch on the rocks. Twice she politely instructed him to add more to what he had already poured, not backing off until the glass was full. She picked up her drink and casually scanned the room.

"Penny!" I called out and waved. Margaret had succeeded in bringing the discussion around to her research on Girnir, but at the sound of my voice all three of them stopped talking and looked in the direction of the bar. The men were obviously interested, Margaret much less so as she watched Penelope cross over to where we stood.

"Stanley," she said, "How wonderful to see you again!" She took my hand and gave it a gentle squeeze. "I hoped you might be here tonight."

I introduced her to the others. "This is Penelope Ainsworth. Penny, this is Professor Davis, the guest of honor."

"Evening," he said, taking her hand.

"And Professor McIntyre."

He bowed slightly, making it clear with a shrug and the same little grin he had shown me earlier that he was incapacitated by his pipe and drink.

"And this is my friend, Dr. Margaret Billings. From Columbia. She's on the verge of overturning everything we thought we knew about Gupta administrative policy." Margaret gave her a polite smile and a perfunctory handshake. "Penny and I met in Agra," I said, "a few months back, when I was there studying Hindi."

"I don't think I've seen you here before," Margaret said. "Are you a fellow?"

"No, I'm not. My research is funded through a private endowment at Oxford."

"That's where you're coming from, then?" Despite her effort to appear blasé, Margaret could not help being impressed by the mere sound of certain charmed names.

Penny nodded and took a swallow of scotch, then set the glass down on a nearby table and pulled a package of Dunhills out of her purse. She extracted a cigarette from the pack and lit it up.

Margaret's eyes flared in the glow of the burning tobacco. "Would you mind a whole lot giving up one of those?" She gestured toward Penelope's cigarette. For an instant I thought she was going to reach over and pluck it out of her fingers. "I just finished my last pack two days ago and I'm already thinking about leaving India if I can't find an alternative to these things." Margaret displayed the Indian cigarette she had been smoking and brandished it disdainfully under our noses; then with a ruthless flourish she crushed it out in a nearby ashtray and stood waiting for relief. Penny produced another Dunhill and lit it for her. One or two drags and Margaret was ready to pick up the interrogation where she had left off. It was evident, though, that Penelope had more or less won her over.

"Are you faculty, or . . ." Margaret hesitated tactfully.

"A graduate student," Penny completed the question. "I'm writing on early Buddhist relief sculpture. I've been doing some work near Agra. That's where Stanley and I met." She smiled and touched my hand again. "But I've shifted now to Bhopal. Photographing Buddhist monuments in the area."

"And what brings you to Delhi?" Once again the mention of Buddhism seemed to have provided Professor McIntyre with an opportunity to join the conversation.

"Partly a social visit, partly research. I'm collecting some information at the archives of the National Museum."

"What's the social part?" Margaret asked, as though she were only trying to make conversation and didn't really care.

"I'm staying with some friends of my parents . . ." She broke off and reconsidered. "They're old family friends, really, with the embassy. I knew them years ago when we lived here. I was just a girl."

"Your parents are involved with the embassy?" Davis asked.

"My father was in the Foreign Office. He retired last spring from his last post in Rome. He and my mother have settled in London."

Margaret pried into Penny's father's foreign-service background a while, then lost interest and steered the conversation back to Girnir. At that point I politely excused myself from the group, inviting Penny to join me for another drink, which I at least wanted badly. She had already polished off the scotch and was ready for a refill. Margaret never stopped talking, but she watched us out of the corner of her eye as we walked over to the bar.

In view of this unexpected reunion I decided to switch to something more festive, and following the art historian's example, I leaned on Balaram to pour me a half liter or so of bourbon over ice. Thus fortified we retired to the couch and immediately fell into conversation. We talked of her work at the archives, then of my own faltering research. I avoided the details of my escalating conversion to Buddhism, though I did touch on some of the intellectual high points. She listened attentively to everything I said. I could tell from her response that Mick had told her something about Judith, but I was not in the mood to find out what. Talk of academia eventually moved into discussion of the food she was being treated to at the British embassy: real cheese, fresh salads, and warm, whole-wheat bread from the commissary kitchen.

She told me an amusing story about her host, a cultural liaison at the embassy. He helped put together concerts, plays, and lectures, working to facilitate an exchange of artists and scholars between England and India. Over the years he had entertained quite a number of celebrities in his home. It was part of his job to see that they were comfortable during their visit and, occasionally, to do whatever else might be necessary to insure that all went smoothly. A pianist from the London Conservatory had insisted on going out to dinner the night before his concert—alone—to Moti Mahal in Daryaganj. He may actually have gone there, but this was probably not the real motive for the trip. He had apparently sought out a postprandial rendezvous with a prostitute somewhere in the back alleys around Turkman Gate. While he was humping away, somebody stole his pants along with everything in the pockets—passport, money, and a Patek Philippe watch. He insisted that this was the work of the woman's pimp, a cab driver who took him there, but he could only describe the man as "an obese chap with a long gray beard. Rather like Father Christmas with a turban." Under pressure from the authorities to come up with a more specific description, he finally managed to produce one other tidbit: the cab had two foam dice and a plastic playboy rabbit hanging from the mirror up front. If the police were to put out an all-points bulletin for a man fitting this description, they would end up interrogating half the taxi drivers in Delhi.

According to the story Penny had heard, the unfortunate pianist was picked up by a motor rickshaw driver who found him wandering along

Asaf Ali Road yelling like a madman. The driver deposited his passenger at the embassy gate in Chanakyapuri, wrapped up in an old sari he had snatched from the whore before storming out in search of the police. Penny's host was now charged with the task of running through half a dozen offices all over the city in order to make sure the musician had a new set of papers processed in time to get him out of India for his next performance in Bangkok.

I reassured myself that this is what the cultural liaison at the embassy is paid for, though I could not begin to imagine how much money would suffice to make it all worthwhile.

While Penny was narrating this story we got up and refilled our glasses yet again. By the time our conversation wound its way around to Agra, I was definitely beginning to loosen up.

"Do you ever go back to Agra?" I asked.

"Now and again."

"Still the same charming city I hold so affectionately in my heart?"

"The same. She's waiting for you to return."

Unbidden, an image of Judith's face rose up in my mind.

"You know what they say: If you have once known the beauty of Agra in the monsoon season, you will never be happy again until you go back." She moved one finger lightly around the rim of her glass. "Sort of like Paris, only different."

"Is that what they say?"

"It is." She looked me square in the eyes.

"Who says that?"

"I think I read it somewhere over at the Ministry of Tourism and Civil Aviation. I was on a lunch break."

"And what news is there from Mickey? Is he still holed up in his room at the college?"

"Still there. He told me before I left that if I saw you, I was to send greetings from the city of the Taj. He says he hasn't been able to find anyone else who appreciates the place nearly as much as you."

"Is that so?"

"Oh yes. He entrusted me with something else, too. A cryptic message. He said to tell you . . ." She paused, trying to remember. "To tell you that falling on the Buddha had opened his wisdom eye. Those were his exact words. He said that you would understand, but that you wouldn't believe it. He said this is his final incarnation."

"Is that all? Why wouldn't I believe that?"

She brushed a stray hair away from one ear. "Don't ask me. I'm just the messenger."

"So what's he doing to pass the time before attaining full and complete enlightenment?"

"Singing bhajans, like always. And painting. Right now he's working on a positively beautiful little court scene. His teacher is letting him use real gold leaf on some of the women's jewelry."

"He's good, isn't he?"

"Yes," she nodded. "He's very good."

Both of us paused for a drink. Penny searched for another cigarette. "Have the two of you taken any more trips to the museum?"

"The museum." She considered for moment. "You mean the museum at Mathura?"

I arched my brows, ever so slightly. "You know, for research?"

"Right." Her eyes narrowed. "I go back every week or so and let Mr. Bhattacharya whack off while I talk about my research. It's gotten to be an obsession. Oh Stanley," she said, laying a hand on her chest and looking around the room as if to see whether anyone was listening, "When I see that little man bouncing up and down behind his desk I . . . I just lose control." She made as if to swoon and spilled half her drink on the couch. It occurred to me that we were both plastered.

"So what's his secret?" I asked.

"Well," she wiped the couch ineffectually with her left hand, the one holding the cigarette, and raised the glass to her lips with the other. I remember watching the ashes fall and worrying briefly that she might set the place on fire. "You have to be there."

"Oh come on," I complained, "that's no answer. I want to know how he keeps you coming back for more." I took a long swallow from my own glass.

"Stanley," she said, laying her fingers gently on my knee, "if I told you that, I would be absolutely under your power. I can't afford to have another Mr. Bhattacharya around."

"So you refuse to tell me anything about . . . about his technique?"

"Don't be silly. Why should I? I'd be running a terrible risk. How would I ever get my thesis written if you decided to keep me in a constant state of sexual arousal?"

All right, I thought, *she's joking. It's a game.* But we were drunk enough at this point that it didn't matter. People had begun to leave the party and we barely noticed. While we were talking, her sari had drifted down from the shoulder, exposing a small bump where one nipple pressed up against the material.

"Penny, I have a suggestion." I tipped back my drink and emptied the glass, nearly losing my balance in the process. She reached out instinctively to steady me. "Look." I showed her my glass.

"It's empty," she replied.

"Yes, it's empty. And I intend to fill it. Yours is empty as well." I nodded toward her glass and she raised it as if to seek confirmation. "I understand your position, which is, uh, delicate. Of course you don't want to tell me in so many words exactly what Mr. Bhattacharya does to keep you coming back for more. But look at things from my point of view."

"What exactly *is* your point of view, Stanley?"

I hesitated. "Well, wouldn't you be curious? I mean, if you were me?"

"I see." A tenuous silence. "So what do you propose?"

"For starters, refill these glasses." We hoisted ourselves aloft and navigated a route back through the group to Balaram, who was ready for us this time with the usual treatment. "Now, follow me," I said, and guided her back across the room and out the door into a hallway, pausing on the way past the couch to retrieve her purse.

"Where are we going?"

"Patience, patience. Watch your drink, there." I took her hand and steadied it. At the end of the hall we stood in front of a shiny brass plaque that had been engraved *Akaljeet Singh, Director*. I ushered her through and closed the door behind us. Then I took her gently by the arm and escorted her across the dimly lit room to a huge wooden desk. I lowered her into Mr. Singh's big, custom-made executive swivel chair. I walked around in front of the desk, pulled up a chair of my own and sat down facing her across a pen and pencil set, manila folders, a stack of ledgers, and a sea of papers that washed between no less than five massive paper weights. I reached over and turned on a small desk lamp, then pushed it off to one side, near a replica to the Taj Mahal that had been made into an ashtray.

"Now," I said, "show me."

"You're joking," she said, rising slightly from her seat.

"Would I joke about something this important?"

She relaxed into the cushion and sat quietly for a moment. "You really want to see?"

"Oh yes. Yes. I want to see."

She picked up her purse, which had dropped to the floor beside the chair, fished out a cigarette, lit it, and inhaled. "Tell me about your research."

"Come on, Penny, I told you everything already, what else . . . ?"

"Tell me again," she cut me off. "I'm interested. Really." Her right hand, the one without the cigarette, had dropped out of sight beneath the desk. Her eyes held mine. "That's what we're here for, isn't it?"

I started talking about Vedanta. I talked about the difference between Ramanuja's theistic dualism and Shankara's abstract monism, between the path of faith and the path of wisdom. I delved into the fine points of Shankara's commentary on the *Brahmasutras*, compared and contrasted what he said there with the position he took on similar problems in other commentaries. While I talked, Penny hung on every word. She nodded her head now and again at appropriate intervals, said "hmmm" and "yes, I see." She leaned back between the arms of the chair, her left elbow resting on the soft material, the cigarette just a few inches from her lips. As I talked she encouraged me to go into specifics, without ever saying more than a word or two of her own. The whole time her right hand remained in her lap, just out of sight below the edge of the desk. I could see the muscles in her forearm contracting, relaxing, then contracting again. I hadn't been talking very long before I heard the rustle of silk below the desk, nothing more than a subtle whisper, but enough to interrupt my learned discourse. I hesitated for a second, my gaze dropped, and I saw the muscles in her arm loosen up.

"Is something wrong?" she asked, pulling my eyes back up into her own. "If you would prefer, we can postpone this discussion to another time."

"Nothing's wrong," I answered hastily.

"Then why did you stop talking?" She continued to look directly into my eyes, and I saw a slight sheen of perspiration at the top of her forehead. A tiny drop rolled down her neck and onto her chest. The sari had fallen even lower. She inhaled again and let the smoke ease slowly from her nostrils. "Please go on, Mr. Harrington." Her voice quivered just a bit, in a slightly lower tone than before.

"What do you want me to talk about? I ..."

She took a last drag on the cigarette, reached over the desk with her left hand, and mashed the butt out on the steps of the Taj. "Why don't you tell me something about Buddhism?"

I started in all over again, only this time I began by dredging up anything I could think of from the texts I had studied during the past several months. I worked my way numerically through a long list of basic doctrines, starting with the three jewels and continuing through the four noble truths, the four bonds, the four perverted views. When I ran out of fours I carried on with the fives and sixes. She had begun to rock slowly back and forth in the big chair. The springs creaked, her silk sari shivered in the light from the lamp. She no longer spoke, but her breathing had become heavier, deeper. Her lids were half closed now, but still she held my eyes, never swerving, never once allowing me to look away.

By the time I got to the eighteen kinds of emptiness her breathing had become a muffled groan of pleasure, and she gave up all pretense. Her hips pumped gently up and down on the cushion, her eyes closed, and she slid back and surrendered to an orgasm that pulsed through her body in waves.

That did it for me. I pushed back my chair and dropped to the floor on my hands and knees. I crawled between her legs and began to chew on one knee, working my way up the inside of her left thigh. She stuck both hands in my hair and began to massage my scalp, pulling my head against her. By now she was squirming in the chair. "Jesus," she moaned. "Please. Oh Jesus *Christ*, Stanley."

I have no idea how long we had been going at it like this—two minutes? ten?—when I heard a voice in the hall just outside the door.

I peered up. "Penny! Listen!"

It was Margaret. Thank god the volume of that woman's speech is at least thirty decibels louder than any normal human being. Otherwise I would never have heard them coming. The few seconds this gave us made the difference between a total catastrophe and an extremely compromising situation. As the knob turned Penny pulled her hands out of my hair and sat up straight in the chair. She was still in the process of rearranging her sari when the door swung open and in walked Mr. Singh with Frank Davis and Margaret. They were so involved in whatever it was they were discussing that they didn't even notice us at first. I backed out from under the desk and looked up directly into Margaret's face. She jumped backward, collided with Frank Davis, and knocked his glasses askew. A spooky, disjointed panic flashed through my inebriated brain as I thought I saw his nose come off along with the plastic frames.

"Stanley! My God, you scared me to death!"

"Oh, hi Margaret." The others just stood gaping at us. I ran one hand through my hair. It was sticking out wildly in all directions. I pulled a handkerchief out of my pocket and swabbed my nose and mouth. "Another of these damn Indian colds!" My pathetic attempt at a laugh was immediately absorbed into the dead silence of the room.

"What on earth are you doing?" Margaret had more or less regained her composure, but so far, neither she nor the others had moved since they spotted us.

I thought fast. Very fast, considering how much bourbon I'd drunk in the past hour. "I'm looking for a cigarette."

"You don't smoke, Stanley."

"Penny dropped it down here somewhere." At the mention of her name all eyes suddenly shifted to where she sat in Mr. Singh's big chair. Fortunately at that very moment she had the Dunhills in her hand and was in the process of extracting one from the pack. She had taken full advantage of the few intervening seconds to rearrange her sari. I was on my knees now and looking across at her through the pen and pencil set, my head even with the minarets on the Taj ashtray. I blew hard on my nose, for effect, then wadded up the handkerchief and returned it to my pocket. I knew that they were waiting for some explanation for our presence here in Singh's office. Before I could come up with anything even remotely plausible, Penny took over with her best uppercrust Oxford accent. Her tone was both dignified and casual, the voice of an English aristocrat on holiday.

"I hope you don't mind too much, Mr. Singh. We came to talk. All the smoke in the other room was bothering Stanley."

Mr. Singh was ill equipped to deal with awkward situations. Terrified of embarrassment, his initial response was to smooth things over, as though nothing out of the ordinary had happened. It was our best card, and Penny played it to perfection, leaving him with just the opening he required to let us gracefully off the hook. He looked at Penny, then at me, then back again at Penny. "Well, this is a bit of a surprise."

Then Margaret mumbled, "If Stanley was having such a hard time with the smoke . . ." She eyed the Dunhill in Penny's hand and her voice trailed off. She obviously decided it would be best not to press the issue.

"We were just preparing to leave," Penny said, standing up briskly from behind the desk. I took her cue and got to my feet. I saw that my chair had fallen over backward on the floor, so I went over, picked it up, and returned it to its original place.

"Yes, please excuse us, Mr. Singh. We really had no right to enter your office like this." I glanced at the desk. "Just talking." I picked up my glass. Then, as an afterthought, I set it down and hauled out the handkerchief again, giving my nose another blast for good measure.

"We'll be off now," Penny said. She took her glass and led the way to the door. As she passed Margaret she turned and addressed her politely. "I'm glad to have had the opportunity to meet you, Dr. Billings. And you too, Professor Davis. I hope your time in India is most fruitful." She paused for a moment in front of Mr. Singh. "Thank you so much for entertaining us this evening. It was delightful." I nodded to everyone and followed her through the door. The whole time Davis hadn't once opened his trap.

We ditched our glasses in the lounge and headed for the door and out into the courtyard, where I grabbed my bicycle and rolled it through the front gate, past the guard who was sipping a cup of chai. Penny hopped sidesaddle onto the flat rack in back, her sari bunched up around her legs, and we fled into the darkness, careening drunkenly through the streets of New Delhi, horny as rutting elephants and immersed in a nonstop laughing jag that surged up in our relief at having escaped more or less unscathed.

It had rained, and the pavement shimmered under the streetlights. Fires from late-night chai shops flickered in pockets of darkness. We glided close by a cow, and Penny reached out, letting her fingers bounce gently over its ribs and along the length of its rough, angular body. Inside a small Hanuman temple a group of old men huddled in a tight circle singing bhajans. They swayed together under woolen shawls and blankets, absorbed in the sound of the harmonium and an ecstatic rhythm of drums and brass finger-cymbals.

Back in my room we tore off our clothes and fucked like animals, grunting and slobbering on my narrow, ascetic bed until we collapsed into each other's arms. During the night I awoke, still mildly drunk, and listened to her soft breathing. The scent of patchouli mingled with the smell of sweat and sex.

The next morning I came back from bathing and found Miss Penelope Ainsworth sitting naked on the bed, her legs crossed, brushing her hair out in smooth, even strokes so that it hung thick and heavy over her shoulders and down across her breasts. It was a tableau, a female arche-type impressed so vividly on my mind and heart that she seemed for one moment less a living woman than a living memory—of someone, of some part of myself—that I had lost a long, long time before.

10

Penny was on the road again a few days later, but she returned to visit me in Delhi several times during my last four months in the city. She was going back to England that summer, and we both knew the time we had together was short. She very quickly became my second real companion in India, after Mick, whom I hadn't seen since leaving Agra.

Penny was ambitious, determined to succeed in the cutthroat world of professional academics, a trait that I found more than a bit troubling. Any concerns I had were overruled—at least for the time being—by my fascination with her enthusiasm for India. She was full of life, a woman completely at ease and in love with the chaos of South Asia. In her company I began, for the first time, to take real pleasure in the wealth of sounds and colors, smells, tastes, and textures that were part of everyday life here.

Together we shared one small pleasure after another: a pyramid of bright oranges stacked high on a rickety wooden cart; the glitter of bangles and heavy silver bracelets on the wrists of the village women; the ghostly, feline cry of peacocks at dusk. She made me stop and notice the way a camel's lips flop up and down as he walks; I extolled to her the charms of the water buffalo with its inquisitive brow, its seductive lashes and sad, glittering eyes. Once, as we sat drinking chai in a neighborhood near Jamma Masjid, she leaned forward over the low table, gasped, and held my arm. Outside the shop a Shaivite ascetic sat bareback astride a white stallion, the reins in one hand, an iron trident clasped in the other. I have no idea why this Hindu holy man was in Old Delhi—much less astride a horse. With his sleek muscles and the dark, wild force of his beard and dreadlocks writhing down over his shoulders, he emerged from the crowded streets of this Muslim neighborhood like some mad Sufi vision of God.

On another afternoon toward the end of February, while browsing outside a used paperback book shop in Khan Market, we were assaulted with the blare of brass instruments, a cacophonous, metallic jumble of sound, a musical freak fathered on India by the ghost of the British Imperial Army: five gaunt figures trussed up in faded military-style coats of red and gold. Heads, hands, and bare feet wrapped in gauze, ragged stumps of fingers and toes. Three dented trumpets. The tortured whine of a clarinet. The thump of a base drum, its torn head bearing the insignia of the Delhi Municipal Corporation Leper's Band.

For me, our time together was a respite, an opportunity to recover my strength. Exploring Penny's body was like renewing an old friendship. I adored simply being in her presence, inhaling her perfume, brushing against her as we talked and wandered through the city. And yet I could not forget the bicycle on the high wire. I was intensely aware of the emotions she inspired, of my growing attachment to her, and of the danger this presented for the tenuous equilibrium I had just begun to discover in India. When she invited me one afternoon to the embassy for lunch and imported English lager, I excused myself after an hour or so and went back alone to my books and meditation. The clown could not trust this newfound happiness, and therefore he could not really be happy.

Nor could I stop thinking of my lost wife. I talked with Penny about everything that had happened before coming to India, of my indiscretion and of Judith's response, of our letters—even of our recent conversation on the phone and the growing distance between us. She told me of her own past. There was someone in London, awaiting her return. He posted long narratives of his life there without her. I saw the envelopes, thick with desire, like the faces of the young men who congregated outside the movie theaters in Connaught Place.

In February, two weeks before my twenty-eighth birthday, I received a letter from Judith, the first since our conversation on the phone. "I've been thinking about this a lot," she wrote, "and I simply don't feel that we will be able to get back together. I think it would be best if we divorced as soon as possible."

It is well known that Kierkegaard was the first to make a clear distinction between fear and dread. Fear, he wrote, is always focused on something, while dread finds no specific target. Dread is a fear of no thing in particular. But this no thing in particular—as Kierkegaard cleverly pointed out—is not "a nothing with which the individual has nothing to do." On the contrary, to dread is to be anxious about one's identity, which is a very personal nothing. To dread is to be troubled about the fragility of that sad little circus clown, the ego; to dread is to worry that one's sense of self may, without warning, slip quietly back below the surface of what is referred to in the first chapter of Genesis as "the deep."

Among the bas-relief carvings on the outer gate of the stupa at Amaravati—one of the most ancient of all Buddhist archeological sites—there is a depiction of the Bodhi tree, its branches sheltering an unoccupied throne. This is where the Buddha should be sitting, but the artist has rendered only a tree surrounded by a group of figures, the demons of Mara attacking an empty throne. This is the throne of memory and imagination, of desire and fear. This is the throne of the exalted ego, and—as the Buddha saw, and we are clearly meant to see—its occupant is missing.

No Buddha.

No self.

Where is the prince who wanted so desperately to find a solution to the problem of suffering? Where is the prince who left behind his wife and small child and nearly starved himself to death while engaged in ascetic practices? Where is he now? The anonymous artist who worked at Amaravati understood that apart from the throne there is nothing to be seen or told.

In the interests of full disclosure, this is as good a time as any to acknowledge my stake in this story. As narrator, I sustain a deeply ambiguous relationship with my protagonist. Stanley and his world are nothing more than a construct, a pastiche of memory and imagination: fiction on a grand scale. His story, though, is indispensible. Stanley Harrington, sitting disconsolately on the vinyl couch in the Fulbright lounge in New Delhi, all those long years ago, a letter from his estranged wife resting open in his weary hands, his head bowed, eyes misting, heart filled with dread. It's essential to get the details of his story right, for the events of his life define the empty throne where I cannot be found; they give form to my absence.

After the initial shock of reading Judith's words, I dried my eyes with the back of one hand and made my exit, brushing past a newly arrived fellow obviously interested in conversation. For the next hour or so—long enough to peddle through the traffic back to my room and prepare a cup of chai—I was fine. Confident even, in a manner of speaking. It seemed as if the fates were conspiring to accomplish something important that I might not otherwise have found the will to do. Ironically, I felt something of what my Sanskrit teacher's son, Krishna, had talked about, the strength that flows from affirming the necessary. I even began to imagine that I could make out, in all of this, the obscure outlines of my own quirky Dharma.

By early evening such fantasies waned and this first wave of courage washed ashore, leaving me high and dry on a polluted beach, surrounded by the familiar detritus of my customary anxiety and loneliness. Judith's words, as I read them over again for perhaps the hundredth time, threw me into an agony of doubt. Unable to sleep, I penned the first of many subsequent confessionals, none of which I ever actually sent.

Dear, Dear Judith,

Your decision to get a divorce arrived with this morning's mail. Was it because of what Beth told you? What she said is true, I have been considering staying on in India. But not without first coming back to Chicago. Not without first seeing you. I'll admit that since we talked I've thought, more than once, that it might be better not to come back. I've wondered if it might not be better to stay here and avoid the possibility of getting together again only to separate for good. I've turned your letters inside out looking for assurance that if I were to return we could make it work. But how could you know what I myself don't?

I almost didn't make the phone call. I was afraid to hear your voice. I was afraid to talk and then to be left alone again. And I'm even more scared to return to Chicago only to say goodbye for the last time. I honestly don't think you have ever understood how frightened I am of giving myself over to my feelings for you. I want to stay here and forget. But I can't make myself forget. We need to have one more chance.

If we're really going to give up on this marriage, we need to do it together. I need to see you. I need to come back.

The letter had barely been written when I fell into a string of elaborate visions of what would ensue if I actually left India and returned. The visions quickly turned sour. Should I force the issue? Would she be able to go through with the divorce if I confronted her? It wasn't difficult to imagine the whole dismal sequence of events as they would unfold: the airport in New Delhi, boarding the plane for Chicago, the grueling flight, the train from O'Hare, standing outside her door, beaten down with exhaustion and fear, one hand gripping my shabby canvas bag. Punching the buzzer. For all I knew she and Bruce would be upstairs together. I should call first, from the airport. We had been separated for seven months now. For the past seven months she had been sleeping with him. They're a couple.

The scene in Chicago that I imagined made Harold Pinter's plays look like a demonstration of faith in life's basic goodness. She would be drinking. I would say anything, promise her anything. She would be forced to decide between me and Bruce. She wouldn't believe a word I said. Why should she? Before it was over we would flay each other on the rack of our anger. Why put us through this when I was not convinced that we could ever live happily together? How could we care for each other so much and still fail so miserably? Was this love?

I came full circle in my imagination and resolved not to go back to Chicago, then changed my mind repeatedly in the days and weeks that followed. There are passages in my journal where I started out headed one way, changed my mind before reaching the end of a single paragraph, and turned a complete about face—without realizing what I had done.

> I can't bring myself to give up on our marriage. The ties will not break. Even after all I've been through here, nothing has changed. I'm still not capable of committing myself to Judith, nor am I able to turn my back and walk away. I have one foot planted in the world we share and the other in whatever it is I've only begun to sense here in India. Both worlds are equally essential. I need them both.

I realized that I had never once been able to tell Judith that I loved her and to know in my heart that it was true.

> I've never believed any of it. Krishna was right—the whole promise of romantic love is a stupid, painful lie and we all know it, but we pretend not to because it's all we have. It's like coming back to the needle for another fix, always with another story. There's always another story.

Amid all of this I had a dream. I was with our old housemate—the woman I had slept with when I set all this misery in motion. Only it was more like a caricature of the actual woman. The woman in my dream was heavy—wide hips, big thighs and breasts, and dark, florid nipples. I was in bed with her and we were having sex, pumping away like machines. We'd been going at it night and day for what seemed like forever when I started to wear out. My penis was sore. Limp. *Not happy.* I said something about taking a break, and immediately the woman in the dream began to harangue me for losing interest in sex. I rolled off her and onto my back and lay there half covered under sweaty, crumpled sheets while she lectured me about how unnatural it was that I couldn't take pleasure in the human body.

In this part of the dream she was hovering over me on her knees, wearing nothing but a pair of faded white panties. I don't know when she put them on—it was a dream—but here's the really weird part: I couldn't pry my eyes away from those panties. I was fascinated and repulsed by a pee stain right in the center of her crotch. It was perfectly symmetrical, like a tantric mandala, a diagram of the psychic universe. All the time she was talking I was totally absorbed in that yellow spot between her legs. A little voice in my head kept repeating: *The pee stain is the key. The pee stain is the key.*

In a flash everything became clear. I knew that I had lived through this whole scene many times before, with just this woman, exactly as it was happening in the dream. I even knew, in some vague fashion, that I was dreaming, but it didn't seem to make any difference. The dream itself was déjà vu. Then the thought popped into my head that this could be the last time. I asked myself, in the dream, why I didn't finish with it, now. This is the last thing I remember before waking up, but that question reverberated in my mind: *Why not be done with it once and for all?*

But what was "it"?

The scene in the dream was disturbingly similar to episodes Judith and I had been through while wrestling with one or another of our endless problems. From time to time I would lose interest in the unceasing drama and simply bail out and become the man in the bubble. Unreachable. Judith would sob violently. Eventually I would come around and try to apologize, or else fly off into a litany of elaborate psychological or philosophical justifications for my behavior. This would go on just long enough for her sobbing to morph into blind rage that invariably culminated in a furious storm of threats and accusations. At last this too would pass, and it would be her turn to apologize. Then the inevitable finale: the two of us lying side by side in bed, crying.

The dream was, in fact, not nearly as bad as what Judith and I had actually experienced in waking life many times.

I sent off a barrage of mail, and at the end of the second week of March I received another letter: "Stanley, my decision is considered and final. I want a divorce. I'm very worried that you will return with false hopes and we will both suffer."

It was over.

If I was afraid to lose her by staying, I was even more afraid to go back. That same day I sat down and wrote to her saying I would not return to Chicago in the spring.

The divorce papers say that I abandoned my wife in June of 1975 without justification and against her will. That's not true. In June of 1975 I left Chicago, bound for New Delhi, but I did not abandon my wife. I didn't leave Judith until early spring of the following year, on the day I mailed that final letter.

After returning from the post office I copied a passage from the *Shikshasamucchaya* into my journal. The original Sanskrit and this, my translation, appear in an entry dated March 17, 1976:

> *Maraṇaṃ cyavanaṃ cyuti kālakriyā*
> *priyadravyajanena viyogu sadā/*
> *apunāgamanaṃ ca asaṃgamanaṃ*
> *drumapatraphalā nadisrotu yathā//*

> Death, departure, new birth, dissolution,
> separation from people and things beloved,
> never to come again or to meet again,
> like the leaves and fruits of the forest,
>   like the current of a river.

11

By the middle of March the sulfurous heat of summer begins to harden and crack the Gangetic plain that extends from northern Uttar Pradesh down through Bihar to Calcutta and the Bay of Bengal. This was my first experience of spring in northern India, a time when the cool days of winter are transmuted almost imperceptibly into summer's dry, ferocious heat, both a change of season and a subtle disintegration of the will.

Dust from the vast baking plains around Delhi was swept aloft by a dry wind and carried for miles until it drifted down over the inhabitants of the great city where I lived. The beggars lay in the crowded streets, more hopeless than ever, roasting like boney, charred rabbits turned over hot coals. Under banks of whirling propellers, accountants at the main office of the State Bank of India were bent low over their desks, surrounded by towers of massive ledgers, wiping the grit from their glasses. In the fashionable suburbs, dust floated through the streets outside exclusive shops and restaurants, gently working its way into each shiny Mercedes Benz, settling quietly over the German pile carpeting and hand-tooled upholstery. Sweepers in the big homes around Chanakyapuri and Jor Bagh kept busy with damp cloths, wiping down tables and floors several times a day. Heavy slatted blinds were lowered against the encroaching light.

For weeks already I had been unconsciously avoiding the direct sun, holding close to the sides of walls and buildings, straying farther out of my way each day simply to follow a sheltered path. At first I was completely unaware of the powerful natural forces at work on my body, contracting and expanding the muscles of my legs, driving my feet down a circuitous route through the shade, where I lingered an extra moment, struggling to recall a neglected errand, when I need only have looked up to the corrosive yellow fire that burned, hotter every day, in the bleached, cloudless sky.

I needed a break from my research. I'd switched again, gone back to my original proposal, working on early Vedanta, but it wasn't going all that well. I felt trapped between the two worlds of Buddhism and Hinduism, unable to decide which route to take. Penny and I began to talk of escaping to the mountains for a short retreat. We studied maps and gathered information on the hill stations north of Delhi. Shimla and Dehradun were out; neither of us was especially interested in exchanging a big city for a small one. Nor did we want to visit any of the busy pilgrimage spots like Haridwar or Rishikesh. After Agra and Delhi, we were both starved for a taste of nature in the raw. I was anxious to see uncultivated plants and wild animals, not more cows and people. One of us spotted a shaded area on the map labeled Corbett National Park. There it lay, beckoning to us from the hills near Almora, only a day's journey by rail from Delhi. I asked around, but no one I knew could tell me anything about the place. The more blank looks I drew, the more perfect it began to seem, until eventually the decision was made and the day of our departure was upon us.

We arose before dawn and set out for the train station in a motor rickshaw, sputtering and popping through the warm, dark air. Paharganj, the bazaar across from the sprawling New Delhi station, was already coming alive in the early light. Scraggly horses stood hitched to their two-wheeled tongas, noses buried in torn canvas bags of feed. Smoke blossomed up from the newly lit fires in the chai stalls where the drivers gathered. Cows roamed freely, grazing on mounds of empty green peapods or the severed stalks of purple eggplant that littered the street in front of a long row of dhabas. From the direction of the tracks came the hiss and shrieks of the big locomotives.

The main ticket hall echoed with the cries of vendors. Hundreds of people stretched out on the stone floor, sleeping under cotton shawls. Others sat together in small groups drinking chai and waiting with their battered aluminum footlockers, rolls of bedding, and a clutter of plastic baskets colored red, orange, or turquoise. Penny and I wove a path over and through the crowd, hopping from one empty spot to the next as though crossing a stream, rock by rock, cautious not to accidentally tread on the fingers or toes of someone's sleeping grandmother.

Somewhere along the way a ragged girl and her little brother appeared in our path, their hands out for change. I dispensed fifty paisa to each one, but this wasn't sufficient to buy them off, and they trailed us up the teeming stairs and over the tracks, then down again onto the platform where our train stood waiting. Having made it this far we could afford to relax—so long as we kept a close eye that the train didn't leave without us. We dumped our bags next to a counter operated by the station and ordered a couple of chairs and a package of glucose biscuits. The little girl planted herself directly in front of me, her brother staked out Penny. Both of them continued to make a big show of it, doing their best to look pathetic. The girl's eyes were half closed, one scrawny arm moving back and forth between her stomach and quivering lips. Her chin drooped and she moaned inarticulately.

I had seen this performance many times since coming to India; the mannerisms were always the same. It's a particular form of street theater usually reserved for foreigners. The basic idea is to act as wretched as you can, and to keep at it until you extract at least ten times the amount you could ever hope to get out of an Indian. The girl performed her role effortlessly, but the little guy next to her was apparently having trouble staying in character. He kept looking over at his sister and smiling in a way that threatened to spoil the whole drama. The longer this went on the more apparent it became that she, too, was fighting back a smile. Every now and again she would reach over and smack him alongside the head or give his ear a twist, but it didn't seem to help much. Despite this obvious handicap they managed to keep it up for several minutes before both of them burst out laughing and ran madly off down the platform, the girl showering her brother with a barrage of mock blows.

We stuffed ourselves into a second-class compartment with a contingent of farmers. Six of us were crammed onto a wooden bench designed to seat three. Penny sat with the open window on one side and me on the other. The day had barely begun, but we were already working up a good sweat. Several of the men were squashed together on my left, smoking bidis. They wore dhotis and dirty white kurtas that flapped around their knees in the wind. A few were barefoot, but most sported the standard-issue footwear for male villagers: flesh-toned plastic slippers with sharply pointed toes. The women squatted on the floor at our feet, saris gathered tightly up around their calves as though each butt had been shoved into a brightly colored cotton bag. Their palms and the soles of their feet had been decorated with ornate patterns of henna. They were all unselfconsciously staring at both of us, laughing and conversing with each other in a dialect I couldn't understand.

One old woman could not take her eyes off of Penny. God knows what thoughts were passing through her head as she contemplated this pale, exotic young female. The old lady didn't have a tooth in her head. She crouched there with her sari drawn up over her stringy gray hair, gumming a bidi. She squinted, tipped her head, then finally yanked off her glasses—a battered pair of heavy plastic frames distributed free by the government—and cleaned the thick lenses with a corner of her sari. This accomplished, she stuck them back on her face and craned her neck for a better look.

Penny seemed oblivious to the attention—an omnipresent feature of life here as a foreigner. She chatted with me for a while, then turned toward the open window and gazed out between the horizontal iron bars.

After Ghaziabad our car emptied out a bit, freeing up a few inches between me and two old Muslim men who now occupied the space vacated by the villagers. There were no more stops, and before long we fell into the soothing, timeless space of the traveler, where, suspended between coming and going, one often finds an unearned respite, a peace that demands no final resolution, freely given and accepted without a thought of gain or loss. The wheels clicked rhythmically over the track, and our bodies rocked and swayed in time with the motion of the carriage. On long, slow curves I could see the full length of the train to where the engine puffed and wheezed, belching dense clouds of steam and smoke that drifted through our window in a mist of fine black particles. Below us the ties rattled by. We passed small herds of goat and water buffalo grazing near the tracks, men peddling bicycles along ribbons of dust, women and girls gathered in the shade. Farther out, the flat countryside stretched away to the horizon. Penny and I barely exchanged a word, but I could feel her weight and the warmth of her body pressing against me.

Moradabad is two hours east of Delhi on the rail line to Banaras. This was as far as we could go by train. From there we caught a bus north to Ramnagar, the last stop for public transportation to Corbett. We each polished off a plate of rice and watery dal at a grubby little dhaba—the best restaurant in town—then assessed our situation. There were still four or five miles to cover, so we shouldered our bags and headed down the road with the intention of hitching a ride or walking the rest of the way to the park if it came to that.

The sun was bright and warm, but the air at this altitude was cooler than it had been on the plain. In the distance, the snow-covered peaks of the Himalayas rose into a cerulean sky. A light breeze dried the sweat on my arms; the sticky scent of pine hung around us like incense. Penny seemed especially beautiful to me as I watched her stoop to tighten the strap on one sandal. It occurred to me that life would never offer anything finer than this moment, that I would never feel more joyous or free than I felt right now, walking down the road with Penny beside me, my bag over one shoulder, an icy stream rushing nearby, the fresh odor of earth and snow in my nose. The cramped university world of Hyde Park was a faded reflection in a distant, cloudy glass. Even the pretentious babbling of the Fulbright office in New Delhi seemed a million miles away.

We hadn't been walking long when I heard the sound of a vehicle approaching. Both of us turned just in time to catch a glimpse of a car as it rounded a bend in the road and disappeared momentarily behind a clump of bushes. I positioned myself behind Penny, relying on the old hitchhiker's ploy of stationing the female out front where she can catch the driver's attention. I hadn't waved my hand more than once or twice when an old Land Rover chugged up next to us and abruptly stopped, stirring up a small cloud of dust.

Two men sat inside. The driver, with his thin moustache, was distinguished in a military sort of way. He was dressed in a khaki chauffeur's uniform and wore a red felt beret tipped jauntily over his forehead. His high cheekbones and almond eyes made it clear that he had been born somewhere in the mountains. The Sikh in the passenger seat, nearest to us, was obviously the boss. He was slightly older, in his mid fifties I would guess, a big man on the verge of becoming too heavy. When the jeep stopped, the passenger leaned out the window and saluted with a leather crop, greeting us in fluent English with just a touch of a British accent.

"Good morning!"

"Good morning," I said. Penny smiled demurely.

He returned her smile. "Going to the park?"

I nodded my head. "That's the plan."

"Come along, then. We're headed that way ourselves."

Before we could grab our bags, the driver was out from behind the wheel and around to our side of the jeep, where he stood at attention, holding the door. We tossed our things in back and climbed in after them. The next moment, we were bouncing up the narrow, winding dirt road that led to Corbett.

Our host turned halfway around in his seat, talking to us over his shoulder while we bumped along. As he spoke he toyed with the crop, holding it in his right hand and lazily slapping the palm of his left. He had about him the robust aura of health and strength of someone who had lived an active, outdoor life. He too had on a khaki uniform, but in place of the driver's beret, an imposing, jet-black turban was meticulously wrapped over his hair. Behind the tightly groomed beard his face was tanned and handsome. His eyes were hidden by a pair of dark aviator glasses. Once or twice he rapped lightly on the dash to emphasize a word or phrase. I concluded that this business of the swagger stick was a military affectation, a pompous vestige of the British Raj. I had to admit that he managed to pull it off with considerable aplomb. He commanded the sort of easy authority that makes for an ideal officer, a strong man who would claim the natural respect and genuine friendship of his soldiers.

"Quite a nice morning, wouldn't you agree?" He glanced up at the clear sky, then back at us.

"Couldn't be better," I answered. "We've just come from Delhi. It's hard to believe the difference."

"Hot down there, is it?"

"Oh yes, it's hot all right," Penny said. "Somewhere around thirty-seven yesterday afternoon."

"But we've escaped for a while," I added.

Once again he looked back and studied me for a minute. "You are from Germany, no?"

"No," I said.

"No?" He looked again.

"United States."

"Ah. USA. I see. And you?" He glanced over his shoulder at Penny.

She had both hands above her head adjusting the clip that held her hair in place, the thin cotton of her kameez pulled snugly up under her breasts. "British."

He seemed to find this amusing. "Ah ha! I would never have guessed. Both of you could easily pass for German, you know."

"Really?" She fastened the clip with a snap and lowered her arms.

"Or Russian, for that matter." He smiled and lightly tapped the nails of his left hand with the stick. "So you're on holiday in India. Arrived recently?"

"Not really. I've been here about eight months now," I said. "Since last June." This plainly caught him by surprise, but before he could respond I continued. "We're here to do research. This is Penelope Ainsworth, from Oxford University."

She nodded. "How do you do."

"My name's Stanley Harrington. From University of Chicago."

"Chicago?" He sounded puzzled. "But isn't that . . . ? Why yes, of course. The place where you Americans kill pigs!" I was about to respond, but he raised the stick, motioning for me to wait. "How does it go? 'Hog butcher for the world . . .'"

Penny repressed a smile.

"Excellent!" I exclaimed. "Hog butcher for the world. That's wonderful. You know American poetry?"

"Only a bit," he replied. I could tell he was pleased with himself. "Mostly it was British poets, but there were one or two of your countrymen. Carl Sandburg, Robert Frost. We were required to memorize them. In school, you know."

"I'm impressed. But just for the record, that city has a university as well. Sandburg didn't mention it, but it's there."

"How interesting . . ."

"Just down the street from the slaughterhouse," I added drolly. "That's where they send faculty who don't get tenure."

Singh gave me a puzzled look. Penny jabbed me with her elbow.

"I'm joking." It occurred to me how delighted Margaret would have been by this exchange.

He turned around and looked out the windshield at the road ahead, clearly uncertain what to make of my humor. After a second, though, he pushed himself around again. "Excuse me, please. I neglected to introduce myself. Colonel Ravindar Singh. Director of Corbett. This is my driver, Suresh." The chauffeur nodded in our direction.

"Very well," he continued, "so you are both scholars out for a bit of a trek, is it?" He ruminated on this. "But is your research somehow connected with Corbett?"

"Oh, no," Penny laughed. "We're here—in the park, that is—on holiday. Just for fun."

"Bravo." He rolled the crop back and forth over his palm. "For *fun*." He seemed to take some pleasure in the word. "And have either of you picked up any of our Indian languages during your stay?"

"*Nishchit rup say.*" I switched into Hindi and, anticipating his reaction, stuck with it. "It would be a shame to spend so much time here without knowing how to carry on a conversation or read the papers."

This positively blew him away. Nine times out of ten, people in India are elated with any foreigner who even makes a stab at a few phrases of their language. Coming out of my mouth, such high brow, Sanskritized vocabulary must have shocked him. He cranked around in his seat and checked to see if we really were the same people he had picked up a few minutes back. "And you, Miss," he addressed Penny in his own rather formal Hindi.

She hoisted a pack of Dunhills out of her bag, flipped back the red and gold lid and proffered it to him. "Do you mind if I smoke?" The Hindi words slid effortlessly from her lips. That did it. He was overjoyed. He and the chauffeur both joined her for a cigarette. Everyone was happy. Even Suresh, who had been left out of things so far, was quite cheery now as we veered along the unpaved road, smoking and conversing in a language he could understand.

We had traveled some distance from Ramnagar by this time, and the terrain now contracted around us in a frenzy of rank vegetation. Teak, oak, and other hardwoods mixed with conifers and stocky palms. The shadows between them crawled with serpentine vines and surreal tropical plants and flowers. We were being swallowed by a primeval jungle. A band of silver langur monkeys romped in the trees near the road. Each black face turned to watch us as the car wheeled by. Rounding a sharp bend we suddenly came upon a luxuriously plumed parrot perched on a branch that jutted over our path. The bird cocked its head, scolding us with a depraved, strangely human cry as the jeep passed below.

While we drove, Colonel Singh narrated the story of the Patlidun Valley, telling us a bit of its checkered history under the Raj and its eventual association with the British naturalist Jim Corbett, who died in 1955. For most of his life Corbett had been known locally for his bravery in hunting down several man-eating tigers that had roamed these hills during the almost eighty years he lived here. In his later years he had earned a small international reputation as the author of a series of adventure stories based on his exploits. It was clear that Singh looked on him as a hero of sorts, which may have accounted for our host's own British affectations.

We had been riding through the jungle for half an hour or so, listening to his stories, when the Land Rover arrived at a juncture in the road, one way leading to the park and the other to a small town nearby. The colonel signaled our driver to stop. He took a last puff on his cigarette, poked out the butt in an ashtray on the dash, and turned around to face us.

"What are your plans, then? Where shall we drop you?"

Penny and I looked at each other and realized that we had not the slightest idea where we would go from here. Our plans had not extended beyond the border of the park.

Finally Penny spoke up. "We hoped to find a government tourist bungalow in the park. Perhaps you could direct us to one?"

He looked at us quizzically. "Tourist bungalow? In Corbett?"

"It needn't be luxurious. Anything at all will do. There must be *something* nearby."

"No, I'm afraid not."

"Nothing at all?" I'm sure I sounded both surprised and incredulous.

He shook his head. "The park isn't designed for overnight visitors. There are no accommodations. *Kuch nahin.*"

Wonderful. This explained why people in Delhi had never been here. For a minute it seemed that no one knew what to say. At last, the colonel spoke up.

"I'll tell you what," he said, shifting back into English. "I have a forest bungalow not far from here. My own place, you understand. Would you be interested in putting up with me for a night or two? It's small, but I could give you a room if you like."

"Are you certain we won't interfere with your work?" said Penny, looking concerned.

"No, no! On the contrary. It will be my pleasure. One grows lonely out here in the bush. It will be an excellent diversion for me. You must understand, however, that I'm not really equipped to deal with guests. But I'm sure my cook can produce something suitable for dinner. And I keep the bar stocked. We can tour on one of the elephants after breakfast tomorrow, as well. Perhaps spot a tiger. A bit rustic, to be sure, but it could be, well, *fun.*" He looked at me, then over at Penny. "What do you say?"

I turned to Penny, who shrugged her shoulders.

"All right," I laughed. "We accept your invitation. With pleasure."

12

SINGH HAD BUSINESS to complete prior to heading home, which presented us with an opportunity to visit some of the outlying areas of the park. Suresh threw the Land Rover into four-wheel drive and took the left fork, abandoning the main road for a path barely wide enough to accommodate a vehicle this size. We hadn't gone more than a hundred yards before we entered a clearing, scattering a group of spotted deer that had been drinking from the brackish waters of a lagoon. They bounded away on agile legs, plunging into the underbrush. I could see them peering out at us from the shadows, turning their ears and sniffing at the air. Remnants of brush dangled from the sprawling horns.

We turned back into the jungle, plying our way along a trail—nothing more than two parallel ruts—that led eventually to the periphery of a wide meadow. It was dotted with compact trees and wiry shrubs that squatted in the grass like petulant dwarfs, their twisted limbs held close under leafy cloaks. On the meadow's far side a small herd of elephants grazed in the sun. They were occupied in gathering lunch, delicately uprooting the dwarfs and dislocating their limbs, but at the sound of the Land Rover, all activity ceased and every head turned in our direction. Nurslings, small and wrinkled with gray sails for ears, stared out at us wide-eyed from under the bellies of the gigantic adults, each miniature trunk coiled around the nearest available leg. As we approached, the larger calves pulled close to their mothers. Singh had the driver stop so we could step outside and get a better look, but it soon became evident that the big females were not pleased by the unexpected guests at their midday meal. Several began pawing and stamping at the dirt. It wasn't long before the closest trumpeted aggressively, which persuaded us to move along.

From there, our path wound up over a ridge and along the rim of an immense gorge that had been cut into the earth by the Kosi River as it poured down out of the mountains on its way to meet the Ganges. We pursued a dramatic, treacherous route, the gorge growing ever wider and deeper. By now the Land Rover was a good forty meters above the meandering water, chugging along the edge of a striated rock wall that plummeted nearly straight down to the boulders below. I had my eye on Suresh, who seemed focused, but totally at ease, when Singh motioned again for him to stop.

While Suresh waited, the rest of us climbed out and walked to the edge of the precipice. Far below, dozens of crocodiles sprawled on the river's bank, scattered in a jumble of dull, mossy scales, dozing and sunning themselves. Now and then one of the giant lizards would yawn, flaunting ragged strings of teeth inside its long, pink mouth.

"We better go," Singh announced, his voice pulling us back. "We have an errand to run, and we need to be home before the sun goes down."

I could not begin to imagine how dark it would be in the jungle at night.

Once in the car he informed us that we were to pay a call on an old anchorite, Kalidas, who lived nearby. According to Colonel Singh the man "watched over things in the backwoods," though it was not altogether evident what this meant. He had been living alone in the bush some fifty years, surviving Singh's two predecessors, who had also known him and tolerated his presence within the park. In India, saints and holy men are allowed to violate not only social conventions but often legal ones as well. His peculiar history had once been a legend among the people who lived in the hills around Almora, but with time Kalidas had gradually been forgotten by the outside world. He came here as a young man hoping to escape society, and though it had taken him nearly half a century, he seemed largely to have succeeded in his effort. For the past fifteen years Colonel Singh and his driver were the only visitors to his isolated sanctuary. They may have been the only two people left who remembered the story of how it was that he came here so many years ago.

Singh told us that the hermit Kalidas had originally been Ramesh Jaganath Mishra, an anonymous midlevel bureaucrat under the British Raj, employed as an accountant at the viceroy's regional administrative offices in Dehradun. Educated at English-medium schools, Ramesh launched into his career after graduation and was soon married to a girl from Mussoorie. He brought the new bride back to his mother's home and settled in, anticipating the security of career and family life. At the end of their first year together a son was born, and Ramesh must have felt that he had everything life could offer. But within months all this collapsed.

Shortly after the birth of their son, the accountant experienced the first in a series of dreams that eventually upset his happiness. The legend has it that he was visited in his sleep by the goddess Kali, usually pictured wearing a garland of severed heads, her long tongue uncurled obscenely over black, shriveled lips. Kali is the only member of the Hindu pantheon who still demands to be worshiped through blood sacrifice. That first night she merely offered him darshan—the blessing of her presence. Other dreams followed, though, and before long she began to lift the corner of her veil, favoring Ramesh with increasingly abhorrent visions. His young wife grew accustomed to being awakened at night by her husband's quick, panicked breathing and by the terrible sound of his cries.

The border between dream and reality eroded, and within months the images began to infringe on Ramesh's waking life. At first it was only the memory of these dreams lingering through the day, but later he saw things—the same, dreadful images—while wide awake.

His waking life became a nightmare. He made the mistake of sharing these experiences with his neighbors. But one can easily understand how impossible it would have been to keep such a thing hidden in a small Indian village. It wasn't long before he was publicly recognized as a seer, favored by the goddess. It was said that he could read the circumstances of each person's death literally inscribed on their features. To look upon the faces of his neighbors was actually to watch each one of them die. For Ramesh this ability to witness the eventual death of his family and friends was a gift of prophecy he had not asked for. Once the visions swept over him, he was incapable of resisting. Accident, disease, and death were with him constantly.

People came from as far as Delhi to sit at the feet of the great prophet. The desire for darshan—to see and be seen by a holy person—is an ancient feature of Hinduism, but in this case it took on a unique flavor. Most of those who came to him were simply pious pilgrims, but as his fame spread, his visitors were increasingly driven by a compulsive need to know every detail of their fate. He complied with their requests, persuaded that the goddess had granted him this power and that it was not up to him to understand why.

The accountant Ramesh was not a sophisticated or ambitious man, and living with these alarming visions must have been an unbearably heavy burden, reading in every face the clear imprint of its destiny, the very moment of death. He resigned from his job and became dejected and withdrawn, passing his days in meditation and worship. Neighbors heard him praying to Kali late at night, quietly sobbing and pleading, gently, unceasingly, for mercy. Hers was a hard blessing.

One of the last to visit him, or so the story goes, was the Mahatma himself. Gandhi is said to have made a trip to Ramesh's home in 1924, shortly after the famous "salt march" to the sea at Dandhi. He had just been released from his first stay in a British prison. If there is any truth to this story, and to the entire legend surrounding Kalidas, then the accountant may have revealed to Gandhi exactly when and where the fatal bullet would be delivered some twenty-four years later. Colonel Singh did not doubt in the least this account of Gandhi-ji's visit. He had heard it all directly from his predecessor, who had in turn heard it from the previous director, a man who claimed to have seen the youthful ex-advocate with his own eyes the very day he arrived in Dehradun to receive the prophecy. The story will probably never be confirmed, but among the local population there was no question as to what followed.

Not long after the Mahatma's pilgrimage to Dehradun, a disaster occurred that once again altered the course of Ramesh's life. Most people insisted that he had seen it coming and had done his best to prevent it but that his puja and meditation had been to no avail, that it had all amounted to nothing more than a desperate and futile attempt to alter his own destiny. Among educated brahmans it was generally acknowledged that things might have been different had Ramesh been stronger, better suited to serve as a vessel for the goddess. The consensus among these learned pundits was that his case was a tragedy; they may well have been correct. Certainly Ramesh was not the obvious choice for the job. He was far too timid, not equipped emotionally to cope with the formidable strain. But then, how many of us are born with the courage to take on the burden of an oracle?

According to Singh's story, Ramesh was up much later than usual one night, praying and meditating long after his wife and child went to bed. The baby had been wrapped and laid as usual on a mat next to its mother, but apparently the boy awoke sometime after and crawled away, falling asleep again off in the darkness where he was not easily visible. When Ramesh entered the room he stepped down on his son and literally crushed the child's tiny body under one bare foot, killing him instantly. A macabre howl reverberated through the household, a primal wail of bottomless despair that woke his wife.

Whether the infant's death could be viewed as an accident was hotly debated. A number of people blamed Ramesh directly for the tragedy. They insisted that he should have run away the moment he saw what was going to happen. Most agreed, though, that even assuming he knew exactly what was coming, Ramesh could no more have escaped his fate than any of us can escape ours. Whatever the truth, the accountant abandoned his wife shortly after his son's death and set out to wander alone in the mountains, eventually ending up in the region of Almora. Here he had dwelled as a hermit ever since. In 1935—almost ten years after his arrival—the area was designated a federal wildlife sanctuary, but he was permitted by the first director to stay on, apparently at the request of Jim Corbett himself.

"The precedent was set almost forty years ago," Singh told us, "and I have had no reason to overturn it. He is an old man now. Every year he becomes weaker. But he will never leave the jungle. Of that I am certain."

I had been listening to all of this with great interest. "You say that he came here for total solitude. To escape society. Why do you bother him, then?"

Colonel Singh drummed nervously on the seat with his fingers. "We bring him a few supplies, some simple things to keep him going. Nothing much. One cannot very well just let the man starve."

"And that's why we're going there now?" Penny asked.

"Yes." He waved a hand toward several burlap bags stowed behind the seat where the two of us were sitting. "Just some simple provisions. And this." He picked up a brightly colored box of incense and held it between us, then tossed it back down beside him. "For puja."

I reached over, lifted the package off the seat and sat turning it over in my hands as though it might contain something more precious than incense, a secret teaching, perhaps, or a prophecy of its own. "So he still worships the goddess?"

Colonel Singh seemed surprised by my question. "But of course. He is extremely devout. He will die here in the jungle, doing puja to Kali."

"Colonel, do you mind if I ask you something?" I said this in English so the driver would not understand. I couldn't resist. "Did he ever tell you anything? I mean, well, you know . . . anything about your own death."

"I have not talked with him about it, Mr. Harrington."

"I see."

"The fact is I have not talked with him about anything."

"About anything?"

"I mean, simply," Mr. Harrington, "that he has not spoken to me, and I have not spoken to him."

"Not once in . . . how long has it been?"

"Almost ten years since I started here."

"Are you saying that you've known this man for nearly ten years and during that time you've never exchanged a single word with him?"

"That is correct. He stopped speaking long before I arrived. He accepts the provisions we bring, but he is not interested in anything else. You'll see for yourself."

"But if the legend is true, then he knows . . ."

"About my death?" The colonel interrupted me, smiling ironically. "Yes, of course he knows. The whole thing must seem very peculiar to you, Mr. Harrington—an American with a university education." He hesitated. "But I have no doubt that he sees clearly what fate has in store for Suresh and myself."

"And there are no other visitors?"

"No one enters this part of the park. Nor do we ever talk about Kalidas outside. His presence here is . . ." He considered for a moment. "It's become our secret, I suppose. I doubt that anyone else knows the man is still alive, or even remembers him for that matter. Which is precisely how he wants it."

Penny had remained curiously silent throughout our conversation. I wondered what she thought about all of this, but it would have to wait until later when we could talk in private. Meanwhile our path led farther into the jungle.

We pulled into a clearing surrounded by dense forest. A ramshackle hut stood at the center, not much more than a bamboo cage covered with a patchwork of palm leaves, the whole thing laced together with a blue plastic cord that must have been included in one of the packages left there by the colonel. As the jeep drew near I saw someone stir inside. A silhouette in the dark interior drifted toward the entrance, then stopped short of the porch and hung back among the shadows, watching cautiously. It would have been difficult for him to see Penny and me in the back seat, and from what Singh had told us, we certainly would not have been expected. I gathered that this was his usual reaction to the colonel's arrival.

Suresh pulled the Land Rover up to the front of the house and cut the engine. Kalidas remained in the dimly lit entrance, a frail old man bent over his cane, barefoot but otherwise fully clothed in the same government issue shirt and pants that the others were wearing. In this case, though, the outfit was several sizes too large for the tiny man, who seemed to have retreated into the baggy folds of worn khaki. His wispy hair and beard fell around his face and down over his hunched shoulders and narrow chest to well below his waist.

Suresh got out of the car, went around and opened the rear gate of the Land Rover, and began unloading a few kilos of rice and lentils, some potatoes and onions. Aside from the food, I saw a can of kerosene for the cooking stove. It didn't take long to finish setting all of it on the porch. Within minutes he was back in the jeep, the motor cranked over, and we were on our way. I turned back for a final look, but Kalidas was no longer standing in the door. I felt suddenly that I had missed out on something terribly important—an opportunity of some kind that would never come again.

We had driven as far as the edge of the jungle when I noticed the incense still lying on the seat next to me where I had let it fall.

"*Ruk jaao!*" I yelled at Suresh to stop and he hit the breaks.

"What is it?" Singh cried out.

I snatched up the package and waved it over the seat. "The incense. You forgot to leave it." Singh was about to take the box from me when I opened the door and hopped out. "Sit still. I'll run it back."

I dashed across the yard and rushed up to the porch just as Kalidas shuffled through the doorway directly into the sunlight. He had come out to retrieve the bags, and my sudden appearance caught him entirely unprepared. We were no more than a few feet away from each other when he looked up and saw me there, standing across from him, close enough that I distinctly heard him draw a deep breath as he stopped dead in his tracks.

I will never forget the expression that swept over his face during those first few seconds, how he recoiled at the sight of me. Perhaps it was nothing more than the shock of being surprised like this by a stranger—a foreigner, no less. And yet, the meaning of the horror that passed over his face is a text that resists any authoritative interpretation, regardless of how many times I resurrect the image of his wrinkled face and scrutinize each ancient, weathered line.

Whatever its significance, the wave of that first reaction washed over the old man's features and left behind eyes unlike any I have ever seen.

They were open wounds. All falseness and artificiality had been scoured away; what remained was just pain, and boundless trust. I felt myself in the presence of a man who needed nothing, a man whose only purpose was to see. We stood motionless across from each other for a few seconds. And then I remembered the incense. I reached out my hand and offered the package to him. He looked at the shiny green wrapper for a moment but didn't seem to realize what it was until I spoke.

"*Aap kaa agarbatti*," I said tentatively, "Your incense." He stared at the box I held between us. "We forgot to leave it with you."

At last one frail arm moved forward, weak and trembling with age, his knuckles knotted and swollen. The arthritic fingers creaked open, hovered over my hand, then descended and closed around the incense, lifting it gently. He withdrew his arm and looked up at me. And then, just as I was about to turn away, he smiled—a shy, toothless grin that spread delicately out beneath the feathery whiskers and floated there for one timeless moment before he retreated into the hut and disappeared among the shadows.

I walked back to the Land Rover. Penny looked at me oddly as I climbed in and slammed the door shut, but no one said a word. The engine roared and we were gone. It wasn't until reaching the spot where we had watched the crocodiles that the colonel said something about dinner, and we all agreed we were starving.

13

SINGH'S FOREST BUNGALOW could easily have been designed for use in an unfilmed sequel to Casablanca: Bogart loses Bergman and retreats to the foothills of the Himalayas. It was as far from civilization as Kalidas's little hut but on the opposite side of the park and built to conform to the British imperial aesthetic.

We entered the compound through a stone gateway, following a broad circular drive of hard-packed clay lined on either side by rows of potted flowers. As the Land Rover approached we were greeted by the colonel's majordomo, a stocky man in a rose-colored lungi and sleeveless white undershirt. His head was clean shaven except for a thin strand of hair left dangling in back. A young male langur perched on his right shoulder. The fingers of one spidery black hand were splayed over the man's bald head, palming it like a basketball; with the other hand the monkey scratched idly at the shaggy fur on his own belly. Langurs have especially long tails—much longer than those of their smaller cousin, the rhesus—and this particular tail looped around the servant's neck and down to his navel, where the tip curled back and forth, obviously looking for trouble. Colonel Singh introduced Penny and me to Jagjit Ram and his hirsute friend, Chota Hanuman.

The house was situated in a clearing not far from the bank of the Kosi. The muted lapping of the river mingled with a screeching and chattering that emanated from the bush: white noise of the jungle. Despite its modest proportions, the bungalow was an icon of British colonial architecture. Wrapped in a deep veranda supported by Doric columns, the wide, sloping roof of ceramic tile absorbed the last rays of the sun as it sank behind the forest. Jagjit led us between the two shutters that framed the entranceway and on into the foyer. Once inside, man and monkey excused themselves—with some prodding, even Chota Hanuman joined two tiny palms and raised them summarily to his forehead—and withdrew.

The interior of the bungalow was shaped by vaulted ceilings and stone floors. On our right was a sitting room with a large, open fireplace reminding me of the mammoth grates one finds in the villas of Tuscany. The flames cast a warm glow. To the left a dining room was furnished with a heavy, rectangular table and six ornate wooden chairs. A brass chandelier hung from the ceiling, fitted out with no less than a dozen candles. The hallway, opening directly in front of us, led off to the master suite and a guest room that would be ours for the next few nights.

"Well," said the colonel, "this is my own jungle retreat, so to speak. I'm here during the hot season and the monsoon, a good seven months out of the year. More, if I can manage it. In the coldest part of the winter I close things up and shift down to Ramnagar."

"It's marvelous," Penny exclaimed. "Really. A dream!"

"You think so, do you?" Singh replied, visibly swelling with pride.

"Oh, yes! I'm quite envious." She turned and gave him a look of mock anger. "A few days here and I won't want to leave."

"Indeed!" Singh laughed self-consciously and began gazing fondly around the room with undisguised satisfaction. Sturdy rattan furniture overlaid with deep cushions had been drawn up around the fireplace on a colorful woven dhari. A tiger skin hung over the mantel, and the rest of the room was strewn with trophies, souvenirs, and curios from the colonel's various adventures. There was a small bar in the far corner. It was early evening and the house was set with oil lamps. The shutters had been drawn against the cool air outside, and a log blazed in the hearth. "Yes," he said, as if to himself, "I have enjoyed myself here."

I followed his gaze to a frame set on the bar, a black and white photograph of the colonel and an attractive, matronly woman in a sari; it had been taken in the circular driveway just outside. They were standing together in front of an elephant, laughing as though someone out of the camera's range had done something to amuse them. A mahout sat astride the elephant's neck, his goad held at military attention. Judging from the colonel's appearance in the picture, it could not have been more than a few years old. His eyes lingered over the photograph, and then, as if to rouse himself, he raised the stick and delivered an abrupt swat to one of his pant legs. "It's quite dark in here, don't you think? I'm accustomed to the poor lighting, but we do have a petrol generator out back. Shall I have Jagjit engage it for us?" He turned to call the servant but Penny stopped him.

"Oh no, please. This is much better as it is. Can we just have the lamps?

It's such a treat to have left the noise and the tube lights behind." She moved near the fire and began to warm her hands.

I wandered over to the bar for a closer look at his photographs; twenty or thirty of them hung in frames above the bottles. Many showed the colonel posing with various Indian dignitaries and military officers. In quite a few I recognized the woman I had already seen standing with him and the elephant. Some were much older than the rest. Yellowed and fading behind the glass, they depicted a world before Singh's time: Europeans gussied up in polished black boots, jodhpurs, and pith helmets, with bushy moustaches and enormous rifles slung over their shoulders—the lost world of the Raj. Several of the photos had been taken in front of the bungalow, and a handsome Englishman turned up here and there shaking hands and smiling with people that appeared to be his guests. I noticed that in several photos he carried a riding crop identical to the colonel's. "Who's this fellow?" I pointed at one where he was saluting a regal looking British officer.

Colonel Singh stepped over to the bar and examined the picture. "Jim Corbett. The park's namesake. I told you about him earlier. He's greeting the viceroy, Lord Irwin, at an official reception for the inauguration of the park. It was called Hailey National Park then, but Corbett was already quite well known in the area."

Penny came over from the fire to take a look. "That's your house in the picture, isn't it? *This* house?"

"Yes, it is. Corbett built it. He was the first to live here. Some of the things you see are just as he left them. This picture, for example, and the tiger skin." He gestured toward the mantel. "One of the 'man eaters of Kumoan' that he wrote about in his books."

Penny and I studied the photo. The colonel had picked up a poker and was making a desultory stab at the coals. "What I want to know, Colonel Singh, is how did you find work like this? You seem to be reaping the fruits of some very good karma."

"Good karma is not enough," he replied with a smile, still gazing at the coals. "It took me twenty years in the Army Core of Engineers. This position was a sort of gift when I left behind my official duties in the service." He laid aside the iron and dusted his hands. "You both must be tired from your journey. Why don't we bathe and change our clothes, then meet back here in . . ." He glanced at Penny. "Will half an hour be sufficient?"

"Certainly."

"Right, then. Jagjit will take your bags." He stopped speaking and cleared his throat, apparently at a loss as to how he should continue. "There is, I'm afraid, only one guest room." Again he paused. "However, if you require separate quarters, I could of course make arrangements."

Penny suddenly became engrossed in an object down at the far end of the bar, an ashtray fashioned out of some unfortunate animal's hoof that had been hollowed out and notched along one edge to support a row of butts. I tried, unsuccessfully, to catch her eye and finally said, "The single room will be fine, for both of us."

Colonel Singh looked at Penny, who lifted her eyes now and returned his gaze. Her expression was impossible to read. "Just so," he said. "If you require anything simply tell Jagjit, and he will be glad to help you out." He gave us a stiff, quasi-military bow and strode briskly around the corner and down the hallway.

Like the rest of the colonel's forest bungalow, the guest room was a vision of the Raj, slightly worn around the edges, to be sure, but absolutely perfect in its own way. The stone floor was covered with a hand-loomed wool carpet tinted to deep russet. In the center of the room the low bed had been positioned under a bamboo frame from which a mosquito net hung loosely. It was suspended at the end of a rope running up through a pulley mechanism that allowed for the entire apparatus to be hoisted up out of the way during the day. There was a vanity table and stool and another comfortable sofa similar to the one by the fire. Two large shuttered doors opened onto the veranda. A familiar aroma wafted out of the bathroom from the Indian-style squatter. Nothing strong enough to be seriously offensive, merely a slight, noisome reminder that we were not altogether removed from the world of Delhi and the northern plains. Someone had lit a stick of sweet incense and set it discreetly on the vanity, next to tea— not chai, but a "full set," as it is called in India: tea as the British preferred it, with milk and sugar served separately.

We had just begun to unpack when Jagjit and Chota Hanuman arrived at the door with two buckets of hot water for bathing. While Jagjit went to deposit them near the tap, the anthropoid began rifling through the contents of Penny's bag until she dissuaded him with a sharp tug at his furry tail. "*Scat!*" She turned to me and laughed. "Cheeky little beast."

When we returned to the main room, Colonel Singh was already there sitting comfortably by the fire. He saw us coming and rose, complimenting

Penny on her sari, an inexpensive, cream-colored cotton, the border printed with a floral pattern in shades of pastel green and cinnamon. It was one of my favorites but not the sort of thing I would have expected a man like Singh to go for. While we relaxed by the hearth, the table was set for dinner.

Despite the unanticipated guests, Singh's cook managed to produce a delicious meal with ingredients already on the premises. Palak paneer; mixed curried vegetables; rich, creamy dal makhani; and tandoori chicken—all of this served with nutty basmati rice and a continuous supply of warm chapatis. I declined to sample the bird, begging off on the grounds that I was a vegetarian, but Penny helped herself to a second large portion and insisted on personally complimenting the chef. Everything was excellent. I made a glutton of myself, giving in to Singh's admonitions to fill my plate again at least two times after I was convinced I could not possibly eat another bite. He maintained that I was desperately underweight for my height. Both Penny and I were much too thin in his eyes, though by the time she finished eating he was forced to concede that it was difficult to understand how she remained so slim consuming as much food as she did.

"Intestinal parasites, young lady," he finally proclaimed, in lieu of any other explanation. "You really ought to have it looked into the moment you're back in Delhi."

When the last of the plates had been cleared away, Jagjit returned with silver finger bowls filled with steaming lemon water and another silver dish containing anise seeds and chunks of crystallized sugar that sparkled under the candles. A round of tea was served, and we sat around the table, too stuffed to move. Soon enough, though, the tea and anise settled our stomachs, and Singh suggested that we withdraw to the other room, where we could relax by the fire with a nightcap.

Before the drinks were poured, however, the colonel suddenly remembered something he wanted to show Penny and me. He escorted us to the kitchen, where we found Jagjit and the cook squatting together in a corner, enjoying a smoke. One of them had given Chota Hanuman a bidi, and when we walked in, the ape had just finished sticking it up his nose. Singh picked up a platter piled with scraps of raw meat and motioned for us to follow him through the kitchen toward a storeroom at the back. The doorway had been blocked off somewhat above waist level with heavy wire mesh. Jagjit followed close behind us holding a lamp so we could peer inside. At the far end of the narrow room a tiger cub crouched in the shadows, eyeing us suspiciously as we leaned over the gate for a better look.

This was no domestic kitty. She was the size of small Labrador, and already considerably heavier and more solid than any dog, with thick, muscular legs and broad paws. It occurred to me as strange and somehow disconcerting that I had never before stood so close, unprotected, to a wild animal. Despite present circumstances she was only a step removed from the jungle where she had lived until recently, when Singh and Jagjit had managed to trap her and transport her back to the house. Her eyes were right out of Blake's poem, blazing with insolent fury and a predator's fierce indignation at having been taken from her rightful home and confined to this dungeon merely for our amusement. It would not be long before the present barrier would no longer suffice to hold her captive.

"Go ahead," Singh said. "Feed her."

Penny stepped toward the platter and sunk her fingers into a thick slice of meat. She lobbed it over the gate and then shook the blood from her hand as she watched the tiger slink forward. Her eyes were riveted on the animal.

The two of us took turns flinging chunks of carrion over the fence to where they slapped on the floor. Each time the cat would pull back on her haunches, hiss and snarl, baring her prodigious teeth, then swipe at the meat with one paw, catch it up in her claws, and devour it whole in a single swift movement.

"What do you think of her?" Singh directed his query at Penny, who had just finished throwing the last chunk over the fence.

"She's gorgeous. How old is she?"

"Not more than four months. We first spotted her mother a few months ago, not far from the house. The kits weren't hard to find. I had my eye on this one, waiting until she was old enough to be taken."

"But why would you do such a thing? It's so sad to see her caged up like this."

"You needn't worry," he laughed. "She will be free to roam again soon enough. But before she goes home I shall teach her a few useful tricks. I've been waiting years for this. Until now the proper animal had not appeared." He handed over the platter to Jagjit, who seemed already to have enough to deal with between the lamp and the monkey, who sat fretting on his shoulder, obviously disturbed by Singh's feline pet. I observed that the bidi was now planted in the servant's left ear.

"A friend of mine manages a park in Bengal," the colonel continued.

"He has a male cat that he trained from just about this age. Ramu. That's what he calls him. I've wanted one of my own ever since I saw that tiger."

Penny's eyes were fixed on the cub, who was returning her stare, crouched low in the corner as she had been when we arrived. "What's her name?"

"She doesn't yet have a name. You may perhaps have a suggestion?"

"Oh no, I wouldn't dare," Penny breathed. The cat curled back her lips. A long, low rumble rolled up from deep in her belly. Her whiskers bristled.

"Some pet," I mumbled, surreptitiously examining the fence. "Do you really think you'll ever be able to trust her?"

"Without question. It takes time, but tigers are extremely intelligent and loyal. It was the loyalty of my friend's tiger that first put this idea into my head. But let me tell you how I met Ramu. I was traveling in Assam and had stopped over with an old friend of mine from the service—Naresh Bannerji. He has a place similar to this one. A bit more elaborate, I would say." He looked around. "Larger, in any case. It was evening—just dusk, to be precise. Several of us were seated outside around a table in back enjoying an after-dinner scotch."

At this point Colonel Singh left off with the narration and looked around again as though he had misplaced something.

"Oh yes! I have entirely forgotten. We ourselves have some drinks waiting for us. What do you say we continue this conversation in the other room, by the fire?" We filed back through the kitchen and were soon comfortably ranged before the flames. Penny and I sat together on the couch, the colonel reclined in one of the other chairs. "Now then, where was I?"

"In back of your friend's bungalow, somewhere in rural Bengal . . ."

"Right. Thank you, Mr. Harrington. So there we were, much as the three of us are now, quite relaxed. Enjoying the liquor and conversation. I can't quite recall everyone who was present." He stared at the fire as though it might jog his memory, then shook his head. "Blast it anyway! What difference does it make who was there? The point is that one or the other of us had just commented on the local political situation. Something about a council in the village that adjoined the park boundaries. Anyway, Bannerji suddenly put a finger to his lips and hushed the conversation. He gestured for us to sit still, then began to gaze intently into the underbrush as though something were out there. As I say, it was dusk at the time. Not yet dark, but certainly none of us could have seen very far into the jungle.

"After a moment or two our host leaned back into his chair. It's nothing, he assured us, nothing at all. But of course we knew better. After some prodding Bannerji finally admitted to having heard a 'crunching about' in the bush. This was a bit disturbing, particularly because there had recently been a nasty incident involving a tiger—we had just been discussing it at dinner. A villager had been killed while walking home one evening along a well-trodden path. One of us recalled having seen an article in the local paper. According to Bannerji the cat had been sighted only the day before not far from where we sat. He apologized for having alarmed us and insisted that we forget all about it." The colonel hesitated, then raised one hand and lightly massaged his chin. "Now, most of us there that night had lived in the bush long enough that something like this was not unheard of. And we also knew that once a tiger tastes human flesh, it must be destroyed."

I interrupted him. "So it's true, what they say?"

"Absolutely. A man-eating tiger will kill again and again until it is stopped. They lose all fear of humans. That is not true for a leopard."

I filed this piece of information away for future reference.

He shook his head. "Tigers have a mind of their own. They rarely take to that sort of behavior, but it does happen. Now and again."

Penny leaned forward a little. "Why is that, Colonel?" Her legs were crossed, fingers twined lightly around the glass she had balanced on one knee. "Why would a tiger suddenly decide to attack humans?"

"Usually because they can no longer hunt their normal prey. As often as not the animal is old and weak. It may be injured. A few years back I had to bring down a man-eater right here at Corbett. Her left forepaw was punctured with a nasty sliver; it was badly infected. She must have been half mad with the pain." He nodded in the direction of a photo on the wall behind the bar. "That's the only one you will ever see with me and a dead cat in the same picture. I'm not a hunter. Never have been. This country used to be crawling with tigers, but they have been hunted to near extinction." He pulled at his beard and gazed up at the tiger skin that hung stretched over the mantle, slightly darkened by years of heat and smoke. The tiger's glass eyes stared back. Its teeth, yellowed with age, gleamed softly in the flickering light of the fire.

"Bannerji's queer behavior left its mark on us. Despite his assurances, we were intensely aware of the jungle all around us. It was a few minutes before the conversation picked up again. We had just begun to relax when suddenly my old friend sat bolt upright in his chair and stuck the same finger to his lips." Singh mimicked the gesture. "This time we immediately fell silent and began studying the leaves for the slightest sign of movement. Sure enough, we could see them trembling way down at one end of the garden. No sooner did we spot those leaves shaking than there was a low growl. The sound we heard that night did not come from any three-month-old cub. There was a big cat stalking out there, just beyond the range of our vision. Every one of us knew it. We were on the edge of our seats, one eye on the jungle, one on the back door to the house. No one wanted to be the first to go. It was Bannerji that suggested we better move, and it was he who stood up before the rest of us. Just at that moment we heard a limb snap and—seconds later—there was a terrific roar. A big male tiger broke through the brush and headed straight across the clearing. Straight for Bannerji. It was a good thirty meters and the animal was loping over the grass—between us and the house by then, blocking any chance of escape."

He looked over at Penny, whose eyes were huge. "Have you seen a tiger move like that? Have you seen how gracefully they run when they know they have plenty of time?" She shook her head.

"Well, young lady, you have missed something remarkable." Under the moustache Singh's lips peeled back in a devilish grin. "We had a professor of zoology there with us from Shantiniketan. I remember him now, because when the tiger appeared he started in yelling as if he'd cracked. Sat there bellowing *Hari Ram! Hari Ram!* The cat ignored him. Never took its eyes off Bannerji. Went right for him. Within seconds it made the table, lunged over and struck the ground just in front of where my friend was standing with his glass still clutched in his hand. There was no question in my mind: that tiger was going to take him down." The colonel cocked one arm back and slashed through the air. He pushed his lips together and shrugged. "It wasn't just me. All of us were certain Bannerji's time had come."

"So," I interjected, "what happened?"

"I'll tell you what happened, Mr. Harrington. The tiger raised up and put those big paws right on the bloody joker's shoulders. That is what happened. One paw on each side of the busturd's neck, and the animal commenced licking at his face. Stood right there on its hind legs with its big tongue all over Bannerji's silly, grinning face. Tame as the proverbial kitten."

Singh laughed out loud. "And that, Mr. Harrington, is how I met Ramu."

"Wonderful," I murmured, then thought to myself that if Singh had pulled a stunt like that on us tonight, I would have shit my pants so bad no tiger would ever want to come near me. The colonel was in stitches.

"I tell you Bannerji never spilled one drop of his scotch! That busturd!"

"Yes sir," I acknowledged, "he is one serious *busturd*." I suggested that his friend might have given someone a heart attack, but Singh kept right on rocking back and forth in his seat, slapping his knee and guffawing.

"Whenever I remember that evening I always picture the professor," he said, struggling to regain his composure: "*Hari Ram! Hari Ram!*" The image threw him all over again into a paroxysm of mirth. "Bannerji, you busturd!" It was apparent that the dignified military man had another, rather perverse side to his character. "By god, I shall have some *fun* with that little girl in the other room!"

14

His story finished, Singh poured another round for all of us and ambled back across the room with the three glasses suspended in a triangle between both hands. We sipped at our drinks and settled in again while he carried on, spinning out one tale after another, escorting us ever more deeply into his world. There was something about the man I could not grasp, something captivating, a kind of ingenuous engagement with life that was deeply appealing. It was enough, for the moment at least, simply to sit and listen. From what I could see, Penny felt the same way. She appeared to be totally at ease in his presence.

He told us of his efforts to save the remaining tigers in India, of his travels in Africa and Southeast Asia. There were more anecdotes of Bannerji and his friends in the game preserves around the subcontinent. We heard about everything from his childhood in Chandigarh to the gritty episodes of army life in a Sikh regiment stationed in northern Himachal Pradesh. The evening wore on, the bottle was eventually transported from the bar to the table in front of the fire, and talk wound around to his days with the Army Corps of Engineers, surveying high in the hinterlands of Ladakh in an area contested by the Chinese.

"I was right in the middle of it when the real trouble began in October of 1962. It was my last action with the army before I retired."

"So you were there," I said.

"I was there all right." He took a swallow from his drink. "Nehru went to England. Hell, he went all the way to America asking for military aid. It was a war." He frowned. "The papers called it a 'conflict,' tried to pretend otherwise. But that's the only word for it. War."

He was quiet for a moment.

"What really happened?" I asked.

"We got our bloody arses kicked, that's what happened. We should have seen it coming long before we did. The Chinese were already building a road up there in 1950. Four years before the 'Panchashul,' the so-called 'five principles of peaceful coexistence.'" His voice was grave. "No one talks about it any more. It's as though the whole thing never happened. But I can assure you, Mr. Harrington, we lost a lot of good men. Too many men died up there. It was a disaster." He turned to Penny. "Do you have a map of India? I mean a British map—printed in England." She nodded. "Where did you purchase it?"

"I'm not sure." She thought for a moment. "In Delhi, I believe. Yes, I bought it at a shop near Connaught. Why?"

"Where was it printed? Was it imported from England?"

"I have no idea."

"Well then, take a close look sometime at the area east of Leh, across the Karakorum mountains. If your map was imported you will see a road that runs right down through the middle of the Aksai Chin plateau. That's where we were stationed. *Kahin nahin say bahut dur.* That's what my men used to say: 'A long way from nowhere.' I was up there with a regiment of soldiers when the Chinese started shooting. We were part of a contingent sent on direct orders from Nehru after the Chinese drew up a treaty with Pakistan. Look closely and you will see that the border west of the Chinese road has been clumsily blotted out with white ink. There is an office somewhere in New Delhi where they paint over the border on every imported map before it's released for sale."

"But I don't understand," Penny said. "What's the point in doctoring the maps?"

"The point is," continued Colonel Singh, "that there are too many politicians in New Delhi living in a dream world. And nobody—not one of them—wants to wake up. We lost the war in Ladakh." He swung the glass up to his lips and took another swallow, then chuckled to himself. "You've seen this sort of thing before. You just don't recognize our Indian style; that is the problem. In the Soviet Union, when something like this happens, they use the finest technology available to systematically dispose of the evidence. Let's suppose the problem is some regional politician who manages to step out of line one too many times—he must be, shall we say, removed from history. Under such circumstances, it obviously won't do to have the man's face appearing here and there in old photographs. A technical problem arises. What to do? Very simple. Photographs must be located and carefully corrected, so that the offending face is erased. If it is done with great care, no one will ever know. And that is precisely what you will see when you look at your map: the Indian equivalent of

Soviet technology. Here in India, some peon is paid fifty rupees a month to squat in the corner with a glass of chai and his paan. We give him a stack of imported maps, a brush, and a can of white paint. That is sufficient." He grinned and expelled a quick blast of air through his nostrils, more a cynical snort than a laugh. "It is damned pathetic. Our leaders are terrified of the Chinese, but their only response is to deface British maps, then sit down with our enemies and make pleasant conversation over a pot of tea, pretending the whole time that they didn't murder our soldiers and steal our land!" He stared at the flames in sullen disgust.

I took advantage of his momentary silence to interject a question. "What's so valuable about a desolate region like eastern Ladakh? Why should China want a piece of it?"

"Why indeed?" Singh asked rhetorically, as if loathe to pursue the matter any further.

Penny spoke up. "The whole area is fascinating, Stanley. Kashmir was a crossroads between China and India for at least a thousand years. There are Buddhist monasteries up there that very few people from outside the region have visited. It's dry enough that things could be preserved virtually forever. God knows what you might find. Frescos, old tangkas, clothing, Kalachakra masks. *Texts*, Stanley. Ladakh was where many of the translations were made from Sanskrit into Tibetan and Chinese."

"She's right," said the colonel. "I've seen those monasteries. Underground rooms full of silk costumes and dusty idols, shelves stacked with old Tibetan books. However, with all respect to Miss Ainsworth," he nodded at Penny, "I can assure both of you that the Chinese were not interested in the Aksai Chin because of its cultural history. No, I am afraid they are not looking for paintings or old masks. There is one very simple reason why they attacked us. The road. Examine the map. They now have an unbroken highway all the way down the eastern Soviet frontier, through Ladakh, and along the northern face of the Himalayas the length of Nepal. And why do you suppose they want a road like that? I do not trust them for a moment. If you doubt their intentions, then just look at what has been done to the Tibetan people, in their own country. In their own country. It is despicable. No, the Chinese are ruthless, absolutely ruthless." He shook his head gloomily, then reached up and adjusted the black turban where it passed over one ear.

The big man pulled himself up from the cushion. He walked across the room and around behind the bar to within a few feet of the pictures on the wall. "Come here and let me show you something." We went over to where he stood. "You see this?" He clicked a fingernail against the glass. The photo depicted two Sikh soldiers in tattered battle fatigues posing against a desolate background of endless rock and sky. They could have been standing on the surface of the moon, except that off in the distance, a range of snow-covered mountains cut a jagged line across the horizon. Both men were on crutches, their uniforms in tatters. "These are two of my soldiers who came back from a visit with the Chinese. They were captured, taken prisoner, and forced to parade through the Chinese camps with no boots in freezing cold weather. The purpose was simply to humiliate them in public. They had their turbans stripped off, their hair and beards cut with a pair of sheep shears. Only then were they set free to find their way back to us. As an 'example,' they had been told. 'An example of what is done to barbarians.'" He looked at us sharply. "Who, I ask you, are the barbarians?"

His question hung in silence.

Singh's eyes moved from one picture to another, from one memory to the next, finally settling on an object that lay in a narrow wooden cabinet to his left. He reached over and took the thing out. It was a small, delicately crafted prayer wheel. Above its wooden handle the miniature cylinder was fashioned out of what appeared to be bone, yellowed with time and use. Letters of some kind had been etched deeply into its surface, the margins of both top and bottom were studded with small pieces of coral and turquoise. One end of a thin copper chain was fixed above the florid script, a chunk of polished amber dangled from the other. A snap of the colonel's wrist sent the amber twirling round and round in a golden blur; the little barrel spun on its axis. "A memento," he said, handing it over to me.

I felt the worn handle as it rested against my palm, nestled in my fingers; a perfect fit. I gave it a few twirls and watched the amber pebble swing out, bob and fall inward, coasting to a stop. "It's beautiful. It doesn't seem to belong here, though. I mean, there's something mysterious. As if it came from another world."

"It did," Singh replied laconically.

Penny reached over and lifted the prayer wheel out of my hand, gave it a few twirls herself, then gently ran her fingers over the surface of the wood and bone, inspecting the workmanship more closely. "I don't know much about Tibetan things, but this looks very old; almost medieval. It's had a lot of use. So small, yet so solid and heavy. It really does feel as if it were charged with some kind of supernatural power." She handed the device over to Colonel Singh and he put it back in its place on the shelf, where it rested among the folds of a faded silk scarf.

I picked up the picture I had noticed earlier and examined the figures where they stood in front of the elephant. "Colonel, who is this woman? Isn't she the same person I see in several other photos here?"

He looked over his shoulder, then turned reluctantly around and took the picture out of my hands. "My wife. She passed away unexpectedly, two years ago. In her sleep. The doctors said it was a heart attack."

"Oh. I'm sorry."

"What can be done? She is gone. *Bas*."

"How long were you married?" Penny asked.

"Thirty-two years." He continued gazing at the picture then set it gently back down. "Thirty-two good years. I only wish we could have said goodbye."

"My grandfather died without any warning." Penny hesitated, "I don't mean to imply that it's the same, but we were very close."

Colonel Singh finished his last sip of scotch, then began to revolve the empty glass round and round under his fingers, as though it were a prayer wheel capable of changing the past by granting him this one wish.

"This is a bit different, Miss Ainsworth. We could have had that chance to say goodbye." His voice was controlled, but underneath there was a note of bitterness. Penny and I exchanged a glance. It was impossible to tell what he meant by this cryptic remark. He took a deep breath and exhaled a protracted, weary sigh.

"My family is from the Punjab. My great-grandfather came to Chandigarh from a small village. I was raised a Sikh, of course, but the truth is my parents were not religious people. I remember my grandfather would take me to Gurudwara when I was a boy. But he died when I was only eight years old, and after that I seldom went. From then on religion was something that came up only on special holidays. At those times we would burn a stick of incense under grandfather's picture of Guru Nanak and recite some prayers. That was all. Our family was wealthy, and I was educated at the best English-medium schools. My father was a career military man, and he pointed me in that direction early on. He taught me to believe only in what I could myself see and touch." Colonel Singh grabbed a fistful of air out of the space between us and held it clenched in the palm of his hand. Gradually the fingers relaxed, drifted back to the empty glass and fell to turning it in the same way as before.

"So it is evident that I am not at all religious." He looked up at us again, "I am not what my father would have called a superstitious man. I have no sense for . . ." He seemed to be searching after the right word. His gaze passed over all the accumulated odds and ends, moving among the books and souvenirs, over the tiger's head above the fire, and back across to the picture of his wife, finally coming to rest on Penny's own green eyes. "For whatever it was, perhaps, that you referred to earlier."

"Me?"

"Yes, when you spoke of the 'power' in that little prayer wheel. Such things have always escaped my attention. I really am quite hopeless in this way, and that is the reason I missed the chance—the chance we might otherwise have had—to say goodbye."

Suddenly I knew where this was leading. "The hermit. You're talking about Kalidas."

The colonel looked up at me. "I told you his only visitors were Suresh and myself. But there was one other."

"Your wife."

"Yes, my wife. We first learned about him from the previous director, as I told you earlier this afternoon. He was already old when I assumed the post here. My wife took pity on him. Not that she necessarily believed the story. To her he was just a lonely old man, barely able to survive out there in the jungle. It wasn't long before she began to visit him. Once in a while at first, then more frequently, especially after he fell and injured his leg. She had Suresh drive her over once every week or so with provisions." The colonel's face relaxed. "She always made sure to bring him something special, fresh sweets or what have you. He was quite old, even then, and my wife became worried. She began feeding him and mending his clothes. She would sit there with him, for an hour or more sometimes, the two of them silent. But then after some time he began to talk. Not much, you understand. Merely a few words now and again, from what she told me. But that was quite something for a man who had not spoken in so many years. For decades, so far as we knew. And he spoke only to her. Never a word to anyone else. Only to her." He looked at Penny and smiled. "She was that sort of woman, you see. Very warm. Everyone felt at ease with Jasmeet." He stared down at his hands. "The old man knew the whole time. He could bloody well have told us."

Once again no one spoke. A minute or so passed, and Penny finally summoned the courage to ask what both of us had been wondering. "How can you be so certain that he knew?"

"Oh, he knew all right. There can be no question. We were visiting his kuti together the very day she died. We saw him only hours before she went to sleep beside me for the last time. She had prepared a big basket of things for him. At the last minute I decided to ride over with Suresh and her. We made a few stops on the way. I remember checking in with one of my backcountry people, a man doing some tagging on a project with elephants. But that afternoon everything was different. When we drove up he stood in the doorway and waved us away. I had Suresh stop the Land Rover at the edge of the clearing. She walked up to the porch alone, but from what I could make out he seemed terrified. He shook his head and waved his arms like a crazy man. Refused to have anything to do with her. Would not even accept the things she had brought. He drove her away, shouting. After some time my wife set the basket on the porch, and we left him alone in the house. I know she was hurt. She could not understand. Of course neither did I." He paused and took a deep breath. "I remember too well the last thing she said to me that night, before she went to sleep." He lifted the picture and held it in both hands. "'Why do you suppose he turned us away?' she asked me. That was precisely what she said to me. I will always remember those words: *Why do you suppose he turned us away?* I was preoccupied with something. With the elephant project or some other nonsense. So I said to her, 'Go to sleep, my dear.' Just to get her to quiet down, you understand? 'Go to sleep, my dear,' I said. 'He is just a crazy old man. The next time you visit him, he will be the same as always. Now go to sleep.' And that is what she did. She closed her eyes and went to sleep."

The last charred log crumbled and fell through the grate into a mound of embers. A melancholy hush descended over the house. Even the nocturnal birds outside seemed quieter than before.

"It's late," the colonel said. "Time for bed. You will discover we rise early here." He gave us a small bow.

As we followed him down the hallway, I heard soft footsteps in the rooms behind us; Jagjit and Chota Hanuman circled through the house extinguishing the lamps.

15

I LAY UNDER the mosquito net watching Penny remove her sari. The shutters had been latched against the possibility of uninvited guests. Moonlight poured between the slats in pale narrow bands, streaming through the darkness and across the walls and floor, illuminating her movements as she unwound the fabric from her body. A faint odor of incense hung in the room, bringing to mind the dank, secret interior of Hindu temples. From outside came the screech of an insomniac bird. Eventually Penny reached the last layer of cloth, peeled it off, folded the sari, and dropped it on top of a pile of clothes in the open bag at her feet. All that remained was the petticoat and a short, tightly fitting blouse. She loosened the silver combs in her hair and let it spill down over her neck and shoulders, then tipped back her head and shook out the tangles. A cool white stripe of moonlight flexed across her stomach.

I thought of the colonel and his grief, and then of Judith, my own lost wife. We had shared so much—the excitement of our first days together, the hastily arranged wedding with our drunken, stoned friends, our endless conversations about art and religion, years of torment and passion. The imprint of her touch was embedded in my flesh like a ceremonial tattoo; the scent of her hair and skin would not be scrubbed away. But she would never know India. How strange that seemed. And how utterly final. She would never know this place. We would not share this room, this night.

Death, I thought. And in my mind I saw an aging black-and-white photograph of an Indian man and woman standing together, laughing in the sunlight. *Departure*, I said to myself, and remembered the evening I had sat alone in Delhi, knowing I would not return to Judith and she would not come to me. I had copied a Sanskrit verse into my journal. I lay on my back, my head propped against the hard foam pillow, and whispered the words of my English translation:

Death, departure, new birth, dissolution.
Separation from people and things beloved.
Never to come again or to meet again.
Like the leaves and fruits of the forest,
like the current of a river.

The nocturnal cloak of the jungle lay heavily against my skin. I inhaled deeply, and the smell entered my nostrils, bending each tiny hair, an ethereal, soundless current flowing like a subterranean river through the moist, hidden cavities of my body. Lungs rise, hesitate, then collapse inward, forcing the spent air back along the same mysterious route. The darkness of the jungle outside and the dark interior of my body are linked by this stream of respiration, joined at the turning point between inhalation and exhalation. Here is the alchemical flask where opposites fuse, inner with outer, life with death, loss with gain, reality with illusion. Samsara with nirvana. Nirvana with the ceaseless repetition of birth and death.

All the yogic traditions of India begin and end here, before creation, where the breath turns back on itself, where the breath of God moves like wind over the waters of the deep. In my memory I am lying on my back in the Himalayan night under a canopy of striped moonlight, watching. And in my body each breath revolves on a gossamer axis, meeting and merging with its opposite: inhalation becoming exhalation, exhalation bending around on itself in the same elusive transmutation. Turning inward I find my way along an ancient path, gathering together what is and what is not. I let my attention rest on the pull of the abdominal muscles, on the lungs filling, expanding, tapering off, on the incorporeal vein of air growing ever more thin, the sensations ever more subtle, weightless, flexible, malleable, alive, still moving in toward the center. With exquisite patience I search for the place of crossing over, the bridge between breathing in and breathing out—that infinitely precious and fragile interface between opposites, a hidden chamber of the heart where self and other meet and trade places in the simplest, most elemental act of love.

But what if the turning point is concealed in the very act of attention? In awareness itself? That would explain why the goal always seems to lie so tantalizingly near at hand and yet forever beyond my grasp. Awareness: present only in its absence, as the reflected image of what it is not. Awareness is always manifest as nothing. Nothing to find and no one to find it. Is the very act of observation, then, the ultimate illusion? *Who sees the seer?*

"Did you say something, Stanley?"

"What?" I looked up at the sagging net, then through the gauze into the dimly lit room. She was not there. "Sorry. Not really. I was thinking out loud."

Her voice came from inside the bathroom where a candle flickered. A shadow climbed up the opposite wall, around and over the ceiling, a distorted black ghost washing and drying itself with a spectral towel that twisted and bent as it danced over the uneven surface of the plaster. A phantom hand swept down like a raven, lifting the candle, and Penny emerged from the door with her fingers cupped around the flame. She walked over to the vanity and set the candle to one side, then sat down and looked at herself in the mirror for a few seconds before beginning to brush her hair. She was still wearing the petticoat and blouse.

"What do you see in the mirror?" I asked.

"A woman brushing her hair."

"That's all? You don't see anything else? Look closely."

She bent forward and stared into the glass. "What? See what?"

"Nothing."

"Nothing?!"

"Yes. Exactly. That's it."

"What on earth are you talking about?" she snapped back, her expression moving swiftly from confusion to exasperated disbelief. "You're being philo*so*phical, aren't you?" She jerked the brush down through her hair. "Stanley, don't *do* that. I was certain you saw some horrible insect crawling in my hair."

I stretched out under the sheets, clasping both hands up behind my head. When I spoke again it was with my best parody of her Oxford intonation. "So tell me, Miss Ainsworth. Perhaps I am mistaken, but were you not a tad uneasy earlier this evening when our host broached the subject of our accommodations? The single room, I mean."

"Uneasy?" She considered. "Yes, I suppose I was."

"And why might that be, my *dey*ah?"

"Are you blind, Stanley? Have you really not noticed?"

"Noticed what?"

"The colonel, he sees me differently now."

"Differently? What do you mean?"

"Shall I spell it out? He knows I'm available. He's interested in your girlfriend."

"*Ra*yally?"

"Yes, *ra*yally, you idiot!"

"Hrumph! Well, then, I must say that I'm not a bit surprised. Surely you must be familiar with that quaint old Punjabi adage."

"No, I am not. But I'll bet you're about to tell it to me."

"Since you asked. How does it go? Let me see . . . oh yes: You can wrap a nice ass in a sari, but men will still want to bite it. There. You see?"

"That's an old Punjabi adage?"

"Damn right it is. You hear it all the time in the streets of Chandigarh. I'm told the original has a sort of rustic elegance that's lost in translation. Of course I don't speak the language, so I can't evaluate such claims. But you get the point."

She continued to brush, unimpressed.

"So Singh wants to bite your ass. But I still don't understand what that has to do with our sharing a room."

"Stanley, sometimes you positively amaze me with your naiveté. Wake up. This is India. I realize that you're a male and therefore have not been compelled to deal personally with all of this. And you're not exactly the sensitive feminist type."

"Whoa there! What's that supposed to mean?"

She ignored the interruption and continued. "But you really ought to be aware of what the rest of us are enduring, at least the Europeans and Americans. I can't claim to speak for what it's like to be an Indian woman. Put down your Sanskrit texts and take a look around. We are walking a very fine line here, Mr. Buddhist philosopher." She drew her hair around one shoulder and down over her chest, brushing the ends.

"How so?"

"Listen closely now, and you will learn something important: class is in session. In India there are five roles for women. No more, and no less. First, mother: threatening in her own way, no doubt, the mother is basically an archetype of pure, nonsexual or spiritual love and total, unwavering acceptance. You come to her and she takes you, as you are. Especially if you happen to be a man. Or, more precisely, a boy who has never grown up. Of course all five roles are assigned from the male point of view, but in India this should more or less go without saying. The second role is sister: still pure, with the emphasis here on chaste. Virginal. Untouched. As you Americans say, her cherry has not been popped. Did I get that right?"

"Yep, that's what we Americans say."

"So that's number two. Woman's role number three is daughter, which is pretty much the same as number two so far as the virgin thing goes. And then we have woman's role four: wife. The operative word here is *loyal*, as in *Sita is the model of the loyal wife, because she was willing to be burned alive to prove her fidelity to Ram*. Of course that's only the ideal. As often as not I suspect the reality is even less pleasant. If you want to call the role sexual in some sense I won't quibble, it's in there somewhere, I'm sure." Her voice trailed off. "So anyway, that's role number four: woman as wife."

"Isn't this maybe, well, just a bit cynical?"

"Maybe. I'd like to think so." She paused in her brushing to fiddle with a recalcitrant tangle. "Which brings me to the last of the five possible roles."

"Let me guess. Uh . . ."

"Think hard and it will come to you, I'm sure."

"Wait a minute! Wait just a minute! I believe I've got it: prostitute!"

"That's it. Now think again, Stanley. Does anything seem to be missing here?"

I gave it a couple second's consideration. "Girlfriend? Lover?"

"Bingo."

"You know, though, prostitute isn't a bad substitute. In a pinch, that is."

"Very amusing," she said dryly, not deigning to glance toward where I lay under the net. "But with a little more reflection I'm sure you'll grasp the point. In Colonel Singh's eyes I am a whore. A sexual woman."

"Hot to trot."

"Marvelous. Another charming Americanism."

"And this explains why you were uncomfortable when he brought up the room arrangements?"

"Now you've got it, Professor. He knows damn well we're not married. Keep the little lesson I just gave you in mind, and I guarantee you will see and understand a great deal that you might otherwise miss."

"So," I said, idly checking out the penumbra cast by the moonlight as it arched around and under her breasts, "aside from the fact that he wants to fuck you, what do you think of our host?"

"I like him. He can't help it if he was raised in this screwed-up society. What the Mughals didn't accomplish in five hundred years, my prudish Victorian ancestors more than made up for. Anyway, I'm accustomed to it by now. I don't take any of it personally. But I've had enough encounters with fellows like Mr. Bhattacharya, whacking off behind his desk. I like to keep on my toes. That way I'm not caught by surprise too often." She paused. "But Colonel Singh really is a charming man. He's quite handsome, too, Stanley. Maybe you ought to be jealous."

I was fiddling with the mosquito net now, trying to grip the sheer material between my toes. "I'll bear that in mind."

She slapped her forearm with the back of the brush, picked up the miniscule carcass of a mosquito and flicked it toward the shutters.

"Getting thick out there?"

"A few. Not bad."

"Tell me, Penny." I loosened my toes and let go of the net, turned around and adjusted the pillow so I could lean back on it and get a better look at her. "What do you make of his story?"

"Which one? We heard about two dozen."

"Not the wild animal act. I mean all this stuff about the hermit. Kalidas."

"I don't know." She examined a few split ends, sifting the tips of the hair through her fingers. "It's interesting, I guess. India is full of these characters."

"Is that all? You don't sound very impressed."

She took a last casual stroke through her hair and laid the brush down next to the candle. With both hands she reached around behind her back and unfastened a row of wire hooks, slipped the blouse forward over both arms, letting it dangle from her fingers for an instant, then dropped it on to the sari. This left only a white silk brassiere and the petticoat. "What do you want me to say?"

"Do you believe any of it? I thought the colonel's testimony seemed pretty convincing."

"I suppose so. But the whole thing seems a bit far-fetched."

"Do you remember what Singh said about the pundits in Dehradun? About Ramesh being a bad choice and all?"

"Ramesh?"

"You know—the accountant. That was his name before he became Kalidas."

"Oh. Well. So he was a 'bad choice.' Whatever that means." For the first time she looked over toward where I lay, then swiveled around on the wooden stool and crossed one leg over the other. "It's a bit disconcerting, Stanley, trying to carry on a conversation with a disembodied voice. I can't see a bloody thing through that net."

"Listen," I said, "I've been thinking about this a lot. It seems to me you could interpret it in two ways. At least. Maybe the pundits were right and the goddess Kali made a mistake: if Ramesh had only been stronger he could have somehow prevented the death of his son. You know—refused to cooperate."

"Do beings of her rank make mistakes?"

"Sure, you read about it all the time. Didn't your Oxford dons ever lead you through a few installments of the Puranas?"

"They don't *lead* us through anything. At Oxford we do it alone."

"Fine," I replied, "but I've read enough to know that even the big guys like Shiva or Ram—or girls, as the case may be—blow it once in a while. If the goddess was wrong, then poor Ramesh has suffered plenty for her mistake. That much is certain. But personally I don't think she was wrong. I think she knew exactly what she was doing when she picked him."

"Why?" She reached down and scratched her ankle, then lifted the petticoat to her knee and flexed one long calf, running her fingers slowly up across the muscle.

"For one thing, after all these years the man is still meditating and doing puja to her. Doesn't that seem significant, somehow?"

"Do you mind if I go to the loo?" Without waiting for an answer she stood up, grabbed the saucer with the candle and disappeared back into the bathroom. "Go on with what you were saying. I can hear you perfectly well from in here."

"What I'm getting at is this," I continued. "Obviously the man has turned his whole life over to the goddess. And why? Because Kali considered him worthy to receive her boon: the power to look directly into the face of death. I mean, how many people could handle that? When you think about it, he's holding up pretty well." No sooner had I said this than the memory of his emaciated form appeared before me, and I saw him all over again as he had looked only a few hours earlier, at the moment when he stepped out the door and spotted me standing there with the incense. "Maybe she gave him even more. Not just the opportunity to see death, but to see right through it. After all, what does the old guy do all day? Think about it."

"I'm sure I haven't the slightest idea." Now it was my turn to listen to a disembodied voice.

"Singh told us. He worships Kali. Nothing but puja and meditation on the goddess, from morning to night."

"So?"

"So he hasn't flipped out. He's holding it together. He's doing all right for himself. No. More than that. Kalidas is doing his sadhana—his spiritual practice. He's going deeper."

"Then why did he kill his own baby?"

My jaw dropped. "Now what kind of total non sequitur is that? How on earth does his stepping on the baby contradict anything I've been saying?"

"If he really knew what was going to happen—which he must have, if there's any truth at all to the story—then why didn't he at least try to avoid it somehow?" She cranked open the faucet down by the shitter, and I heard water spewing into a plastic cup. I heard her pouring the cup of water over her fingers, washing herself off.

"Come on," I said, "that's the point here. That's the key to the whole thing. He couldn't avoid his fate. He had to do it. The only difference between him and all the rest of us is that he knew he had no choice and we don't. We think we have this mysterious thing called 'free will' that allows our little ego to get whatever it wants, if only it's clever enough. Like the universe is this huge cafeteria with all these wonderful dishes to choose from and we've got endless credit."

She emerged from the bathroom, bladder emptied, hands washed, and paced over to the vanity, where she sat down on the stool and plunked the candle at her side, letting the saucer fall the last half inch so that it rapped against the wood.

I looked at her through the net, sitting there in silence. "You still don't get it, do you?"

"I guess not."

"Look. He was pushed into a corner with no way out. No exit. But much worse than anything Sartre could imagine."

"If what you say is true then I feel sorry for the poor man," she said.

"Well I don't. That's exactly what it means to follow a spiritual path. Or to receive some kind of vision. That's the real significance of fortune telling, astrology, and all the rest of it—to show us that the feeling of choosing is an illusion. An ego game. I suppose you could call it the 'esoteric significance.' But the gift of prophecy is only one kind of spiritual vision. The most debased kind, so far as that goes, because almost no one appreciates its real power. In other words, for most people it just doesn't work. They're only interested in using it to make money or get laid. Or maybe to become a better person."

"And what's so bad about wanting to be a better person?"

"Nothing. Except that it doesn't have anything to do with spiritual vision. How can improving yourself solve the problem when your self *is* the problem? There's no more disgusting vice than believing you're a 'good person.' The whole preoccupation with self-improvement is just another stupid mental game, another distraction for the ego. Obsessing over its so-called 'virtues' and 'sins,' forever swinging between pride and guilt. But you're right. It's probably just as well most people don't see how terrifying all that stuff really is, or astrologers and fortune tellers would be out of business overnight."

"Okay, Stanley." She looked toward the net, straining to see inside. "You're obviously the expert here. So tell me what you mean by 'spiritual vision,' since that's what we seem to be talking about."

"What do I mean by spiritual vision." I hesitated. "Do you really want to know?"

"Don't be patronizing. I asked, didn't I?"

I took a deep breath, closed my eyes, and let my head sink back against the pillow. "For starters, you see something. Something you don't want to see. Something about the world, something about yourself. About the way you live. It's like seeing everything you normally take for granted from some new perspective, and this new perspective—or whatever you want to call it—sort of begins to take over your whole life. It's like you were always sick but you somehow never noticed before. That's the meaning of the first noble truth of Buddhism. For a person who sees clearly, the life of the ego is nothing but a kind of sickness. Seeing this is where spiritual vision begins. Everything—not just the sad stuff, but all your pleasures and joys, too—you see it all for what it actually is: a sick, self-centered delusion."

There was a long silence while I waited for her reaction.

"That's all?" She sounded perplexed. "That's it?"

"Should I keep going? I mean, I could definitely keep going, but maybe you've had enough."

"Not at all. I'm learning something about you."

"About *me*?"

"Just go on, okay? This is interesting."

"Well, all right then. Where was I?"

"You were talking about the ego being a kind of sickness or something. A delusion."

"Right. Okay. So you may have some sort of warning with all of this. Or then again, maybe you get no warning at all, like with Ramesh. Either way, however it happens, the really important part is that once you see things from this perspective, it's as if you're suddenly conscious of being infected with an incurable disease. At that point you give up on the whole project of self-improvement. It's like that old Zen metaphor: you can polish a brick forever, but it will never become a mirror. The big *me*—the ego, with its pride and jealousy and petty ambitions and all the rest of it—is the center of all experience. Everything—I mean not just your personality, but your whole world—takes shape around the ego, in its image. And the ego is nothing but a fucking brick. It just sits there. You can't get rid of it, and you sure as hell can't make a self-centered delusion into anything other than what it is. Once you see this—I mean really see it—all bets are off. You just give up. Let it all go. It's like someone sticks a knife into your stomach and then gives the blade a sharp twist. You need that twist to make sure the wound is lethal. All interest in the ego has to die. For Ramesh, the twist was not only that he knew exactly what was going to happen but that he himself had to do it. If anyone else had stepped on the baby, it could have been called an accident. Then Ramesh the accountant might have felt anger, or even compassion. That would be the saintly response. Right? Saints are good people. Holy people. But because of the particular way his son died, none of the usual reactions were possible. He had to see for himself that the ego is nothing but an imposter. A liar. *A baby killer.*

"So anyway, that's what I mean by the 'twist.' It can come in an infinite number of ways, but it's got to be there. That way, once the knife goes in you are completely, totally fucked. You become a desperate person. A haunted person. You can't go back to the way things were before. You're good for nothing to yourself or anyone else. So far as other people are concerned, you're clinically deranged, because you're already disconnected from the world of shared reality. If the spiritual path, or whatever you want to call it, didn't work this way—by trapping you like this—then no one would go through with it. No one would give a shit. Why should they?"

I didn't wait for an answer.

"Look at most people. I mean *normal* people. *Reasonable* people. People like that always imagine they have a choice—that they can somehow or another intervene in events and influence the outcome by choosing to do the right thing. And what do they do? Go to church or temple or fiddle around with lofty ideals of universal peace and brotherly love. Work in a soup kitchen, maybe, or go for therapy. The truth is, of course, we don't really *choose* anything, no matter how much we like to think we do. What we call 'making a choice' is just something that happens, like the weather—like rain or wind, like the movement of the breath or the beating of your heart. Like thoughts arising and passing away. Nobody *makes* this stuff happen. Let's face it: you never actually know what you're *going* to choose, since you can always change your mind at the last second; you only know what was *chosen*—after the fact. So all the pride and guilt is for nothing. We're all every bit as trapped as Ramesh was. Every one of us. But like I said a minute ago, the difference is that almost no one actually *sees* how utterly hopeless the situation really is. So far as I can figure it, this is the gift of spiritual vision that Kali gave Ramesh. Unlike most of us, he knows that he is up against the fucking wall. *The house is on fire and the doors are locked.* What kills me is Ramesh is actually cultivating that way of seeing things. I don't feel sorry for him at all. I envy him. It takes enormous courage to actually give up—to just let go of the whole project of being somebody. I don't even know how to *try*."

For the past several minutes Penny had been sitting there filing her nails, waiting for me to finish. When I finally stopped talking she glanced up.

"Is that it now? Are you through?" She looked at me out of the corner of one eye while examining a minor hangnail with the other.

I let out a sigh. "Yes, that's it."

"So if I get this right, what you're saying is that you envy a lonely, tormented old man who killed his infant son. And you envy him because he's trapped in his shitty life."

I didn't respond.

"Stanley," she said, "you're sick. You know that, don't you? I mean, you *really are* sick."

She got up from the stool, her hands slipped around back again, and off came the bra. Once free, her breasts seemed to swell in the fluttering light of the candle. Bending low she stepped out of her petticoat one leg at a time. Stark naked now, she leaned over to blow out the candle. Her body appeared to me flawless, perfect—a divine vision sprung from my own desire. The flame was just about to go when I asked her to wait, to stay where she was for a minute longer. She stood up and turned slowly around, looking at me as though I had finally gone over the edge.

"Do you mind all that much?" I said, a bit sheepishly. "This is sort of interesting."

"Oh for God's sake, Stanley. Can't we continue the conversation with me in bed?"

"I'm not concerned with the conversation. I mean you. Out there naked, bent over the table like that."

"And what about Kalidas? Spiritual vision, Stanley. The twist!" She snapped her fingers. "Remember?"

"What can I say? My attention was distracted."

"I still can't see you under there," she said, lowering her head and straining to make out my form where I reclined inside the net.

"I can see you fine. Can you just stay where you are for a little while longer. *Please?*" I was honestly pleading with her now, and she knew it.

"What am I supposed to do out here?" She folded her arms indignantly under her breasts; they stood at attention, pointing directly at me where I lay. If this is righteous anger, I thought, then please Lord, give me more.

Out loud I said, "Be a sport! I'm living out a fantasy. Would it hurt so much to cooperate just a little?" She remained standing as before, staring at the net. "Are you cold?" I asked.

"Not yet," she replied, with a disgust that was half serious, half feigned. I could tell from her tone she was already coming around.

"All I would like for you to do," I said, "if you don't mind, is to cup your breasts from underneath and hold them up for me. What do you say?"

Grudgingly she uncrossed her arms and her fingers glided up over the bare skin. She raised her breasts tentatively, a bit higher than they had been already.

"Very nice. Could you sort of massage them a little?"

She gave both a gentle squeeze and continued holding them aloft. The nipples were stiff in the cool air. Everything about Penny's body was delicate—you could almost say innocent—except for her nipples. They were unusually prominent, and with the slightest provocation they swelled up into dark, hard nubs of flesh that jutted out like thick pencil erasers. I found them unbearably erotic.

"How's this?" she said, her voice softer. She had a nipple between the forefinger and thumb of each hand and was twirling them back and forth. Her lips were parted, head tipped slightly back. "Now what do you want me to do?"

"That's good." I took a deep breath and exhaled slowly. "Turn around and bend over the vanity in front of the mirror, the way you were a minute ago." I spoke rather abruptly, aware that I was no longer asking. I decided the time had come to go for broke. We were gathering momentum with every second.

She did as I asked, showing me her back and the full length of her hair cascading down over her shoulders. Leaning low, she pressed her chest flat against the vanity. One arm up over her head, her fingers splayed against the mirror. She spread her legs, and with the other hand reached down between them and began rubbing with an easy motion.

"Just like our first night together in Delhi," I said. "I love to watch you play with yourself."

Her hips were rotating now in slow circles.

"Come out here," she said. "Please." Now she was the one doing the begging.

I wasted little time crawling out from under the net. Once out, I stripped off my shorts, grasped her waist from behind, and pushed myself against her. She had both arms up now, hands gripping the edge of the vanity. In front of us the big hermeneutical mirror reflected the whole sordid scene. There I was, the young Fulbright scholar from the University of Chicago, making the most out of my opportunity to study abroad. *The clown is happy tonight.*

"My, my," I said. "Look what happens when we come to the jungle on holiday. You've become a little animal." I reached down and around her stomach, cupping my hand under her, and slipped a finger up inside. She was drenched. "What do you see in front of you?" I asked.

She lifted her head and looked into the glass. "Two nasty people." Her eyes met mine in the mirror. "Don't play around, Stanley. Not tonight."

"How about something special then? A jungle fuck."

She began to writhe up against me.

"Do it," she moaned, more a low growl than language.

I hesitated at the tiny flower of her anus, felt the resistance and the urge to give way. I made sure it was wet and then entered her slowly, pushing in and down, watching each sensation with total attention. I buried myself in her, taking my time, feeling every tiny spasm. Down I went, all the way down to that same incomprehensible turning point, beyond fear and desire, beyond death, beyond nothing and nobody to the same empty space that I found between inhalation and exhalation, the same impossible joining of opposites where in becomes out, meeting and merging with its hidden partner, vice becoming virtue, motion turning back on itself, crossing over, and starting up again out of the void, upward toward goodness and beauty, back to light and life, but always moving toward another turning point—another miraculous void that would be reached just when the head of my cock was about to escape through the taut ring of her muscle. There at the apex I paused, the outward pull slacking off and transforming, somehow, into its opposite, once again descending into darkness. I clamped on with one hand, the flesh hot and slick with sweat under my fingers. With the other I reached underneath and massaged her, giving myself over to every shiver of her flesh, her body telling me what to do, when to ease off, when to press harder or more quickly. I could feel her climax building, an earthquake beginning to rumble, the tremors of pleasure rolling up from deep inside.

"I can't wait any longer," she managed to groan. "Oh god, Stanley... *Fuck me.*"

I pushed myself forward one last time, down into the abyss.

16

NOT LONG AFTER SUNRISE the next morning, our chamber door was assaulted by a series of brash knocks. My eyes cracked open reluctantly, rebelling against the early morning sunlight coming through the shutters.

"Chai, Sahab!" It was Jagjit.

I pushed myself up and out from under the net, snagged my pants off the floor, and yanked them on. When I pulled the door open there they were, man and beast, both faces baring their teeth in a good-morning smile. Jagjit was holding a tray with two cups, a pot of tea, a small bowl of sugar, and a silver pitcher of boiled milk. The monkey was perched in his usual spot, his fuzzy, dwarfish head and pointed ears bobbing right alongside his master's own barbered pate. This morning the servant was sporting a trendy synthetic kurta over a pink lungi. Very stylish. The embroidered collar was open, and for the first time I noticed the pendant that dangled from a silver chain strung around his neck. It was a miniature figure of Chota Hanuman's divine namesake, the monkey god Hanuman, loyal servant of Lord Ram. It was Hanuman who had rescued the goddess Sita from her captor, the demon Ravana.

The monkey swung down and stood waiting at his master's side while I took the tray and deposited it on our vanity. When I returned to the door, Jagjit tilted his head slightly forward in the customary Indian fashion, affecting an abbreviated bow, palms joined in front.

"The colonel invites you to meet him for breakfast on the terrace as soon as you are ready." His Hindi was marked with the same lilting accent I had first heard in Ramnagar when we stopped for lunch.

I acknowledged the invitation with my own small bow. Just then, from somewhere behind me, I heard a metallic tinkling and knew right away that Chota Hanuman had once again surrendered to his obsession with Penny's jewelry. He was rummaging through her bag. Jagjit bounded across the room and scooped the little bandit up in his arms, extracted a glass bangle and two silver rings from the grip of those furry fingers, and deposited him back on his perch, after which the recidivistic anthropoid gave a shriek of protest and promptly began to twist his master's ear with unrestrained zeal. Jagjit batted the offending paw away and flashed me a sheepish grin as he exited the room.

Singh speaks the truth, I thought. The show starts at dawn.

I roused Penny and poured us both a cup of tea, serving it to her where she lingered, supine under the royal canopy. The brew was hot and strong and worked its magic. I was sitting beside her, poised for a last sip, when a shrill trumpeting pierced the early morning silence. I sat down my cup, went over, and opened the shutters.

Beyond the veranda an elephant swayed heavily in the brilliant Himalayan sunlight, an enormous gray battleship rocking on waves of parched yellow grass. Her trunk curled back over her forehead as she cut loose with another blast that echoed into the emptiness of the mountain sky. The mahout straddled her neck and rocked up and down, one bare calloused foot nestling behind each of the elephant's magisterial ears. He was a small, wiry man, naked except for a short dhoti rolled up between his legs like a bulky diaper. His head was wrapped in a ribbon of indigo cotton; the last meter of cloth hung free in back, rippling in the breeze like the tail on one of those kites I had watched in the sky over Banaras. He nudged a heel sharply up behind the elephant's left ear, and she pirouetted on the grass and sauntered obediently out of sight around the corner of the house. I remembered the colonel's promise of an outing. Was this to be our mount? Downing the last few swallows of tea, we hurried through our morning ablutions.

When we arrived on the terrace, we found the colonel sitting over his cup perusing some official-looking papers stacked in his lap. His ever-present stick reclined across a corner of the table. We exchanged greetings, prompting him to shift the stack of papers to the floor, rise from his chair, and favor each of us with his characteristic, stiff-waisted military bow. I watched closely this time as his eyes swept over Penny's body, from the tips of her long lashes down to her bare, sandaled feet. Her outfit—a light blue salwar kameez with subtle gold stitching along the hem—seemed to meet with his approval.

"Well," he declared, his eyes coming to rest at last on Penny's face and neck, then on mine, "it looks as though your mosquito net may have a few holes." Our skin was, in fact, dotted with tiny red bumps. Only then did

I realize that he might have heard us in the other room; we had not been discreet. Penny took firm control of the situation before I could begin to assemble a viable response to the colonel's remark. She didn't miss a beat.

"It was my fault. I'm so clumsy. I got up to go to the loo and tripped over the chair. Poor Stanley . . ." She glanced shyly over at me where I stood dumbfounded, waiting to see what this brazen little liar would say next. "He leapt up to help me and the net got tangled. I do hope we didn't wake you with all the commotion." She lowered her eyes demurely and rounded off the whole charming show with a sweet, impeccably innocent smile.

Penny's acting skill, this ability to project a poised and convincing facade, was more than a bit disconcerting. I had problems with anyone who could just whip up fictitious tales like this on the spur of the moment. I held myself tightly to a pristine ideal of truth. That's why I told Judith about my infidelity the very day it occurred. I actually thought she would prefer to know. Once, when I took Penny to task for cooking up these bullshit stories on the spot, her response was equally swift: "It's not lying, Stanley. It's simply an embroidered version of the truth." Of course my own brutal integrity was every bit as self-serving as any lie, but at the time I did not see it that way, and during the few months we shared, I often experienced a twinge of panic when I thought about what it would mean to fall in love with such a woman. Penny seemed capable of saying absolutely anything that would work toward her own, present purposes, and saying it with utter conviction. I couldn't trust a word that came out of her mouth. I could not even trust her beauty. There was nothing about her that I could hold on to, nothing that could not conceivably be turned against me. In any case, Singh was obviously satisfied with her response.

Over breakfast, he told us we would be going on an adventure. He had given orders to prepare his elephant, Sita, a spry, middle-aged female that had served the previous director as well. It was she we had seen cavorting on the lawn. We finished our vegetable cutlets and toast, and when the final pot of tea had been drained, we left the table and followed a stone path through a grove of aromatic mango trees to a clearing outside the stables. Sita was in full harness now and awaiting our arrival. Several layers of stiff, colorful dharis had been draped over her back, an intricately carved teak howdah set in place and cinched from below with leather belts that circled down and around her belly. She was standing alongside an ingenious scaffold that permitted us to mount her by ascending a small platform abutting the expanse of her ribbed flank. A single brown eye followed our progress up the staircase. One by one we stepped into the howdah and found our seats. I slipped my legs under the banister and let them swing free; the heels of my black converse sneakers brushed against the pachyderm's coarse hide. Smooth and warm to the touch, the wooden rail pressed against my palms.

Evidently a man of many talents, Jagjit had for the present occasion assumed the guise of lookout and guard. He sat immediately to the rear of the mahout, an ancient and colossal gun cradled in his arms. The leather ammunition belt was strapped diagonally across his chest, the shells down along its length like a row of dormitory beds stuffed with fat cylinders, each one wearing the same copper nightcap, each one quietly dreaming of violent, explosive surrender. Chota Hanuman was not in attendance. He had been left behind, perhaps out of concern that he might decide to reach over and trigger the weapon.

Once everyone was comfortable, Singh barked out an order, and we lurched off, lumbering across the yard and directly into the high grass. Within a hundred meters of the house the undergrowth became so tall it grazed our feet. Penny reached out and let the stalks brush against her fingers as we plunged forward, blazing a path through country that would have been inaccessible to the Land Rover.

After some time we paused at the edge of a steep bank and surveyed the clear waters of the Ramganga. The river stretched out in front of us, its gravel bed strewn with smooth, chalky white rocks. The mahout pushed both heels forward, and before we could catch our breath, Sita plunged over the edge and straight down the side, leaving us clinging insanely at the balustrade. I understood then why the wood under my hands had been worn to a high gloss over the years. Once at the bottom, the elephant waded knee deep into the river and repeatedly submerged the tip of her trunk, each time sucking up one or two gallons of water that was summarily hosed into her waiting mouth. Thirst slaked, she moved farther out into the swift current, and within seconds the water was churning up around her stomach.

"Colonel, what would happen," I asked, "if she chanced to step over a steep drop-off?"

"She knows what she is doing," he assured me, with obvious confidence.

Exactly like Penny at her best, I thought, as I listened to him speak. I was about to ask if elephants can swim when Singh continued, preempting any further reference to the subject.

"Mr. Harrington, this is *her* world, not ours."

Sure enough, we made it safely across, only to face another harrowing trip directly up the opposite bank and then back into the relative security of the high grass.

"Amazing creatures, elephants!" our host exclaimed. "Sure footed and silent."

Singh went on to tell us that the previous director had come across Sita wandering alone, an infant in the jungle, not far from where we had stopped to watch the herd of elephants on our first day in the park. He had found her half starved and desperate for attention. It was not clear what had become of her mother, nor was it evident why she had not been adopted by the other matriarchs of the herd. Rather than leave her to an almost certain death, the director had led the small elephant home and personally nursed her back to health. His original intention had been to set her free as soon as she was strong enough to fend for herself, but when the time arrived it seemed she had no interest in leaving.

Twice she was set loose at considerable distance from the house, and twice she returned. The second time it took her almost a week to find her way back, but in the end she appeared one morning outside the kitchen, lazily grazing on the high grass at the edge of the yard. The director made up his mind to keep her and raise her himself, and in the months that followed, she was subjected to a rigorous education. Among other things, she had been trained to spot tigers by relying on her prodigious olfactory powers. Singh explained that an elephant's sense of smell is legendary and encouraged us to pay close attention and we would see for ourselves. In this we were not disappointed. From our perch on her back, we watched her halt from time to time, uncoil her great trunk and let it rise, bobbing and swaying like a cobra, mesmerizing us with the gentle rhythm of its dance as she sampled a stray breeze for traces of the elusive feline perfume. At such times I too would inhale deeply, drawing in the musky odor of the jungle, redolent with the secrets of life and death. I asked myself what it was she sought—something so familiar she would recognize it instantly and without question. Something I could not discern. What is the scent of a tiger in the wild, untamed and free?

This is her world, not ours.

More than once Sita picked up the aroma of a cat lurking somewhere nearby. On four occasions she raised her right front foot, offering us the prescribed sign, softly pawing the ground. Each time we scrutinized the surrounding brush, suspicious of every leaf that swayed, every blade of grass that stirred in the light breeze. The third time this happened, we were poised, holding our breath, looking and listening, when without the slightest warning, a large male boar shot out of the underbrush not more than thirty feet off to the right. Something had apparently spooked him, and he bolted straight toward us. One look at Sita, though, and he veered away and ran shrieking along a different course. In the excitement, Jagjit swung the shotgun around and almost blasted the hell out of one bristly, frightened pig. Even Singh was caught off guard. Penny latched onto my wrist so hard that her nails left visible marks. We still had not seen a tiger, but early in the afternoon, just before turning back, our luck changed.

"Look!" Penny pointed up into the foliage. Just above us a sloth was suspended upside down from the branch of a venerable sal tree, hanging there like a furry Christmas ornament. Its head was thrown all the way back, slowly rotating so as to keep an eye on us as we passed below. This was the first of these comical little creatures either of us had seen, and we were talking and laughing about it when suddenly Sita froze at the edge of a broad, flat marsh.

"Quiet!" Singh whispered, holding his hand up between us.

The elephant raised her trunk and sniffed. I became suddenly conscious of the smell of stagnant water and rotting vegetation. And then I heard the faint sound of Sita's ponderous foot scraping the dirt. I felt a tug at my sleeve, and I turned, straining my eyes in the direction Singh indicated, straight out over the open marsh.

A large Bengal tiger was crouching in the grass, so near I could see its flesh ripple, its ribs swell and contract with each breath. The animal turned and glared at Sita. The muscles of the neck and shoulder bunched up, the eyes narrowed.

Here was a lethal, compelling beauty, unlike any I had known and infinitely more seductive. A beauty that fed on life, erotic and irresistible.

17

WE RETURNED IN TIME to rinse off at the tap before late afternoon tea, followed by dinner and the colonel's ritual nightcap. It was hard to believe that this was only our second evening together; I had already become attached to the house and its comforts, and to the alien, savage intensity of the jungle outside. But we were to leave the following morning. Singh had made arrangements to send us back with his driver to Ramnagar, where we would catch the train for Delhi.

While Penny was getting ready for bed, I went out to stretch my legs. The fresh night air was sobering after having spent the last few hours settled back by the fire with the colonel's whiskey. I walked unsteadily around the drive for a while, my head tipped back, gazing up into the immensity of the cosmos. The sky looked like one of those cheap velvet paintings, the plush carpet of the universe plastered over the inside of a gigantic dome, a blackness so dense it absorbed time and space and then let them rip through again in a billion points of cold white fire. On an impulse, I headed toward the stables to check in on Sita. I wanted to see if elephants slept on their feet like horses and cows.

I crept up to the huge door and peaked in. Sure enough, there she was, standing motionless, her big head dipped forward between those magnificent ears, eyes closed like some hoary sage immersed in deep samadhi. The expert nose drooped limply down into the straw. Was she dreaming of tigers? I studied the mountainous silhouette of her body as it loomed over me in the darkness. All at once I realized that I was utterly exhausted. I found my way back to the room, climbed in bed next to Penny, and immediately fell into a fitful sleep.

That night I dreamed that I was being pursued through the jungle by Kalidas. He was accompanied by a trained tiger able to track me down by following my peculiar scent—the smell of Regenstein Library at the University of Chicago. I was running for my life. Stumbling through the brush I jettisoned my bag, which was stuffed with heavy dictionaries and grammars. I kept hoping to come upon a river, so I could use that trick you always see in the movies when convicts escape the bloodhounds by swimming downstream. In my panic to shed the library stench, I began frantically to strip off one piece of clothing after another, until at last I was crashing naked through a dense tangle of vegetation. But it was to no avail. My skin itself exuded a telltale aroma of bound periodicals, xerox fluid, and those foul little ammonia wafers they put in urinals. I entered a clearing and sprinted for the other side, then tripped and fell. Within seconds, Kalidas and the tiger burst out of the jungle. The old man barked a command, and the animal lunged toward me where I lay in a crumpled fetal position, knees drawn tight against my chest, arms thrown up around my head.

I must have cried out in my sleep and woken Penny, for the next thing I remember is the warmth of her arms wrapped around me. Half lost in dream, I drifted into her embrace, giving myself over to her touch. We lay together in silence, legs entwined, while she stroked my hair, gently kissing my face and neck. And then we made love, our bodies moving together and merging as the early morning light filtered through the shutters.

At breakfast the colonel seemed uncharacteristically jumpy. Twice he asked how we had slept, then called for a fresh pot of tea. While we waited, he fidgeted with his napkin, rearranged his chair, and commented repeatedly on the weather. At last the tea arrived and Jagjit circled the table, filling our cups. Only then, after the servant had once again disappeared, Singh let it be known that he intended to name the tiger cub in the back room after "Miss Ainsworth." He made quite a production of the announcement, stressing that he had, until now, been unable to reach a decision on this important matter. He obviously intended for Penny to take it as a considerable honor. He ended by formally requesting permission to use her first name.

"Oh, no," she shook her head, "it's too much. Really." She actually blushed.

"Not at all, my dear. I insist. My mind is made up. But this means that you *must* come again to visit." He glanced in my direction, then back at Penny. "Both of you must return, when the tiger is older and fully trained."

"We will!" Penny exclaimed, without a moment's thought, turning a gleeful smile in my direction. "Won't we, Stanley?"

"Sure," I said, with a slight shrug of my shoulders. "Why not?"

Penny continued looking in my direction, searching my face for some sign that—against all odds—such a thing might in fact be possible. But what could I tell her that she didn't already know? By the time that tiger cub was trained, she would long since have returned to England. After a few seconds her smile faded, ever so slightly, and she turned back to our host. "Thank you, Colonel Singh. For everything. For opening your home to us, for allowing us to share these magical days with you. I shall never forget your generosity."

This time it was Singh who seemed to be at a loss for words. Whatever his feelings may have been for Penny, at that moment the silence between them was both intimate and tender.

That breakfast—our last meal together—is now little more than a mélange of fading images spread out across the canvas of Colonel Singh's poignant, solitary world. I see the three of us seated around the white linen table-cloth with our tea and toast, talking together under the weathered tile roof of the colonel's forest home. The dull luster of a silver teapot polished with wet ash and clay. Three china cups and matching white plates. Three yellow omelets speckled with thin slices of green chili. Penny's hair pulled back and tied with a scrap of silk, the supple curve of her neck, a slender finger hooked through the cup's small handle. The precise creases of Colonel Singh's khaki shirt and trousers, his gleaming boots, the black military turban wrapped proudly above bronzed cheeks.

18

We arrived back in Delhi on a late train. The very next day Penny traveled to Bihar, where she had arranged to photograph Buddhist archeological sites. Our plan was for her to visit me in Manali later on in the summer.

My final weeks in the capital were consumed with preparations for the transition to a new life in India. It was already late March, and at the end of April the period of my official status as a Fulbright scholar would be over—I would no longer bear the institutional imprimatur. I would need to create a new identity from scratch, establish my own boundaries, reasons, justifications. But I had managed to save virtually all of the considerable funds that came with the original award. By continuing to live even more frugally in Banaras, I figured that I would be able to hang on in India indefinitely. I planned to go first to Manali, a village in northern Himachal Pradesh. There in the high elevations, I could wait out the hot season, studying Pali and Sanskrit until late August, when the monsoon had cooled things down a bit on the plains. Then I would relocate permanently to Banaras.

A few days after I got back to Delhi from the Corbett trip, while sorting through the mail in the Fulbright office, I ran into Margaret Billings. Not surprisingly she was aghast at my plans to stay on in India.

"Frankly, Stanley, I'm stunned." She extracted a cigarette from the box and pushed one end between her lips, torched the other with a blue Bic, and sucked in a lungful of smoke. "From a professional point of view," she said, "this is certainly a mistake. But I'm talking to myself again." Two gray clouds spewed out of her nostrils like diesel exhaust. "Why should I care if you ruin your chances for an academic career?"

I didn't know how to respond. After all, why *should* she care about me? I never had understood. The attention was flattering, in a perverse way, but also annoying. I stood there mute, hanging my head like a recalcitrant child.

"You know, this could very well jeopardize your ability to get scholarships through your department. There's only so much you can expect Sellars to do for you—especially if it begins to look like you're not serious about your work."

"I appreciate your concern, Margaret."

"But you don't care *yourself*." Her tone had softened.

"Honestly, I appreciate your advice," I interjected. "I really do. I plan to be back in the States by next fall. I'm just going to spend the summer in the mountains, working on my Hindi." All those opportunities to watch Penny had paid off. I lied. Brazenly. Margaret knew it too, but there was nothing more to say. She simply shrugged her shoulders. Clearly she was giving up on me.

We were each weaving the fabric of our lives: I would remain here in India, without any clear idea why; she would return on schedule with the results of her research to tie it all up neatly in a paper that could be presented at the next meeting of the Association for Asian Studies, with no need to wonder why. I left her sitting on the same couch where we had met, the butt of a cigarette glowing faintly between her fingertips.

Seeing Margaret again made me realize how much had changed since the afternoon of our first encounter, how my mood had shifted from the disorientation and despair of those first few months to a sense that things were finally moving in the right direction. After the whole miserable business with Judith and the bleak loneliness of those early months in Agra and Delhi, I had managed to surface with a tenuous faith in my decision to stay on in South Asia beyond the period of the Fulbright award. Meanwhile, my past life was growing ever more remote. I rarely thought about Chicago and Abe Sellars. Research for the dissertation had all but stalled. Reading the Sanskrit texts had become an end in itself.

Since arriving in India I had accumulated a small stack of photographs from home. They came one or two at a time in the mail—pictures of my mother and father, my sister and my brothers, of the Thanksgiving turkey, of Christmas, the tree and gifts, the winter snow, aunts and uncles and cousins. I kept this sheaf of curling photos in an aluminum trunk, wrapped in a handkerchief like a Lakota medicine bundle. Viewing them had become a ritual act. I would bring the little package to my desk, carefully unwrap the square of cotton cloth, and make my way deliberately from one snapshot to the next, allowing them to conjure up a chain of memories that led backward in time to a world both intimately familiar and eerily distant. Everything was just as I had left it, except for one, small detail: these people—people I knew so well—were now living a life I did not share. It was as if some clever censor had airbrushed me out of my own past.

I still have that anachronistic collection of Kodachrome photos tucked somewhere in a drawer. The colors have bleached with the intervening years, but this only contributes to the disconcerting sense that the entire world they depict never did really exist. Each fragile photographic image has become a thinly layered testament to the continuing sequence of losses on which a life is built. I study the two-dimensional faces, those effervescent holiday smiles, and I see all of us somersaulting through a world that is, according to the *Lankavatara Sutra*, "neither as it appears, nor otherwise."

One night I dreamed that I was back in America, in an unfamiliar, dingy apartment somewhere in Chicago. I somehow knew that this was an apartment where Judith had once lived, though at the moment it appeared unoccupied—furnished, but otherwise empty of any personal belongings. I was going through drawers and closets, looking for something, though I did not know what. Finally, in a box under the bed, I discovered a fluffy purple beach towel that I immediately recognized as a gift I had given to her on Valentines Day in 1971. Her favorite color was purple, and she had treasured that towel. One afternoon when we were camping in northern Michigan, at Sleeping Bear Dunes National Lakeshore, she left it on the beach. We didn't realize it was missing until much later, after we had returned to our campground, and by that time it was too late to go back. We never saw it again. Oddly, when I found the towel in my dream I knew immediately what it was, and I knew I had to get it to her. She would be thrilled. But where was she? I hadn't the slightest idea, and I was seized with a desperate longing for her company.

This dream and the terrible poignancy it provoked remained with me long after waking. For the first time, I sensed just how much had been irretrievably sacrificed in order to cut my ties with Judith. I realized how I had literally been saved by forgetting, how this ability to simply not remember so much of what we have lost serves as a natural escape from the otherwise unbearable weight of the past.

About this time I began working my way through the Sanskrit text of the *Bodhicharyavatara*, a medieval poem describing the inner life of a bodhisattva. I was drawn to it not only because of the beauty of the original language, but also because of the passionate voice of the author, a Buddhist monk named Shantideva. The tone of his writing is deeply personal; his question goes to the heart of the spiritual life: how can we open ourselves fully to the painful contradictions of our love for this world, a world so fragile, so tenuous and fleeting, that it can never truly be our own?

I copied a stanza onto the first page of my journal, where it remained as a sort of maxim guiding my life through the following years. Without making any special effort, I committed it to memory and began unconsciously reciting the Sanskrit several times a day . . .

> *Yā avasthāḥ prapadyeta*
> *svayaṃ paravaśo 'pi vā/*
> *tāsvavasthāsu yāḥ śikṣāḥ*
> *śikṣettā eva yatnataḥ//*

A free translation of my understanding of the Sanskrit might read something like this:

> Whatever happens—
> whether through your own resolve or the will of another—
> circumstances conceal a deeper import.
> See this, and learn.

What I loved about this verse is the suggestion that there is something in our present experience that we fail to notice—something profoundly worthwhile. Whatever it is, this "deeper import" is always available, and in this sense it's completely ordinary. But we don't trust what is common and easy; we want the exotic, the complicated, the *extra*-ordinary. Of course the irony of traveling halfway around the world in search of what is most common was not lost on me; but then, what's more common than irony? The verse called to mind the Vedantic idea of the Satguru—the True Teacher who is always present and available but unnoticed. We recognize the Satguru only when we're particularly vulnerable, in a rare, unguarded moment of trust and self-surrender. And the lesson he teaches is always the same: Here I am, your own real self in the guise of the other.

Back in Delhi, it was not the Satguru that I found when I looked within or without. There was only the white clown, anxious of losing his balance and tumbling off the high wire into the abyss. Amid the crowds and the traffic, immersed in classes at the university and conversation at the Fulbright office, the abyss was always and everywhere present, for it was none other than this world. This conditioned world, as the Buddhist texts say—this world of endless desire and fear. *Samsara*. I found myself retreating into solitude. I became more guarded than ever. When Penny once again went on the road I missed her, but I was relieved to have her gone.

A few weeks before I left Delhi, Ed Rivers passed through on his way out of the country. He had written to me from Banaras, requesting permission to stay a night or two at my place while he tied up the final arrangements with people at the Foreigners' Registration Office and the airlines. During the few days we shared, what struck me most was his apprehension in the face of his impending departure. He did his best to hide it, but his distress was obvious. He was jumpy, on edge. I couldn't help but recall how on our first meeting back in Chicago, Ed had appeared so comfortably self-contained, as though drawing energy from an inexhaustible source. Even in Banaras, during my Christmas visit, he had been calm and grounded. What had happened now to account for this disturbing transformation?

Pondering all of this it became clear. This wouldn't be a short visit home with family and friends. This time it would be for good. Very soon—in a matter of hours—India would be, for Ed, nothing but a memory. It's hard to imagine any context in American society where the preceding eight years of his life would make sense. He had been floating free in a strangely privileged, hermetic environment, a vast, eternal present. But the clock would start ticking with a vengeance the moment his plane touched down in New York. What skills did he have that might help him pull through what was just over the horizon? What had he learned during his long sojourn in the holy city?

As far as I could tell he had mastered two valuable lessons: how to survive on almost nothing and how to work hard with no thought of reward. Perhaps this would be enough. I watched him arrange his few possessions before leaving for the airport. Did this small bag contain all he had in the world?

He spoke vaguely of a plan to go into business with a friend, importing village handicrafts from India into the States. He folded his lungi and packed it.

"You're taking that?" I suppressed a smile, imagining him walking the streets of an American city in a brightly patterned, cotton wraparound skirt.

"I'll wear it at home." His tone was mildly defiant. "It gets hot in New Jersey in the summer. How can I live without a lungi?"

"Sure." I replied, abruptly contrite. I asked why, after eight years, he was leaving.

"You can't stay in India forever," he answered, as if this were obvious.

But I didn't see why not. There must be a way.

At about ten o'clock a taxi arrived. It was dark, but the night air was still hot. Ed fastened the catch on his bag, picked up the sitar case plastered with *fragile* stickers, and thanked me for the hospitality. He was wearing the same polyester shirt and pants he had worn that night in Chicago.

19

In mid April I had my last Sanskrit lesson with Anantacharya. These quiet evenings had been a routine part of my life in Delhi, and even before our final meeting I was mourning their loss. I loved everything about this weekly event, beginning with the long bike ride to Anantacharya's home through streets filled with children and peddlers. He lived with his family in a bleak, middle-class housing development, row after row of concrete stucco stained from years of heat and rain. I turned into a section marked Block C and peddled up to number 139, where I dismounted and pulled my bicycle under the covered porch. Krishna greeted me and showed me to my customary place on the couch, then disappeared into the kitchen.

There was one chair in the front room. Like the couch, it was a lacquered wooden frame with wide, flat arms, the back and seat a web of white plastic strings. In front of the couch was a coffee table, and a waist-high metal bookcase stood against the wall opposite my seat. High above the bookcase, only a few inches below the ceiling, a black-and-white photograph of Anantacharya's father hung from two wires: a stern, dignified man with a magnificent moustache that completely obscured his upper lip. He was shown from the waist up, shirtless, the sacred thread looped over one shoulder. The photo had been partially colored by hand and mounted in an ornate gilded frame. On either side were similarly framed pictures of Hindu gods. Windows above and behind the couch had no glass, only vertical bars painted green. The shutters were open, and a ceiling fan turned slowly overhead.

Before long Krishna returned with a glass of water on a saucer, which he placed on the coffee table. Having seen to my immediate needs, he excused himself to summon his father. Meanwhile, I looked fondly around this room where I had passed so many enjoyable hours.

There is something indescribably precious about the deliberate, meticulous work involved in mastering a classical language—memorizing conjugations and declensions, splitting long compounds, unraveling grammar and syntax in order to decipher a message that has miraculously survived its journey through the centuries. Such intricate, all-consuming labor demands great patience, and it had carried me through much of this first difficult year in India. I owed a debt to Shri Anantacharya much greater than he would ever comprehend.

To commemorate our final evening together, my teacher's wife served me masala dosa and sambar, topped off with a cup of strong, South Indian coffee prepared with sugar and water-buffalo milk. Anantacharya sat to my right, in the chair beside the couch, watching me eat. He was dressed as usual in a dhoti and long kurta. At the bank he must have worn Western-style clothing, but he changed as soon as he got home; I never saw him in anything but a dhoti. Usually he was perfectly groomed, but tonight his long, silver hair had been carelessly pushed back over his ears, and his cheeks were covered with gray stubble. He looked tired. It occurred to me that he was an old man. When I finished the last of the coffee, he rose stiffly and shuffled over the smooth concrete floor to the bookshelf where his beloved library rested. He carefully withdrew a slender volume and examined it, wiping off some dust with the hem of his dhoti.

"You will please take this," he said, gently depositing the book in my hands. "It is a Sanskrit edition of *Raghuvamsha*, one of Kalidasa's finest poems. I worked for many years, collecting and collating every manuscript I could find. So many quiet hours in my father's study in Madurai. I have also attempted to capture the meaning in English, but I am afraid this was a difficult task. I requested fifty copies printed and bound at my own expense."

I tried to insist that with my poor knowledge of Sanskrit I was not in a position to appreciate such a gift, but he would hear nothing of it.

"You have traveled all the way from America only to learn our language. I want you to have this."

I held it carefully. The cover bore an English inscription, in gold lettering, to his father. While Anantacharya continued to speak, I slowly turned the pages.

"I know that you are most interested in Vedanta, and also in the poor grammar of your Buddhist dialecticians—a serious error of aesthetic judgment which I nevertheless forgive." Here he tilted his head to one side and shrugged his shoulders in mock surrender, as if to imply that he had tried his best to help me refine my taste. "Mr. Stanley," he said, "we have an ancient saying in Tamil. May I tell it to you?"

"Please do."

"Let me see . . ." He was clearly attempting to come up with a suitable translation. "Ah, yes. Here it is. We say, if two people are talking, and the speaker understands of what he is speaking, while the listener also understands of what he is hearing, then it is *business!*" He smiled cagily. "Do you follow?"

I nodded. "Is that all?"

"Oh no, no." He waggled his head back and forth. "Very amusing, Mr. Stanley. That is only first part. It goes on in this way: If two people are talking, and the speaker understands of what he is speaking, but the listener does not understand of what he is listening, then it is *grammar!*" He got quite a kick out of this, Sanskrit grammar running a very close second to poetry and drama on the list of his favorite subjects.

"Very good," I said. "I see that I'm not the only one who has trouble with Panini's *Asthadhyayi*." Panini was the most famous of all Sanskrit grammarians.

"Yes, indeed. But this last part is especially for you. Listen: If two people are talking, and the speaker does not understand of what he is speaking, nor does the listener understand of what he is listening, what is it then, Mr. Stanley? What is the subject?" His eyes sparkled.

"I should know, right?"

He grinned so broadly that I spied two gold teeth I had never before noticed, set way around in back among the molars. "It is philosophy, Mr. Stanley. *Philosophy!*"

He looked at me and continued to gloat for several seconds, then spoke up again without waiting for my response. "All in fun, you understand." The grin gave way to something with a bit more gravitas. "But allow me to tell you something serious now, and I hope you will not let what I have to say slip away without giving it some thought."

I assured him that I would give his words a great deal of thought. Throughout this exchange he had remained standing in front of me, leaning heavily forward onto his cane. At this point he commenced to wobble slightly, as if he were about to topple over. At the last instant he redirected the vector of his fall, deftly spinning his body around so that he landed, with a little springing motion, dead center on the plastic webbing of his armchair. He let the cane fall to one side, where it clattered to the floor, then settled in like a Zen master, taking his time, meticulously rearranging the folds of his dhoti.

"Mr. Stanley, this is our final time for meeting together. We have labored to complete the foundation on which you might, if you choose, build a temple. You are young. You have time. A lifetime to use as you wish. I hope you will continue with your study. You may discover that, for Kalidasa, philosophy and poetry are not really so different."

This last remark brought my eyes up out of the pages. Since Corbett, the name "Slave of Kali" had taken on new associations. The greatest of India's classical poets was also a devotee of the goddess. I had never really thought about it before. What had she taught him, I now wondered, and what price had he paid for her instruction?

"If you have no objection," Anantacharya continued, "let us read the first shloka together. Some day you will open this book, far away in America. You will read this same shloka again, and you will fondly recall our time together. You may perhaps remember this very evening, this little room in Delhi where you sat with your old Sanskrit guru." He spoke with such ingenuous warmth that I became suddenly self-conscious.

I opened the book in my lap, and Shri Anantacharya began to recite the first verse while I followed along with the Sanskrit text.

> *Vāg arthāviva sampriktau*
> *vāg artha pratipattaye/*
> *jagataḥ pitarau bande*
> *pārvatī parameśvarau//*

At the end of the verse he paused, allowing the sound of the words to re-enter the silence out of which it had arisen. Then, as was our custom, he proposed an English translation of the text for me to consider. This evening, he lifted the words from his own book:

> Salutations to Parvati and her Lord.
> May I attain supreme knowledge
> of this divine couple,
> mother and father of the universe,
> inseparably bound together,
> like a word and its meaning.

"Parvati's 'Lord' here is the Mighty Shiva, her husband, whose home is in Varanasi on the banks of the Ganga. Like a mother and father, Lord

Shiva and Parvati love all creatures and guide us. Marriage, you understand, means two people are joined together forever. Man and woman become one."

I nodded vaguely.

"Here Kalidasa makes a comparison to words and their meaning. The Mimamsaka . . ." He broke off and raised one bushy white eyebrow. "You are familiar with Mimamsaka, Mr. Stanley?"

Again I nodded. I knew it was an early Hindu school of philosophy concerned with interpretation of the Veda. That's about it, actually. But I wasn't going to stop him for a disquisition on the Mimamsakas.

"That is good. Then you may be knowing that Kalidasa is using the ideas of Mimamsaka, that the sound of a word and the meaning of that word are joined like man and wife, for all time. Mimamsaka also speaks of supreme or 'self-luminous' knowledge. It is like the flame of a candle, which simultaneously illuminates both itself and the objects around it. It is knowledge that encompasses not only the word and its meaning but the knower himself as well. With supreme knowledge comes *moksha*."

He paused to catch my eye, then held it in his portentous gaze.

"You understand what I am saying, Mr. Stanley? Liberation. One knows oneself in the sound of the words and in their meaning. One sees oneself as inseparable from words and ideas. Knowing oneself in this way, Mr. Stanley, one is free from samsara. All this is present here in the first shloka of this great poem of Kalidasa. So you see—you may read these lines as poetry or, if you wish, as philosophy. It is your choice. For in India, the greatest of philosophers wrote in verse."

"Excuse me, Anantacharya-ji."

"Yes? Please speak up." He raised both bare feet off the floor and tucked them in under the folds of his dhoti.

"I was taught—maybe I simply assumed—that Indian philosophers wrote in verse to make it easier to memorize the texts. Is that so?"

He studied my face. "And why we should memorize now, when written word is so easy to find?"

"Well," I began, intensely aware that I was wading into deep waters. Anantacharya had repeatedly lectured me on the value of memorization. "Maybe the custom survives from a time when everything was passed along orally, before things were written."

"Survives?" He tipped his head to one side, like that dog in the old RCA Victor ads. "You are suggesting our Indian custom of philosophical poetry is anachronism?" He pronounced the word slowly, as if taking the full measure of its weight on his tongue. "An old tradition we might want to avoid now, in modern world. Is that it? Is that your meaning?"

"No, well not exactly." I was on the spot. The truth was that I had always more or less taken it for granted that classical Indian philosophy was composed in metered verse. I suppose I thought of it as a form of scholasticism. Anantacharya seemed to be hinting at something more.

Neither of us said anything. For a while he pulled at one earlobe, then switched to massaging the tip of his nose.

"Mr. Stanley," he said at last, "let us consider *Raghuvamsha*. *Raghuvamsha* is epic poem, *mahakavya*. You will find only five mahakavya in whole of Sanskrit literature, for there are many strict requirements. An epic poem must begin with salutation, as we are just now reading together. Subject of mahakavya must be some very important event. There must be great councils, messengers and embassies, armies engaged in battle. Mahakavya must include cities and villages, seas, mountains, and change of seasons, sunrise and sunset. And moonlight. Yes, Mr. Stanley," he smiled knowingly, "moonlight must be there. Moonlight is necessary for scenes of amusement in garden, scenes of drinking sharab and dalliance between man and woman. This is *raga*, Mr. Stanley. What do you say in English? Passion. Love. But not only joy. *Raga* means also sadness and grief, from losing all those things we love. Mahakavya must show us both joy of victory and misery of defeat."

Here he halted long enough to cough once or twice, catch his breath, and call out for a glass of water. The glass appeared in seconds, delivered by one of the younger boys who handed it to him, hanging back just long enough to smile shyly in my direction. Anantacharya took a long drink and deposited the glass on the floor next to his cane. He cleared his throat with alarming force—I thought for a moment he might be choking—then adjusted himself in the chair and rubbed one palm over his freshly shaven crown.

"Philosophy and poetry—they are having the same subject: life. But not only some abstract idea of life. They speak to me of *my* life, the life I am living, here and now. Is it not so? For if the poet is skillful, then the story he is telling becomes *my* story. I see the meaning of his words in my own life."

He leaned over, lifted the book from my hands, and demonstrated, holding it stiffly at arms length while he pretended to read. "Not like this,

Mr. Stanley. No indeed! Not like this." He let his arms relax and drew the book in to where it settled gingerly against his paunch. "You see? I let the words enter into me. I am in*vol*ved."

He closed the book and folded his hands across its cover.

"Poetry and philosophy cannot be separate from life. What good to have words and ideas, up here"—he thumped his knuckles against his skull—"like rupees locked inside vault. No, no . . . words must *live* in me. When words come into my heart," he laid a hand on his chest, "their meaning becomes my own."

His lungs rattled into another coughing fit. He thumped on his chest and finished off the last of the water, which restored him enough to continue.

"And so we have cities and seas, mountains, passing of seasons, sunrise and sunset, moonlight and dark of night. Passion, hatred, war, and all the rest of it! Suffering, sadness, despair, and death. Yes," his voice softened, "we must have death."

I wanted to say something—if only to show him I was paying attention—but I didn't know what. Anantacharya often spoke at length about the texts we read, but never like this. Never from such a personal point of view. I knew he was ill. His son Krishna and I frequently sat together after the Sanskrit lessons, speaking of this or that, and he had alluded to concerns about his father's health.

"Now, Mr. Stanley, let us try to understand what Kalidasa is saying in this shloka." He leaned forward slightly. "Life and death, you know? They too are only words. But they are words we have taken deeply into our heart. This world is here with us because we have made these and so many other words our own." He sighed.

"Words can not be avoided. We are human. This is as it should be. This is not a problem. At Bank of India, for example, we have two very serious words: peon and *malik*." He smiled at this use of the Hindi word for "boss." "So it is among Indians, you know? One is peon, another is malik. The difference is very real. We need not pretend otherwise. This is our modern world."

His voice modulated when pronouncing the word "modern," as if he weren't entirely reconciled to its use, as if he would much prefer not to let this particular word enter into his heart.

"It is true, some ugly words we must use. Fortunately these are not the only words we have, and this modern world is not our only world. There is also the world of Kalidasa, a world that he gives to us in his

Raghuvamsha. Nevertheless," he seemed to be considering how best to proceed, "even beautiful words reveal their deepest meaning only when we do not allow ourselves to be fooled." He paused. "What is it to be fooled? I will tell you."

"Our life and our death are inseparably bound together with words and ideas. All of this," he swung his arm in a wide arc, "is made of words: *shabda-mayi.* Words, and only words: *shabda-matra.* This is Kalidasa's meaning. This world of words—this life and death—it is nothing but *bara tamasha.*" He examined my face, as if unsure whether I was familiar with the Hindi expression. "Big drama. You know? Theater."

He raised his fist and let it hang in the air like a knot at the end of a rope, nails pressed tightly against the flesh of his palm. "*Ma-ya.*"

As if chanting a mantra, he lingered over each syllable of the Sanskrit word. One by one the fingers relaxed and fell away, his hand turned slowly at the wrist and drifted gently down to his lap, leaving the space between us empty.

"We bind our hearts to this illusion—this big drama—and for that we must suffer. But when there is supreme knowledge of word and meaning, then at last we are free. Words may be a tool for doing business, or an incantation for casting of spells. But in the end—in the end, Mr. Stanley . . ."

Once again his voice grew hushed, as if he intended to share with me some intimacy, some piece of wisdom ordinarily gained only at great personal expense.

"Words are a burden, to be set aside."

This Vedantic perspective was astonishing, coming from a man who had immersed himself in the world of Sanskrit poetics. A man who had seemed—until this moment—totally identified with the language and literature of classical India. We sat together in silence. I waited to make sure he was finished. I did not wish to appear impertinent. At last I spoke.

"A burden, Anantacharya-ji?"

He responded without the faintest hint of irony. "Oh, yes. Most certainly. Words can become a great burden. Just as a philosopher may eventually tire of the endless search for reasons, similarly a poet may grow weary of the constant repetition of victory and defeat."

He closed the book and handed it back to me.

"And so it is, Mr. Stanley. So it is. But you are young. And you have Kalidasa. Such beautiful words."

It was a good time to get out of town—and not only because of the heat. During the previous nine months of Indira Gandhi's Emergency, some 140,000 people had been arrested and sentenced without trial. The press was heavily censored, but even so, in the last several months, newspapers had begun self-consciously joking that India had become "the land of the rising son." The reference was to Sanjay Gandhi, the youngest of Indira's two adult children, and despite the clever journalistic humor, no one was laughing.

The Prime Minister's son was an aggressive, ambitious man who appeared to be universally despised. Before the Emergency, Sanjay had been in England training to be a Rolls-Royce mechanic, but Indira had summoned him back to India to assume leadership of the party's youth wing. Much of his time was apparently spent at a local garage, where he fiddled with cars and honed his macho image among a growing band of hoodlums. They were recruited to the party as his loyal followers and were anxious to prove themselves in his service. Sanjay wanted to make himself known as a man of action—someone who knew how to get things done—and high on his agenda was a campaign to rein in India's formidable and steadily growing population. Under Sanjay's new programs, lower-level government employees were not paid unless they motivated a prescribed number of Indian males to sign up for vasectomies. Reports of abuse were rampant, especially toward Muslims and low-caste Hindus; stories circulated about men in rural Bihar being offered transistor radios and watches in return for submitting to "the operation," or men in Delhi who were dragged from a cinema and forcibly subjected to surgery.

It was difficult to know what to believe, but the public's fear and hatred of Sanjay was palpable. Most recently, his name had been associated with a government-sponsored initiative to clean up Old Delhi's infamous *bastis*—the slums associated in particular with the area south of Jamma Masjid, where the pianist in Penny's story had lost his pants. Residents in the crowded neighborhood of Turkman Gate were ordered to evacuate their homes and resettle a considerable distance away, across the Yamuna on the outskirts of the city. The entire area was scheduled for demolition. Most of the people affected were Muslims who had been living in the narrow lanes for centuries, running tailor shops, chai stalls, and other small businesses. They objected that the relocation would not only destroy their homes and their means of their livelihood but also force them to commute by bus into the city every day at a cost that was prohibitive. When they refused to comply with the evacuation order, Sanjay called in the police.

On April 18 a phalanx of armed militia faced off against thousands of people who had gathered to protest. When the crowd did not disperse, the soldiers opened fire, killing six protestors and wounding scores of others. News of the massacre was censored from the Indian press, but because it was reported over BBC and other international news agencies, it didn't take long for word to spread, and then all hell broke loose. Nevertheless, in the end, the Turkman Gate neighborhood was bulldozed as scheduled, and Sanjay rolled on.

The Fulbright people were distinctly on edge. Still jittery about Indira's well-known paranoia of the CIA, they once again cautioned Americans to stay clear of any kind of political gathering. But it was increasingly difficult to avoid the demonstrations that seemed to be everywhere. It was, as I say, a good time to get out of Delhi, and—at Ed River's suggestion—I had already decided where to go. I carefully packed up my things and left them in storage at the Fulbright office; I wanted to travel light, to leave behind everything that weighed me down.

For most of the years he lived in India, Ed had maintained a small cabin in Himachal Pradesh, at the northernmost end of the Kullu Valley. There, near the town of Manali, he had escaped not only the extreme heat of the summer but also the pyrotechnic insanity of the autumn holiday season—a time when everyone who can scrape together a few rupees invests in bombs and rockets powerful enough to blow small craters in the road. I had already experienced Durga Puja and Diwali in Agra, and once was enough. The state of Himachal, with its relatively sparse population, offered the possibility of a respite. From the forested hills of the Terai up into the remote hinterlands of Lahaul and Spiti, the landscape is staggering. Ever since the visit to Corbett, I had wanted to return to the mountains.

There is an ancient Chinese legend recounted by the fifth-century poet T'ao Ch'ien in an essay titled *Peach Blossom Spring*. The story tells of an isolated community where people live in simplicity, in harmony with the natural order. The Tibetans, as well, have their own tales of *beyul*—"hidden worlds"—said to be nestled in the most remote and treacherous peaks of the Himalayas. These stories have entered European and American culture through the mythology of the kingdom of Shangri-La popularized by the novel *Lost Horizon*. Both the paperback and the Hollywood film tell the story of a group of Europeans attempting to flee China during the early days of the revolution. Caught in a blizzard, their plane goes down somewhere high in the mountains of central Asia. The pilot is killed, and the survivors are eventually rescued by a mysterious party of Tibetans, who escort them through snow and wind, finally arriving at the cramped entrance to a cave. Passing through the cave, they emerge in a lush, temperate valley inhabited by a community of immortals who have no desire to re-establish contact with the outside world.

The tricky thing about a beyul is that it cannot be discovered through any kind of intentional search. No map will ever point the way. As the British imperial forces well knew, a map is primarily a tool of conquest, a visual embodiment of the desire to capture and hold a specific territory. To imagine forced entry into a beyul is like planning to storm the gates of Neverland. Even to harbor a desire to find such a place is to be irredeemably lost in an oxymoron; the valley of T'ao Ch'ien's *Peach Blossom Spring* will never be found through yearning and striving but only through unconditional surrender. In Manali—if only for a short while—I stumbled into just such a magical world.

The ride from Delhi was a grueling twenty-four hours by bus through the dusty, flat expanse of Haryana and the Punjab, up into the Terai and, finally, along a poorly maintained road that wound northward through the Kullu Valley. It was almost dark by the time we reached Chandigarh, and there was still an entire night and part of the next day in front of us. Most of that time I was half-awake, smashed upright into a crowded seat, my head bouncing and jerking with the motion of the bus as it rounded one sharp turn after another, following the switchbacks that clung to the steep walls of the Beas River. By the time we arrived at our final destination, early the following afternoon, I had long since sunken into a kind of hypnogogic trance. My eyes itched and burned, and the muscles of my neck and back were contracted like iron straps. It was pure joy to climb off the bus and find myself standing in the relative silence of the Manali bazaar, breathing in cool, clear mountain air.

On both sides the valley rose in a network of terraced rice-paddies and apple orchards that gradually gave way, at higher elevations, to deep forests of Deodar pine, fir, and spruce. To the east was the towering peak of Deo Tibba; to the west a craggy line of snow-covered mountains leading off into the Solang Valley and the source of the Beas River—an immense amphitheater of glaciated ice and rock situated over twenty thousand feet above sea level. Looking northward, I could just make out the striated cliffs of the Rohtang Pass, an angular rock wall thrown up against the mind-boggling emptiness of the Lahauli sky. The Rohtang is closed by snow most of the year, but as I stood there outside the bus, I could sense the presence of the vast Tibetan plateau as it spilled over the pass, charging the northern Kullu Valley with its elemental power. The village of Manali stands guard like a sentry here at the boundary between this world and another, alien realm of monstrous proportions, a land of ice and stone sliced by frigid torrents of foaming whitewater.

Outside the wooden storefronts, men in baggy woolen pants and short coats clustered in the street smoking and talking, every one of them wearing a kind of small, brimless cap with a swatch of brightly colored fabric sewed along the front. The women, too, were all wearing versions of the same dress: a plaid wrap-around blanket fixed in place at the shoulders with two brass pins. It seemed like every other person was carrying an amorphous ball of fluff tucked into the waist-belt of their clothing. While they talked, they worked it with their fingers, stretching and pulling the fuzz into a single long strand that led downward to a whirling wooden top that twirled just above their feet. It took me a moment to realize that they were spinning yarn.

I had no idea where to stay; all I wanted was to find a room where I could stretch out and get some sleep. I figured I'd start looking around for a more permanent place the next morning. I was trying to decide which way to go when a teenage boy emerged from nowhere and approached me just outside the bus. He was wearing blue jeans and a shabby, chocolate-brown suit coat. Under the coat was a V-neck argyle sweater emblazoned with the name of an Indian cricket team. The toes of his grimy rubber thongs were scuffed to a thin edge. His hat—the same style as the other men were wearing—was cocked at a rakish angle, which gave him a breezy, confident air. Tufts of unruly hair poked out over his ears.

"Hello sir." He pronounced the English words with great confidence, simultaneously extending one hand. "My name Ramnath."

I shook his outstretched hand.

"You want good room?" He smiled ingenuously, as though he desired nothing more than to assist a needy traveler.

I looked him over. My immediate impulse was to tell him to get lost. He was obviously a hustler—a kid accustomed to working the hippies and the occasional tourist who somehow got this far up into the mountains. He probably had a contract with a local hotel owner from whom he collected a commission. But I was desperate.

"What kind of 'good' room?"

"Very good room, sir." Again the smile. "You come with me. See this room."

He gestured for me to follow, then started walking. After a few steps he turned back and saw me still standing. "Come. This way, sir." Again he motioned for me to follow. "You no be sorry."

What the hell, I thought, lifting my bag, which was full of heavy books and dictionaries.

He watched me struggle, then came over and took the strap from my hands. I protested, but he waved me off and eased the bag over his shoulder. "No vurry, mahn!"

I followed him for a block or so down the main street, keeping close behind. We turned left into an alley between two buildings, scattering some chickens that ran squawking and fluttering ahead. He was walking surprisingly fast, considering the weight of the bag, and within moments we were free of the buildings, heading out of the bazaar and up the western side of the valley, plying our way along a well-trodden maze of pathways that led between the flooded rice paddies. All the while my guide was whistling and singing. Every now and again he glanced over his shoulder to make sure I was still there, flashing the same innocent grin. After twenty minutes or so, we took a fork in the trail that led up to a two-story, wood and stucco house enclosed by broad, covered porches at both the lower level and above.

The room Ramnath offered me was in his own home. It was one of two on the ground floor; the other was used for storage. Inside I found a small, wood-burning stove in one corner and a straw sleeping mat on the floor. In the course of our negotiations, it became clear that the boy could speak very little English, and when I switched into Hindi he was genuinely thrilled. He agreed to rig me up a desk, using a few old crates, and the deal was closed.

Ramnath and his family lived in the single, large room above. His mother, Durga, was a sturdy, strong-featured woman with ears pierced all the way around and hair tied back in a bright red scarf. His father was a raw-boned, cheerful man, with stubbly cheeks and bad teeth, someone who had obviously worked hard all his life. Both Ramnath's parents departed for the forest early every morning and came lumbering back home after dark, buried under two mountains of wood strapped to their backs. When not busy with the wood, they worked the small vegetable garden near the house or tended to a few chickens that scratched around in the dirt. Ramnath's sister, Kaladevi, also lived upstairs. She couldn't have been more than twelve years old. Most of the time she carried their younger sister, a toddler named Priya, on her hip. Among themselves the family spoke a Kullu dialect virtually unintelligible to me; but when we conversed, they effortlessly shifted into something approaching the language I had studied in Chicago and Delhi. During the month I lived with them, I barely used a word of English.

Water for drinking and washing dishes had to be hauled from a nearby stream in a twenty liter plastic container, and I was responsible for splitting my own firewood. All this took up a significant part of my afternoons. Since I was cooking for myself, I had to get fresh vegetables every other day. It took a couple of hours to hike down to the bazaar, purchase what I needed, and get back up to the house.

I learned that a Tibetan refugee community had settled at the south end of town, around a Geluk monastery and a smaller Nyingma temple. To the northeast, a steep hike up from the river, there was another monastery that belonged to a famous Kagyu meditation master named Apo Rinpoche. He was renowned for his teaching of *tumo*, a form of meditation designed to recalibrate the body's thermostat. People told me that hermits who know this practice could survive subzero weather in a cave without firewood or warm clothing. I heard stories about how Apo Rinpoche trained his monks outdoors in the dead of winter. While the lamas sat cross-legged in the snow, absorbed in meditation, he would walk back and forth, upending buckets of freezing water over the motionless row of bodies. Ramnath and his mother both insisted they had seen—all the way across the valley—clouds of steam rising from the courtyard of the monastery.

I had no idea what to make of such tales, but I was taken with the Tibetans, spinning their prayer wheels, chanting mantras, and laughing. Their broad, weathered faces, framed by black braids, turquoise earrings, and necklaces of coral and silver reminded me of Edward Curtis's old photographs of Native Americans. One afternoon I stood for the better part of an hour watching a group of men huddled on their knees in a tight circle, gambling. They took turns shaking several dice in a small wooden cup, which they slammed down with great flourish onto a leather mat. The slap of the cup as it struck the mat was accompanied by enthusiastic cries of *AH-LAY!* and *TSOK SUNG!* followed by a great deal of cajoling, teasing, sighing, punching, and shoving. *Who are these people?* I wondered. Like so many other Western visitors to the Himalayas back then, I desperately wanted to pry into the secret source of their joy.

Not withstanding all the novel distractions of life in Manali, I made an effort to resume my work with Sanskrit and Pali, and my meditation practice. It quickly became apparent that Ramnath would be a problem. No matter what I happened to be doing or how engrossed I was in my work, he would simply invite himself into my room and announce the plan of the hour. Driven from the room, he would then pace back and forth on the veranda just outside my open window, observing me from the corner of his eye as I sat on the floor in front of my makeshift desk, reading and writing. For the first few days I did my best to ignore him. But on the third day after I moved in, he explained to me that he was going to help a nearby family plant rice and asked if I would like to come along. Before I knew it, I was wading knee deep in water behind two slick, wet buffalo, clutching at the handles of a wooden plow, with black muck oozing up between my toes. I had not had so much fun in a long time.

What really took me away from my books, though, was the discovery of an entirely unanticipated pleasure. There were two handcrafted looms on the veranda outside my room, and when there was no more pressing business, everyone took their turn weaving. The blankets made by the family were sold wholesale to a vendor, who then—from what I gathered—would pass them along to a buyer who traveled up from the plains. Ramnath put in several hours a day, which seemed to be his main contribution to the domestic economy. When he offered to teach me, I immediately accepted.

The very next morning we hiked to the old village of Manali, some forty minutes away, to help shear a herd of sheep. Everyone was involved and having a good time. Even the small children made a game of it, gleefully collecting the wool and stuffing it into burlap sacks. Along with several other men, I was given the task of restraining the sheep while the scissors did their work. The animals were bleating and wild. I wrapped my arms around their chests and plunged my fingers into their thick, tangled coats, down through twigs and grass and hard pellets of shit, hugging them tight against me. Their warm bodies smelled of rain and snow, pine needles, grass, and earth.

Late in the day, after the work was done, I sat around a fire with the others, chewing on doughy paratha and drinking *chang*—a kind of milky, homemade beer. A few of the men began to sing, and before long the whole group joined in. Someone suggested that I sing an English song, and in a moment everyone was yelling and clapping, insisting that the videshi perform. The only thing I could think of was *Swing Low, Sweet Chariot*, so I went with it. The moment I began to sing, everyone stopped talking—even the children wandered over to listen. The only sound, other than my voice, was the crackling of the fire.

Ramnath and I came home sometime long after dark, wobbling drunkenly through the woods. I was filthy and exhausted and absurdly happy. Over my shoulder I carried a bag of wool that I would spin into yarn, for a blanket that I myself was going to weave.

The next morning I skipped meditation and slept in. I awoke with a manageable hangover, made a cup of Nescafé, and spent the morning sitting on the porch with my host, relaxing in the sun, lost in aimless conversation. From that day on, for the remainder of my stay with Ramnath and his family, I never opened another book.

We soon developed a routine. While my tutor worked at the loom next to me, dispensing occasional instructions and encouragement, I sat ensconced behind an intricate network of strings and levers. Two peddles at my feet controlled the mechanism that lifted and dropped the combs, separating the strings of the warp in alternate directions. Gradually I learned to synchronize the movement of my feet with the back-and-forth motion of the shuttle as it slid between my hands. It did not take long before I fell into a natural rhythm that required no conscious thought. From where we sat on the front porch, I could look out for miles north and south along the valley and all the way down to the bazaar. Far below, people went about their business like Lilliputians, moving among streets lined with tiny houses and shops. Now and again the faint sound of a bus horn would reach my ears. Otherwise there was only the hypnotic swish of yarn and the expanse of Himalayan sky.

One morning, about a week after the sheep shearing, we were sitting together on the porch having coffee, and during a lapse in the conversation I spotted a bright green lizard on a boulder just in front of the house. It was doing pushups on its front legs, moving up and down on the stone in deliberate, jerky motions. I asked Ramnath if they were dangerous.

"*Bahut khatarnaak*, Stanley-ji," he responded, vigorously nodding in the affirmative. "These creatures are very poisonous."

"But they're everywhere!" I exclaimed.

It was true. They were as common as the squirrels in Jackson Park, skittering over rocks and across the paths where we walked. I had even seen them, more than once, right here on the porch.

"They won't hurt you," Ramnath said, waving a hand vaguely in my direction, as if to brush away my worry.

I continued watching the lizard, who did not seem to be at all concerned with us. Indeed, he was still moving up and down, just as before.

"So what are they doing?" I inquired.

Ramnath looked at me quizzically.

"The little pushups, I mean." I put two fingers on the plank next to where I sat and bent them up and down a few times at the knuckles. After a second he seemed to get my meaning.

"Puja," he responded. "It is worship, you know? These are prostrations."

"*Prostrations?*"

"Yes, they are bowing to Lord Shiva, requesting permission to bite humans."

"Wonderful," I said drolly.

"But Lord Shiva will never allow it," he responded quickly, apparently in all seriousness. Then he added, with a smile: "No vurry, mahn!"

Ever since the night in Old Manali, Ramnath had been after me to teach him to sing *Swing Low, Sweet Chariot*. This proved to be something of a chore, largely because he absolutely refused to quit until he had it right. He made me repeat each word over and over, shaping my lips and tongue, holding the sounds in place while he watched and listened attentively. I was surprised by his perfectionism. He had particular trouble with the *swa* sound in "swing" and "sweet." He pronounced the words with great care, laboring to get it right. At first I was surprised at his diligence, then dismayed. We worked at it for several hours, until, at last, he was satisfied.

> *Su-ving low, su-veet chaar-ee-yaahat,*
> *cahming furto*
> *cahr-ee me aum . . .*

From that day on, it seemed as if he never stopped singing that song, and oddly, I never grew tired of hearing it.

> *. . . A bah-und of ahn-gels,*
> *cahming furto get me,*
> *cahming furto cahr-ee me*
> *aum.*

At my urging, Ramnath patiently coached me through a folk song in Kullu dialect. I still remember the melody—a sequence of wavering quartertones that sounded, to me, like the music of gypsy caravans and campfires . . .

> *Ghora vay tsan*
> *aah low,*
> *bhanga ray-lee*
> *begee yaah.*

I never learned the meaning of the words. It never occurred to me to ask. Neither one of us knew what we were singing, and neither one of us cared. The sound was enough. And even now, after all these years, the sound of the words I learned from him is still enough to conjure up the hidden world of Ramnath's front porch, where I was held, for a brief time, secure and content in the arms of the mountains. It was a place where what needed to be done was simple, and good, like throwing a shuttle back and forth, from one hand to the other, the same movement repeated again and again.

> *Ghora vay tsan*
> *aah low,*
> *bhanga ray-lee*
> *yaah.*

Late one morning in the first week of June, I hiked down to the bazaar to buy provisions. On an impulse, I decided to stop by the post office. I had given my address to the Fulbright office with instructions to forward my mail.

There in the wooden box labeled *Poste Restant*, I found a blue inland letter with my name on it. The return address read Block C, no. 139, Baba Nagar, New Delhi.

I took it outside and sat down on the curb next to a group of Tibetan pilgrims from Spiti who had chosen that spot to rest. The peaks all around us glittered in the sun, cutting a stark line against the blue sky. I inserted a finger under the envelope's flap, carefully tore it open, and unfolded the page. In small, meticulously crafted script, was a short message:

> Dear Mr. Stanley,
>
> On the morning of 25 May my father passed from this life to the next. I felt that you would want to have this information, as you were his chela, and I know that he enjoyed so much reading Sanskrit with you. Please come to visit us when you are next in Delhi.
>
> Aap kaa,
> Krishna
>
> P.S. The wedding is postponed to later date. As eldest son, it is my duty to give pinda.

Pinda: Offerings for the dead.

Shri Anantacharya is dead.

He had been my first teacher in India—a living tie, through his father and his father's father and on and on, backward in time, to the world of classical Sanskrit literature and poetry. And now, so swiftly and so surely, he was gone. This is death, I thought. This is the meaning of the word. A man goes away and behind him a doorway closes, and that doorway will never be opened again.

I knew in that moment, sitting there with the letter in my hand, that I had to find a place of my own.

I began that very afternoon to search, inquiring here and there in the bazaar. Within a few days I found a secluded, one-room cabin about half an hour's climb up a steep trail on the eastern side of the valley.

The morning of my departure I packed up my clothes and books and papers, along with the blanket I had finished weaving only days before. I tied my two new cooking pots to the outside of my bag. When I left my room I found the entire family assembled on the porch outside. One by one I thanked them for their hospitality and said goodbye while Priya slept in her sister's arms. Ramnath was last in line. I told him how deeply grateful I was for all he had done, but he barely looked at me. It was time to leave.

I walked maybe a hundred feet, to where the path took a steep turn, and hesitated. Before losing sight of the house I looked back one last time. The family was still standing where I had left them, so close together their bodies touched. Only Ramnath held slightly to one side, watching me go, both fists planted deep in the pockets of his old coat. I joined my palms together, put my hands to my forehead, and bowed low, then straightened up and shouted "No vurry, mahn!" I saw him smile.

21

My hut was built of stone plastered over with a mixture of clay, straw, and cow-manure. The tiny square room was lit through a single window and a shuttered doorway that I kept open during daylight hours. An alcove carved into the back wall could be closed against foraging creatures. My only furnishings were a circular tin stove about ten inches high, like the one I'd had at Ramnath's, and a desk I made out of a split log laid lengthwise over two apple crates. I purchased a straw mat to sleep on, and I spread out a torn burlap sack in front of the stove where I prepared my nightly rice and vegetables.

Everything about my new home was ideal, except for the roof. The beams over my head supported several tons of slate shingles that did a good job keeping out the rain but were much less effective when it came to discouraging the occasional rat and the not-so-occasional lizard that would slip through the cracks. All too often, as I sat reading, one of them would lose its footing and plummet with a resounding smack, striking the floor as if someone had slapped the stones with a rolled-up newspaper. They never seemed to be injured, but it always scared the shit out of me. Once, while I was working out the translation of a tricky passage of Sanskrit, some kind of obese red-and-yellow-striped chameleon dropped through the roof and landed squarely on the back of my hand. I don't know who was more startled, but we both recoiled in horror and made a break in opposite directions.

Like it or not, I shared my space with a variety of living beings. On the whole we kept to ourselves and things went smoothly, though there were some unpleasant moments. One early morning, not long after I moved in, I made my way groggily across the porch and accidentally stepped on a huge black slug; its body blew apart under my bare foot like a water balloon.

It was the tarantulas, however, that really taxed my coping skills. What most disturbed me about these giant spiders was that I never, ever saw them move. They simply *manifested*. I might be absorbed in reading and would chance to look up, and one of them would be clinging to the wall, absolutely still, its body the size of a golf ball, shaggy legs radiating up and out like tentacles. My landlord assured me they were harmless. I wanted to believe what he told me, and I suppressed the urge to flee in terror from my new cabin. But it was hard to ignore them. Especially in those first few weeks, I rarely let the spiders out of my peripheral vision, which was not easy. They would routinely stay in one spot half the afternoon without so much as twitching. Eventually I would get distracted and glance away. And then, when I remembered to look . . . *vanished*.

Spiders notwithstanding, I knew I had found the perfect hermitage. All alone, perched on the rim of a flat, terraced area amid an apple orchard, it was only a fifteen-minute hike to the forest, where I went every few days to collect firewood. My nearest neighbor, a German woman who passed her time reading Hegel and practicing sitar, was a good twenty-minute walk away. I hardly ever saw her—or anyone else, for that matter. Water came from a nearby spring. I shat in the woods like a wild animal, squatting under a tree with the cool breeze tickling the hairs on my naked butt.

One night not long after my move to the new cabin, I woke up and stumbled out, half asleep, to pee off the edge of the porch—a drop of some ten feet to the steep slope below. Across the valley, the sky opened up between the jagged, snow-capped peaks like a hole torn out of the cosmos, black as death behind the great, curving arc of the Milky Way. It was like pissing off the bridge of the starship Enterprise. Standing there balanced at the edge of the void, it was easy to see how our conventional, everyday experience is itself suspended somewhere between the infinite reaches of space and the groundless, subatomic realm of quantum probabilities—extreme frontiers of the mathematical imagination.

I stocked up on provisions and cut my trips to the bazaar to a minimum. When the vegetables ran out, I ate onions, rice, and lentils so as to extend my solitude for a few more precious days. I was in retreat, hiding from the world.

22

Toward the end of June Penny came for a visit. From here she would go on to Ladakh for a festival at Hemis Monastery in Leh. Manali was considerably off her course, and the only reason she came was to see me.

By the time she arrived, loaded down with expensive photography equipment, I had long since settled in at the new cabin and was thoroughly absorbed in my monastic routine. I had not talked to anyone in weeks. Penny was consumed by her academic work and could talk about little else. She had been selected to sit on a panel at a big conference in Paris, and she was thrilled. I could not share her excitement, and although I made a real effort to hide my feelings, my reservations were difficult to conceal. We did all right the first night, but things boiled over the next day.

It was a gorgeous summer afternoon, and we were drinking Nescafé on the porch. We sat facing each other, our backs resting against two posts that supported the stone roof. Penny was telling me the details of a book she was reading, something by the art historian chairing her panel. I had been listening for quite a while without saying a word, but at last I could no longer restrain myself.

"All of this struggle to climb the ladder of academic success seems pointless," I finally blurted out.

"What do you mean, Stanley?"

"I guess I just don't see what it has to do with Buddhism. That's all."

She looked at me like I had just stepped off a flying saucer. "You mean, you don't see what the book—or is it the panel?—has to do with *practicing* Buddhism? That's what you mean, right?"

I didn't respond.

"Studying Buddhism isn't the same as practicing Buddhism. Is that what you're saying? Because if that's all you're saying, then okay, fine. I think we know that already."

"I just mean, well . . ." I considered, choosing my words carefully. "Why do you care so much about what these people think?"

"People?"

"Like this guy in Paris."

"This *guy* in Paris happens to have been a student of Henri Focillon. Do you even know who Henri Focillon is? He . . . "

I shrugged my shoulders and took a sip of coffee.

She stopped talking in mid sentence and put down her cup. Her eyes narrowed. "Oh, I get it. Now I understand. It's the whole *evil ego* thing? Right? Isn't that it?" She didn't wait for my response. "Like the academic world has a monopoly on big egos."

"I didn't say that."

"You didn't say it, but that's what you're thinking. I know exactly what you're thinking. Just because you hate your advisor . . ."

"I don't hate him. He's an arrogant jerk, that's all. People like Abe Sellars don't care about India or Buddhism or anything, really. The texts—or whatever it is they're studying—inscriptions, rituals—it's all just some kind of proving ground, a way of jockeying for position in the big race to the top. All they care about is their own reputation as some kind of murderous intellectual."

"Okay, so maybe he is a jerk, but that doesn't make everyone in the entire academic world a jerk. And it sure doesn't mean that there aren't a whole lot of insanely egotistical people outside the university. That's for sure. Because there are."

"It just seems sort of, you know, all about ambition, this need to be recognized as somebody important, somebody with power. It's like this huge competition for status."

"And of course you don't care about *status*." There was an unfamiliar, and distinctly unpleasant, edge to her voice. She stared across at me. Her legs were stretched out straight between us, the tin cup of coffee resting on one knee, wrapped in the web of her fingers. "I suppose you intend to live here in this little cabin, all alone, for the rest of your life? Reading your Sanskrit books and meditating. Like your hero—that old man what's-his-name."

"Kalidas," I mumbled.

"Kalidas. Right. *Giving up on the whole project of being somebody.* Is that it? Is that your plan?"

"I don't know. Maybe."

"Stanley the hermit. Stanley who doesn't need anybody or anything— least of all status. Gazing down from his mountaintop retreat on the rest of us with our sorry lives, like some Olympian deity."

"Look, I'm sorry. What do I know? *I'm* the arrogant jerk."

"What you are is hurtful. You *hurt* people." Her eyes were clear and wide and glistening with tears. She set the cup to one side and looked away. "You don't think about what you're saying. And you don't even care about anybody's feelings."

"I'm sorry. I really am."

No response. She sat quietly, looking out over the valley.

"It just bothers me, that's all," I said, aware now that I was pushing it, but I couldn't make myself stop. "I don't know why. People have this terrible need for recognition."

At this she brought her eyes quickly around and cut me off. "Well it bothers me that you seem so judgmental. Like *you* don't have a huge ego that tramples over *everything*."

"I just said I'm an arrogant jerk, didn't I?"

"Mmhmm." Her lips were pressed tightly together.

"But that's not . . ." I reconsidered.

"What? What were you going to say?"

"I was going to say, that's not the point."

"That's not the point." She folded her arms. "If that's not the point, then what exactly *is* the point, Stanley?"

In the few days she stayed with me I found it impossible to make any but the smallest concessions in my rigid schedule of meditation and study. These practices were my refuge. And we did not have sex, which pretty much says it all. Not exactly because I didn't want to have sex, because I did. Sort of. But mostly I did not want to, because it was my very desire for her that was most disturbing to me. It was as if I had been thrust back into my own past, back to the early days when Judith and I were first together. Only now I felt like I could see the whole thing all too clearly, every move in the game, and the game was going nowhere. She had a boyfriend in London; I was staying on in India. As for her feelings, I can only guess. She may actually have been in love with me. The sad truth is that I would not have noticed, and I did not ask.

The day she left we made the long hike down to the bazaar in virtual silence. She bought some bananas and an apple for the journey, and I went with her to the bus station and waited while she got her ticket. From Manali she was headed to Dharamsala—a long trip through mountainous roads. We stood outside drinking chai, talking around the fact that we had made no plans to see each other again. People started to climb aboard the bus.

"I better go," she said.

"Yeah," I said, "you better go."

I wanted to put my arms around her—and I would have, but that was not possible in India in a public place. So we just stood there awkwardly looking into each others' eyes. There was nothing left to say. And then, without a word, she slung her bag over one shoulder, turned, and stepped up into the bus.

She must have sat on the aisle, because I circled the bus several times and could not see her through any of the windows. Still, I waited, and watched, hoping to catch a glimpse of her inside. At last the driver leaned on the horn, the engine kicked over, and the bus lumbered away, moving through the gears. It gained speed, becoming smaller and smaller, finally disappearing into the distance.

I went immediately to the sharab shop and purchased a flask of Old Monk rum. That night the white clown got seriously plastered. He sat on the porch alone and drank the whole bottle and thought long and hard about what a pretentious asshole he was.

Overnight the weather changed; the next morning was windy and cool. Puffy white dragons roamed the sky. The sun made fleeting appearances over the flooded rice paddies, shimmering in a maze of mirrors until another cloud cast its shadow half a mile wide across the valley, where it crawled over orchards and roofs of golden straw. Without a fire, the interior of the cabin was cold. When the sun shone I was comfortable, but when it was cloudy, a chilly breeze sifted down through the pines carrying the smell of snow and ice, and the coffee at my side steamed in its battered porcelain cup. I had a dreadful hangover and an even more dreadful sense of loneliness and self-loathing. I spent the morning on the porch, bundled up in woolen socks and a sweater, writing in my journal.

> My head is pounding and I feel like shit.
>
> Penny is gone.
>
> She was with me for only a few days, cooking, washing dishes, reading, but somehow she managed to make the place more hers than mine. More ours, I should say. Even while she was here I knew I would miss her. Even when I was most impatient,

there was always that familiar, comforting warmth. And today, now, her absence dominates everything.

I don't understand. I was doing fine. Then she walked into my cabin—a serene, self-contained environment, complete in every detail before her arrival—and from that moment nothing was the same. She was everywhere. Hair pins, a brush, the skirt tossed over a nail by the door, a bottle of perfume alongside my books and papers. And now she's gone and I'm lonely and miserable.

How is it that when I say goodbye to Penny it's like I'm saying goodbye to everyone I've ever known?

That turned out to be my last entry. I began to feel conflicted about the whole project, to distrust my desire to remember. I put the journal away and before long forgot all about it.

Two days after Penny left, I discovered several of her broken bangles under some papers on my desk and spent most of one morning tying them onto twigs with lengths of black thread I had purchased to mend my socks. I carefully assembled the twigs into a set of wind chimes and hung them outside my door, where they revolved in the breeze, the tinkling of glass lulling me to sleep at night and greeting me first thing every morning when I awoke.

In July I received an inland letter from Ladakh, nothing more than a few words telling me she would soon return to Delhi, and from there back to England. I didn't hear from her again until sometime after I had moved to Banaras, when I wrote to her with my new address. She wrote once or twice after that, short, noncommittal letters, and I responded each time, narrating my daily routine, reminding her of all the mundane wonders of India, the kind of details that had so delighted both of us in Delhi. After the last of these exchanges, quite a while passed with no word from her, until one day, long after the fact, I realized it was over.

There is an epilogue, of sorts, to the story of Penny and me.

Only a few months ago I was in Manhattan visiting friends, and one afternoon we went to the Strand to browse. Downstairs, in the religion section, I ran across something on Tibetan tangka paintings, published under a grant from the Collège de France—one of those heavy, expensive art books with lavish color plates and a scholarly commentary. I turned idly to the flyleaf in back, and there was a photograph of the author, an attractive middle-aged woman with silver hair and green eyes. Penny's eyes. Such beautiful eyes.

23

IN THE WEEKS that followed, I immersed myself again in meditation and study. There were days when I did virtually nothing but sit motionless on my porch, from dawn into early evening, settling into the rise and fall of the lungs, watching the passing thoughts and sensations. By mid August, the hot season was over, and India was well into the monsoon. It was time to leave the mountains. The cabin had been swept clean and its single cupboard stocked with tins of sugar, powdered milk, and instant coffee in anticipation of my next visit, whenever that might be. I was headed first to Delhi, to pick up my things, then on to Banaras.

I left Manali just before sunrise on a rickety, broken-down bus. The road south was a strip of asphalt winding between a sheer rock wall on one side and, on the other, a gravel shoulder crumbling away into the Beas River hundreds of feet below. I knew from the ride up that even under the best of circumstances the return trip would be a punishing, overnight journey. And this time of year, during the monsoon, circumstances were far from ideal. Only two hours out we had to stop where heavy rains had brought down tons of rubble, blocking the road. Workers labored with shovels and wicker baskets to clear a path through the debris; the loads they carried were so heavy that it took two people to lift them up onto the head of a third. Men and women filed past my window, alternately filling their baskets and emptying them over the edge.

It seemed like we had barely gotten moving when we ground to a stop once again an hour or so north of Mundi. This time the entire road was washed out. A section of asphalt had collapsed into the swirling whitewater of the river, leaving only a rocky footpath clinging to the wall along what had been the inside of the road. It was obviously the end of the line for our bus. Within seconds everyone clamored for the door, and I was swept along with the crowd. The men rushed around to the ladder in back and climbed up to the jumble of cargo piled high in the rack on top of the bus. I had no idea why they were in such a hurry, but as it turned out, we were playing a game—something like musical chairs. The bus waiting for us on the other side would not have room to seat everyone, and since no one had a reserved place, it would be first-come, first-served. Many of us would be left standing, packed into the aisle for the next five hours it took to reach Chandigarh. The point of the game was to locate your baggage and fling it over the edge to family members waiting below, then negotiate your way as quickly as possible over and through the rubble to the other bus. If you were among the first to arrive, so much the worse for the others.

It was quite a spectacle: a spindly legged grandpa tottered along with his cane, as fast as he could manage, with bent, arthritic grandma trailing not far behind. A young woman in salwar kameez clutched her howling infant. Men and women staggered under the weight of bags and boxes, plastic satchels, and burlap gunny sacks stuffed with onions and cabbage. Everyone was scrambling over the rocks, stumbling and falling, pushing and shoving to be among the first on the opposite side.

By the time I figured out what was happening, the whole thing was pretty much over. I ended up making the trip across with a group of stragglers, the truly feeble and infirm. When we got there, the new bus was waiting for us, its engine idling impatiently. Emblazoned just above the windshield in bright red lettering were the words *Super Fast*; before and after these words the artist had painted the Sanskrit symbol for *Om* surrounded by wiggly golden lines, as if each mantra were emitting rays of light. We were the last to board; most of my group had people waiting for them, seats saved. I, however, was stuck standing in the aisle, shoulder to shoulder with the other losers, gripping the metal bar on the back of the nearest seat, my bag on the floor between my feet.

We stopped in Mundi for lunch—potatoes and cauliflower partially submerged in a viscous, shimmering concoction of oil and green chilis, with a side dish of dal and a steady stream of hot tandoori roti, their edges charred and crispy. In the days before Starbucks, I used to rank American diners on the merits of their coffee. In Indian dhabas, dal served the same function. On the quality end of the spectrum you have a thick, richly seasoned pastiche of lentils, garlic, and onions that can be mopped up with warm chapatis or heaped onto a plate of rice. The other extreme is the watery, pale-yellow broth I had for lunch that day in Mundi. It may have been the dal that got my stomach churning. Within minutes after the last bite I left the table in search of relief.

The men's lavatory at the bus station was an open sewer. I sloshed through the door and was nearly knocked over by the acrid stench. A man stood at the opposite wall with his back to me and his dhoti hitched up over one leg, pissing on the floor in front of the broken urinal. Nearby were three stalls, battered wooden doors hanging askew. Inside each was a standard South Asian squatter splattered with shit. One look was enough to propel me posthaste for the hill out back, where I stepped cautiously between piles of fresh and not so fresh human excrement. Behind a scraggly pine I dropped my pants, without a second to spare.

On my way back, I rounded the corner of the building just in time to spot the bus as it began to roll slowly out of the station. I sprinted after it, waving and yelling, enveloped in a dense cloud of diesel exhaust. Fortunately, someone noticed me back there and called out for the driver to stop. An affable, burly Sikh, he laughed out loud as I flung myself through the door and up into the crowded aisle.

An hour or two later we pulled over for a routine stop at Sundernagar, a cluster of dilapidated tea stalls huddled together near a bend in the road. Until then the bus had been traveling along one side of a deep gorge engulfed by steep, forested mountains. At Sundernagar, on the southernmost rim of the Himalayas, the valley abruptly opened up to a breathtaking view down and out over an endless expanse of verdant plains.

Grateful for this respite, I dragged myself out of the bus and over to a wooden bench, where I found a spot among several local patrons. My legs and feet throbbed. I ordered a chai, milk and sugar mingled with a hint of cardamom and the gritty taste of red earth. Behind me the high peaks rose into the late afternoon sky; in front, to the south, the hills tumbled down into the flat Punjabi haze. From far away the odor of jasmine drifted up. The air in Sundernagar was hot and humid, and for the first time in months, I was drenched in sweat. But it felt good; it felt like I was returning home. This was India in the monsoon, India at its most *Indian*. It was like being born, all over again, into an exotic, magical place that was, now, deeply familiar.

I was reflecting on such things, sipping my chai, when I looked over and noticed, for the first time, that the driver was sitting beside me. His gray beard was tightly braided, drawn upward and tucked into the turban; his eyes shone darkly under luxuriant brows. He was unwrapping a tiny parcel, carefully folding back the paper along worn creases. He saw me looking at him and smiled.

"*Charas.*" He nodded toward the sticky black ball that now rested in one palm, broke off a small piece and offered it to me. *"Zaraa khaa-lijiyay, sahab.* Have a bite!"

I hadn't smoked dope for over a year, much less eaten hash. Of course I'd done plenty back in Chicago—grass and hash was the least of it. Friday nights Judith and I usually got roasted with a group of friends and went dancing at one of the clubs uptown. There was a period, in our prime, when her idea of a good time was a fifth of Southern Comfort and several hundred mic's of blotter acid. But all this was ancient history. Although ganja was a staple of the Indian scene, since arriving here I had completely lost interest in getting high. On this particular late afternoon, though, something felt different. Maybe it was the driver's congeniality, or—more likely—the lingering effects of Penny's visit. Since her departure, a month earlier, I had been totally isolated, doing nothing but reading Sanskrit and sitting meditation. I missed her. A lot. In particular, I missed the wild sense of possibility that I had felt with her, the sense that anything could happen and that whatever happened would be an adventure. I had grown accustomed to thinking of Penny as more cautious than me, more bound to convention, but the ironic truth was that in her absence, my life had become rigid and closed. And now I was returning to the plains, a place that, in many ways, she had helped me to love. What's more, I *wanted* to return— not simply to the plains, but to the world. I reminded myself of what I took to be the core teaching of Vajrayana Buddhism: salvation flows not from avoiding what we fear as impure but from embracing it as our own. So when the driver offered me a piece of his oily hashish, I took it from him, placed it on my tongue, and washed it down with a swallow of chai.

This is the
body of Christ.
Amen.
This is the
blood of Christ.
Amen.
Gatay
Gatay
Para gatay
Para sangatay
Bodhi
Sva
Haaa!

It was dusk when we reached Chandigarh, and I desperately wanted to get out to find something to eat. The charas was kicking in pretty heavily, though, and I wasn't sure if I could navigate the crowd and find my way back to the bus. It had occurred to me sometime after we left Sundernagar that the driver's so-called hash was black and oily because it wasn't hash at all; it was opium—or maybe a mixture of hash and opium. One way or another, I was extremely high and apparently getting higher by the moment. Everyone in the station was floating several inches above ground, like a school of fish, only it was all happening in slow motion, as if the fish were swimming in honey. I leapt, very carefully, off the last step of the bus and joined them, propelling myself in the direction of a centrally located refreshment stand.

There I managed to order two samosas and a Limca. While the man behind the counter watched me with curiosity, I painstakingly sorted through a twisted knot of paper money. I selected a five-rupee note and handed it to him, my arm telescoping oddly out of a luminous void into the space between us. At what appeared to be a very great distance, the bill dangled from my fingers, then set itself free and sank, languidly settling at last on the marble surface of the counter. I laughed self-consciously, then immediately regretted it.

A number of passengers had disembarked in Chandigarh, and when I got back to the bus, I found an empty seat directly behind the driver. This was a stroke of exceedingly good fortune. Here I could hide out in relative comfort, eat my dinner, and watch the activity outside through the open window next to me without fear of being left behind again. We wouldn't be in Delhi until sometime early the next morning, so all I had to do now was settle in for the ride. As I bit through the warm crust of the samosa, sinking my teeth into a spicy mixture of potatoes and peas and onions, I was feeling pretty good about the situation.

It was dark by the time we pulled out on the final leg of our journey, through the Punjab and Haryana, where the monsoon earth was wet and the one-lane blacktop rolled straight out to the horizon between hulking, bulbous trunks of palms. The curves were gone now, and so were we, gone full throttle, as if pursued by some unseen diabolical force. The bus sped forward into the darkness, a mountain of battered steel hurtling blindly past villagers on foot and bicycle, veering around cows and ox carts, between goats and children, chickens and sleeping dogs. In the black emptiness of night the demonic shriek of the horn substituted for eyes. The shapes ahead were winged spirits flying in and out of the darkness as we tore past. I slumped forward over my bag, drifting between waking and sleep, my knees pressed against the short barrier that separated me from the driver.

God knows how long we had been traveling—several hours, maybe— when without the slightest warning, the bus skidded to a stop and I was thrown violently forward, my face slamming hard against a metal bar. People in the aisle were catapulted to the floor. A woman screamed, and I felt my heart knocking against my ribs like a jackhammer. From some remote corner of my brain adrenaline sirens wailed, and I struggled to pull the world into focus. A baby bawled loudly two or three rows behind me. I saw a dark wet spot on my bag, touched my lip, and brought my finger away smeared with blood.

Just outside my open window, a large crowd had gathered under a fluorescent streetlight that cast a pallid glow over their faces. I could see the shadow of something lying crumpled in the dirt. A man stooped over and picked it up, and I watched as he cradled a small, limp body. One whole side of the child's face had been crushed, the flesh was badly torn, and a dark spatter of blood covered his head and chest; he appeared to be either unconscious or dead. The man was staring down at the boy, his jaw slack, mouth hanging open. All around him women wailed and clutched at their saris. The sounds they made were appalling; I have never heard anything, before or since, so rawly human, so saturated in despair. Their cries rose up from a dark world buried deep beneath the earth.

I barely had time to take all of this in before I realized we were once again creeping forward, forcing our way through the crowd, horn screeching mercilessly. I heard a loud thud, then another as the bus door strained and buckled under the weight of men throwing their bodies against it, trying to force their way inside. People were yelling and banging on the metal sides of the bus with their bare hands. One man had a long stick that he swung crazily through the air. He brought it down hard against one of the headlights, and the glass exploded into darkness. Several others perched on the front bumper, obscuring the driver's vision. They were clinging at the windshield wipers. I could make out human faces contorted in fury and indignation, some of them pressed against the glass, demented, frightful masks ripped from the medieval Flemish countryside of Pieter

Bruegel and transferred here, through some cruel majesty, to rural northern India. A man hung from the rearview mirror by one hand, running alongside the bus, legs pumping wildly. His other hand was clenched in a fist that slammed repeatedly against the driver's window with such ferocity it was a miracle the glass did not shatter. All the while the bus was picking up speed. One by one the men relinquished their grip and leapt or tumbled to the side, rolling head over heels in the dirt. Within seconds we gained the open road, and it was over. The tires hummed; wind rushed past the open window next to where I sat gripping my bag.

The whole ghastly episode could not have lasted more than a few minutes, from beginning to end. One or two of the passengers shouted halfheartedly at the driver, who leaned forward now, gripping the big wheel before him as if he had the power to wrench it free, intent on putting distance between himself and the nightmare behind. No one seemed to know what to do or say, and as the road whipped by we retreated into a stunned, delirious silence. I remained frozen, waiting for someone to act. But we plunged into the darkness, and at some point I realized it was not going to happen. The bus would not stop. We would not go back. We would continue on, together, just as we were.

I retreated into a frightful, trance-like stupor, staring fixedly at the back of the driver's head, my lip throbbing. This man had most likely labored all his adult life behind the wheel of some vehicle or another. And on this particular night, of all those many years of nights, he had struck and very likely killed a child. His bulky shoulders were hunched, locks of gray hair curled from under the folds of his turban. The threadbare collar of his shirt was grimy and soaked in perspiration. These and other details of his appearance now held my attention with unearthly urgency, as if placed under a high-powered microscope. Our driver had suddenly become other than human, a demon or a fierce deity of some kind—Lord Shiva himself, perhaps—but no longer one of us.

24

SOMETIME AFTER THE ACCIDENT I fell into a deep, dreamless sleep and awoke just before dawn, as the bus was sputtering into the Inter State Bus Terminal in Old Delhi. The driver was up and gone almost before the engine died, vanishing into the crowded station. The rest of us stumbled bleakly out the door. I was still drifting in a weirdly detached state from having partaken in the driver's stash almost fifteen hours earlier. I briefly considered trying to report what had happened, but I hadn't the first clue where to go, and I was worried what would happen if I—a foreigner—spoke up. From everything I'd heard about the Delhi police, I wanted nothing to do with them. It seemed best just to get the hell out of there. I had no trouble finding a motor rickshaw to take me to the Fulbright office and my things.

The chaukidar at the gate let me pass with a nod. It felt strange to be back in that unbelievably quiet and clean office, surrounded by expensive furniture and carpets—especially given what I'd just been through. The lobby was deserted at this hour, the air conditioning turned up so high the place felt like a meat locker. I went immediately to the bathroom and took a look at myself in the mirror. It was not a pretty sight. My clothes were rumpled and filthy, my hair an oily mess. I hadn't had a proper bath in months, and I'm sure I was casting forth a righteous odor. But there was nothing to be done for it. I washed up as best I could, rearranged my hair, and stepped out to find Mahmud waiting for me with a glass of chilled water. He greeted me as if my sudden appearance after three months, looking like I'd just escaped from a train wreck, was nothing odd. The expression on his face revealed nothing. I would have loved to find a hot shower and a bed, but the train for Banaras would be leaving early that afternoon, and I was determined to be on it. I no longer had a room in Delhi, and despite my utter exhaustion, I didn't want to spend the night in a hotel.

I walked to the nearest chai stand for a quick snack, and when I returned the staff had begun to arrive for work. The next few hours were consumed with organizing my financial affairs and taking care of other mundane business. By lunchtime I was ready to leave. The director, Mr. Singh, was in his office doing paperwork, and I stuck my head in to thank him and say goodbye. He rose from his big chair to shake my hand. I'm sure he washed immediately after. Mahmud summoned a taxi and helped me load the aluminum footlocker crammed with books accumulated in Agra and Delhi. Fifteen minutes later I was in the New Delhi train station, where I purchased a ticket on the Kashi Vishwanath Express and made my way to the platform with plenty of time to spare.

From Delhi to Banaras would be another sixteen hours. I was traveling second class, which meant that I would have a berth of my own where I could finally get some sleep. The train was already there waiting, so I found my bogie, climbed on, and pushed my way down the aisle followed by a porter dragging my luggage. My compartment was full of soldiers; the locker was too big to fit underneath the lower berth, so it had to remain in the middle of the floor, where it was immediately pressed into service as a footrest. There was the usual argument with the coolie about baksheesh, which amused the gathered troops—especially when they saw me capitulate and grudgingly pull another few rupees from my pocket. I had no energy for fighting over money. Fortunately, the top berth was empty; I flung my bag up there and hoisted my body aloft. I used the bag for a pillow, stretching out with my head pressed against the canvas.

The train left on time, crawling out of the station with the whistle blasting, the powerful engine heaving our weight forward. I lay on my back staring up at the curved metal ceiling only a few feet above. For the first time since leaving the bus station I had nothing to occupy my attention, and scenes of the previous night percolated into consciousness. I tried to read, but it was futile. Eventually I lost myself in the clatter of the wheels on the track and collapsed into an agitated sleep. I remember waking once or twice during the night, vaguely aware of the soldiers below me playing cards on my trunk, laughing and smoking bidis. And I recall hearing the cries of vendors when the train stopped at Lucknow. Distorted images of the bus ride passed in and out of my dreams: the man cradling a child's body, women sobbing, a fist pounding relentlessly on the window, the driver's shoulders looming just in front of where I sat huddled over my bag.

Early the next morning I awoke with a start. Someone was shaking my arm. It was a young private, his khaki sack hung over one shoulder, a heavy rifle over the other. "*Pahunch-gaayay!*" He looked at me and grinned, teeth glistening under a pencil thin military moustache. *We have arrived!* As I lowered myself down from the bunk, the whistle blared, brakes sung up and down the train, and the long string of cars rattled and clanked to a stop. From outside I heard the amplified sound of a tabla and the reedy whine of shehnai, a scratchy recording pumped through loudspeakers that dangled over the platform amid a tangle of wires. *Raag Bhairav.* A morning raga. Music of surrender to the power of Lord Shiva. I had entered the sacred precincts of Kashi.

Graveyard of the Cosmos.

Forest of Bliss.

25

I HAD BEEN ANTICIPATING this move ever since my visit the previous winter. Here I would take up my new life in earnest, no longer affiliated in any way with Fulbright or the University of Chicago. Here, at last, I could sever my ties with the past—beginning, I now hoped, with my memories of the past forty-eight hours.

For the first few days I crashed with Richard. He was looking for a housemate, and he offered to share his place, but I wanted to live alone. After making some inquiries, I located a room on the second floor of a building not far from the river.

The east wall of my new room was lined with shuttered windows looking out over the street leading down to Assi Ghat, the oldest entry point to the waters of the Ganges. At that time Assi Ghat was still as it had been for centuries—a bare, earthen bank sloping to the sacred water, its slick clay surface packed solid by the passing of innumerable bare feet. The world I viewed through those windows no longer exists. An ancient silence has been lost.

I shared a latrine and water tap on the ground floor with several other tenants, but the room itself was mine. The landlord had a fresh coat of whitewash applied to the walls, and the first thing I did was get down on my hands and knees to scrub the floor. It had a drain in one corner, so I could simply push the water across the ceramic tiles and out. Once the room was clean, I went to the bazaar near Chowk and purchased a few domestic necessities: a plastic bucket and cup for bathing, a kerosene pump stove, a pot and a few other cooking utensils, a desk, and a single electric bulb housed inside a string cage that could be suspended either over the bed or the desk. I unpacked the trunk of books I had carried from Delhi and arranged them on two sets of stone shelves built into the wall opposite the entrance. Between the bookcases, a set of double doors opened directly out onto a shallow veranda above the street. The room came furnished with a wooden armchair, a chest of drawers, and a threadbare rug. There was also a *chowki*—a raised wooden platform that I used for a bed and meditation area. I placed it lengthwise, with the head against the west wall, so that the room was divided in two; the desk sat at its foot, in front of one of the east-facing windows, where I would have a clear view down to the river while I worked. I covered the planks of the chowki with an old cotton quilt and the shawl I had woven in Manali. The rug found a spot on the floor to one side, nearest the books, and on the other side I unrolled two narrow straw mats that gave the room a vaguely Japanese air that somehow pleased me. After some deliberation, I went out and bought three potted palms for company and placed them near the windows, where they would get plenty of light. While in Manali, I had painted a watercolor of the house where Ramnath and his family lived; it looked a little like one of those paint-by-number kits, but all the same I liked it. I found a cheap wooden frame in the bazaar, installed the picture, and hung it on a narrow strip of wall to the left of the desk. A ceiling fan rotated overhead.

On the day all this was finished I went outside in the hallway and shut the panel doors, then opened them again, stepped in, and looked around, as if I were seeing everything for the first time. And what I saw was a clean, orderly room, an ideal place from which one could venture out into the chaos of Banaras and to which one could, thankfully, return.

My windows, like most windows in Banaras, had no glass—only iron bars to prevent unauthorized entry and shutters that could be closed from the inside to keep out sun and rain. I soon found out, the hard way, just how long and skinny monkey arms are, and how quickly they can be inserted between the bars. In one swift raid I lost several pencils, a new copybook, and a pen I had carried over from the States. All of this was taken while I was actually present in the room, reading. And the windows were not the only place the monkeys posed a threat. They loved to play on the roof where I dried my laundry. A few mornings after moving in, I lost my favorite khadi shirt and very nearly lost a pair of trousers that I had fool-ishly left hanging unattended on the line. Luckily, my neighbor—a young housewife—happened to be watching from her own roof, and she spotted several culprits wandering around up there, checking out the scene. I was sitting at my desk working when I heard her cry out for my attention: "*Sahab! Sahab!*" I looked up from my book and saw her out there, just across from my window, where she had a clear view of the top of my building. "*Bandar loag aa gaayay hai, chat par*!! The monkey people are on the roof!!" I sprang for the door, but before I got out of the room I heard her call again, telling me to take some food—anything at all that could be used to attract their attention. I had gone shopping earlier, and there was a bag of rice, one of lentils, and half a dozen potatoes. I grabbed a couple potatoes and bounded up the stairs.

When I rounded the corner onto the rooftop, there they were, two big males, perched on a stone railing at each of the far corners. The one on my left had my shirt stretched out between all four of his little hands, methodically tearing it into strips with his teeth. Meanwhile, his friend combed through the pockets of my pants. The shirt was already a total loss, so I rolled a potato over toward the ape on my right. He had one greedy paw buried in the front right pocket, but when he saw that spud coast to a stop only a few feet away, he froze, eyed it for a second or two, then chucked the pants and went for the bait. This gave me just enough time to pitch across the intervening space before he realized what was going on. When I dove for the pants he assumed I was charging directly for him with intent to kill. His eyes popped out of his wrinkled pink prune face and the hair on his head bristled with fear. He flew off the roof, his companion in hot pursuit. The last I saw of my shirt was a white flag fluttering in the wind as the little bastards leapt over the rooftops and into the haze of the holy city. I shuffled back downstairs, grateful, at any rate, to have salvaged my pants.

This was my first face-to-face encounter with the monkeys of Banaras, and it set the tone for an ambiguous and often strained relationship that persisted throughout my years in Assi. Just outside the bars, they loped back and forth in their oddly listless fashion or lounged on the ledge, picking lice from each other's fur, not more than three feet in front of where I sat immersed in my work. It wasn't long before I could recognize the regulars by their characteristic features or the quirks of their body language. The males had easily identifiable battle scars, but several of the females and even the youngest of the monklets became familiar too. I came to know them not only by their appearance but also by their personal habits and the regular hours when a particular troupe would pass by each morning or evening. I fed them, talked to them, tried to play with them, and dearly wanted—on more than one occasion when they managed to sneak into my room—to kick their furry asses.

After the quiet, solitary summer months in Manali, Banaras offered endless possibilities for socializing. The city was home to many of India's top classical musicians, and once the music season began in November, there was a constant succession of both public concerts and smaller, private musical programs organized in homes all over the city. Through Richard I gradually came into contact with a number of local musicians and scholars—including Pundit Trivedi, my new Sanskrit teacher—and with a loosely knit community of foreign expatriates, people who had traveled to Banaras from all over the world and for every imaginable reason.

I remember one such person in particular, a young French Canadian woman who called herself Parvati. I had only been in town a few days when our paths crossed for the first time. I parked my black Atlas bicycle outside Arora Medical Stores—a pharmacy in the neighborhood of Lanka, near the imposing entrance to Banaras Hindu University. I had stopped to get a soda from their cooler, one of the only functioning refrigerators on the south side of the city. When Parvati walked in, I was leaning against the counter sipping my Limca, relishing the powerful blast from two ceiling fans that whirled above me like jet propellers. She entered the relative darkness of the store's interior like a goddess descending from some ethereal, heavenly sphere.

The first thing I noticed was her height. Parvati was tall, strikingly so in the context of Banaras, a good four or five inches above the heads of the men who crowded against the counter, pushing, waving their arms, and shouting to attract the attention of clerks who hurried back and forth in front of shelves crammed with all manner of bottles, torn packages, and dusty vials. Combined with her fair complexion and a frenzy of blond dreadlocks that exploded from her head, her height would have been sufficient to attract attention. But Parvati also possessed an astonishing figure, the mythological body of her namesake, Lord Shiva's wife: long, shapely legs, wide hips and breasts that bulged like two ripe mangos below the lungi wrapped under her arms like a beach towel. The thin cloth was dyed saffron—the color of renunciation—symbol of Parvati's status as a female anchorite, and it was, at this moment, fluttering under the fans in a most provocative manner. As she strode toward the counter, everything about her seemed to sway. Could she possibly have been oblivious to the effect she had on the men who fell back to let her pass, swept aside in her wake? Did she care?

I was on the verge of prostrating myself at her lotus feet when the clerk, who was himself having some difficulty accommodating the situation, tried to charge me for whatever it was she got. Before I could move to correct him, Parvati took over and patiently explained, in fluent Hindi, that she was *alone*. She handed him a ten-rupee note, received her change, and turned to leave, never so much as glancing in my direction. I watched dumbly as she stepped across the open sewer in front of the shop and disappeared into the throng of bicycles and rickshaws.

In time I discovered that Parvati was something of a legend. A student at McGill University sometime in the late sixties, she was studying abroad in France when she decided to quit school and take the Magic Bus from Amsterdam to Delhi. Apparently she was an accomplished yogini, known and respected well beyond the neighborhood of Assi. I heard there was an ashram in Rishikesh where she resided during the hot season; pilgrims who came there worshiped her as Mata-ji, a manifestation of the Great Mother. She had taken a vow to drink nothing but water from the sacred Ganges and to consume only the gifts of the sacred cow.

Now and again, over the months that followed, I spotted her in one or another of the city's myriad sweet shops, poised over the cloudy glass of a counter, below which were displayed the endless varieties of milk and sugar that provided a good share of her diet. One evening, while out for a walk near the Ganges, I saw her sitting in full-lotus posture, deep in samadhi. She was practicing the traditional "penance of the five fires": four mounds of dried cow dung burned close to her body, one at each of the cardinal points, the fifth in a clay pot balanced on her head. I saw her there again the next morning surrounded by a small crowd of interested spectators. She had remained as she was, unmoving and silent, through the night.

I never spoke to Parvati. She left in the spring for Rishikesh, and after that I never even saw her again. But plenty of other eccentrics remained behind. Banaras was a three-ring circus of spiritual seekers and lost souls, musicians, crooks and saints, dope heads and scholars, down-and-out drifters and trust-fund hippies—all of us running away from one dream and toward another.

Mickey—my old friend from Agra—arrived in late September. He had written to me in Manali announcing his intention to move to Banaras in order to pursue his training as a classical vocalist. His teacher in Agra had recommended him to a famous singer from a family here in town, somewhere in the neighborhood of Kabir Chaura. In addition to singing, he immediately fell in with a group of wrestlers who belonged to an akhara near Assi Ghat, devotees of the monkey god Hanuman. Most mornings you could find him working out in a large open-air pit of sand, swinging heavy maces called *jori* to the sound of rhythmic chanting: *Jai Bhajrangbali!* He took to drinking several liters of milk a day and swimming over and back across the Ganges, dodging bloated animal carcasses and the occasional human corpse, all in an effort to maintain his impressive physique.

Despite my occasional forays into the city's social scene and my association with Richard, Mick was my only real friend—though I can't say I really knew him. He was above all an enigma, a deeply private person. He did not associate with any other foreigners, so far as I knew, and the local Banarsi greasers he called friends were not the sort of people who placed a premium on sharing the details of their emotional life: deadbeats, lechers, thieves, pimps, small-time thugs, the sort of people whose character is perfectly captured in the Hindi word *goonda*. One of them was rumored to have been involved in a local political scandal that ended in murder. I could not understand the attraction these people held for Mick, and I did not have much patience for the demands they placed on our friendship. It was virtually impossible to go to a public place with him and not be accosted. We might be sitting together at the Sindhi restaurant in Belapur or drinking chai at Ravi's, deep into debate over some point of Buddhist doctrine—an interest he had maintained since the days he was a monk in Thailand—when a gaggle of these creeps would suddenly appear, arm in arm, and slouch down beside us. They always traveled in groups, and they all dressed the same: skin-tight polyester, hair slicked back, red betelnut dribbling from the corner of a self-satisfied smirk. I don't recall Mick ever turning them away.

"What on earth," I once asked him, "do you find to talk about with such obvious losers?"

He looked at me with his usual uncomprehending expression, the one he saved for such occasions—just the hint of a frown, eyebrows ever so slightly arched—as though I ought to know better than to pose such a silly question. After a moment or two, he answered with an air of mild unconcern: "Oh, you know, stupid things . . . nothing, really."

It's his life, I told myself. None of my business. And I suppose the truth is that I enjoyed Mick's company in part precisely because he moved so fluidly along the seedy margins of Banaras society. I knew very little about his life before India, but he had told me a few stories about the rough neighborhood in South Boston where he grew up. There was a stint in reform school, where he had been sent as a juvenile offender. He had been involved in a robbery where the clerk was badly beaten. He mentioned this only once in passing and never brought it up again.

In any case, my own life kept me fully occupied. There was my new Sanskrit teacher, Pundit Trivedi, with whom I met every day. And I managed to finagle a visa by gaining admission into a Tibetan language program across town at Sampurnanand Sanskrit Vishwavidyalaya. Sanskrit University, as it is often called, is a small college founded in 1791 by British officials committed to the preservation of India's classical literature. The Tibetan program was something new—an effort to work with Tibetan scholars now living in exile to retranslate Indian Buddhist texts from Tibetan back into their original Sanskrit. It was a perfect arrangement for me: without Fulbright, I needed the visa, and since Manali I had grown increasingly interested in the living tradition of Tibetan Buddhism.

In other respects, though, things were not going so smoothly.

The social and cultural scene was more than a bit distracting, but that was only the beginning of my problems. I was consumed by ideas of what I *should* be doing, and such ideas often conflicted with the realities of living in a busy Indian city. On any given day I was likely to be detained indefinitely by some mindless bureaucrat at the bank or the Foreigners Registration Office, where I spent a good deal of time working out the provisions of my visa. As I had learned in Agra, a seat behind a desk means, first and foremost, the power to make people wait. And I spent a lot of time doing just that: waiting.

One way or another, it seemed, half the time I spent outside the blissfully sequestered precincts of my room was flat-out wasted, and on such occasions, the bug up my ass would *sting, sting, sting*. I had a difficult time adhering to the advice I had found so attractive in that verse from the *Bodhicharyavatara*, the one I had memorized back in Delhi:

Whatever happens—
whether through your own resolve or the will of another—
circumstances conceal a deeper import.
See this, and learn.

Despite everything, I did my best to structure my life in Banaras like a retreat. Immediately after waking I ran through my early-morning exercise routine, then bathed downstairs, came back up, and sat meditation. After sitting I made coffee, had some yogurt and bananas, and read Sanskrit or Tibetan until lunch, which was usually at the Sindhi. In the afternoon I met with my teachers. I returned home in early evening, rinsed off at the tap, read more, had a snack in my room, sat meditation again for several hours, and went to bed. Every day followed the same schedule, and every day began before dawn with the furious clanging of a cheap Indian wind-up alarm clock I had purchased way back in Agra. It ticked so loudly I hadn't been able to sleep at night until I grew accustomed to the sound.

In Manali I had met a Canadian from Vancouver, a student of Apo Rinpoche, who told me he went into a six-month solitary retreat with one of these same clocks. He allowed himself only a short period of sleep, the remaining twenty or so hours of each day scheduled tightly with meditation, rituals, and prayers. The clock was essential to maintaining his schedule, but within the first week it began acting up, the alarm going off unpredictably, depriving him of precious sleep and interrupting his strict routine. For six months he worked with the situation, tinkering with the controls, propping the clock in odd positions, or muffling it while he slept, in the hope that it would be less of a jolt when the bell went off. Nothing availed, though, and for the entire six months, he lived at the mercy of those erratic wheels and levers. The day his retreat ended, he calmly placed the infernal device on the ground outside his cabin and pulverized it with blows from a large rock he had carefully selected weeks before and stored in plain view under the altar, just below an image of the Buddha, in anticipation of this great event—the culmination of six months of intense spiritual practice. He assured me that full and complete awakening could provide no greater satisfaction than he felt the moment the clock shattered under his hands.

I too would gladly have destroyed anything that interrupted the strict regimen of my days—the pattern of my expectations and desires—if only I could have found a mighty enough rock.

26

I was haunted by memories of the bus and by an irrational conviction that I was somehow implicated in the child's death. It wasn't as if I could have forced the driver to slow down, and once the accident happened, I certainly could not have stopped him from fleeing the scene. Nor was I naïve: I knew what would have happened had the crowd outside managed to get at him. I recalled an article in the *Times of India* that I had read way back in Agra, about another bus that had struck and killed a child; the driver had his hands chopped off by angry villagers. Since then I had heard many such tales of retributive mayhem. The point is, I knew there was nothing I could have done to change what happened that night in the Punjab. So why did I feel somehow responsible?

We bind our hearts to this big drama, and for that we must suffer.

No doubt my old guru's words were true, but it's one thing to suffer out of compassion for others and quite another to feel culpable. Why should an innocent bystander feel guilty? The question was very much on my mind when, one morning just before waking—less than a month after moving to Banaras—I dreamed I was back on the Super Fast.

In my dream it was nighttime, and I could see myself there in the bus sitting just as I had been, behind the driver, bent forward over my bag. It was as if I were looking over my own shoulder—an oddly disembodied point of view that I take for granted in my dreams, though in waking life I've often wondered at this capacity of the mind to somehow climb outside of itself and simply watch as it creates a world out of nothing but memory and imagination. It wasn't until I'd been meditating for years that it occurred to me I was consciously cultivating a perspective already familiar from my dreams. In any case, the angle in my dream abruptly shifted, and the detached observer suddenly found itself firmly lodged in my dream body and staring at the back of the bus driver's head. From this new vantage point I could now see over the driver's shoulder to where his face, caught in the glow of a small illuminated portrait of Guru Nanak, was reflected in the windshield. The image of his face floated there on the dark surface of the glass like a spirit trapped in the bardo realm between death and rebirth.

At first I couldn't take my eyes off it, but I soon discovered that by simply refocusing my gaze, I could look right through the reflection, out to where the glare of the bus's twin high beams vanished into darkness. I experimented shifting the focus back and forth, looking directly at the reflected image and then through it—a game that once again I found absorbing—until something outside caught my attention: far off in the distance a single point of light emerged out of the void. It was as though the bus had been a rocket drifting alone through deepest space, but now, with this solitary star as a point of reference, I was suddenly aware that we were hurtling directly toward it at a fantastic velocity. Very soon, where the star had been I could make out the fluorescent glow of a streetlight, and then, under the light, a chai stand with people sitting on benches in front and a few children playing nearby. It seemed like the closer we got, the faster the bus moved, as if it were being sucked forward by a powerful gravitational force, until at the last possible instant a boy stepped out of the darkness and the bus plunged into the light and the horn shrieked and I was thrown violently forward.

I lay on my back, engulfed in silence, still half asleep and lost in the feeling of the dream. Over my head the fan revolved slowly, churning the sultry air. My first thought was, *That's not the way it happened. On the real bus I wasn't awake. I didn't see the boy until it was over.* But how could I know if I was awake or asleep on that bus? How could I know anything for sure when I was stoned out of my mind on opium? And then it occurred to me: maybe the whole thing had been nothing but an extremely realistic dream.

It was an extraordinary thought. The very idea that the accident might not have actually happened seemed, at first, beyond comprehension. And yet, on the bus that night after leaving Chandigarh, I had been totally blasted, sliding in and out of consciousness—and opium is notorious for producing hallucinatory dreams. But even ripped on opium, is it possible, I wondered, to conflate waking and dreaming experience so completely? I'd no sooner asked myself the question than I remembered a woman I'd known in Chicago who told me that when she was applying to graduate schools, she once dreamed that she got a scholarship to Harvard. The dream had been so vivid that she actually believed it was true. It wasn't until she was on the phone telling her father, and he asked about the details, that she realized her mistake. She'd been wandering around literally for days feeling this huge sense of relief that had nothing whatsoever to do with waking reality.

At the time, I'd found her story far-fetched, but now I could empathize—for the past month I had been feeling guilty about the death of a boy who may never have existed. Perhaps the most disturbing thing was that I probably could never know for certain whether I dreamed it or not. I tried to imagine what it would take to get at the truth. Maybe somehow I could go back and make inquiries at the station, or with the police—surely they must keep a record of such things. But then again, maybe not. The accident may well have gone entirely unreported. All sorts of horrible stuff happens in India that never makes it into any official police record. To find out if the accident really happened, I'd have to go back to the Punjab and visit every chai stand between Chandigarh and Delhi.

The feelings were real enough, even if the event wasn't. So how could real feelings be generated by an unreal event? But of course it wasn't the event itself that generated my feelings; it was the *memory* of the accident—or the memory of a dream—which obviously had a power of its own. In fact, it's amazing how powerful memory is, how everything about our present experience is interpreted through its lens—even sense perception is based on recognition. But if I were only remembering a dream, then the sense of culpability I'd been carrying around was *doubly* groundless. I lay there for several minutes pondering all of this, growing more and more disoriented, then finally gave up and threw back the sheet, forcing myself out of bed.

It was late September and the monsoon was winding down, but even at this early hour the air was uncomfortably hot and humid. When I finished my morning calisthenics, I was soaked in sweat. I took my towel from where it hung, picked up the bucket and the clay jar I used for drinking water, and stepped out into the hallway, heading downstairs to rinse off at the tap. I remember pulling the doors closed after me and fastening the chain in case a monkey happened to come down the stairs from the roof. Just as I turned from the door I smelled a faint, repellent odor. Following the scent I walked down the stairs and around the corner to the crawl space where I and the other tenants went for water. There, directly under the tap, a dog had collapsed on the cool, wet stone. The outside door to the alley was open—someone had obviously forgotten to latch it—and the dog had come in looking for a safe place to rest.

Her hairless gray skin was corrugated with oozing sores; the nipples hung slackly from her chest like tiny withered fruits. She was so still that at first I thought she wasn't breathing. On closer inspection I could just make out the feeble movement of her ribs, a tenuous rise and fall of shallow respiration. Instinctively, I clapped my hands. She did not respond. Again I clapped and shouted in Hindi: "*Hut!*" I stamped my bare foot on the floor a few inches away from her muzzle. *Move it!* Still she did not stir, so I gently shook her with my toes. This time the ragged ears flopped back, and her head rose, ever so slowly. As though she were pushing upward against an overwhelming force, she struggled to lift her brittle, stinking body and drag it out into the hallway. Her spine had been severely twisted and both hind legs appeared to be paralyzed. I had seen dogs like this sprawled in the street, half alive, still lying where they had been caught under the iron wheels of a passing horse-drawn cart. After a few steps it appeared she could go no further, and when she started to lie down, once again I nudged her with the ball of my foot. I distinctly remember that it felt different this time, I was suddenly hyperaware of the sensation caused by her matted fur brushing against my bare skin. She stumbled, regained her balance, and continued to pull her useless, crippled back legs slowly toward the open door.

As I watched her struggle, I was overwhelmed with disgust at what I was doing—driving her out in this way. And then, as if in response to my feeling, I heard a voice say, *This dog cannot remain in this place where I bathe and clean my dishes and take my drinking water.* I realized then that ever since the first moment I had seen the dog, this same sentence had been repeating in my mind like a military command, with all the authority of reason. But now I was not just thinking this thought, I was aware that I was thinking, which was a whole different experience. And not only this thought, but everything else as well was now intensely clear and present—the smell of rotting flesh and dank air, the sound of claws scratching against stone, and a swirl of conflicting emotions that fell over man and dog like a shadow across the floor as early-morning sunlight broke through the open doorway and the dog emerged, working to catch her breath, her front legs folding, her chest dropping to the pavement.

I stood staring down at the animal, then turned quickly and walked back through the door, latching it behind me. I went to the tap, rinsed and dried myself, filled the clay jug with water and walked up the stairs.

Back inside the room I changed out of my wet shorts and put on a light lungi, then went over to the bed and positioned myself on its hard surface, crossing my legs one over the other in a half-lotus posture. I sat without moving, hands folded in my lap, eyes closed, following the sensation of the air as it passed in and out of the nostrils. With my attention focused, I began watching the memories of what I had only moments earlier seen and done and felt—the abject fear in the dog's eyes, the texture of her fur against my skin, the stink of her wounds, the scratching of her nails on stone, my thoughts and reasons and justifications, the horrible mixture of compassion and guilt that swelled up in my heart as I drove her out the door. As I sat quietly watching, these and other, more distant memories took shape and faded away again, along with an endless stream of thoughts and feelings and sensations, all of them perfectly clear and present, held in the mind's eye like shimmering reflections on the glassy surface of consciousness.

But with the subtlest, involuntary lapse of attention, the glass would become a lens, awareness passing through the translucent images like light through film, filling the darkness with the captivating spectacle of a world where the play must go on no matter the cost. At such times I felt myself falling into the picture, and I needed to begin all over again, patiently adjusting the focus, bringing attention back to the present moment, to the sensation of breathing, to the memory itself as an object that arises and passes away.

I opened my eyes, very slowly, and looked around the room, taking in my books, the desk and chair, the aluminum footlocker, the jug filled with water. According to the clock I had been sitting for almost three hours. As I unwound my legs I felt the muscles tingle and burn, felt myself rise and stretch and walk over to the stove, where I put on water for coffee.

It was midafternoon before I summoned the courage to leave my room. When at last I walked down the stairs and opened the outside door, I found the dog lying exactly where she had fallen. The crows had already eaten her eyes. Her body lay there, stiff and covered with flies, all that afternoon and through the next night, before a sweeper finally came and dragged it down to the river.

27

I FIRST HEARD ABOUT Pundit Trivedi through an earnest young student from Kyoto who was then studying at Banaras Hindu University. Pundit Trivedi was well known around the university as an erudite and highly orthodox scholar who had a particular expertise in the literature of the Sankhya—India's most ancient systematic philosophy. I was told that he had accepted some foreign students in the past; the last of these had been a number of years ago, but at this point in life he was no longer willing to teach anyone. Nevertheless, I decided to try.

Pundit Trivedi's home was located in the maze of narrow alleyways behind Tulsi Ghat. Twice I knocked at his door, and both times I was turned away by a servant, apparently on the direct order of the pundit's wife. On the third visit I encountered an elderly man sitting on a chowki on the front porch reading the local Banaras newspaper. He was wearing a white dhoti wrapped around and through his legs, the sacred thread of his brahman heritage looped diagonally over his shoulder and down across the bare, wrinkled skin of his chest. His face was pressed between two pendulous, wing-like ears, and he had a truly imposing raptorial nose on which rested a pair of reading glasses. I was immediately reminded of the magnificent and yet somehow comical Garuda, the mythological bird associated with the great god Vishnu.

I introduced myself in Hindi and inquired if I might speak with Pundit Trivedi. I was told to go ahead and say whatever I had to say. I briefly described my interests and my previous experience and said that I was searching for a suitable teacher to help me deepen my facility with Sanskrit. The old man listened in silence until I was finished, at which point he folded the newspaper and quietly set it to one side. I thought for a moment that he was about to rise, perhaps to go inside. Instead he began questioning me in some detail about my training at Chicago. He wanted to know exactly what I had read, both the root texts and the commentaries. But it was only when I mentioned my evenings with Shri Anantacharya that he warmed to my request. He proposed a trial period of two weeks, during which time he would reserve the right to terminate our associa- tion, no questions asked. I accepted these terms immediately. But when I offered to pay him for his time, the reply was curt and evidently non- negotiable: "My home is not a shop."

We met the very next day, late in the morning, and every day after that. Two weeks passed in this way, then four, and I gradually began to appreciate just how fortunate I was to have found my way into the world of this kind, learned man and to have him as my teacher during the final years of his long life.

Pundit Ravendranath Trivedi was the last surviving Sanskrit scholar in an unbroken line of brahman intellectuals that stretched back hundreds, if not thousands, of years, perhaps as far back as Vedic times, when, he assured me with great solemnity, his ancestors had presided over the elab- orate rituals that brought human society into harmony with the implicit order of the cosmos. Pundit-ji occasionally told me stories about his father, a landed aristocrat and well-known scholar among the Banaras intelligentsia during the days of the British Raj. It was here in the very courtyard where we met for my lessons that his father had conversed with the wise and holy men of Banaras. It was here, as well, that his father had announced his intention to become a sannyasi, as had his own father before him, after seeing the first faint streaks of silver hair over his son's temple. Astrologers were called to determine an auspicious date for the symbolic funeral, the first essential step toward renunciation. The service was performed, and from that day on he was, ritually speaking, dead to the world, released from the all-encompassing web of obligations that Hindu society imposes on every householder. These domestic responsibilities now fell to his son, my teacher.

Years before his father left home, Pundit Trivedi had been groomed for his role as patriarch. His marriage had been arranged with a woman born in the family's ancestral village in eastern Bihar, and within a few years of their wedding, she gave birth to a son and two daughters. In deference to the times, all three children were sent to an English-medium school. A modern education was important if the girls were to marry well. For the boy, though, learning English was something of a formality, as it had been for Pundit Trivedi, since as the only son he would of course remain at home to take over for his father, to assume his place in the long succes- sion of brahman scholars who had walked this same path. Pundit Trivedi tutored his boy from an early age, as he himself had been tutored by his father. The two of them sat together in the garden, every morning, reciting declensions and conjugations, reading the folk tales of the *Hitopadesha* and the abstruse verses of the *Laghu Siddhanta Kaumudi*, an introduction to Panini's sublime vision of Sanskrit grammar.

Who could have predicted what would follow? Who would have thought that so much could be lost so quickly? But we live in the Kali Yuga, the fourth, final, and degenerate epoch, a time when even the most ancient, revered traditions are slipping away.

When the girls reached an appropriate age, they were married and sent off to live with their respective families, just as they were expected to do. It became clear, however, that the boy was not interested in pursuing his studies in Sanskrit. Instead he attended a technical college, where he trained to become an electrical engineer. How this decision was made— how such a thing was permitted to happen, with what amount of conflict and heartache—I can hardly imagine. By the time I met Pundit Trivedi, all of this was history. The prodigal son and I were never introduced, and I saw him only once, as I was leaving from a lesson; he was a distinguished man with graying hair.

With his son in New Delhi, Pundit Trivedi did not renounce the world to take up the life of a sannyasi. Had he gone away, who would have watched over Mata-ji and the complex domestic affairs? It may be that he too had fallen under the spell of the decadent Kali Yuga, for in 1945 he did something else altogether without precedent: he accepted a non-brahman as his student—an Englishman, a magistrate at the high court of Banaras—and began tutoring him in Sanskrit in the same quiet garden where he had passed so many hours with his young son. Since that time he had taught only a handful of Westerners, all of whom were attracted to Banaras because of its reputation as a center of traditional learning.

His most recent student before me had been a prominent German philologist who studied in Banaras during the sixties. The professor had arranged for Pundit Trivedi to receive a post at Humboldt University as a lecturer in Sanskrit. For Pundit-ji to accept this offer would have entailed the final break with his orthodox roots. Of the many difficulties involved, perhaps the greatest was that traveling to Germany would open the unimaginable possibility of death outside the precincts of Shiva's city, the triangle of land bordered on the east by the Ganges and on the north and south by the Varana and Assi rivers. *Kashyam maranam muktihi.* So says the *Kashikandika*: "Death in Banaras is liberation." Death in Banaras is death that brings an end to death. And so it was that the invitation to teach in Germany was respectfully declined. Pundit Trivedi elected to remain in the holy city, supervising the family property and discussing politics and philosophy with old friends.

I arrived for our lesson one cool December morning and found my teacher reclining, as usual, on a stone bench in the garden, absorbed in his newspaper. Nearby a cow stood under a canopy of palm leaves, studiously working her way through a mixture of water, oats, and hay. Pundit-ji leaned against a large cylindrical bolster—his "wisdom pillow." "Without my wisdom pillow I could not remember even one shloka!" This was his standard claim, and it was generally accompanied by a solid slap to the white cloth and a sly smile. He was wearing heavy wool socks, a bulky sweater, and an incandescent orange stocking cap pulled tightly down over his head. A pair of wooden sandals rested on the ground at his side, each one with a single peg made to fit between the first and second toes, each peg rubbed to a soft luster from years of service.

As I stepped from the shadows into the sunlight, Pundit Trivedi looked up from his paper. I saluted him by bowing slightly and raising my hands, palms joined.

"Oh ho! The great Buddhist scholar has arrived! Please, come. Sit down, sit down." His eyes glittered and he smiled enthusiastically, directing me over to the bench in characteristic north Indian fashion, his right arm outstretched, palm downward, cupped fingers moving rapidly back and forth as though digging a small, invisible hole in the air. He sat leaning slightly forward, back straight, arms at his sides, the way a musician sits with his sitar—his right knee bent sharply over the fulcrum of the left thigh. I went to him and touched my fingers to his feet and then to my own head, after which I settled into my spot on the bench. For a moment we simply sat there silently beaming at each other as though this were the happiest occasion of our lives, the culmination of all our hopes and plans.

"Mata-ji! *Chai laao!*" Through the backdoor of the house I could see the broad silhouette of his wife as she moved toward the kitchen to prepare tea. "You will have some chai, no?"

"Yes, please. How's the new calf doing?" We both turned to examine a miniature white cow that hovered near its mother, wobbling on four bony stilts. She blinked her long lashes uncomprehendingly, as if this new world had been made just a bit too bright for her taste. The servant, Madhav, rubbed her body vigorously with a large towel, causing her head to bob up and down.

Pundit Trivedi studied the young cow, giving my question serious consideration. "These cold nights are too much for a newborn. She needs to be watched over carefully or we will lose her." He called out instructions to move the calf away from its mother and into the sun. Madhav acknowledged his words with a nod and began to pull the tottering animal out from under the shelter. This resulted in a loud exchange of plaintive cries between mother and daughter, both of whom were clearly uncomfortable with the new arrangements.

When Pundit Trivedi's father became a sannyasi, he left behind much more than the single great stone house. The house and surrounding property marked the center of a modest feudal estate. Madhav's family had served Pundit Trivedi's family for generations, bound to them by loyalty, tradition, and expediency. According to a long-standing agreement, the land where Madhav and his relatives lived was entirely at their disposal in return for services rendered. So far as I know only one of Pundit-ji's several household servants, a deaf mute who slept in a shed with the cows, did not come from Madhav's extended family. I was told that she had been an orphan child begging near Kashi Viswanath temple. One day, for reasons of her own, Mata-ji singled out this particular girl from among all the other wretched beggar children and brought her back to the house. Here she had lived for over twenty years, earning her keep by washing clothes and cleaning up after the cows. I never heard her called anything other than *Goongi-ji*—from the Hindi for "deaf and dumb."

Engaged in her various duties, Goongi-ji skulked around the house and garden in a clumsily wrapped, soiled cotton sari, her hair a tangled nest. She communicated with the rest of us through a frenzied jerking of her arms, hands, and fingers, accompanied by spasmodic facial contortions, grunts, and squeals, which her interlocutor was obliged to imitate by way of response. It was more than a bit disconcerting to see her and Pundit Trivedi squared off in conversation, flailing their arms at each other, faces twisted, eyes bulging crazily. Under the mass of snarled hair *someone* was keenly alert, forever watching and thinking. At the moment she squatted in a corner of the garden making a great fuss over her lunch—dal and chapati that she bolted down with the aid of both hands, smacking and chomping—all the while keeping one eye on Madhav and the rest of us.

204 | C. W. HUNTINGTON, JR.

I opened my book and arranged my notes on the table between us. We were reading the *Buddhacharita*, an elegant narrative poem of the Buddha's life composed in the third century. Ashvagosha, the author, was a master stylist, and I had selected this text hoping that my teacher would appreciate the language in spite of its Buddhist subject matter. I presumptuously imagined that reading a beautifully written Buddhist text might expand his intellectual horizons. He repaid me adequately for my conceit. We hadn't finished the first chapter before he began teasing me by punning, in Hindi, on the Buddha's name, referring to him as Bhagavan Bud*dhu*— Lord Blockhead. This wasn't just about Buddhism, though; regardless of the context, Pundit-ji derived enormous pleasure from puns like this, concocted from an imaginative blending of Sanskrit, Hindi, and English. There was always some danger that our work would be sidetracked at any moment with an obscure linguistic joke or an amusing anecdote only vaguely related to the reading. These interruptions were relatively brief, though, compared to the ever-present possibility of unannounced guests; at such times I had no choice but to sit back and wait, and perhaps to discover, as I did on this particular morning, that there are many ways to learn.

With the calf now basking happily in the warm sun, Pundit-ji appeared suddenly to remember our purpose together. He opened the text that lay before him and leafed through the pages, carefully moving one long index finger down the margins until he located the place where we had left off the previous morning, and began to read. Pundit Trivedi did not speak Sanskrit; the language spoke through him, just as it had spoken through his father and grandfather and all the others. To hear him read aloud was to grasp, in an immediate, visceral way, that I was hearing the ancient language of the Aryas, warriors who inhabited the Indian subcontinent over three thousand years ago with their horses and chariots and their elaborate sacrificial rituals. The very name *Sanskrit* means "polished," "cultured," "refined," and above all else, it is the *sound* of Sanskrit—its most sacred treasure—that has been closely guarded over the centuries with uncompromising devotion. The power of the mantra, the capacity of Sanskrit to heal and transform, is entirely dependent on its correct enunciation. These sounds emerged from the crucible of visions, shaped through poetry and metaphor into words that echo the primordial vibrations of the cosmos. Sanskrit is a bridge between conceptual thinking and the elemental forces of nature, a gateway opening backward out of the mind into the divine realm of fire and earth, thunder, wind, and rain.

Pundit Trivedi taught in the old way, first reciting the sounds himself, then listening closely as I repeated what he said, mimicking, as best I could, his pronunciation. After reading each verse, he analyzed its syntactic structure, split compounds, and deciphered particularly rare or thorny grammatical forms, if necessary rehearsing the appropriate conjugation or declension. Finally, almost as an afterthought, we discussed the meaning of the words. In this fashion the two of us plodded along at the majestic pace of water buffalo, with great deliberation—no more slowly as we labored under the plow, no more quickly as we headed for the river to bathe. Reading Sanskrit with Pandit Trivedi was in essence a ritual act, a sort of linguistic *darshan*, in itself sufficient to insure a more favorable birth next time around.

We were already deep into our reading when Mata-ji arrived with chai; one glass for Pundit-ji and the special "foreigner's cup" for me—a flowered ceramic mug that could be easily identified so as never to accidentally enter the ritually pure kitchen. This business of the foreigner's cup was something that took a bit of getting used to, and during our first week together I committed a crude faux pas that succeeded in embarrassing everyone present. I had reached out to take Pundit Trivedi's glass from Mata-ji to hand it to him. Fortunately, an instant before my fingers made contact with the untainted glass, she deftly pulled it out of reach.

This morning Mata-ji was accompanied by a Hindu gentleman who stood politely to one side while she served us our chai. He was perhaps forty, dressed in carefully pressed slacks and a Western-style shirt, his hair and moustache neatly trimmed. He had the appearance of an office worker or a government bureaucrat. The muscles in his toes flexed uneasily in the dirt as he watched us receive our glasses. I had seen him before, several times in the early evening, performing puja at a small Vishnu temple near the shop where I went for black-market kerosene. Once the chai was served he stepped forward and knelt, palms joined. He brought his fingers to Pundit Trivedi's feet, then raised these same fingers to his head.

"Namaskar, Guru-ji."

Pundit Trivedi accepted these formalities with the easy grace of a man accustomed from childhood to the life of an aristocrat. "Namaskar,

Chotilal." Madhav fetched a dilapidated cane chair, placing it at a discrete distance from the bench where we sat. Meanwhile I leaned back on my cushion and prepared to be kept waiting indefinitely. "*Baiteeyay*," Pundit-ji said, motioning for him to be seated. "Tell me, how is your wife?"

Chotilal shook his head gloomily. "Not well, Pundit-ji. Her digestion is worse. The medicine prescribed at the clinic does not seem to have helped her at all. She has taken up an Ayurvedic treatment now, but so far there is no improvement in her condition." He averted his eyes for just a moment, then turned back to Pundit-ji. "She has a good deal of pain."

Pundit Trivedi frowned, which had the effect of pulling his nose down over his upper lip. "I'm very sorry to hear that. Please tell her so. And your daughters?"

"They are fine, Pundit-ji. The eldest will be fourteen this month. I have completed arrangements for her marriage to a boy from a very good family." He hesitated. "The dowry they are requesting is more than we can afford. But they will not agree to anything less. *Kyaa kiyaa jaayay*? What is to be done?"

"And the others?"

"Sita and Anju are in school. But soon enough they too will require husbands. We . . ." His voice dropped away into an embarrassed silence. "I did not come here to complain to you about these mundane problems."

"What is it, then?"

Chotilal stared at the wooden chappal resting on the ground near his feet. After a few seconds he glanced in my direction and seemed to look right through me, then turned to Pundit Trivedi.

"Guru-ji, I have been reading and studying the *Bhagavadgita*, attempting to go deeper into the meaning of Shri Krishna's words. For this purpose I turned to the explanations given by Shankaracharya in his commentary."

I perked up on hearing the name of my former dissertation subject but tried not to appear nosy.

"I see," said Pundit Trivedi. "No doubt Shankara's philosophy of non-dualism is most profound, but his views are subtle. Do you find the commentary worthwhile?"

Chotilal sat forward, causing the chair to creak. I noticed that through the repeated clenching of his toes, he had dug two small trenches in the packed earth. "It is difficult. In the beginning—before reading Shankara—I felt I understood what Krishna tells Arjuna, that he must fight." He recited, from memory, the Hindi translation he had been reading:

Better to die fulfilling one's own dharma;
to take up the dharma of another is filled with peril.

I watched Pundit Trivedi as he reflected on the significance of this verse, one that must have figured prominently, years ago, in discussion with his son. "The meaning is clear, is it not?"

Chotilal nodded. "Arjuna cannot escape his duty as a warrior. This much I understand. But the explanations of Shankara . . ." He sighed. "The more I study, the more confused I become. I no longer know what to think."

Both he and Pundit-ji seemed to have forgotten all about me as I sat quietly, pretending to be absorbed in the text we had been reading. It may be that Chotilal assumed I could not understand Hindi; although he really did not seem to care. Nor was he the first to converse with Pundit Trivedi in this way, as if the foreigner sitting nearby had no ears. In Banaras, the most intimate details of one's life become the shared property of family and neighbors; maybe under such circumstances people don't need, or expect, privacy. Pundit-ji now looked at Chotilal with obvious concern. Before he could respond his guest continued in the same bookish, formal Hindi.

"Shankara writes about Brahman, a state beyond all distinctions—beyond all the worry and pain of this illusory world. Beyond even the need to fulfill one's dharma."

Pundit-ji's brows arched almost imperceptibly. "Indeed, this is one interpretation of Shankara."

"But how can it be, Guru-ji? Is this world really nothing more than maya?" He appeared genuinely exasperated. "Is all that we do for nothing?"

"*Hari Ram!*" Pundit-ji exclaimed. "You are becoming a philosopher, Chotilal. What is the point in worrying about such abstruse matters?"

But Chotilal was clearly in no mood to back down. "Is this," he threw out his hand in a nervous arc that took in the garden, the cows, even Goongiji, who had finished eating and was now following our every move with great curiosity, "all of it . . . *not real?* I want to understand, Guru-ji. I need to understand Shankara's meaning."

"And what if it were?" Pundit-ji responded pointedly. "What if all of it—the whole world—were nothing but a dream? *Kyaa fark hai?* Would knowing this change anything?" He seemed to have suddenly become aware of his neighbor's heartfelt distress.

Chotilal let both hands drop to his lap in a dramatic gesture of resignation. "*Bardhaa fark*, Guru-ji. If this life is no more than a dream, then why should I worry to pay my daughter's dowry? And my wife's pain—if it is not real, then why should I care? Why should I care about anything?"

"Is that what you would prefer?" Pundit-ji's voice was flat, betraying no emotion. "Not to care about your daughter's marriage? Not to care about the suffering of your wife?"

Chotilal did not immediately respond. He bent forward in the chair, his elbows resting on his knees, and began to massage his forehead with both hands. "It would be easier, Guru-ji . . ." He looked up, his face framed between two open palms. "Would it not?"

A solitary crow circled in the sky, a shadow fell across the garden as the bird descended, coming to rest on an empty branch. The crow extended its wings, ruffling the feathers, then closed them neatly, rearranging a few errant plumes with his beak. On the wall behind us, two monkeys had paused in their rounds. One of them was grooming the other, searching his companion's fur, picking out the lice. In the distance I heard the faint sound of a radio playing a popular film song.

Chotilal had nothing more to say and seemed to be awaiting some response to his question. By this time the holes under his toes had grown into miniature canyons. Pundit-ji studied his face with a curiously detached expression I could not begin to decipher. He may have been uncertain how to respond to such ingenuous pathos. After what seemed a very long time he spoke.

"Few of us can doubt that life includes a great deal of discomfort. But this teaching of maya is very tricky, and if one is not careful with it—as with a strong medicine—it can bring more trouble than it solves." He considered for a second or two. "Have you heard of Kela Baba?"

"No, Guru-ji. Who is Kela Baba?"

"A swami I once met, when I was a child. During the winter months he lived alone, somewhere in the Vindhya Mountains. But he occasionally traveled to Banaras. On one of his visits he came to our home. He sat here. Right here." He patted the stone bench. "He and my father talked. I was just a boy at the time, but the memory of that afternoon is still clear. Kela Baba was said to have attained deep realization of Shankara's teaching. People came from far away to receive darshan and to hear him speak. In return for his instruction they would offer him bananas, which he loved."

Pundit Trivedi adjusted the wisdom pillow, fluffing and patting it into the proper shape.

"I will tell what I myself saw and heard."

He leaned back on one elbow and settled in.

"One morning Kela Baba was discoursing just outside the gates of the Durga mandir . . ." Pundit-ji gestured southward with his free arm, in the direction of the temple to the goddess. "My father and I had gone there to perform puja. As we were coming out onto the street, we saw Kela Baba talking to a group of villagers on the subject of maya. We had just walked over to listen when one of the men suddenly shouted very loudly and people began to run off in every direction. An elephant had some-how gotten loose from its trainer and was stampeding through the bazaar, overturning vegetable carts and trampling everything in its path. When the swami saw this huge beast, with its trunk lashing wildly, he snatched up several bananas that had been given to him by disciples and fled for his life. For some reason, the elephant took a particular interest in him and charged in his direction."

"Bananas," Chotilal interjected thoughtfully.

"What?"

"Bananas," Chotilal repeated. "The elephant went after him because he carried those bananas. He should have left them behind."

"You are correct," acknowledged Pundit-ji, who really did not seem to have considered this before. "The elephant went after the swami to get his bananas." He hesitated for a moment before continuing, mulling over Chotilal's observation, as if this single detail might suggest some new meaning to everything that followed. "Yes, well, in any case, the bananas were the least of his problems. Not far from where the swami had been talking, there was an abandoned well. It had long ago dried up, and for some time sweepers had been filling it with trash. In his haste to get away from the elephant, the swami stumbled and fell over the edge, down into the well. The rubbish broke his fall, but he was too far down to climb out. The elephant came close and looked over."

Pundit-ji raised both brows and peered down into the imaginary shaft. Placing one hand in front of his nose as if it were a trunk, he began sniffing and snorting.

"Kela Baba and his bananas were out of reach, so the elephant soon lost interest and went away. When they were quite certain it was safe, my father and the others who had been listening to him speak came over and looked down. There he was, lying amid the refuse—a pitiable sight. One of them called out, '*Aray*, Swami-ji! Are you hurt?'

"'My friends! Please get me out of here!'

"Someone went for a bamboo ladder. Now, as it happened, among the group there was a student from BHU—very proud of his modern scientific views. He looked over the edge of the well and called out. 'Baba-ji, you told us everything is illusion. If the elephant was not real, then why were you afraid? Why did you run away? Even you do not believe this maya talk! You are a fake and a liar. From now on I will call you Garbage Baba, since that is where you belong—in the garbage.'

"'Get me out of here,' the swami called back, 'and then we will talk.'"

"But it's *true*," interrupted Chotilal, whose mood had once again shifted. "Why should the swami be frightened of an elephant that is not real?"

Pundit-ji waved a hand to silence him and continued. "Certainly Kela Baba was in a . . . a compromising position. When they pulled him up he was covered with manure and other rubbish, and he gave off a strong odor that did not seem the least bit pure." Here the great pundit paused in his narrative and daintily pinched his nostrils between two long fingers, all the while fanning the air between us with his other hand. "But he dusted himself off as best he could, then looked out at the group, a few of whom had begun to smile. 'Listen closely,' Kela Baba said, 'and I will explain. The elephant was indeed an illusion. That it became angry and charged through the bazaar was another illusion. And it was also only an illusion that I *appeared* to run away.' The student was about to object, but Kela Baba pointed at him and continued, 'Even he—this one who thinks himself so clever, so certain of his views—even he is not what he believes himself to be.' Then he turned to face the young man and addressed him directly, 'What you see, my son, is nothing but a distorted image of your own face, reflected in the mirror of fear and desire.'

"At that the young man stepped forward, right up close to the old sadhu, and spoke boldly. 'If only you had told us this while you were still in the well, then we would not have taken the trouble to raise one illusion out of another! Why should we care?!'

"*Why should we care*?! You see, Chotilal? This was his problem, as well. Those were his very words. I remember well, because what happened next was—for my father—quite distressing. This arrogant young man gave the swami a push that sent him tumbling over the edge into the filth. He then turned and walked away, without so much as looking back. He may have done this in order to prove to everyone present that he himself really did *not* care; it was certainly a shock—and not only to my father. Of course, once again the people helped Kela Baba out, but this time as soon as he was free, the swami left without a word. And that was the last time he was seen in Banaras. We heard later that he was living as a hermit in the Himalaya, somewhere in the mountains near Kedarnath. I do not know if it was true."

I glanced over at Chotilal to see what effect, if any, Pundit-ji's story might have had on him. It could have been lifted right out of the pages of any number of classical Vedanta texts. That's not to say all of this didn't actually happen, but I had to wonder. Judging from his expression, though, Chotilal was quite obviously troubled.

"But Guru-ji, was Kela Baba only pretending to be afraid of the elephant?" His gloom had returned, and I could see he was working himself up all over again. "What good is it to know that the world is maya if . . . if . . ."

He suddenly became animated, throwing up both hands in frustration. "He *ran* from the elephant, Pundit-ji! He ran to save himself! There is no reason to run from a dream!"

"Exactly." Pundit Trivedi pounced on his words, speaking calmly, but with great authority, almost before Chotilal had finished this last sentence. "There is no escape from a dream, because even the *idea* of escape is itself only a part of the dream. You have grasped Shankara's essential point. The dream of escape is the final illusion. When you see this, there is nothing more to understand."

It was as if a trapdoor had abruptly opened beneath my feet, and I felt myself falling through endless space. I had been studying Vedanta for years, but with these few words Pundit-ji had turned everything on its head. Of course he was right. But what does it mean to say that life is a dream when there is no possibility of waking up from the dream? What, then, is the meaning of "liberation"? For all I know, Chotilal was struggling with the same conundrum. Pundit Trivedi had so swiftly turned his own words back on him that the poor man appeared speechless. At any rate, I'm quite sure this was not the lesson he had come here to learn. I thought he might break out in tears. Pundit-ji must have sensed this, as well, for when he resumed speaking he struck a different tone.

"But enough, I think, of this maya talk, which can so easily lead to confusion and trouble. Let us set aside Shankara and his theories and look to the *Gita* alone. There are certain shlokas to which you should pay particular attention." Before Chotilal could respond Pundit-ji began to recite a Sanskrit verse, after which he offered his own Hindi translation:

> One must know what it is to act rightly,
> and one must know wrong action, as well.
> But most important, one must know the meaning of nonaction.

"Do you grasp the distinction? Right and wrong actions we know; this is not difficult to understand. But what is this other type of activity? What is the meaning of nonaction? This is explained in the very next shloka:

> He who refrains from action while acting
> and acts while not taking action,
> he alone is wise among men.
> He alone lives in peace
> while accomplishing all that need be done.

"Here, Chotilal, Lord Krishna offers the profound teaching of karma yoga. We have no choice but to act—even to *refuse* to act is a kind of action. Of course we must always act in accord with our dharma, but Krishna explains, here, that any action aimed toward achieving some result—even a good result—only brings more suffering. What the Lord calls *nonaction* is action that seeks no reward. Action that has no goal or purpose other than to serve Lord Krishna. Already in the third chapter of the *Gita*, the Lord explained this to Arjuna:

> In doing his work without attachment to its results,
> a man attains liberation.

"This is a most useful teaching. Please contemplate its meaning carefully. Then do what you must, and let it go."

For the first time Chotilal acknowledged my presence with a fleeting, self-conscious glance. "It is late," he said. "I have interrupted your lesson."

"Do you understand, Chotilal? Whatever comes of your action, it is not your concern. You have only to act." Pundit Trivedi held out both his hands, palms down, and gently patted the air between them. "Do what you must. And then let it go."

Chotilal pushed himself up from the chair and moved his hand in a single motion from Pundit Trivedi's feet to his own forehead.

"Namaskar, Chotilal." It was a simple goodbye, but Pundit Trivedi's voice held the power of a blessing.

Chotilal backed away a few steps, then turned and walked slowly across the garden and into the house.

When he had gone Pundit-ji sat staring at the text we had been reading. At last his lips began to move. He spoke in Hindi. "I have known this man all his life, since the time he was born. He is a good father, a good husband. We must pray that his wife regains her health." He looked up at me, the great nose suspended between us like a bridge between two worlds. His eyes were as soft as shells polished by the sea. "And you!" he said sternly, in English. "You have not touched your chai! What's the matter—too much sugar?"

"Pundit-ji?"

"What?"

"The story about Kela Baba. Is it true?"

"I told you already. I saw it myself. That is its truth."

"What do you think?"

"Think?" He eyed me suspiciously. "About what?"

"About Kela Baba."

"What about Kela Baba?"

"Did he understand Shankara's teaching, the meaning of maya?"

He smiled. "Why ask me this question? What do I know of such things? I am an old man telling stories. That is all."

"I'm curious. What do you *think*?"

"He waved one hand in the air, as if to brush away a fly. "All is illusion! All is real! What is the difference?" He paused, then answered his own question. "No difference at all. This is precisely Shankara's teaching, is it not? All distinctions are merely apparent; all difference is ultimately false: *Neti, neti*. It is a lesson as old as the Upanishads: *Not this, not that*. Very simple. But illusion or not, we must live here, in this world." He rapped the bench with his knuckles. "A world filled with hope and disappointment. In any case," he huffed, "this teaching of maya is not found in the *Gita*."

"But Shankara's famous commentary . . ."

He held up one hand like a stop sign. "Shankara is an illustrious philosopher, but he has imposed his monistic philosophy, his nondualism, onto the *Gita*. It is not there. The philosophy of the *Bhagavadgita* is Sankhya, not Vedanta. This much, at least, should be obvious to any knowledgeable person. But all of this is not important, for what is most distinctive about the *Gita* has nothing to do with philosophy. Krishna teaches Arjuna not how to think but how to act. How to live in accord with his dharma."

"This word *dharma*, would you tell me what it means, Pundit-ji?"

Pundit Trivedi was accustomed to my endless questions, but this time I appeared to have stumped him. It was as if I had asked why he stood upright and walked on his hind legs rather than crawling about on all fours. I believe it suddenly struck him just how far I had traveled to sit here in his garden on this perfect December morning.

"Dharma," he said, repeating the word. "It is from the root *dhru*—to hold, or support. Dharma is the foundation on which everything is built. Dharma is our duty, our obligations to others. It is the life given to each of us, the life to which we surrender. It is the life of a son or daughter, a father or mother. It could be the life of a warrior, as it was for Arjuna. Or the life of a farmer, a sweeper, or a scholar . . . the circumstances are of no particular importance. To live in accord with your dharma means simply that you do things the way they have always been done. You choose nothing, and nothing is yours." Pundit Trivedi looked over at the new calf, so small and vulnerable and, now, so apparently content, as it lay curled and sleeping in the warm winter sun. "In such a life, even the joys and sorrows are not your own."

28

ON JANUARY 23, 1977, Indira Gandhi announced that she intended to bring the Emergency to a close and to hold free and open elections later in the spring. She immediately released her opponents from prison and allowed them to speak publicly. It was as if she had tossed a stick of dynamite onto a dam. The censors were fired as summarily as they had been installed, and the press went on a rampage. All the pent-up animosity, all the fear and resentment, spilled out into the streets. Her fiercest critic, Jagjivan Ram, immediately allied his Congress for Democracy with the newly formed Janata Party, and the stage was set for all-out war. Everyone was on edge, talking and arguing about politics in anticipation of the coming elections. And yet none of this had any appreciable impact on my life. Completely dissociated from the dramatic events unfolding all around me, I moved like a ghost through streets crowded with demonstrators. My days were marked, as always, by morning and evening meditation, by the meticulous reading of Sanskrit and Tibetan.

One morning in early February I returned from my meeting with Pundit Trivedi and found an official-looking manila envelope that the postman had slipped under my door. It had been sent from the States via registered mail; a form was affixed to the outside with a space for my signature. Of course, in India all of this meant nothing. The seal had been broken by customs agents, who had obviously inspected whatever was inside. In itself, this was not unusual. My mail was often opened and then clumsily resealed with wide swaths of glue that occasionally leaked through, making it necessary to tear apart the pages of my letters. This time, however, the reader hadn't bothered to reseal the envelope, and the contents slid easily out into my hand: a single piece of legal-size, pastel-blue cardstock folded back on itself in thirds. The cover bore the following message:

NOTICE OF ENTRY

To:—The Defendant in Person

Sir:—Please take notice that the within is a (certified) true copy of a judgment duly entered in the office of the clerk of the within named court on, September 14, 1976.

Yours, etc.,
Frederick W. Klostermier
Attorney for the Plaintiff

The printed cover opened like a little door, swinging to the left; underneath was another little door that swung to the right. Inside, a paper had been stapled lengthwise, so that I needed to turn the whole thing ninety degrees in order to read it.

At a Special Term, Part 7C of the
Illinois Supreme Court at the
County Court House, Cook County
on September 14, 1976.

Present: Hon. Samuel Hook Special Referee

JUDITH L. HARRINGTON, *Plaintiff*, DIVORCE JUDGMENT

— against—Index No. 67003

STANLEY D. HARRINGTON, Defendant, Calendar No. 43555

(a) This action was submitted to me for consideration
on 5 / 13 / 1976
(b) The defendant was served within the state, personally outside the state.

(c) Plaintiff presented a verified complaint.

(d) Defendant appeared has not appeared and is in default.

(e) The Court accepted written proof of non-military service.

Now, on the motion of <u>Frederick W. Klostermier Esq</u>., attorney for the plaintiff, it is:

ORDERED AND ADJUDGED that:

1.Plaintiff shall have judgment that the marriage of the parties is dissolved on the evidence found in the Findings of Fact and Conclusions of Law in accordance with Domestic Relations Law, Section 235, Subd. 3;

2.~~The husband shall pay the wife for support of the above named child(ren) $ per week and alimony for the wife $ per week;~~

3.~~The Separation Agreement , executed _____, 19 ___ which is annexed to the Findings of Fact, shall be incorporated by reference in the Judgment and shall survive;~~

4.The woman may resume the use of her maiden name, which is <u>Reusswig</u>.

Judith and I were married in July of 1970; I was twenty-two at the time, she was twenty-one. Our friends were startled that we chose to have a traditional Christian ceremony performed in a church. But a wedding is—or, at least, so it seemed to me—the quintessential ritual act, and I subscribed to Victor Turner's understanding of ritual as a peculiarly potent form of theater. This was one time Judith and I were in complete agreement on the value of dramatic effect. Any theatrical performance is enhanced by suitably majestic architecture, and Bond Chapel—a small, Gothic church on East 59th Street—was the perfect setting for our transformation from man and woman to husband and wife. And if the setting is important for good theater, finding the right script is essential; ideally, the vows spoken on stage should resonate with indisputable literary and historical significance. Measured by this criterion, nothing wields more authority than the Anglican *Book of Common Prayer*, unchanged from 1662 to the present and used by every one of Jane Austen's couples:

> I, Stanley Harrington, take thee, Judith Reusswig, to be my
> wedded Wife, to have and to hold from this day forward, for

better for worse, for richer for poorer, in sickness and in health, to love and to cherish, till death us do part, according to God's holy ordinance; and thereto I plight thee my troth.

So I was on familiar territory. Like the *Book of Common Prayer* held by the minister who had stood before Judith and me at the altar, clothed in his black gowns and prompting us with these words in stentorian tones, the slender blue triptych resting in my hands was also a ritual object imprinted with ceremonially charged words. Employed, as these words had been, in the appropriate context of the municipal courthouse, this was language that brought to an end what other language had once created. No great mystery here, no mystical juju. Anyone who's read J. L. Austin's work on speech acts knows all about the power of performative utterance, the capacity of language—mere words—to create and demolish whole worlds.

I read carefully through the legal jargon one more time, absorbing every tortured locution, then closed the two small doors and laid it aside. For quite a while I just sat there at my desk, staring out the window and down the street. I could see one of my neighbors, the press-wala, standing at his bench next to a mountain of laundry, smoothing out a shirt and straightening the cuffs. Beside him the heavy iron rested on a grate, suspended over a red-orange glow of coals. A solitary rickshaw drifted by, coasting around the corner by Ganga Mat.

I had known for almost a year that the divorce was in the works. But still, to hold in my hands this tangible proof that our marriage was over, a legal certificate generated in some anonymous courtroom in Chicago and sent all the way here to Banaras: it was exceedingly strange. My life with Judith had become a distant memory. Nevertheless, this document was an object of undeniable power, invested with all the ritual authority of the court—the call to order, the judge in his robes, the banging of the gavel. By the sheer force of these words, I knew that something terribly real, something I had once dreamed of and desired with all my heart, had now been irrevocably destroyed.

I couldn't plunge into my usual routine today; I decided to get out of my room and go for a walk.

Near the little temple at the corner of Assi crossing, I paused for a moment, immersed in the tumult of human speech. A group of fifteen or twenty old women—pilgrims from the country—passed by on their way to the river. They were bunched together like gaily colored birds, singing bhajans in a high-pitched, nasal drone. In the gutter at my feet, squatting behind baskets heaped with fresh coriander, two village girls argued loudly in the local Bhojpuri dialect. A few feet to their left a group of Muslim shop-keepers dressed in checkered lungis and white kurtas stood knee deep in a swirling tide pool of Urdu. The prime minister's name was cast up now and again on a velvety swish of fricatives, only to be sucked back into the guttural undertow. One of the men was waving his shabby briefcase to emphasize a point—something about Sanjay Gandhi.

Several rickshaws were parked in the shade. On each red vinyl seat a driver leaned back and puffed at a hand-rolled bidi, his feet extended straight out over the handlebars. Wound round each head was a swath of vibrantly colored cloth. Sweet clouds of smoke drifted in the air, mingling lazily with the drivers' rough Bihari patois. Nearby, two middle-class babus wearing dhotis and black, pointed slippers were carrying on a sedate discussion in cultivated, Sanskritized Hindi—"Standard Hindi," as it was called by the linguists at the university in Delhi. Their pronunci-ation was quick and sharp, each crisp syllable grafted onto the next with surgical precision. A young French couple crossed the street with their long stringy hair, gaudily embroidered Afghan vests purchased in Kabul, and bare, grime-coated feet. A languid succession of round, heavy vowels rolled from her pursed lips while he listened, self-consciously wagging his head in agreement. All around me, men, women, and children quarreled and bartered, discussed, joked, scolded, and bantered in a multitude of lan-guages and dialects. The rhythm of their voices was captivating—a grand, invisible realm of sound, dominion of the mighty Logos, the Maharaja of Nomenclature and his Court of Verbosity.

Behold the cavalry of sturdy substantives on horseback, troops of light-footed participles, a humble, exploited peasantry of pronouns and prep-ositions. Cloistered in the harem and languishing under fans of woven grass wielded by a core of eunuch articles, definite and otherwise, are the adjectives, vain and prone to excess. Some are clothed seductively in diaphanous diphthongs; others are wrapped in gowns of richly embroi-dered phonemes, their feet pressed into tiny sibilants. Necklaces of semi-vowels shimmer at their throats; their fingers are adorned with clusters of surds and chunky, garish sonants. The atmosphere is thick with labial perfume. Outside the palace the bazaar teams with offensive idioms and guttural riffraff. Here and there in the crowd one spots an old, worn-out cliché hobbling along, an offensive quip darting among the shadows, or a charming expression from the village decked out in her best sari. A gang of ugly remarks lounging around the nearby paan stall eyes her as she passes. Not far away an overworked metaphor sits hunched behind his chai, brooding on the continuing string of accusations he cannot afford to feed and clothe. The holy city is home to an endless succession of gross insults, bold assertions, and redundant misnomers that are born and die in the streets; but it has, as well, spawned generations of subtle discourse and eloquent turns of phrase. The citizens of Banaras are born in the shadow of Bhojpuri, raised by Hindi, educated in English, and die with Sanskrit whispering in their ears.

In Chicago, I once consumed several weeks working my way through a small shelf of medieval texts known as the Pancharatra, an amalgam of Vedic exegesis and early tantric lore. According to one of these treatises, the *Ahirbudhnya*, the appearance of the self and its world is an emanation of Lord Vishnu's all-encompassing mind. During the period between the destruction of one world and the creation of another, when neither time nor space exists, Vishnu falls into deep, dreamless sleep; his awareness is present only as *nada*, described as "the long, drawn out sound of a temple bell." When he begins to dream, this elemental vibration rises into divine awareness "like a bubble floating up from the depths of the ocean." At the surface the bubble bursts into consciousness, spilling forth the fourteen vowels and thirty-four consonants of Sanskrit—the stuff out of which the dream of self and world takes shape and into which both ultimately collapse once again.

These same primal elements of language are visualized by the yogi in the form of a serpent, the kundalini, lying dormant at the root of the spine, in the lowest of the seven chakras. With adequate practice, the kundalini can be roused in meditation through the use of specific mantras. Once awakened, it moves upward along a central channel, through the navel and heart chakras, and into the throat, where it emerges in audible form as the seed syllables, or *dhatus*, of Sanskrit, each one associated with a particular tantric deity who protects and dispenses the energy of universal consciousness. As the kundalini approaches the crown chakra, the yogi effectively becomes God, reversing the process of creation, moving from waking consciousness into dream, from dream to dreamless sleep, and from dreamless sleep to an unborn, undying state known only as "the Fourth," characterized in the texts as Pure Being, Pure Awareness, and Pure Bliss: *Sat, Chit, Ananda.*

* * *

Absorbed in these ruminations and adrift on the voices all around me, I was jolted back to my senses by the furious clanging of rickshaw bells. The driver had veered to avoid colliding with a cow that stood placidly in the center of Assi crossing eating a cardboard box; the rickshaw now careened straight toward where I stood paralyzed, unable to decide which way to jump. For a split second I met the driver's eyes and my stomach wrenched. The center of the man's face was rotted away with leprosy. Where the tip of his nose and his upper lip should have been, there was a naked, suppurating wound, a single hole punched above a crooked ring of paan-stained teeth rushing down on me. He flung out a warning cry—no word, but a rough, wet ball of sound—and shot past, disappearing around the corner and down toward the river.

I caught my breath and looked around. To my left the girls sat, quietly now, behind their baskets of coriander, arranging leaves in neat piles; the Muslim men were gone.

"Stan? You okay man?"

"Oh. Hey."

It was Richard. Since my move to Banaras the previous August, we had bumped into each other from time to time, mostly at concerts. In the interims between his periodic liaisons with the foreign women who passed through town, he visited the prostitutes near Chowk. This afternoon he was, as always, well dressed, in a carefully pressed, tailored kurta-pajama of raw silk.

Richard was not what you would call a contemplative person; he showed little interest in philosophy or spiritual things of any stamp. I remember one time when a group of us were sitting around a table at Ravi's chai shop. Ruth, the German musician who had a cabin in Manali, was talking about how she always performed puja to Sarasvati before practicing her flute. Richard had remained silent the whole time, listening, but at this point someone asked him if he did any kind of regular puja or meditation. At first he said nothing; he simply gazed at Ravi, watching him flip an omelet. I thought he hadn't heard the question, but then he responded, laconically, something to the effect that practicing his tabla was as close to religion as he ever wanted to get.

Before coming to India Richard had worked as a carpenter somewhere near Bristol in the UK. In the off-hours he was a musician—drummer in a garage band that played the clubs. Then the Beatles released *Revolver*, with George on sitar, and Indian classical music was suddenly everywhere.

A friend took him to a tabla performance in London, and according to Richard that was it. As he told me one afternoon while tuning his drums, "Somethin' just sorta come over me, and I split." He packed a small bag, withdrew his life's savings, and took the ferry from London to Amsterdam. From there he traveled for two months in a haze of hashish and Hendrix, riding the Magic Bus through Yugoslavia, Turkey, Iran, and Afghanistan. Finally arriving in Delhi in late summer of 1968, Richard eventually found his way from there to Banaras, where he began studying tabla. He had never returned to England.

Richard and I had few common interests, but we talked together now and again. I liked his unpretentious, working-class edge. He devised an endless succession of entrepreneurial schemes to supplement his dwindling savings, and recently we had begun to see more of each other as the result of his latest enterprise, a flourishing business in whole-wheat bread. He baked it himself in a big tandoori oven constructed in a friend's courtyard near Sonarpur. Early every morning he stoked up the fires—both the one in his chillum and the one in the oven—and prepared several dozen loaves, which he delivered by bicycle, still warm, to his enthusiastic customers.

His route brought him through Assi and by my place every other day. On such occasions he would stop in to drop off a loaf of bread and report whatever gossip was going the rounds. Lately it was some tidbit about Marie, a French nymphet who occupied Harold's old room in Lanka. "You remember 'arold, right? The American fella who ate an eggroll from the Winfa an nearly died a food poisnin? So his visa expired and he left for Nepal, and now this dishy chick from Paris lives in his flat. Apparently she's got some famous guru in Poona. What's his name? Oh yeah, Rajneesh. That's it. Has everyone doing somethin he calls ruddy 'sex yoga.'" Before Marie, the news generally included some mention of Dieter, a German sitar-wala whose blatantly racist views provoked frequent arguments and the occasional fistfight. Dieter detested India and Indians and made no effort to cloak his feelings, yet through some profound karmic irony he had been living in Banaras for years and showed no inclination to leave anytime soon. Richard knew them all. It was no surprise that he should happen to appear now, just as I was nearly run down by a rickshaw.

"Looks like he clipped you." He gestured toward my pant leg, which had been torn open, apparently by the rear axle of the rickshaw as it swept past. Through the tear I could make out a small cut.

He inspected the wound and offered a long, low whistle. "Could a' been worse. He was an ugly bloke, that's for sure." He looked up. "Hey man, how 'bout a chai?"

I was in no hurry to go back to my room and the blue notice, so I accepted his invitation.

He led the way across the street and up four or five stairs to a small clearing under a pipal tree that provided shade for a nearby chai stall. We found a seat on a circular concrete platform that surrounded the tree's immense, ribbed trunk; the stone was cold and polished to a smooth finish from years of service. The French couple I had seen earlier in the street now occupied a bench across from us. He was holding forth while she listened, her fingers nervously twisting a thick tangle of ash-blond ringlets that fell down over her neck. The air smelled pleasantly of ganja and incense. Just inside the tiny shop—not much bigger than a packing crate, really—a skeletal man with greasy, shoulder-length hair crouched behind a stove, fanning the smoldering dung with a tattered mat. He was barefoot and shirtless with blue-black skin; the bottom half of his lungi had been tucked in at the waist to form a short skirt that hung around his knees, leaving the stringy muscles of his calves exposed. When he saw us, he pulled himself up and peeled back his lips in a broad, crooked smile.

"Namaste, Richard!"

"Namaste, Chai Baba. *Doe chai pilaao.*" Richard brought up two fingers and tapped them against his forehead, at once a greeting and an order.

Chai Baba's eyes slid around to me and he raised both hands, palms joined in formal greeting. "Namaskar, Babu."

Chai Baba made it a point to know every foreigner who stuck around town for more than a week. He talked with them, hung out and smoked ganja, did business with them, made connections. *Networked.* I was not one of the regular crowd at his shop—stoners that flew by with the seasons between Kathmandu and Goa like migratory birds, touching down en route for a month in Banaras in fall and spring, but still he knew all about me. He knew everything about everybody, but nobody seemed to know much about Chai Baba. He was reported to have a wife somewhere, but no one I knew ever actually saw her. And I was told that the child who worked around the shop was his son. There were plenty of other stories I never bothered to confirm, like the one about how he had once traveled to Germany in a VW bus with half a dozen Euro-hippies. They supposedly made it all the way to Berlin before the authorities sent him packing back to India at the Reich's expense. He was even said to have wandered as a sadhu for some years, studying under an Aghori master.

I nodded at Chai Baba and summarily pushed my palms together, which was sufficient for him as he turned and went back to the fire. He took up a blackened, dented pan and set it over the coals. He filled the pan with hot water that fell in a steaming arc from the spout of an aluminum kettle. He then pried open the lid of a yellow Dalda can and measured out two heaping spoonfuls of powdered tea leaves, tossing each of them into the pot with considerable flourish. From a second can he spooned out twice that amount of sugar and repeated the process, ladling milk from yet another container. Finally, he selected a single green pod of cardamom from a tiny jar, delicately cracked it between the nails of his thumb and forefinger, and let it fall into the boiling liquid. He picked up the pan and swished it around once or twice, then poured the mixture through a plastic sieve into two smudged glasses and delivered them to us where we sat.

As he handed me my tea, Chai Baba's eyes flicked to the rip in my pant leg, and once again the bottom half of his face curled back in a toothy smile.

"Rickshaw nail you?"

He spoke his own peculiar dialect of English, an eclectic ragbag of words and phrases gleaned from years spent listening to nonnative speakers. He was similarly conversant, from what I could tell, in French, German, Russian, and Japanese.

"Bummer." He laughed. "Rickshaw also nail Chai Baba." He indicated a jagged red scar just over his left knee. "Many years before. Hard lesson, no?"

I was already in a foul mood, and the supercilious grin began to irritate me. I responded abruptly in stuffy, formal Hindi: "What lesson?" Immediately that verse from the *Bodhicharyavatara*, my mantra from the early days in Delhi, flashed to mind.

Chai Baba cocked his head to one side, as if he hadn't understood my question, then switched to Hindi himself: "*Rastay say hut jaao, babu, nahin to chot lag jaaega.*" Maybe he thought the answer was so simple it should be obvious: "Get yourself out of the way, Babu, and you won't get hurt."

At that moment the French hippies called out for another round. Chai Baba went over and collected their dirty glasses then slouched back inside the shop.

In the street a camel sauntered by with a load of firewood strapped to its back. A man walked in front of the big animal, holding a long tether that was secured, at the other end, to a bridle. The two of them moved leisurely in the direction of Harishchandra Ghat. Richard and I sipped our chai and watched the camel's head as it faded into the distance, swaying gracefully, high above the crowded street, like a cobra dancing for a snake charmer. Richard put down his glass, removed a package of bidis from his *jhola* bag, and lit one up. The tip crackled and spit.

"Yesterday afternoon I may a' passed up the opportunity of a lifetime," he remarked casually, plucking a piece of tobacco from his tongue and flicking it into the gutter.

"How's that?"

"Guru-ji took me with him to a concert at that girl's school over near Lahurabir. You know the one. Up toward Sanskrit U."

I tipped my head slightly in the Indian manner, indicating I was familiar with the place. It was an English-medium school catering to the daughters of well-off families—the kind of people who considered themselves "modern."

"There were at least three hundred girls in the audience—teenagers, you know? Guru-ji had me up on stage with him. Must a' been waiting an hour, I bet. The principal and three or four other blokes up there talking. You know how they do before concerts—bloomin' malas and everything. Guru-ji tuned his tablas, and I just sat there looking out at all those girls giggling with each other and whispering back and forth while the old men talked."

I could easily picture the scene. Garlands of bright orange marigolds strung around the musicians' necks and draped over the stage. The pristine white cushions where they sat, cross-legged, behind their instruments. Richard's teacher powdering his hands and fiddling with the ring of wooden pegs that ran around the periphery of the drums, each peg tucked under a rawhide string that could be stretched by whacking it up or down with a small silver hammer, altering the tension on the head and changing the tone. Richard the handsome foreigner, doubtless the center of attention during those interminable speeches, sitting up next to his teacher in a position of real status. The girls and he could stare at each other to their hearts' content, something that would be entirely inappropriate under any other circumstances.

"Guru-ji is always tellin' me I should get married, how it would be good for my music. You know, sett'le down, get a woman to do the cooking an' shopping an' all. Mostly I just ignore him, but lately he's made a bloody crusade of it. So get this: after we'd been sitting up there for a bit, he turns to me an' he says"—at this point Richard puts on his best Indian-English accent—"'Richard, while I am playing I want that you should be taking opportunity to examine these girls. So many girls. Surely one of them will make a good match for you. When I finish you will please show me your choice.' Can you imagine, Stan? He was gonna try to fix me up—you know—with a *wife*! I swear to God I'm not joking. Cross my heart."

He waved a hand vaguely over his chest then shook his head in consternation.

"For *Chrissake*, Stan. What would you a' done?"

I doubt that Richard knew I had been married. He knew very little about my life before coming to India.

"I mean, there was nothin' to say. Guru-ji started in playing, and that was it. So I sat there, you know, for the next two hours, sorta checking out the talent—as if I were a bloody nabob and the school was my private zenana. At first I just looked, but after a bit I came up with a system. I move slow, see, from one girl to the next, up one row and down another, get some good eye contact with each one. Make certain she knows I'm looking right at *her*, you know? Then, when I've got her attention, I give her a good, close, run over—hair, skin, lips. Imagine what it'd feel like to, you know, shag each one of 'em."

He stopped here for a second to re-light the bidi. "I tell you, it was tiring. By the time the concert was over I was fagged." He took another drag and leaned forward, resting his forearms on his knees, the cigarette dangling between two fingers.

I stared at him, incredulous. The whole thing was beyond belief, truly a case of worlds colliding. Obviously, though, Richard was dead serious. "So, when's the wedding?" It was all I could think of to say.

He shook his head. "No wedding, man."

"Why not?"

"Stan, this was not a game." He looked up at me and frowned. "All the time I was sittin' there, I couldn't help wondering what it would mean to *really* get married. I'd never given it much thought. I mean, you know, man, marriage isn't all just about sex and food."

A single sentence exploded into my mind: *Marriage is about learning to love.*

In my memory it was early evening and I was sitting in Anantacharya's home in Delhi. I was talking with his son, Krishna, and Krishna was saying, "Outside of marriage there is only passion. Love is built on commitment to one's dharma, on surrender to a sacred duty much greater than personal desire." I had never forgotten his words: "There is no mystery, Mr. Stanley. Love is not about getting what we want. Love is about how we live with what we are given."

Dharma: the foundation on which everything is built.

But is that really all there is to love? Duty and obligation? Sticking by a vow, for better for worse, for richer for poorer, in sickness and in health, in drunkenness and in fighting and in cheating on each other, till death do we part?

I glanced over at Richard, who was rummaging through his jhola, looking for a match to relight his bidi.

Thank God, I thought, it's not my world. I'm not bound by caste, not born to be a warrior or a sweeper—or a businessman, like my father. I don't have to marry a stranger. I don't have to marry anyone, for that matter, and I obviously don't have to *stay* married. There's always another option. I'm free to do whatever I want.

But what if I want to stop wanting?

Asking this question was like looking at one of those optical illusions where you stare at it forever, and then for no apparent reason the ground all of a sudden shifts, and you see everything from a radically different perspective.

Who am I kidding? I can't *stop* wanting. My entire identity is built on picking and choosing. If I stopped wanting one thing and not wanting another, I'd totally cease to exist—just pop like a bubble! It's exactly like Pundit Trivedi said, just like one of those fucking Chinese finger traps: The whole idea of escape—wanting to stop wanting—just gets you in deeper! There's no way out. The truth is, I'm not free to do whatever I want—I'm *compelled* to do whatever I want.

"The truth is," Richard was saying, "I got it down to two girls—both of 'em pretty, too. Real little charmers."

I struggled to find my way back into the conversation. "And . . . your guru?"

"Right. The whole time he's playing, he's givin' me the eye. When he finished, he asked me to show him the girl. I said I'd come up with two. No problem, he says, just show me which two and we'll see what we can do. Honest to God, Stan: he would not quit. It was damn scary. But here's the best part. I mean the really weird part. When I refused to point out the girls, Guru-ji got angry. Seriously. He was pissed."

Richard stopped short and stared sullenly at his chai.

"Off his trolley, he was. All because I wouldn't lay claim to some fifteen-year-old virgin. What kind of nuthouse is this, anyway?"

He continued grumbling to himself, until I spoke up. "That's it?"

He shrugged his shoulders and let the cold bidi slip from his fingers to the ground between his feet, then planted his elbows on his knees, his chin resting on his palms.

The scrape on my leg was throbbing, and I'd had all the conversation I could handle. I downed the last of my chai and was about to beg off when Richard let out an anguished groan. I followed his gaze to the side street that led down to the river. There was the same line of rickshaw-walas I had passed earlier, but now every head was turned, every eye focused on the statuesque figure of Parvati as she walked by, oblivious to the attention.

"God damn it, Stanley. How the bleedin' 'ell does she get away with that in this town?"

A shadow swept over the crowded street, and I looked up and saw two immense wings spread wide against the sky. A vulture soared downward then dropped heavily onto the edge of a nearby rooftop and settled in, his bald pate bobbing obscenely between steep, feathered shoulders.

29

AMONG THE VARIOUS MATERIALS distributed to new Fulbright fellows prior to their departure for India, I had received a packet of information on health issues in which I was told that during my stay in India I should treat even the slightest abrasion with care. In the language of the institute's glossy brochure: "If the surface of the skin is broken, the chief line in the body's defense system has been compromised, rendering the site vulnerable to invasion by a variety of pathogenic bacteria peculiar to the subtropical regions of South Asia." The military trope achieved its intended effect: since my arrival I had been zealous about keeping every superficial scratch scrupulously clean and slathered with antibiotic ointment. Nevertheless—almost two weeks after my encounter with the rickshaw—the scrape on my leg was still inflamed and crusty and sore to the touch. In addition to using an antibiotic salve, I had recently put myself on a course of oral cephalosporin. A man behind the counter at the Lanka pharmacy thought it would be a good idea; he sold me a bag of capsules.

Fear, it has been said, is the recollection of pain endured, a peculiar form of memory inscribed on the mind like a wound that will not heal. Desire, too, is a form of memory: the memory of pleasure. But desire wanders free, homeless and incorporeal, a hungry ghost forever reaching out to eat, perpetually searching for a way back into the flesh.

One morning, after cleaning and dressing my leg, I went over to the book-shelf and ran a finger along the row of bindings. I located a familiar, thick black volume bulging with paper markers and removed it. The cover was embossed with gold lettering: *Visuddhimagga*, or *The Path of Purification*. This medieval text, originally composed in Pali by an Indian monk named Buddhaghosa, is as close as you come to the Bible of the Theravadan Buddhist world, a world that extends north from Sri Lanka through Thailand, Cambodia, Laos, and Myanmar. A quick check of the contents located a chapter titled "Foulness as a Meditation Subject." I thumbed through a few pages and began to read:

> This is the body's nature: it is a collection of over three hundred bones, jointed by one hundred and eighty joints, bound together by nine hundred sinews, plastered over with nine hundred pieces of flesh, enveloped in the moist inner skin, enclosed in the outer cuticle, with orifices here and there, constantly dribbling and trickling like a grease pot, inhabited by a community of worms, the home of disease, the basis of painful states, perpetually oozing from the nine orifices like a chronic open carbuncle, from both of whose eyes eye-filth trickles, from whose ears comes ear-filth, from whose nostrils snot, from whose mouth food and bile and phlegm and blood, from whose lower outlets excrement and urine, and from whose ninety-nine thousand pores the broth of stale sweat seeps, with bluebottles and their like buzzing round it, which when untended with tooth sticks and mouth-washing and head-anointing and bathing and underclothing and dressing would, judged by the universal repulsiveness of the body, make even a king, if he wandered from village to village with his hair in its natural wild disorder, no different from a flower-scavenger or an outcaste or what you will. So there is no distinction between a king's body and an outcaste's in so far as its impure stinking nauseating repulsiveness is concerned.
>
> But by rubbing out the stains on its teeth with tooth sticks and mouth-washing and all that, by concealing its private parts under several cloths, by daubing it with various scents and salves, by pranking it with nosegays and such things, it is worked up into a state that permits of its being taken as "I" and "mine."

I skimmed the rest—something about how men delight in women because men fail to perceive how "in the ultimate sense there is no place here even the size of an atom fit to lust after." I closed the book and replaced it on the shelf, making a mental note to share this passage with Richard the next time he dropped by. It had been a favorite of Judith's. Once when I was studying Pali in Chicago, I made the mistake of reading it to her, and she had never forgotten. From then on, every ache and pain, every case of the flu, every menstrual period, it was the "foul body" acting up, or the "foul body" with its persistent demands for food, clothing, sex.

Opposite my window a gang of male monkeys strolled insolently along the ledge looking for trouble. They were strangers in our neighborhood, so far as I could tell, exploring new territory. Perhaps for this reason my neighbor was out on her roof, keeping an eye on her laundry drying on the line. She was also, I noticed, watching me. This was the opening move in a discreet game we had been playing, repeatedly, for several months now—ever since she had spotted those monkeys on my roof and called out to me.

A very extended Bengali family lived next door. I had counted some fourteen people, give or take an infant that may have been visiting or was accidentally counted twice. Most mornings, though, this girl—she was maybe seventeen or eighteen years old—was up there working all alone. A scarlet gash of vermillion sliced through the part in her hair, leaving no question as to her marital status. I assumed she was the newest bride, which would mean that she occupied the lowest station in the family hierarchy. This would explain why, in my observations, she appeared to be saddled with more than her fair share of domestic responsibilities. A few of the other women showed up now and again to boss her around, but I never once saw her husband on the rooftop. I was pretty sure, though, it was him I spied coming and going through the front door below, while just upstairs his young wife and I pursued our respective labors, separated only by a few iron bars and three feet of open space that spanned the alleyway between our buildings. Of course, she never left the house. He would not have permitted such a thing. It would be out of the question for an orthodox, new Hindu bride to traipse around in public under the gaze of other men. Under the circumstances, then, I alone was allowed to gaze.

It was shortly after that first encounter that I realized that my west windows overlooked the otherwise secluded rooftop of another man's one-woman harem, and I soon became aware that she seemed to be watching me at least as closely as I was watching her. It didn't take long to appreciate the erotic significance of this peculiar arrangement and to formalize the conventions of a protracted flirtation that could only make sense in a situation where a young woman is virtually imprisoned in a household, where the days and months pass and she is thrown into regular, surreptitious visual intercourse with a man outside of her family circle, where that man is a foreigner, and where that foreigner is himself otherwise devoid of female companionship and randy as the proverbial goat—despite the obvious fact that "in the ultimate sense there is no place here even the size of an atom fit to lust after."

But what about the soft brown slope of a woman's neck where it curves to meet her shoulder? Or the supple turn of her ankle, a delicate bare foot, tender toes adorned with silver rings? What of a narrow nose, a small mouth, and moist lips painted red like a ripe strawberry? And what of those eyes—two luminous pools rounded by dark shores of kajal?

The game. I sit at my desk untangling Sanskrit syntax; she squats across from me on the rooftop, sorting laundry or perhaps combing through a pile of lentils, searching for and removing tiny stones and scraps of debris. One end of her sari is pulled demurely over her hair, trailing low across her forehead; her lashes curl against its hem. She peeks out from under the sari and watches me where I sit at my desk for as long as I can endure the caress of those eyes as they move from the top of my head slowly over my arms and hands and shoulders and chest, ruffling every blond hair on my body, exploring every exposed inch of my pale, alien flesh. In short, she is allowed to have her way with me, to stroke my body with those invisible fingers, until—and only until—I look up from my books. Until that moment we are still gathering momentum, rising, slowly and tentatively, toward a point of no return. But when I look up, at the very instant our eyes meet, all the rules are broken. This coming together of the eyes is a moment of exquisite intimacy, a shameless, brazen violation of every societal norm, an indecent coupling that never lasts for more than two or three seconds at the most before she reluctantly turns away, prolonging our misery and our exultation in a smoldering sidelong glance straight out of the pages of Kalidasa's *Abhijnana-Shakuntala*:

> If love will trouble her
> whose great eyes madden me,
> I greet him unafraid,
> though wounded ceaselessly.

Where all of this left my neighbor, I was never sure, but in my solitude this very uncertainty about her feelings provided an opening for endless speculation. After one of our scandalous encounters, she would retreat back under her sari, rise, and walk briskly to the far side of the roof, occupying herself there with one or another innocuous chore. More than once she disappeared down the stairs, only to resurface five or ten minutes later with a heartbreaking expression of calculated insouciance. As for myself, I would generally collapse forward onto the open text I had been reading and let my face sink into the page. And when I raised my head, the whole thing was likely as not to start all over again, only this time with me in the role of aggressor.

I stare at her unflinchingly, mauling her body with my eyes, while she in her turn feigns total indifference to my attentions. She lolls on the rooftop, stretches like a cat in the sun, runs her small hands down along her hips, stands on tiptoe draping her husband's kurta over the line with her naked stomach exposed to the warm winter sun. All of this, I somehow know, is for me.

The apes were strung out along the ledge between us now, pacing back and forth suspiciously. Something was up, and I wasn't the only one who noticed. My neighbor's body language had shifted, from ease into a wary and anxious crouch. Her nostrils flared; the gold ring in her nose caught the sunlight and flashed. Her fingers coiled slowly around the bamboo stick that lay at her side, soundlessly tightening their grip. Her eyes narrowed, scanning the pack as it spread out along the top of the wall.

The monkeys were clearly deploying themselves for whatever was about to come. One contingent fanned out along the ledge in front while several more circled around in the other direction, completely surrounding the rooftop. A single skinny male lowered himself head first down the inside of the high wall in back, gripping the edge with his toes. He dangled there, moving cagily up and down, all the while shifting his line of vision between the laundry and the rod clenched in my neighbor's hand.

It suddenly occurred to me that this might be a gambit of some sort, intended to distract her attention. The thought had no sooner passed through my head than my neighbor took the bait: springing to her feet, she lunged toward him with a truly vicious open-mouth threat. Sure enough, the monkey she went for was nothing but a decoy, for at precisely that moment the biggest, ugliest member of the gang leapt through the air behind her, snagged the clothesline with his tail, and swung out along its length grabbing frantically at the laundry.

"*Pichay dekho!*" I yelled, waving both arms in the air over my head. "Look behind you!"

She spun around, the bamboo stick tightly clasped in both hands, and as she turned she swung it like a samurai sword—straight from the waist—cutting through the air with a *whiz* that caught the big monkey smack on his ass and sent him flying into a basket of clothes. He cried out with a terrified yelp, and the whole troop panicked and scrambled for safety, leaping wildly, one after another, into the maze of power lines or onto my veranda. A few hurdled straight over the side and down the sheer face of the concrete wall toward the street—anywhere out of reach of that stick. Meanwhile the big guy was left alone, tearing around the rooftop in wide circles, tumbling through shirts and pajama pants, through knotted dhotis and a couple dozen brightly colored socks, all the while clawing madly at a purple sari-blouse that had gotten wrapped around his head like a blindfold. My neighbor was in hot pursuit, her sari streaming behind, hair flying. Her bare feet slapped against the stone, ankle bracelets jingling like crazy sleigh bells as the pole sliced through the air and one stinging blow after another landed on the monkey's radiant posterior. At last he managed to rip the blouse off his head, and with a final desperate howl, he leapt out across the alley, arms and legs flailing. It was as though he had been shot out of a circus cannon directly toward my window. He slammed against the bars in front of my desk. A final poke of her stick sent him up over the edge of the roof.

My neighbor was now stretched over the wall in front of me, leaning forward at the waist, the dreaded stick still held aloft in her hands. She was breathing heavily and glistening with perspiration. Her sari had fallen over one shoulder and her braid had come undone; her hair rippled in a shining confusion down the length of her back. For a good thirty seconds she remained as she was, poised at the edge of the roof, eyes raised, scrutinizing the spot where the monkey had disappeared. In the excitement she seemed to have forgotten all about me. But now, as she lowered her gaze, we unexpectedly found ourselves just a few feet apart and looking straight into each others' eyes.

Never had we been this close. Never this unguarded. Her lips were slightly parted, cheeks flushed. I instinctively bent forward and inhaled the air between us; it was saturated with the smell of her—an indescribably foreign, carnal perfume. I wanted desperately to do something—anything to keep this moment from slipping away. I wanted to reach out through the bars for her hand. I wanted to plead with her to run away with me, to flee to Kashmir. No, to *America*, where her husband would never find us.

She lowered the stick, without once taking her eyes from mine. As she did this, I leaned closer and brought my hands up and circled the bars with my fingers and clung to them.

Even as I struggled to find some way to hold on to the promise of those fleeting seconds, she was already letting go, backing off, forcing me to exchange my fantasies for her own flawlessly innocent smile, the artless, bashful smile of a teenage girl, a young Hindu bride. Now a thousand times more desirable and more impossibly distant than ever before, she pulled the sari up over her head—that familiar gesture—and turned brusquely away. She began collecting the laundry, seeing to it that everything was sorted and hung on the line.

I waited for her to look back. I don't know how long I stood frozen like that before it dawned on me just how ridiculous I would in fact appear should she chance to look over and see me still there, clutching at the bars like some forlorn prisoner, all puffed up with myriad implausible cravings that—if gratified—would have brought ruin upon us both. Immediately I released my grip and dropped into the chair and pretended to straighten the books and papers on my desk. When finally I dared to look up again, she was gone.

> Thus does a lover deceive himself.
> He judges her feelings by the measure
> of his own rank desire.

* * *

That night I dreamed once again that I was on the Super Fast, plunging through the monsoon darkness of rural Punjab. I saw myself propped forward over my canvas bag, poised somewhere between sleep and waking, knees pressed against the barrier that separated me from the driver, who in his turban and soiled shirt, monstrous, sat gripping the wheel. Over his shoulder I could see the pavement rushing by under a glare of headlights. Silhouetted people and animals sprung up out of nowhere and vanished again like spirits fleeing the light.

This time I knew what was coming: I was waiting for a boy to appear out of nowhere and to die. What I did not know—and what I struggled to understand as I lay in bed, asleep—was *where* the accident would take place. Would it happen in a dream or in waking life? The border between the two worlds had inexplicably ruptured, and somehow my uncertainty about the past had insinuated itself into this dream as an uncertainty about the future. Memory and imagination had fused.

What I was feeling was, in a way, the same odd sense of detachment from my own experience that was so familiar to me in my dreaming life, as in my meditation practice. But now there was something new in the mix, for my confusion meant that I realized in some inchoate fashion that things were not as they appeared.

30

IN EARLY MARCH, I received a letter from Abe Sellars, my advisor at Chicago. He wanted to know how my research for the dissertation was going. He wanted to know when I planned on returning. What he really wanted to know, I suspect, was exactly why he had consented to write me a reference for the Fulbright in the first place. After the party in New Delhi, Frank Davis had no doubt informed him about my decision to abandon the proposal for which I was awarded the money I'd been living on for almost two years now. In that time, I hadn't written Sellars even once. I couldn't face his disapproval. He had an international reputation as an Indologist, but what he truly excelled at was withholding approval. I don't think I ever expressed an idea that (according to him) he hadn't already considered. I remember going into his office one day just after finishing *Eros and Civilization*. I was on fire with Marcuse's mesmerizing hybrid of Freud and Marx, literally vibrating with excitement. Sellars was chairman of the department at the time: a very busy man. He endured my babbling for several minutes, until I sort of wound down in the face of his monumental silence, after which he commented, "I went through my Marcuse period in prep school."

Maybe in his mind this sort of thing was intended to goad people into doing their best work. I honestly have no clue. But the effect it had on me was totally demoralizing. One of the best things about living in India was that it was pretty much as far away from him as I could get. His letter unearthed a landfill of repressed insecurities, all the old conflicting emotions I still nurtured about power academics.

Meanwhile, at Sanskrit University, things were not going well. This was particularly unfortunate because I needed to hold on to my research visa in order to remain in India, and since bailing on the program at BHU, the visa was now tied to my study of Tibetan across town. The problem was that the Tibetan class at Sanskrit University was a farce. My classmates—

all five of them—were noncommissioned officers in the Indian army. Ever since the Sino-Indian border dispute, Nehru, and after him Gandhi, had made it a point to keep a division of soldiers patrolling the Aksai Chin, where Tibetan is the native language. Ostensibly enrolled at Sanskrit University to learn Tibetan, the real incentive of my classmates was money. They apparently received a sizeable bonus simply for agreeing to study this strategically valuable language. It seems to me it might have been wiser for the payoff to be contingent on their actually achieving an acceptable level of proficiency. As it was, they didn't give a shit if they learned a word of Tibetan. They didn't even come to class.

So it boiled down to just me and the teacher, Tsewang, a young Nepali who had been hired specifically for this job. He had no previous experience teaching Tibetan and was profoundly uncomfortable in his new role. Twice a week he and I sat together conversing in Hindi about whatever crossed his mind. Most of our conversations ended up being about life in the US. I couldn't even get him to speak Tibetan. Since I needed the visa, I really had no choice but to more or less acquiesce in the situation. To make matters worse, I felt a genuine affection for Tsewang, so I didn't dare complain to anyone about his incompetency. I met his wife once, after class—a slight, timid girl dressed in a *chuba* robe and colorfully striped apron, cradling their infant son in her arms. The last thing I wanted was for him to lose his job.

Nevertheless, I plugged away, trying to learn Tibetan on my own. At the Motilal Banarsidass store near Chowk, I found a beat-up edition of Roerich's old *Textbook of Colloquial Tibetan*. This and Jäschke's *Tibetan-English Dictionary*, originally published in 1881, were pretty much the only tools available at the time. I was deeply enmeshed in reading the Indian Buddhist texts in the original Sanskrit, but most of them had long since been lost. Access to this literature was possible only through Tibetan translations made centuries earlier. I needed to learn the language, and to do that I needed someone who, at the very least, would consent to answer my questions. I knew there was a Tibetan temple in Sarnath, so I decided to take the bus out there and look around.

In 1977 there could not have been more than a few dozen lamas living in Sarnath, all of them housed in a series of concrete cells built along the southern periphery of the compound surrounding the Gelukpa temple. Two plump concrete snow lions greeted me, one on either side of the gateway into the courtyard. They sat on their haunches, teeth bared, forepaws resting on what looked very much like two plastic beach balls. Walking through that gate I was suddenly back in Manali; even here, in the plains, I felt the peculiar sense of entering a "hidden world." I was greeted by a young monk. Speaking in Hindi, I briefly explained who I was and why I had come. He listened politely then motioned for me to follow him up to the second floor of the residence hall.

It was still early in the day, but the March air was already hot, and I felt the first hint of perspiration on my stomach and chest as I climbed the stairs. At the top we entered a veranda and passed a succession of rooms, finally stopping in front of an open doorway hung with a set of white curtains that blocked our view. An "endless knot" of interlocking orange and red ran around the edges of each panel. From inside came the rich, spicy-sweet smell of Tibetan incense. My guide disappeared through the curtains for a few minutes and then returned.

"Geshe Sherap will speak with you," he whispered in Hindi, holding the curtains aside.

I thanked him and stepped through.

It took a moment for my eyes to adjust to the relative darkness of the interior. A large tangka hung on the wall directly in front of where I stood. The image depicted a blood-red buddha with thin, serpentine eyes and wearing a crown set with jewels. In his lap, embracing his waist with her legs, sat a white naked female. Her arms were raised in the air, elbows bent, her head held in profile and tilted provocatively to one side, electric blue hair falling down over her shoulders. Rainbows undulated from the couple, fanning out into a background of open sky dotted with stylized wisps of cloud. Below the tangka, on a small table, someone had arranged a series of silver bowls filled with water. In front of them were a brass bell and dorje.

"*Aaiyay. Baitiyay.*"

The deep voice emerged out of silence like the throaty rush of air from a baritone sax. I turned and saw a big man sitting just to the left of the table, on a chowki platform covered with a thick wool carpet emblazoned with woven patterns of leaves and flowers. The man had his legs and feet drawn up under his robes. Above his waist he was wearing only a sleeveless yellow singlet. He had broad, muscular shoulders and arms. In front of him lay the leaves of a text he had obviously been reading before being interrupted.

"I am Dorje Sherap," he said, somewhat perfunctorily, in Hindi. "Please, sit down." He gestured toward a nearby chair—the only other piece of furniture in the room.

My host was a middle-aged Tibetan with luxuriant silver brows and stern eyes. A scar ran diagonally across one cheek, beginning just below the left eye and continuing to the angular hinge of his jaw. It looked like it had been made by a sharp blade in a single swift stroke. On the floor next to where he sat, a tiny kitten pounced and leapt, tossing itself into the air like a piece of downy fluff. The little cat was tethered at one end of a fine golden chain looped, at the opposite end, around one leg of the chowki. I remembered this kitten several months later, when I first heard the story of Gampopa and Milarepa, intended to illustrate the danger of becoming attached to Buddhist teachings. "If fettered," Milarepa had once cautioned his disciple, "one may as well be bound by an iron chain as a gold one, for there is no real difference."

I introduced myself and described my training at Chicago and my work with Indian pundits. I also told him, in some detail, what I had read in Sanskrit and what I hoped to read in Tibetan. I then proposed that we exchange lessons with each other: I would tutor him in English in return for instruction in Tibetan. He heard me out, then courteously declined my offer. He was fluent in Hindi and this, in his view, was sufficient for his purposes here in India. As it turned out, Geshe Sherap was a celebrated professor with extensive administrative responsibilities; he had neither time nor inclination for such an arrangement. He had been recruited to help create the institute's new library and already had plans to return to Drepung Monastery, in South India, when his work in Sarnath was complete. Nevertheless, I seem to have provoked his interest, for he questioned me about the details of my studies. As it happened, I had only recently begun reading, in English translation, *The Perfection of Wisdom in Eight Thousand Lines* and was totally absorbed in the text. I mentioned this and was about to go on when the geshe interrupted me midsentence.

"*Nortul* . . ." He pronounced the Tibetan name warmly but with dismay, as if he were greeting an old friend who had unexpectedly appeared at the door. I remember that I actually glanced over my shoulder, expecting to see someone standing there. But we were alone.

After a long silence he spoke again, this time to me. "There is . . . a Nyingmapa lama . . ."

"Yes?" I waited.

"I think he might be interested in your proposal."

I felt myself becoming excited. "This lama lives here, in the monastery?"

"Oh no. He is in Delhi."

"In Delhi?"

"You would need to go there to meet him. Of course I cannot say for certain that he would accept."

I was about to object—*What good is a teacher in Delhi when I live in Banaras?*—but Dorje Sherap was obviously not concerned about this relatively minor inconvenience. He appeared to be preoccupied with some other, more pressing concern.

"Yes," he said, almost as if he were talking to himself. "I think he might be interested. But it is curious . . ."

"What?"

He frowned. "That you should come here now, at this particular moment—just when I have once again found him. After all these years."

"But why curious?" I repeated the same Hindi word he had himself used: *ajib*.

He did not answer. Instead, he pushed his legs off the chowki and stood up. "Excuse me." He walked briskly out the door and returned with a china cup. He cleared a spot on the table and set it down next to his own, then lifted a massive thermos from the floor and filled them both with what looked like chai. "Please." He indicated the new cup. "It is Tibetan tea." He watched me closely, smiling in anticipation.

I thanked him, picked it and took a sip. The liquid was hot and salty, with a slight oily flavor. My face must have betrayed, in that first moment, some hint of discomfort.

"Have you tasted this tea before?"

I swallowed and shook my head. "No . . ."

"How do you find it?"

"It's . . ." I searched for the appropriate words. "It tastes like soup. Like some kind of buttery soup."

He laughed out loud with delight. "Yes. Think of it, then, as soup! Forget all about tea and it will taste better. Everything depends on how you think. Isn't it so?"

This time it was me who smiled. "It's good," I said, reassuringly. "I like it." I took another sip.

"Very well." He settled back down on the chowki, rearranging the robes around his legs. "Now, let me tell you about Nortul Rinpoche."

"I first met this lama in Tibet—before the Chinese. This was my final year as a student. I was living then in Lhasa, training at Drepung Monastery. But I had gone on pilgrimage to Samye Monastery. You know Samye?"

I nodded. I knew that the monastery at Samye was revered as Tibet's most ancient center of learning. Almost a thousand years ago it had been the central clearinghouse for Buddhist teachings streaming in from India, a place where the early translation teams had worked to recast the Sanskrit texts into a form of Tibetan that had been constructed for this purpose.

"At the time of my visit," he continued, his Hindi marked by a distinctly Tibetan accent, "Nortul Rinpoche was also there on a pilgrimage. He had walked to Samye from his monastery in eastern Tibet in order to do a retreat at Chim Puk—a meditation cave not far from the monastery. He had been in the cave for several months, I think. But the very day I arrived, he finished his retreat and came to the monastery for a brief stay."

Dorje Sherap went on to tell me how, in that first chance meeting, the two men passed four or five days in each other's company, engrossed the entire time in conversations that clearly left a strong impression on him. Back in Lhasa he had puzzled over the memory of this unusual Nyingmapa lama. Here was an old man from an unknown, provincial monastery—somewhere out in the boondocks of Kham—who was deeply conversant in a genre of literature rarely studied but held in the highest esteem among the intellectual elite at Drepung.

"I had never before encountered such unpretentious erudition. He is a great scholar, with a remarkable knowledge of Indian Mahayana doctrines. But he is especially interested in *sherchin*—you know? What is the Sanskrit?"

"Prajnaparamita?"

"Yes, yes," he nodded. "That is it. What you are yourself now reading. These texts, they are very important for his practice.

"When we parted at Samye," he continued, "there was no reason to expect we would ever see each other again."

And they wouldn't have if not for the violent upheaval of 1959 when the Chinese army clamped down on Tibet.

"I remember everything." The geshe pressed his lips together. "Everything. From the moment the Chinese army first entered Lhasa. We had just finished morning puja when we heard, from the streets below, the faraway sound of canons and guns. Shortly after this some laypeople came to the monastery and told us that the Chinese were killing monks—that we should all leave Lhasa immediately. I and some of the other senior students went to the abbot. He told us we should do as they said and go quickly into the country. There was no time to prepare. I left with ten others, in a small group. We assumed that the fighting would be over in a few days, and that we would then return to our old life. I took with me only one thing—a copy of Tsongkhapa's *Lamrim Chenpo*—a text I was studying at the time. I still have it. It is all I have from Tibet.

"When we reached the first village, the people told us that the Chinese had already been there and they might return at any time. It was not safe. They told us we should go farther into the mountains. So we went on walking. And everywhere we went people told us, 'Do not stop.' Still, two old lamas were with us—one of them my teacher—and they were unable to continue. I did not want to leave them behind, but my teacher insisted. He would not allow us to stay with him. We left him and the other lama with a family of nomads who were camped high in the mountains. They gave us some tsampa and balep to carry with us to eat, and we continued on to India. By this time we were only a few days from the border, but the crossing was not easy. The pass was very high. Snow was falling. We slept huddled together at night, changing positions frequently so that some of us could be in among the others for warmth."

Dorje Sherab and Nortul met for the second time in a refugee camp set up by Nehru's government to accommodate the influx of Tibetans streaming across the border at Misamari, near Tezpur in the North Indian state of Assam. Here the two men were thrown together again under circumstances quite different from the tranquil security of Samye. This time their paths crossed in a place that still conjures up nightmarish memories among the generation of Tibetans who were forced to flee from the Chinese. Thousands of them were marooned there in the jungle, oppressed by the low altitude and monsoon heat, by the swarms of malarial mosquitoes. Fetid water and lack of adequate latrine facilities contributed to an epidemic of hepatitis among the displaced men, women, and children who camped there waiting to be redistributed. It was a time of sickness, of uncertainty and apprehension, a time of endless waiting.

"When we arrived in Tezpur, I was taken to a large tent with bunks, and there he was: Nortul! He had walked all alone from Kham. Of course, I was very surprised to see him again. It was in the camp where I learned what little English I know. Nortul and I studied the language with an old British lady. We were there together for over a month before I was transferred to a settlement in South India."

Once again he and Nortul parted ways. And that would certainly have been the end of it, if not for one further, very recent development.

It was obvious from what Dorje Sherap told me that since arriving in India, he had established a reputation as an eminent scholar. When plans took shape for the founding of a new Drepung Loseling Monastery in Karnataka State, he had been among an elite core of intellectuals recruited by the Dalai Lama to help. The previous fall—just about the time I moved to Banaras—he had been sent north as an emissary of the abbot of Drepung to assist with the creation of the Institute for Higher Tibetan Studies in Sarnath. In this official capacity he had traveled to the Indian capital only a few weeks before we talked. The purpose of his visit was to confer with librarians at Delhi University regarding several crates of Tibetan texts that had been in storage there since the time of the Sino-Indian border conflict in 1962. The university had no use for such materials, and arrangements were underway to have them donated to the Institute in Sarnath. The boxes had lain neglected for all these years in a storage facility, uncatalogued and, in point of fact, unopened. Or at least this was what the geshe had been told by his abbot. But when he actually arrived at the university library in Delhi, he was startled to hear that someone else had apparently gotten there before him.

"I knew nothing about this," Dorje Sherap exclaimed. "Nothing at all. The arrangements certainly had not come through our office at Drepung."

The director of the library told him that only a few weeks before, an old lama had appeared at the library one afternoon and produced an official letter of introduction signed by someone at the Ministry of Home Affairs authorizing the bearer to inspect the contents of the crates from Ladakh before they were released for shipment to Sarnath.

According to what the librarian told Geshe Sherap, since his arrival the mysterious lama had apparently been working nonstop. Every morning when they came to open the building, people from the library staff found him waiting outside the door, an enormous flowered thermos of chai suspended from one shoulder by a plastic strap; every evening at closing he was escorted out. Or rather, this had been his schedule prior to when he had somehow managed to get himself locked in for the night. One evening the peon assigned to the task of fetching the lama had apparently neglected to do so. No one realized this mistake until the next morning. When the lama didn't show up at his usual post outside the main entrance to the library, the director went to check and found him in the basement, still sitting at the table where he worked, brooding over a stack of long, narrow woodblock prints. The most astonishing part, however, was not simply that this enigmatic Tibetan monk had been at it for almost twenty-four hours without any break but that he appeared to be completely unaware of how much time had passed. He thought that the library was only then closing for the night.

This story made the rounds, and the monk's assiduousness won him the affection and respect of the library staff. After that incident, he was permitted to remain overnight now and again at the discretion of the director.

Naturally enough, Dorje Sherap was curious to make the acquaintance of any scholar so diligent as this. He was escorted down into the storage facilities, where he saw a squat man in shabby robes that had obviously been restitched and repaired countless times over the years. The old fellow was at that very moment working away with a pry bar, laboring to open yet another crate, but when the two men entered he looked up from his work. Imagine the learned geshe's surprise when he recognized the same Nyingmapa lama he had first met at Samye almost two decades before. Geshe Sherap made a point of telling me that he had himself immediately recognized Nortul, whose appearance and demeanor had not changed in the slightest over the intervening years.

"I will never forget this lama," the geshe said with conviction, as he leaned forward to offer me more chai. "He is a very intelligent man."

He finished pouring and paused, as if weighing how best to continue. And then, for no apparent reason, he abruptly switched from Hindi to heavily accented English. "But you must understand . . ." Still bent over my full cup, the thermos held aloft, he looked me square in the eye and lowered his voice. "Nortul Rinpoche is *eunuch*."

I stared at Dorje Sherap, who returned my blank look with a portentous widening of his own eyes.

The smell of *tukpa* wafted up through the bars of his open window. Lunch was being prepared in the courtyard. From the temple nearby I heard the monotonous drone of chanting, the clear ring of a bell used in tantric rituals.

For God's sake, I remember thinking, *why is the man telling me this?* The sudden shift out of Hindi had taken me by surprise. But this business about Nortul Rinpoche being a eunuch was something else altogether. I was aware of such practices in China, where beginning around the eighth century, emperors retained castrated slaves as guards in their harems. This had apparently continued up until the end of the Ching dynasty in 1912. In fact, I had read somewhere that as late as 1960, there were still a small number of Ching eunuchs living in Beijing. And then, of course, there are the Hijra in India, who undergo ritual castration in an operation called—bizarrely—*nirvan*, the Hindi for nirvana. But I had no idea until this moment that the custom played any part in Tibetan culture.

"You mean . . ." I, too, switched to English now, and the words felt weirdly intimate. I waved two fingers more or less in the direction of my balls and snipped them open and shut, like scissors.

He raised one eyebrow a bit, contemplating the significance of my gesture. After a second or two he repeated exactly what he had just said, this time shaping the English syllables with extreme care, in an obvious effort to drive his point home. "Nortul Rinpoche is *eunuch*." As before, he laid considerable stress on the last word. His tone was decidedly ominous. "I want only warn you."

He tipped the thermos upright, shoved in the plastic cork, and drove it home with a swift thump from the heal of his palm. Once secure, it was replaced on the table.

I let my hand drop to my lap in astonishment. "Warn me?"

"Yes," he replied. "This lama, he like play funny trick sometime."

"What kind of funny trick?" I hadn't the slightest idea what he was talking about.

"*Drupnyen* kind of trick. You know?" He studied my face, perhaps trying to determine if I grasped his meaning, which I did not. "Is many years alone in cave." He folded both hands in his lap, one palm on top of the other, and sat up straight, back rigid, as if meditating. "Big yogi power." His jaw hung slack, eyes wide open and staring blankly out into space, as if he were gazing right through the wall. The effect was disturbing.

I nodded dumbly, unable to imagine any other response.

"*Eunuch*, yes. No doubt. But good scholar. Very good scholar. And in Delhi he tell me very interest in learn English. He speak more English . . ." He hesitated, apparently unable to find the right expression. "Uh, more English . . ."

"More English *than you?*" I interjected.

"Yes, yes," he nodded vigorously. "More *than you.* Rinpoche speak English good, but still he very interest learn more. You go Delhi and see him. I give you letter."

He reached over and picked up a pen and paper from the table and set down a short note in Tibetan introducing me to Nortul Rinpoche, which he folded carefully and thrust into my hand, gently pressing my fingers closed around it.

31

Holi, the great Indian festival of renewal, is celebrated every year on the vernal equinox in March. It is one of the archetypal "spring fertility rites" documented, most famously, by Sir James Frazer. In Europe, as Christianity supplanted earlier pagan cultures, the cruder elements of the old symbolism were displaced by the Easter story of Jesus's death and resurrection; nowadays all that remains in the West of that long-forgotten past are bunnies and colored eggs. In India, though, Holi still proudly bears the marks of its prehistoric origin in a complex of rituals invoking blood, sex, and death. It is a day where normal social hierarchies are turned on their head, a day, I was told, when caste and gender discrimination is overturned and people are free to meet as equals and friends.

I had first experienced Holi the previous spring, when I was living in the rented room in New Delhi. Mahmud urged me to go to the old city, where—according to him—the holiday was celebrated in proper style. "In my neighborhood," he boasted, smiling broadly, "on the day of Holi the women *beat* the men."

"But why would they do that?" I objected. Without waiting for his answer I continued, "And anyway, it's not a Muslim holiday." In a seminar on Hindu festivals at Chicago, we had read an article explaining that Holi is associated with the worship of the Hindu god Krishna.

"Go there and see for yourself," was his laconic response.

So I did. Just after sunrise on the morning of Holi, I caught an auto rickshaw to Old Delhi.

I had the driver take me around behind Jamma Masjid and drop me off at the entrance to one of the many narrow alleyways that wound their way deep into the bowels of the neighborhood near Chandni Chowk. Normally, even this early in the day, there would have been people everywhere, but on this particular morning—the morning of Holi—the streets were uncannily quiet. I set off, somewhat apprehensively, into the labyrinth. I had been walking for maybe three minutes when, no more than a hundred feet ahead, four women rounded a corner. They were dressed in salwar kameez and carrying knotted ropes. One of them immediately spotted me. I saw her stop short and grab the arm of the woman next to her, pointing in my direction. And then they were running toward me, cackling hysterically and twirling the ropes over their heads like rodeo cowgirls. I had no idea what I was supposed to do, so I stood there smiling stupidly in anticipation of an interesting cross-cultural experience.

Within seconds the women surrounded me and lashed out with their ropes. I ducked low and threw up my arms in an effort to protect my head and face. The coarsely woven hemp fell hard across my thin cotton shirt, the knots biting painfully into my flesh. It was like having BB guns fired point-blank against my exposed back. I involuntarily cried out—playfully, at first, but very soon in dead earnest—for them to stop. In response to my protests, the four women closed ranks, forming a tight circle with me at the center, all of us revolving around in some mad contra dance as I dodged and shuffled to avoid the stinging blows. At last I shoved them aside, pushing my way violently through the ring, and sprinted back in the direction I'd come. I made it to the open street and kept running, without looking back. At the taxi stand across from the Red Fort I caught a motor rickshaw back to New Delhi. For a good week afterward my flesh was ornamented with ugly, red welts, souvenirs of my first Holi.

Now, in Banaras, I received repeated assurances that ritual beatings were *not* part of the celebration. Quite the contrary. Everyone told me that the women of the holy city did not dare to go out in public on the morning of Holi; the streets were too dangerous for any female of marriageable age.

In the weeks leading up to the festival in Banaras, I watched with interest as massive piles of combustible materials accumulated in the center of every major intersection in the city. Scraps of lumber and the splintered limbs of saplings were heaped up along with broken furniture, old tires, and various other detritus—anything vaguely flammable was tossed on.

Every child in the city was anxious to tell me the story of Holika, the evil daughter of King Hiranyakashyap, how she had accidentally cremated herself in the attempt to murder her husband. Some people said that her effigy would be fixed atop the fire on the eve of Holi. Others insisted that it was not Holika but Putana who would be sacrificed to the flames. Putana was a witch who had tried to kill the baby Krishna by offering him her breast filled with poison milk; the divine infant had sucked her dry, and the elated villagers burned her carcass. There were other stories as well, all sorts of fanciful tales about villains and hubristic demigods. No one seemed to really care that the various accounts didn't match up. The point was simply that there would be bonfires all over the city and crowds of people watching as *someone* went up in flames.

As Banaras prepared for Holi, All India Radio blared from every chai shop, the voices full of nothing but the coming election and how it would bring an end to Indira's Emergency. And then, in mid-March, we heard that two shots had been fired at Sanjay Gandhi's jeep. He was campaigning somewhere in the rural areas north of Delhi when the attack took place, and despite his entourage of guards, the shooter somehow managed to escape. Surprisingly, everyone I talked with was convinced that this apparent assassination attempt had been staged by Indira herself in order to gain sympathy for her favorite son. If so, then the plot failed miserably; people now seemed to hate the man even more than they had before.

One afternoon, riding my bicycle through the busy intersection at Belapur, I noticed that a rustic human scarecrow had been fastened upright atop the mountainous pile of accumulated combustibles. Affixed to its face was a plastic mask with Sanjay's trademark bushy sideburns and square black glasses. There he perched, high above the snarl of traffic, a man of stuffed straw dressed in white kurta-pajama, his head tilting ineffectually to one side, arms drooping in the afternoon heat.

As the holiday grew near, vendors multiplied everywhere along the edges of the city's streets. Rows of enterprising men, women, and children squatted behind precise, conical piles of brightly colored powders and an array of esoteric Holi paraphernalia. The most popular item appeared to be the *pichkari*—a type of giant syringe capable of propelling streams of liquid dye some ten or twenty feet through the air. Local sweet shops displayed racks of gujia, mathri, and other Holi delicacies. Thandai, the special Holi drink, a kind of marijuana milkshake, was readily available at the bhang shops in Godowlia crossing and also at most of the city's myriad chai stalls. Whipped up with little paddles twirled between two flat palms, thandai was obviously going to serve as the launching pad for all the mayhem to follow.

Clearly, this was going to be a major deal.

* * *

As promised, on the eve of Holi the mounds of debris at every intersection were soaked in gasoline and torched, the thandai flowed freely, and
all hell broke loose in the Forest of Bliss. The revelry continued unabated
through the night; by next morning when I finished breakfast, a significant percentage of the city's population appeared to have gone genuinely
insane. Given my experience in Delhi, I decided that it would be in my
best interest to observe the festivities from the relatively safe confines of
my second-story room. As I watched through the window, men and gangs
of prepubescent children galloped through the street below, untamed and
howling with glee. They assaulted each other with pichkaris and handfuls
of powder that erupted, filling the air with dense clouds of aquamarine,
chartreuse, and indigo.

I spent the first half of the morning trying to read Sanskrit, while just
next door the entire female wing of the Bengali family was on the rooftop
upending buckets of tinted water onto anyone unlucky enough to pass
below. My girlfriend was out there with the rest of them having the time
of her life. Since the recent business with the monkeys our relationship
had cooled down, but I still nurtured a terrible crush. She seemed particularly gorgeous as she threw herself unselfconsciously into their games.
It was impossible not to watch. I finally gave up trying to work and went
outside on my veranda to get a better view.

A raucous crowd of drunken BHU students was at that very moment
marching up the street in our direction from Assi Ghat. Above their heads
towered a colossal papier-mâché model of an erect phallus next to a sign-
board depicting Indira Gandhi having anal sex with Morarji Desai, the
Janata Party's candidate for prime minister. He was an eighty-year-old
best known for consuming a glass of his own urine every day during the
months of his imprisonment—apparently it was some kind of Ayurvedic
regimen. The artist had done a remarkably good job. Indira was por-
trayed bent over with her sari hiked up around her waist exposing a huge
ass, amply suited to the formidable dimensions of Morarji's penis. As
the disorderly throng of students moved within range, torrents of color
spilled forth from above. The mob scattered in every direction, cursing
and shaking their fists at my neighbors, who were shrieking in delight. At
that moment a clump of cow shit flew up from below and struck the wall
behind me with a loud slap.

"*Aray, bhosadi-wala, zara gobar khaa lo!*"

It was Mickey.

"Eat shit," he bellowed in Hindi, "you lover of large cunts!"

I hardly recognized him at first. The women had obviously scored a direct hit, and he was completely drenched. The colors blended in a mélange of fantastic streaks that streamed through his hair and down over his face. His clothes were awash in the same riotous palate. He looked like some bizarre hallucination rising out of the jungles of Vietnam, a soldier in psychedelic camouflage.

"Stan!" he bellowed. "Come on down, *bhaiya*! You're missing all the fun!"

I shook my head, slowly and unequivocally. From somewhere off to my left another ball of cow shit flew up out of the crowd, traversing the air in a wide arc. I ducked and it soared over my shoulder and straight into my room, where it landed with a wet *plop* on the floor beside my bed. I scrambled inside and slammed shut the veranda door.

I was on my hands and knees wiping up the mess when what sounded like a herd of buffalo came thundering up the stairs. Before I could get to my feet, the door burst open and in reeled Mick, followed by three of his greasy friends, all of them obviously stoned off their respective asses.

"You are *not* staying in your room today, Stan. It's Holi! Look what I've got." He dipped a hand into his pocket and pulled out several pellets of bhang. "Medicine for the doctor."

I sat back on my heels, the rag still clasped in one hand. "No way."

"It'll loosen you up. Get you in the holiday spirit, you know?"

Against my continuing protests he went over to the clay jug where I kept my drinking water, pulled a cup off the shelf and filled it. Meanwhile, his friends were surveying the contents of my room, presumably checking it out for any interesting foreign valuables I might have left in view. One of them I recognized. He was a regular at the Kerala Café in Belapur, where I had often seen him stuffed into a booth with six or seven of his friends, all of them talking and laughing ostentatiously. Our eyes met and he joined his palms, greeting me a big, paan-stained smile.

"Okay, here you go." Mick stood before me, the glass of water in one hand, a chunk of bhang the size of a marble in the other. I was kneeling in front of him like a supplicant. "If you don't take your medicine, you'll never get well."

I looked up at him. His hair was plastered against his head, streaks of blue and green water ran down his face and neck. To our left, on the desk, Vaidya's edition of the *Prajnaparamita* lay open where I had left it next to my notes. Outside a rowdy cheer erupted from the rooftop next door as the family let loose with another deluge. In my peripheral vision I could see my neighbor leaning out over the railing, a plastic bucket held upside down in her hands. Her sari was soaking wet, clinging to the curves of her body like a second skin. I reached out and took the bhang from Mick. He handed me the glass of water, and I tossed it back. This elicited a boisterous applause from my guests, who threw their arms aloft and commenced gyrating around my room, obscenely swiveling and pumping their hips, performing a dance called, in Punjabi, the *bhangra*.

"*Chaliyay*," Mick said, gripping my arm and escorting me toward the door. "Let us go down into the world of mortals and see how they amuse themselves!"

Within half an hour I was toast. What remains of the morning and most of the afternoon is a hazy, dissociated pastiche of dreamlike visions. I see the white clown dashing through the streets pursued by hoards of screaming children, all of them engulfed in a multihued fog. Cows cruise by us like tie-dyed battleships. High above, a giant, translucent monkey dances gleefully along the wires brandishing a pichkari from which pours a luminescent stream of orange flame. Everywhere people are laughing and shouting. An elephant paddles through the crowd, ears flapping like canvas wings, legs pumping in slow motion. His flanks are draped in scarlet bunting, his tail adorned with golden streamers. He is floating like the Goodyear blimp, inches above the surface of the street. A skeletal musician plucks at the single string of his instrument, singing of his devotion to a God without name or form. One long, angular tooth thrusts upward from the ridge of his gum. The man's clothes are dirty and torn, his hair flies in oily strings as he twirls round and round. Nearby someone hammers at a drum, pounding out a frantic, syncopated rhythm. The singer's voice is mesmerizing, the beating of the drum erotic and irresistible. The white clown is dancing. We are all dancing. Beggars and holy men, shopkeepers and tattered children, monkeys and goats and water buffalo, the living and the dead, the righteous and the damned—we are all of us dancing together in this glorious, twisted, heartbreaking carnival of love.

By early afternoon the various magic potions were beginning to wear off. People blearily made their way home through painted streets. They would bathe and change clothes and go out, once again, this time to visit with friends and enjoy the rest of the holiday with chai and sweets that the women had spent the last several days preparing. I had long since lost track of Mick. It occurred to me that I was ravenous. I caught a rickshaw to the Sindhi, which was closed, so I made do with half a dozen samosas purchased from a peddler. Hunger sated, I returned to Assi and my room. There I cleaned up and flopped down on my bed, exhausted.

I must have fallen asleep, and when I awoke it was twilight, that mysterious time out of time when the world drifts, rudderless, between day and night. The streets outside were quiet. I lay on my back and looked around the room. The books stood side by side on the shelves, desk and chair in front of the window. I sat up, turned, and slid my legs off the bed and pushed my feet hard against the surface of the floor, feeling the smooth tiles press against my calloused soles. I stood up and stretched, then took a couple steps over to the almari and pulled out the kerosene stove for chai. But where are the matches? I went over to the desk and sat down and looked halfheartedly for them near the little Garuda incense holder. Things were still a bit fuzzy around the edges. It would take another twelve hours or so for the effects of the bhang to totally wear off.

Just outside my window a lone rhesus monkey rested on the narrow ledge that ran along the perimeter of my neighbors' rooftop. A large splotch of purple dye covered his back. I recognized him from the jagged scar on his forehead; it was the same big male that often paused here for a moment, at this hour, before continuing his rounds through the city. He sat hunched over like a yogi, his limbs drawn close, staring blankly off into the distance, absorbed in solitary rumination. He had not yet noticed me. Every now and then he raised a hand and idly picked at his scabrous belly. His head was a scrawny ball bristling with sparse tufts of red hair. The sagging flesh of his ears appeared distressingly human, as did his sorrowful pink face. I had seen this same face more than once, back in Chicago, among the winos who sat nodding on the benches in Jackson Park. My visitor gazed out at the world through restless, pensive eyes, as though a single piece had somehow been removed from the puzzle of life and this one omission had cast the whole affair into disarray. He seemed to be on the verge of an insight, a crucial revelation that would change everything. The line between us was razor thin, and he was poised to cross.

We sat so close to each other that I could see the muscles twitch under one eye where a fly probed its moist edge. Carefully, so as not to startle him, I reached behind me to the bed and retrieved a small paper bag containing the remains of some Holi sweets I had carried back with me. I took out the last small square of pista barfi and placed it gently between two bars. As I withdrew my hand, the monkey's eyes darted around and stopped cold, riveted with burning intensity on my offering. He looked quickly back and forth between the delicacy and me, sizing up the risk, then pitched forward across the open space and snatched it up in a one swift motion that had him instantly back again on the ledge. His spindly fingers picked furiously at the prize, skillfully breaking off one crumb after another and tossing them up between whiskered lips. Very soon it was gone and he looked hopefully at the spot between us.

Now I raised my hands and laid them palms up on the desk to show my guest that there was no more but also to make it clear that I had no weapon. As I did so, I found myself seized with compassion for this half-starved, injured being. On this holiday, this celebration of love, I desperately wanted to make some kind of genuine contact with this sad, fuzzy old man whose path across the rooftops of Banaras had inexplicably intersected with my own. I sat looking at him, my empty hands stretched out over the desk, while he continued to scrutinize the ledge where the barfi had been. After a few seconds the monkey lifted his eyes and locked them on mine with a tense, penetrating stare. I had the eerie sensation that the lost piece was about to fall into place. I was certain that I saw, in his eyes, a hint of recognition, a possibility that I appeared as familiar to him as he did to me. Are we not evolutionary brothers? *He must realize this*, I thought. I remained absolutely still, holding his gaze with infinite tenderness, my hands relaxed and welcoming.

All at once the glimmer in his eyes ignited and blazed across his face. With a savage hiss the monkey flung his body directly toward where I sat and struck the bars with the full force of his weight, gripping them tightly with all four hands, digging his frightful black nails into the iron. The ferocity of his charge literally propelled me backward out of the chair. My legs caught under the desk; I tripped and fell, and then laid there sprawled on the floor, frozen in horror while the livid animal bared his teeth and— still clutching the bars—heaved his body against them, again and again, as if to wrench them free with the sheer enormity of his rage.

And then it was over. He sprang back across the alley and bounded along the wall, leapt to the power lines and onto a veranda across the street, disappearing over the rooftops that spread out against the dusk and the last vestiges of smoke from the Holi fires. He was gone.

After several minutes I pulled myself up, leaning on the desk to get my balance. My hip throbbed where it had slammed against the floor. I stood and looked out in the direction the monkey had gone. Finally, I picked up the chair and returned it to its place, then found the matches, limped over, and lit the stove. When the chai was ready I took it to my bed and crouched there with my back to the wall. The ceiling fan turned slowly, its breath brushing against my damp skin. It was dark now, and through the open window, I could already see the garland of the Milky Way, billions of stars slung in a low arc over the black water of the Ganges.

32

I'M ON THE SUPER FAST again. High beams reach out into the darkness like hands clawing their way over hot asphalt, opening a narrow tunnel of light through which the bus pitches forward. This time I know for certain that things are not as they appear. It's nothing but a trick of the mind: I have dreamed this dream before.

Has he already died? I lift one hand and feel my lip. No blood. It hasn't happened yet. To my left, just outside the window, a light flashes in the huge rearview mirror, and a jolt of fear rockets up my spine. I shiver and turn away, averting my eyes from the glare. Something's not right. Where's the driver? He's not where he should be, just in front of me. Instead, two arms stretch forward out of empty space, fingers wrap around the big steering wheel. The grooves on its plastic surface are smooth to the touch and slick with sweat. The accelerator thrusts itself up against my foot with a sense of urgency.

I'm going to kill a boy.

RAAAAAANNNNNGGGG! The alarm rips through the veil and yanks me out of the dream.

Je-sus Christ.

I reach over and hit the button to shut it off, then lie there on my back watching the still blades of the ceiling fan. No electricity. It's unusually humid for March. The disturbing images from the dream are still vivid in my mind.

I'm going to kill a boy.

I push the heels of both palms hard against my eyes, rake my fingers back through my hair.

A dream. Nothing but a dream.

With great effort I drag myself upright and force my legs around, feet off the bed, pausing only a few seconds before I drop to the floor amid my library and force myself into the morning exercise routine. Fifty pushups, fifty sit-ups, fifty leg lifts. Touch the toes, stretch, run in place. My feet pump up and down, toes digging in. Calisthenics finished, I pick up the plastic bucket and towel and step through the door, pulling both panels shut behind me.

I can't shake the dream, an eerie sense of unreality clings to everything—or is it a heightened sense of reality? In the dim light from the electric bulb, the hallway feels too narrow. The curved steel handle of the bucket pushes down into the crook of my fingers, as if it were a living thing, calling for attention. A repellent odor hangs in the darkness like the smell of rotted flesh.

The dog.

I'm still dreaming.

Now I'm hunched over in the dank, triangular crawlspace below the last twist of the staircase. The dog is lying on the concrete in front of me, struggling to move. I'm pushing her with my foot; her fur bristles against my skin, stiff as wire. *This dog cannot remain in this place where I bathe and clean my dishes and take my drinking water.*

RAAAAAANNNNNGGGG! All over again the alarm rips through the veil and yanks me out of the dream. I swing my hand over and hit the button hard.

Je-sus fucking *Christ.*

My fingers remain where they fell, and I lie still for several minutes, disoriented and apprehensive, staring at the blades of the ceiling fan as they revolve slowly in the hot, dry air. Could this, too, be a dream? Cautiously, I withdraw my hand from the clock, sit up, and look around the room. The books stand side by side on the shelves like dutiful sentries. Desk and chair rest quietly at the foot of my bed, waiting to serve. I run my fingertips over the cotton sheet, touch the grain of the fabric and the knotted stitching along the hem. How would I know? I turn and slide my legs off the bed, wiggle my toes against the floor, feeling the glaze on the tiles hard against the soles of my feet.

By the time I've finished the exercise routine, my skin is sticky with sweat. I pick up the bucket and soap and towel, step cautiously through the door, and make my way down the stairs. At the faucet I pause to scrutinize its dull brassy sheen. A single drop of water clings to the spout, iridescent, then falls like a tiny jewel into the dark mouth of the drain. Everything is exactly as it is every morning. I take a breath, inhale the odor of wet stone, then exhale slowly, stoop, and place my fingertips against the cool metal of the tap.

33

PEOPLE AND PLACES fall away like dry leaves. Borders shift and fade. I have grown old now, and it is so much easier to forget, so much more difficult to distinguish truth from fiction. Memory is an abandoned mineshaft cut deep into the earth; it absorbs the narrow beam of light cast downward from above. Toss a stone over the side, and it disappears, tumbling soundlessly through space.

There are times when one is thankful not to remember. The psychologist Carl Jung wrote about islands of consciousness washed by the dark waters of forgetting. In the *Bhagavadgita*, Lord Krishna confides to Arjuna:

> I have entered into the hearts of all;
> from me come memory, knowledge,
> and forgetfulness.

All of us harbor memories we might prefer to forget. A careless deed, an indiscreet word. We know the meaning of remorse. But forgetting can never be deliberate. The blessed lapse of memory comes to us while we sleep, a thief in the night. And what is stolen will never be missed. In these matters one may justly speak of grace. The structure of reason and of history—the material out of which identity is forged—depends as much on what is consigned to the depths as on what adheres to the troubled surface of thought.

It would soon be two years since my arrival in India. When I recalled the image of Ed Rivers as he had appeared that evening in my room in Delhi, departing for the airport with his sitar and lungi, the memory elicited a kind of primal terror. I dreaded the thought of a return to my own past in Chicago. Now I was one of the foreigners who had made a home in India, one of the travelers who had ceased to travel, spirits crossed over into a land beyond time.

We survived on our accumulation of merit, profiting greatly from an international exchange rate that made us wealthy beyond our means. Or, like Richard, we lived by our wits, moving from one clever moneymaking scheme to the next. We were not Indians, nor were we tourists. We were not there to save the starving poor, to work for an NGO, or to cut deals with politicians or businessmen. Nor were we academics—that peculiar class of merchants whose business it is to trade in ideas. We had left all that behind. Whatever we might have been in a previous life, it was no longer important. Our path to salvation rested on a single, minimal requirement: no return ticket.

All alone, with past and future erased, one's sense of linear time undergoes a curious transformation. One day becomes the same as the next. Morning opens like an exotic flower, a gift freely given and received. The heat, the smell of burning flesh, the temple bells and the call to prayer, the beggars and peddlers and pilgrims—all of it is simply present, taking shape in the imagination and passing away cleanly, imperceptibly, into a past that might just as well be a dream.

> For the born, death is certain.
> For the dead, there will be birth.
> Therefore, as this purpose is given,
> thou should not mourn.

In traditional Hindu reckoning, to remember is to imagine a future that has already happened an infinite number of times, for the world is periodically created and destroyed in the course of immense, repetitive cycles of time. Each cycle—from creation to destruction—is divided into four epochs, or *yugas*, taking their names from the four throws of dice in an ancient Indo-European game of chance: Krita, Treta, Dvapara, and Kali. Like the classical Greco-Roman ages, the Indian yugas begin in purity and decline as they pass by in a gradual, irreversible descent toward chaos and despair. Time moves, unwavering, from the point of creation toward an age when property confers rank, when wealth becomes the only mark of virtue, passion the sole bond of union between husband and wife, dissimulation the key to success, power over others the only means of enjoyment. An age when the trappings of religion are mistaken for spiritual purity, and intellectual prowess for wisdom. This, according to the *Vishnu Purana*, is where we are now, in the

Kali Yuga, which began—according to certain obscure calculations—on Friday, February 18, 3102 BCE. In the Kali Yuga, our best efforts are condemned to fail.

The Kali Yuga will endure for 432,000 years. The preceding Treta Yuga lasted 864,000 years, the Dvapara Yuga 1,296,000, and the Krita Yuga 1,728,000. This comes to a cumulative total of some 4,320,000 years, a single complete run of yugas, thus a *mahayuga* or "great cycle"—the period of time between the creation and destruction of a world system. One thousand mahayugas, or 4,320,000,000 human years, makes up a *kalpa*, one day in the life of Brahma, creator of worlds. Elsewhere, a kalpa is said to be equal to the length of time it would require to wear down Mount Meru, the cosmic mountain at the center of the world, by brushing it once a year with a feather.

And here is what we know of the great god Vishnu: Conscious, but wrapped in deep slumber, Vishnu begins to dream. A white lotus arises from his navel and opens to reveal the four-headed Brahma, who will shape a world from the stuff of Vishnu's reverie: birth, aging, sickness, and death, heavens and hells without number, demons, ghosts, and animals. We are now in day one of the fifty-first year in the lifetime of "our" Brahma, and it will unfold in a gallery of marvels as time moves forward like the hands of a clock sweeping over the same numbers again and again. Victories of the demigods followed by their inevitable defeat at the hands of the titans. The sporadic incarnation of divinity: Lord Vishnu taking birth in his various animal and human forms. Everything from the creation of the universe to the last exhalation of a beggar dying in the streets of Banaras is forever fixed in its position in the circle of time, the same events repeating themselves in the same order, forever.

For the born, death is certain.
For the dead, there will be birth.

Only accomplished seers and yogis can bear to shoulder the full burden of the past. To see that the future already exists in memory is a blessing that shatters the pretensions of the ego. Even the great warrior Arjuna pleads for blindness when granted an uncompromising vision of the Lord's maya—the memory of all memories, the endlessly repeating dream of birth and death. And yet, scattered through the scriptures, there are clues for the discerning, tiny epiphanies that could easily be ignored or explained away—just as we so easily ignore or explain away the experience of déjà vu.

For example, we are told in the Puranas that during the first Manu Interval of the present kalpa, Vishnu incarnated as a boar and plunged into the sea in order to rescue the goddess Earth. She was at that time a young virgin who had fallen into the lascivious hands of Hiranyaksha, the Golden-Eyed One. In the ancient story we hear how the demon is slain and Earth rescued. As Vishnu ascends to the surface, the willowy goddess draped over his powerful tusks, he inadvertently reveals his awful secret when he whispers in her ear,

Every time I carry you up this way . . .

It is so much easier to forget, and in any case the act of remembering brings with it another kind of loss. Pompeii, Freud observed, was truly destroyed only when it was excavated and raised up into the light. For Freud, as for the Buddha, it is repression and denial—and all the other various intricate mechanisms of forgetting—that invest the past with its tremendous power to shape entire worlds of experience. All the joys and all the sorrows of existence have their roots in this dark, fertile soil.

Letters from Judith. Bleached photographs of family and friends. Messages from my past; light from distant nebulae. The infant. The schoolboy. The lover. The husband. The scholar. The traitor. The recluse. The seeker. The one who grows old.

Sicut eram in principio, et nunc, et semper, et in sæcula sæculorum.

As I was in the beginning, am now, and ever shall be, unto the ages of ages.

I SIT MOTIONLESS before the first gray light of dawn, settling into a timeless gap between night and day, where the breath of God moves over the surface of the deep. One leg is crossed on top of the other, back straight, eyes closed, watching. A gentle, even pressure of the lungs and diaphragm. In . . . out . . . in . . . out . . . expanding and contracting. Thoughts fall through the silence like snowflakes in an empty sky, melting into an immeasurable sea of darkness. Hopes and plans, memories and regrets, intangible seeds of joy and despair, all these ghostly spores returning to the source. The stream of breath enters, tapers off, hesitates, and turns outward, tapers off, hesitates, and turns inward again, completing its journey through the invisible circle of respiration that revolves at the center of the body, marking the entrance to an ancient path that still leads home. Sweat collects under my arms, forms rivulets, trickles down along my elbows and drips onto the cushion. A single mosquito whines at my left ear, surveys the terrain, spirals down onto the auricle and hangs there, insubstantial and irritating, like the lingering memory of an unfaithful lover. I sit still and bear witness, settling back into the open space of awareness, watching as she delicately probes the tender flesh, observing the faint tickling sensation as she punctures the skin, exchanging poison for blood.

By the time I finished my morning meditation, purple light streaked the sky above the Ganges. From where I stood at my window, I saw people lying along the edges of the street stretched out next to each other in parallel rows—husbands, wives, and children, ancient grandmothers withered and bent even in their dreams, beggars and holy men, pilgrims collapsed after their long journeys—all of them covered from head to foot with soiled cloth, like so many corpses in the pictures I had seen of villagers killed during an air strike somewhere in the Vietnamese jungle. They had begun to stir now, rising to join the growing stream of humanity that wound around the corner of Ganga Mat and down Assi Ghat to the river for morning ablutions.

A single, sturdy old pipal tree grew at the end of the street, not far from the Ganges. At its foot a Shaivite ascetic sat rapt in silent contemplation, back erect, legs knotted in a full lotus. His body and hair were smeared with ash from the cremation pyres. An iron trident impaled the hard clay at his side, a replica of Lord Shiva's own weapon on top of which the Holy City of Banaras is said to rest, outside space and time and beyond the reach even of the law of karmic retribution.

I had looked out over this same scene every morning for months, but on this particular morning nothing was quite the same. There was no precedent in my experience for the lingering sense of ambiguity that permeated everything. It was as if I'd been turned inside out. What normally belonged to the subjective world of feelings, thoughts, and sensations had, for a time, spilled over into the world of the senses, so that even now the smell of my neighbor's incense and the sound of the Muslim call to prayer were no longer simply out there in the world but were, at the same time, somehow intimately mine, elements of my own psyche that had drifted into consciousness and would soon drift out again. And yet the old, well-defined structure of things was regaining its hold; the line between inner and outer was steadily being redrawn by an invisible hand. Such elemental habits of mind do not easily loosen their grip.

I brought out the brass Ajanta stove from its spot in the corner and filled it with kerosene purchased from a neighborhood black-market cloth merchant. In the few months since Indira Gandhi had rescinded the stringent regulations on black-market profiteering, the city's alternative economy had returned.

With the water heating for coffee, I sat at my desk with a bowl of yogurt and bananas. Before me a copybook lay open to a passage from the *Prajna-paramita* I had recently finished translating. The Buddha is speaking with Subhuti, one of his closest disciples:

> Here, Subhuti, the bodhisattva, a great being, reflects as fol-
> lows: "There are measureless, countless beings who should be
> led by me into nirvana. And yet there are neither those who
> should be led to nirvana nor those who should lead them."
> However many beings he might lead to nirvana, still there is
> not a single being who has attained nirvana, nor anyone who
> leads others. Why is this? Subhuti, for one who apprehends his
> illusory nature, this is in accord with the essence of things. It is
> as if a skilled magician or a magician's apprentice were to con-
> jure up a large group of people at a crossroads; and then, having
> conjured them, he were to make them disappear. What do you
> think, Subhuti: Has anyone been slain or killed or destroyed
> or made to disappear? In just this way, Subhuti, a bodhisattva
> leads measureless, countless beings to nirvana, and yet there
> is not a single being led to nirvana nor anyone who does the
> leading. If a bodhisattva, a great being, hears this teaching and
> is neither afraid, shocked, or otherwise shaken, then, Sub-
> huti, that bodhisattva, that great being, may be known to be
> well prepared.

The elegant flow of the Sanskrit was completely lost in my stilted English. I reached over and selected a stick of Tibetan incense from a nearby bundle, lit it, and fitted one end between Garuda's tiny palms. Since meeting Geshe Sherap, I had become more interested in the old Indian scriptures on the perfection of wisdom. But this morning, in light of my dream of waking, this ancient Buddhist text reverberated with new associations.

The water almost boiled over, but I heard it just in time and lunged for the stove, twisting the valve closed. The flame died with a tiny hiss. I waited a minute while the grounds settled in the pot, then filled my mug and took it over to the desk.

I had been working for over an hour when someone knocked at the door.

"*Kaun hai?*" My first thought was the sweeper. Lately she had been coming around asking for baksheesh, and I was not in the mood to listen to all the stories of her various problems. "Who is it?"

"*Aray, bhaiyaa!* Open up."

The muscles in my shoulders spontaneously relaxed. I rose and walked over to the door, released the chain, and drew both panels back. "Good morning, Mick." And it did feel good to see him standing there, radiating ordinariness. His presence made everything seem safe and normal. He already had the blue rubber flip-flops off his feet and was edging his way past me, sniffing at the aroma of South Indian coffee that filled the room.

"Hey man, how's it going? Look what I brought you." He handed me a small sack made from recycled newspaper. It was saturated in warm syrup. "Jalebi. Still hot."

"Thanks." I put the bag on the desk and gestured toward my mug. "Want some?" I didn't wait for him to respond but instead went over and fired up the stove and put some water on, mixing in a big spoonful of fresh grounds. While the water heated I munched on a jalebi. I offered the bag to Mickey, who took one and popped it into his mouth, then sank down onto the bed. He began to swab his head and neck with the cotton gamcha he carried over one shoulder.

"You know something, Stanley? It's hot."

"You're in India, Mick. This is what they call 'the hot season.'"

"I mean," he let his arm fall limply, "it's fucking seriously hot." He ruminated on this observation. "I saw a fist fight yesterday afternoon out in front of the Lalita. They were really going at it. Two BHU students."

"People you know?"

"Yeah. It's a union deal that sort of went sour."

The Lalita was a local cinema in Belapur, and I could easily picture the whole chaotic scene, what is called, in Hindi, *tamasha*. A crowd would have gathered instantaneously, some to egg on the fight, others struggling to pry the men apart. Most would simply be spectators watching absent-mindedly while the contestants flailed at each other, their arms revolving like the blades of a windmill, like the arms of the girls who used to fight in the parking lot outside my high school.

"I've been tempted myself to take a swing at someone," Mickey continued. "Which reminds me . . ." He stuck one hand into his jhola, drew out a small piece of stiff gray cardboard, and tossed it onto the book that lay open on my desk. "Here's your ticket. Leaves at two o'clock tomorrow afternoon."

"Thanks, Mick." I picked up the ticket and examined it, the Kashi Vishwanath Express for New Delhi station. "Was the station crowded?"

He shrugged. "Don't worry about it. I had it taken care of, you know?"

By which he meant that he had one of his friends—someone with connections at the station, no doubt—pick up the ticket. Anyway, I was deeply grateful. Offering him a cup of coffee was the least I could do.

He took a sip, then gazed out the window, looking down toward the river. "So who exactly is this guy you're going to meet?"

Mickey knew I was studying Tibetan at Sanskrit University, but I had told him very little about Geshe Sherap and our conversation.

"He's a lama. A tulku. You know, the reincarnation of an earlier teacher."

"Oh, yeah. The Tibetan thing."

"This is true," I said. "It's a Tibetan thing." Mick's stint as a Theravadin monk had left him with a healthy skepticism when it came to certain Tibetan beliefs and practices, and this whole business about reincarnate teachers struck him as over the top. As with so many other things in the world of Tibetan Buddhism, I reserved judgment.

"So what's his name again?"

"Nortul Rinpoche."

"Sure you don't want company?" He grinned.

I returned his smile and shook my head. "I don't think so. Not this time."

"I could use some air-conditioning—like at Nirulas. And an ice cream sundae, all slathered with hot fudge and nuts."

The ends of his mustache twitched as he smacked his lips. Sometime after arriving in Banaras Mickey had grown a Nietzschean affair with long, waxed tips, precisely the sort of thing in vogue among the wrestlers and miscreants with whom he hung out.

"It'd be great to get out of this madhouse for a while. See the big city, you know? Something different." His eyes drifted over to the papers that lay scattered on my desk. "What's this?"

"A translation I'm working on."

"What is it?"

"*Ashtasahasrika Prajnaparamita*—the *Perfection of Wisdom in Eight Thousand Lines*." I considered telling him about the dream but then decided against it.

He picked up my copybook and began to read out loud. "'What do you think, Subhuti, has anyone been slain or killed or made to disappear?'" He studied the page for a few seconds and then continued reading. "'If a bodhisattva hears this teaching and is neither afraid, shocked, or otherwise shaken, then, Subhuti, that bodhisattva, that great being, may be known to be well prepared.'"

Mick had learned some Pali in Thailand, and he loved to argue about philosophy. One time back in the Agra days we took a bus to Bhopal. We were going to visit Sanchi, an ancient Buddhist site. After hours of nonstop discussion about some abstruse point of Abhidharma, the conversation gave way to the roar of the engine and the sound of rubber turning against hot pavement. I had nearly fallen asleep when out of nowhere he began to sing a bhajan—one of those irresistibly seductive Hindu prayers, a song of yearning for the warm flesh of an adulterous lover, for reunion with the divine. It's possible he didn't even realize he was singing. The melody was barely audible over the sounds of the road. One by one, though, the men and women around us stopped talking and turned to listen, filled with wonder at the sound of this foreigner's voice, a beauty sufficient to move the heart of God.

Mick looked down at the paper in his hand and considered for a moment, draining the last of the coffee. "This Mahayana stuff is crazy shit, Stan."

I didn't respond.

"What's this mean—'well prepared'? Prepared for what?"

"Maybe that's not the best translation," I said, a bit defensively. Vaidya's Sanskrit edition of the text was lying on the desk. I picked it up and located the long compound. "*Mahasamnaha-samnaddho*. . . It means something like 'he has put on great armor.' You know, 'girded his loins.'" I smiled. "Hey, how about that? Shall I use it?"

He continued to study the English text. "As in, like, he's prepared for war or something."

"Yes," I replied. "Like in the *Bhagavadgita*, where Arjuna is preparing to go into battle."

"Against his relatives." As he said this, he looked up and caught my eye. I nodded.

"So the bodhisattva is well prepared to go out and kill his relatives."

"I don't think so, Mick."

"But that's what the *Gita* is all about, right? Arjuna doesn't want to kill his relatives, and Krishna—you know, God—tells him it's his duty. His dharma. He's a warrior. Warriors kill people, Stan. That's what they do. This bodhisattva is a warrior."

"It's a metaphor, for Chrissake."

"Okay, then you tell me what it means."

I felt myself growing impatient. "Doesn't it seem like, well, sort of a stretch, that the bodhisattva is someone 'well prepared' to go out and *kill* the people he loves?"

"Maybe so," Mick replied. "But then what about this?" He picked up the copybook and tapped his finger on one line. "'Has anyone been slain or killed or made to disappear?' It's pretty obvious the answer is no. People aren't really born—right?—so they don't really die, either. So it doesn't matter if the bodhisattva kills them because he won't really have killed anyone. That's what it means, Stan. Just like in the *Gita*. It's obvious."

He cocked an eyebrow, as if to say *I just cashed you out, Dude, so admit it.*

"For God's sake, Mick, it doesn't say he kills them. It says he leads them to nirvana."

"So what's the armor for?"

"Mick . . ." I took the copybook out of his hands and laid it back on the table. "You can't just go and read a Buddhist Prajnaparamita text as if it were a chapter from the *Bhagavadgita*."

"Oh?" Again with the eyebrow. "Why not?"

"For one thing, according to Sankhya—the philosophy behind the *Gita*—there's a fundamental distinction between the body and the 'self' or soul; they're completely different substances, but both of them are equally real. In the Sankhya view, the true self is pure awareness, something called *purusha*. The body is *prakriti*. All sensations are prakriti. So are thoughts and feelings, and everything else, for that matter. So the body is born and it does die. Really die. That's a big difference. In Mahayana Buddhism there's no such ultimate distinction between body and soul or between consciousness and its objects. It's just like you said—in the Mahayana, at least, everything's equally unreal. It's all *shunya*—empty of any kind of absolute or ultimate reality."

He blinked. "Sounds to me like some kind of bullshit philosophical hair-splitting."

This was beginning to piss me off. "Look, Mick, I've got things to do. Okay? I'm really grateful to you for getting that train ticket. I am. But, well, I'm sort of busy now. I've got stuff to do to get ready for the trip."

He wandered over to the window and looked down at the street, which was busy now with people moving to and from the river. "Life is a war zone, you know? Someone's gotta die so someone else can live. Even if you're a vegetarian, you have to kill the goddamn carrots in order to survive."

"Oh come on," I broke in. "You don't really think killing a carrot is the same as . . ."

He ignored my interruption. "If you're here at all, you're guilty."

"Guilty? Is this some kind of Catholic thing?"

"Sure. Why not? Even God is a killer: *He giveth life and he taketh it away*. Right? Nobody's hands are clean. Sometimes I think the hardest part is just finding a way to live with yourself—with what you do every day, you know, just to exist. Why should a bodhisattva be any different from the rest of us? Has he, like, been granted some kind of reprieve or something from the Buddha? I don't think so. All he's got, so far as I can tell, is compassion. Isn't that right? Compassion. That's all he's got."

"And wisdom."

"Wisdom," he repeated the word. "Well, I hope he has the wisdom to gird his fucking loins."

He turned away from the window and stared at me with his trademark blank look, then reached over and extracted a jalebi from the bag, which I had left lying on the desk. "Anyway, that's the way I see it. But it's not my problem. You're the scholar." He dropped the jalebi into his mouth and slung his jhola over one shoulder. "But remember, the quality of your translations will help shape the future of the Buddha's teaching in the West."

"I'll remember that."

"So I guess I'll see you when you get back from Delhi?"

"Yeah. And thanks again, Mick. You know, for the ticket and all."

"No problem. Have a hot fudge sundae for me, okay?"

"Sure thing."

I watched him slip on his rubber sandals and step through the door. The slapping of his feet echoed against the concrete stairwell as he descended. Through the window I could see him in the street, fiddling with the rusty lock on his bike.

I had to admit he was right—at least he was right about the *Gita*. Krishna had told Arjuna that it was his duty—his dharma as a warrior—to kill his relatives. It's all there in the opening scene, and every commentator from Shankara to Mahatma Gandhi has struggled to reconcile those verses with the teaching of *ahimsa*, or nonviolence, the cornerstone of the spiritual life in India. I went over and pulled a copy of the *Gita* off the shelf, opened to the first chapter, "The Despondency of Arjuna," and read,

> I do not want to kill them, O Krishna,
> even if I myself am to be killed.

Turning to the index of first lines, I scanned down and found what I was looking for in chapter 11, where Arjuna is granted a vision of Krishna's real identity:

> I am time, almighty destroyer of worlds,
> appearing here for their annihilation.
> They have already been destroyed by me.
> You will be the mere instrument, O warrior!

And then it struck me: Kalidas.

36

On March 22, election results were announced. Indira had been defeated by a coalition of her enemies. A few days later—on the very morning that Mick delivered my ticket—she officially resigned. The whole country was in the streets celebrating the news. It was not the best time to be traveling to Delhi, but I had my reservation and was determined to go. Geshe Sherap's letter of introduction was tucked securely between the pages of my passport; the passport was zipped into a cloth pouch I wore on a belt under my shirt.

The train left as scheduled at two in the afternoon. I was traveling second class, which meant I had no guarantee of a place of my own until sometime after dark. My compartment was already full beyond capacity—eight of us were crammed into a space designed to seat six. For the rest of the day people would be getting on and off every time the train stopped. But I had long since figured this out. No one wanted to be in an upper berth during the daytime, so unless things got really crowded it was uncontested territory. If I grabbed it early—as I did this time—it was mine for the duration. I shoved my old canvas bag up there, then went to one end of the car and stood in the open doorway, where I could lean out, feel the breeze, and watch the tracks rattle past. Looking out on the rural Indian countryside, I imagined Prince Siddhartha wandering there, searching for a way to live in the face of old age, sickness, and death.

We sped through an endless network of raised pathways dividing the earth into small, sunken plots of land. In the monsoon they would be flooded with water, muddy and lush with grain; in March they were nothing but open graves, brittle tubs of cracked earth. From time to time we passed a cluster of adobe huts squatting in a common yard of packed clay, a single bucket suspended over the low, circular opening of the well, women in saris threshing wheat in the shade of a gnarled tree, a stone image of the village deity installed at its root.

An hour or so outside of Banaras, near Jaunpur, the train slowed at an intersection, and a group of children gawked, then waved, laughing and pointing at the foreigner who had appeared out of nowhere and was already vanishing into the distance. In the early evening we stopped at Sultanpur, where I purchased chai from a vendor and drank it on the platform. Sometime after dark I climbed up into my berth, opened my bag, and dug out a beat-up copy of the *Rupachandrika*—a compact book containing some seven hundred pages of essential Sanskrit conjugations and declensions. I worked on memorizing irregular verbs and then read a novel Richard had given me. After a while I dozed off. I woke up around eleven o'clock at night, just as we were entering Lucknow.

Lucknow is a large city, and the station was a madhouse. It was impossible to know how long we would stop before moving on, so for people waiting to board, there was no time to waste. Men and women rushed the train, yelling at the porters, who struggled with enormous bags and trunks. We had not even come to a stop and people were already leaping in the door and pushing their way through the narrow aisles of our car. Everywhere children clung to their mothers and whined, babies howled, and vendors hawked their wares. "*Chaaii! Garam chaaii!*" Up and down along the length of the train, people shoved steaming clay cups through the open windows. Peddlers crowded around with an endless assortment of cheap plastic toys and water bottles, stainless-steel tiffins, glass bangles, and colored prints of Hindu gods. One man balanced a straw basket on his head; it was stacked high with freshly severed slices of mango and bright orange papaya that had been neatly arranged in an ascending series of smaller and smaller concentric circles. Another man stood behind a hammered brass tray heaped with unshelled peanuts carefully banked around a small aluminum pot filled with hot coals. He scooped up the dry husks, letting them fall from his fingers into a hand-held scale. Next to him a man in baggy kurta-pajama had transformed himself into a sort of living shop. The red frames of his sunglasses—lenses shaped like two huge hearts—obscured the entire upper half of his face. Several dozen pairs of similar plastic frames were pinned to his hat and every square inch of his pants and shirt. Overhead, loudspeakers buzzed with announcements in English and Hindi while the locomotives groaned in and out of the station.

I hadn't eaten since early afternoon, and I was hungry. I went outside to stretch my legs and stuff down some sabji-puri, being careful to stand outside the window to my compartment, where I could keep an eye on my bag. The puris were hot and greasy, and I used them to scoop green chilies, potatoes, and peas out of a shallow bowl fashioned of dried leaves that had been stitched together with their own stems. From my left a wobbly, box-like cart approached. An old man, barefoot, bald, and naked except for a scraggly gray beard and a loincloth, leaned heavily against one end of the cart, pushing with every ounce of his strength. It appeared to be all he could do to keep the thing trundling along on its tiny casters. There was an A-frame rack in the center of the cart; on it was fastened a collection of magazines in Hindi, Urdu, and English, all of them bearing glossy photographs of Bollywood movie idols—a gallery of smug, meaty-faced demigods with puffy lips and dazzling white teeth. Eyelids at half-mast, they pouted at the camera, as if to make it absolutely obvious, by such prosaic signs, that they were sated with hedonistic pleasures far beyond anything we mortals could possibly conjure up in our wildest, most intemperate dreams.

I had finished eating all but the last couple of mouthfuls of my meal when I noticed a hairless, skeletal dog hiding under the train. I tossed what was left over the edge of the platform and watched him lick the leaves clean. He looked up hopefully, then spooked and ran under the next car and stood cowering in the shadows. As I was crouching there, attempting to coax him out with a Milk Biki, a peddler walked by lugging a brass bucket filled with ice and bottles of soda. I purchased a cold Limca and downed it in one gulp. When I looked back, the dog was gone. I tossed the biscuit over the edge, then boarded my car and climbed back into the upper berth.

Not more than a foot over my head, a fan attached to the curved ceiling rattled in its metal cage like a trapped rat. The night air was cooler, but I was still damp with sweat. I wrapped myself in a lungi, closed my eyes, and was soon rocked to sleep by the clacking of wheels.

I was awakened by an eerie silence; the train was not moving. A dim light filtered into my compartment from outside, and from the bunk below me I could hear the faint, wheezing sound of a man snoring. At first I thought we were on a side track, as often happens, waiting for another train to pass. But after a few minutes I leaned out of my berth and peered down through the window and saw that we had stopped at a small, rural station. I was wide awake now and terribly thirsty from the sabji-puri, so I decided to see if I could find something to drink. Careful not to disturb the people sleeping below me, I climbed down from my bunk, slipped on my sandals, and walked quietly along the aisle and out the door.

The platform was deserted. Inside the station house a neon tube hummed faintly, its sterile light illuminating half a dozen small, translucent lizards that clung to the wall. Otherwise everything was silent and empty—not a person in sight. And then I heard someone shout *sahab* and I turned, and there, several hundred feet off to my right, where the platform descended to the ground in a long, sloping ramp, I spotted a ramshackle chai stall. The proprietor—a middle-aged Sikh—squatted under a single electric bulb; in front of him I could see the orange glow of coals. He waved in my direction, beckoning me. If I were lucky, I'd have just enough time to get a chai.

I walked as quickly as I could, holding close to the train in case it should start to move. I had just reached the foot of the ramp when a child emerged from the shadows and came toward me, his hand extended. Judging from the boy's size, he was maybe eight years old; his skin was so pale it seemed to glow in the dim light. At first I thought he was an ascetic; devotees of Shiva often paint their skin with ash gathered from a funeral pyre. But then I realized he was an albino, and I immediately remembered that other child from so long ago, the schoolboy in Agra throwing rocks at a sow and her piglets. The memory made me shudder. The child's head was cleanly shaven and covered with scabs. Thick rivulets of snot had coagulated on his lips and chin. I dug a worn five-rupee note out of my pocket and placed it in his outstretched palm, depositing the tattered paper there among the few small coins he had collected. Five rupees was much more than he could have hoped for from any Indian. We both knew this, and I knew it probably wasn't a good idea, but I did it anyway—perhaps because I wanted to buy him off, to make him go away. I managed to smile as I handed it to him and said something polite in Hindi, one human being to another.

As I turned to go the boy asked for more, his voice a low moan. "*Sahab ... Bhukh ... Bhukh ...*" I was a foreigner and obviously had money to burn. And I had spoken to him, a few kind words. I instantly regretted it.

"*Aray*, child. *Bas*. That's enough." He moved one hand feebly back and forth between his belly and mouth. I ignored him, turned, and continued to walk toward the chai stand. I hadn't taken more than a few steps when I felt him grab my pant leg.

"*Mat chuuo!*" I swiveled and bent toward him and spoke the angry words loudly. I was genuinely offended by this patent breach of etiquette: in India, strangers do not intentionally touch. He would never for a moment have dared to make physical contact with any Indian. He did it only because I was a foreigner. In his eyes, I was an ignorant person unworthy of this most basic sign of respect. This sort of thing happened to me often, which only made it worse. Mostly I just let it pass, but this time all my resentment boiled up. I had been living here for almost two years now, and during that time I had worked hard to find a legitimate place in the culture. I was fluent in Hindi. I even read Sanskrit. In many ways I felt more at home in India than I did in my own country. And despite all of this, everywhere I went I was still treated like a "red monkey," a stupid hippie fresh off the Magic Bus. Obviously, I could stay here for the rest of my life and nothing would change. And I had just gone out of my way to be nice to this kid. "Do not *touch* me!" I scolded him, wagging a finger inches from his startled face, then pointedly walked away.

When I felt his fingers brush my leg again, they burned like fire. I lost all patience and was seized with a blind, self-righteous fury. In a single swift motion I whirled around and slapped his hand away. He lost his grip and the coins he had been clutching scattered on the ground, rolling and skipping across the platform. For a second he looked up at me, his face contorted in an expression of disbelief, then panic, as he dropped to his hands and knees and scuttled around in a frantic effort to retrieve the money. The five-rupee note I had given him fluttered onto the tracks, and he clamored after it, vanishing under the train. Filled with shame, I no longer cared about the chai. I wanted simply to run and hide. At just that moment the whistle blasted and couplings rattled up and down the line, as one car tugged against the next.

I'm going to kill a boy.

At first the words came to me as a vague, indistinct memory, the memory of a dream. Then they returned as a thought. And finally—all in a matter of seconds—they flashed into my mind with the full strength of a realization.

I'M GOING TO KILL A BOY.

The train was rolling forward, heavy steel wheels clanking over the rails. I stood and watched in horror, my eyes fixed to the spot where the child had disappeared—where he was now trapped. I was paralyzed, frozen in place, overcome with fear and guilt and a wild desire to flee while I still could. The train was rapidly gaining speed; very soon it would be going too fast for me to get on, and I would be stranded here in the darkness—god knows where—left to confront the consequences of my pride and arrogance. It was too much to bear. I wrenched my eyes away from the tracks and sprinted up the ramp and along the platform, running hard by the cars, passing a succession of square windows, each one a miniature proscenium opening onto its own cramped world where people slept and dreamed amid the chaos of things they had brought with them on their journey. The train picked up speed, and very soon it was overtaking me, the windows moving by me now in the opposite direction, the same scenes I had just witnessed repeating themselves in reverse order, as if I were sliding backward in time, losing ground, falling into the past.

This cannot be happening. Oh Jesus fucking Christ. Please. This cannot be happening.

The train was moving fast, and I reached out in desperation and grabbed a handrail and held on, my feet flailing in midair as I was yanked off the platform and up into the open doorway. Within seconds the station was gone—lost—and I was once again hurtling through the void.

37

I AWOKE TO A FRENZY of activity, just as the train was entering New Delhi station. Up and down the aisle people struggled with their luggage, pushing their way toward the door. There was no point in moving, so I lay in my berth and waited until most of the passengers had gotten off, then climbed down and made my way through the crowded station. Outside I flagged a motor rickshaw and had him take me to the YMCA on Jai Singh Road.

Fortunately they had a vacant room. Once inside I secured the door and collapsed onto the bed and attempted to dispel the image of that boy from my mind.

I told myself that it wasn't my fault he got trapped under the train. It had been a terrible accident. Buddhism teaches that the karmic consequences of any action are rooted in its intent; murder is not murder unless there is a clear intention to kill, and I certainly had no such intention. And anyway, I asked myself, how do I know he actually died? He could easily have crawled out on the opposite side of the train, where I wouldn't have seen him. Or else kept low against the tracks and waited for the cars to pass. I remembered reading about someone who had done just that with a CTA train in Chicago. The man was completely unharmed.

This reasoning went nowhere. It wasn't enough to *not know* whether I'd unintentionally killed a boy. Especially when I had to deal with the abject cowardice that had driven me to abandon him and run for the train—which was the only reason, after all, that I didn't know if he were still alive. The truth was that I hadn't even wanted to know. All I'd wanted was to get away.

So what did I want now?

I wanted to forget. I wanted to bury the memory of those few horrible moments deep down under wherever it is that memories get buried. Unfortunately, that was not possible. All of it was there, vividly present in my mind. Or at least most of it was there.

I remembered waking up in the middle of the night, and everything that followed—right up to the point where I flung myself into the train. But from there on things got hazy. Try as I might, I could not recall making my way back through the cars to my berth. After leaping into the train, the next thing I remembered was waking up in the New Delhi station. Obviously, it would have taken a while to find my way through the cars and get settled again and fall asleep—especially after what had just happened. So why couldn't I remember any of it?

But of course there is so much we don't remember or remember incorrectly. Nevertheless, this question triggered a string of other questions, for the more I puzzled over that mysterious lapse of memory, the clearer it became that there were several other peculiar things about the station. For instance, why did no one else get on or off the train? Even at the time the absolute silence of the place had struck me as odd. And why was the boy wandering all alone out there so late at night? And why would a chai shop be open at that hour, the chai wala way down there off the platform making tea for nobody? And why, it occurred to me now, would the Kashi Viswanath Express stop in the dead of the night at a tiny station in the middle of nowhere? Express trains don't make such stops.

And behind it all, suffusing these questions with an ominous, indecipherable portent, was the dream I'd had just before leaving Banaras where I was driving the bus. *I'm going to kill a boy.* The words sent chills up my spine. They had freaked me out before, but now it was a hundred times worse. And all of it seemed to go back, somehow, to the original accident in the Punjab, which could itself have been a dream. And then, as I lay on the hard mattress at the YMCA, dissecting these subtleties, I recalled a detail of my experience on the Super Fast that had until that moment entirely slipped my mind: the cut on my lip.

That night when the bus skidded, just before striking the boy, I had been thrown forward against the metal bar separating me from the driver, and I had cut my lip. The memory was still crystal clear. But later when I was cleaning up in the bathroom at the Fulbright offices I hadn't noticed any sign of the cut. No blood, no swelling or discomfort. Nothing. At the time I was too preoccupied to think about it, but it seems highly unlikely that I could have been bleeding like that on the bus and not found so much as a trace of dried blood when I looked in the mirror only a few hours later. Sitting on the bus I had distinctly seen and felt blood on my fingers and—as I now remembered—on my bag. Yes, a drop of blood had fallen on my bag. This could be confirmed.

I got up from the bed, went over and found the bag, and took it outside on the veranda. In the bright sunlight I meticulously examined every square inch of the canvas fabric. There was no hint of the dark stain I remembered seeing that night in the Punjab. Of course the bag was dirty, and the spot could have faded with the passing of time. Or maybe in the poor light of the bus I hadn't really seen what I thought I saw.

Things are not what they seem—memories and dreams, whole worlds that exist only in the mind—*nor are they otherwise.*

It was mid morning and I had been lying in bed wrestling with this conundrum for too long when I finally gave up. I went down the hall to the communal bathroom and took a hot shower and then ordered tea through room service. I hadn't eaten a proper meal since the day before in Banaras, so when the tea was finished I left the hotel and walked across Connaught Place to the Glory—a dhaba on the outer circle, one of several among the maze of shops near Shankar Market. I found a seat among a crowd of mechanics and auto-rickshaw drivers. All around me men conversed loudly, laughing and eating with relish. It was a relief to get out of the hotel room and stop obsessing about something I could not influence, one way or another. And it felt good just to eat: I consumed a saucer of pickled red onions, a fiery plate of mattar paneer, two thick, steaming tandoori rotis, and a saucer of mung dal.

When I finished eating, I went to the back of the restaurant to rinse my hands and mouth. Bent over the small metal sink, massaging my gums with the water from the tap, everything seemed at once both familiar and remote. I was doing something I'd done dozens of times before in exactly this place. I splashed the cool water over my face and stood up from the sink feeling somewhat refreshed. Since I had no intention of looking up Nortul Rinpoche today, I had the rest of the afternoon free.

I hailed a motor rickshaw and had him drop me on the south end of Lodi Gardens, near the mausoleum of Shah Sayyid, the fifteenth-century sultan of Delhi who had claimed to be a direct descendent of Muhammad. I paid the driver and walked through the gate. It was mid afternoon now, and the sun was blistering hot. A man slouched in the shade, watering bushes, waving a nozzle aimlessly back and forth over a tangle of thorny leaves. There didn't seem to be anyone else around. I climbed the cracked masonry steps, passed under the arcade, and paused near the entrance to the tomb. The cool air of the interior smelled of stone and earth. Two mynahs swooped and soared in the shadows under the dome with its arabesques. Beneath them the grave was marked by a heavy slab of sandstone. I sat down to rest under the high lintel and looked out over a nearby grove of eucalyptus. Behind me the faint swish of the birds' wings reverberated off the stucco walls. A peacock moaned.

I thought about those other afternoons when I used to stop here on the way back from my Sanskrit lessons with Shri Anantacharya. When the goal is liberation, he had assured me in his solemn tone, one cannot afford to exclude anything. Poetry as a path to moksha. But I was not convinced he really wanted such a liberation from cities and seas, from mountains and the passing of the seasons, and certainly not from the poems of his beloved Kalidasa. In any case, I thought, Anantacharya is gone. And his son, Krishna, will soon be married to a woman he barely knows. *Love is about how we live with what we are given.* I recalled how Penny and I had walked here one morning, after sex and coffee, exploring a newly enchanted world. We had been entertained at the foot of these very stairs by a man with two trained monkeys. The male was clothed in absurd little cotton pants, the female with a tiny frilled smock. "*Shaadi karo!*" Their master snapped an order and they pretended to "be married," gripping each other in a furry embrace, their long tails curling upward like the handles on a vase.

The man with the hose was down on his hands and knees now, pulling grass from around the flowering plants. Seeing him there, an image of the boy in the station flickered into my mind. All over again he was crawling at my feet, groping for coins, his face contorted with panic and confusion. And I wondered, all over again, if it really might have been a dream. The mere fact that I could imagine such a possibility seemed altogether too fantastic. I must be losing my mind even to consider such a thing. And then I remembered what Mickey had said about how life is a war zone, and a big part of the battle is waged in the effort just to live with yourself—with the guilt, as he put it, of being here at all. So is that what this is about? Guilt? If so, I asked myself, then just how much am I willing to doubt or to believe or to simply *forget* in order to avoid confronting the consequences of my own pride and arrogance? There is no way to calculate the extent of our obfuscation, no way to know who or what might already have been sacrificed simply in order to keep going. No way to know how deeply I could be fooling myself. Or trying to fool myself, by turning an actual child into a bloodless fantasy.

But then, it occurred to me, maybe it's not that far-fetched. The border between memory and imagination is notoriously porous. This business about fooling oneself is a double-edged sword. Don't I fool myself every night when I dream without knowing I'm dreaming? And that's the least of it. In Banaras I had dreamed of waking up and gotten all the way downstairs before I even suspected I was still in bed asleep. So if I can be that wrong about a dream, then why couldn't I be wrong about a memory—the memory of a dream?

"Sahab." I looked up and the man was standing directly in front of me, his arm extended, a key dangling from his fingers, addressing me in Hindi. "Is it yours?"

It was the key to my hotel room. But how I had managed to drop it in the grass I don't know. I took it from him, thanking him profusely, and stuck it back in my pocket as I stood up. He remained where he was, motionless, palms joined. It took me a second to realize that he was waiting for baksheesh. I dipped into my pocket and dug out a few coins and dropped them into his outstretched hands, then walked quickly down the stairs and out to the road, where the auto rickshaw I had come on was still parked.

On an impulse I decided to stop by the Fulbright offices, and ten minutes later I was walking through the front gate. The chaukidar was someone new; he raised his palms in greeting. Where was Mahmud? I pushed open the door and entered the lounge, where I immediately succumbed to an array of conflicting emotions. The first thing that hit me was the frigid air-conditioning. Such ostentatious, technologically controlled comfort immediately suggested everything good and bad about the institutionalized world of academia—all of it bound up with money. Work hard, play by the rules, publish, and network and—if you're among the fortunate few to be anointed with tenure—your future is secure. No one was anywhere to be seen. I recalled that on this very day Morarji Desai was being sworn in as prime minister; the staff probably had the afternoon off. I stood and surveyed the all-too-familiar room. To my left was the couch where I had sat talking with Margaret Billings on our first meeting. The sound of her patient, maternal voice still lingered in the air, advising me on strategies for professional success. And that grueling conversation at the party, with Frank Davis cross-examining me about the dissertation.

I peered down the hall to the director's office, the scene of debauchery. I was overwhelmed with an old sensation that I had not experienced since moving to Banaras. All over again I was the child, the clown, the intruder—the one who must wear a mask. The one who does not belong. Suddenly I wanted out. Out before I had to shake hands with anyone. Out before I had to answer a single pointed question about my research.

I turned to leave and my eye came to rest on the row of mailboxes by the door. I stepped over and peered into the one marked "H." There was a pile of envelopes. I drew it out and began to sort through the various letters and cards. Surely there couldn't be anything here for me, not after all this time.

Wrong.

There, on the bottom of the stack, was an airmail envelope from the States, addressed to Stanley Harrington. I thrust the rest of the letters and cards back into the box and scrutinized the sky-blue paper, the row of canceled US postage stamps, as if I were holding an artifact that had somehow been carried over intact, through the bardo, from a previous life. On the back of the envelope, in a scratchy, grade-school hand that I immediately recognized, was the return address: Judith Harrington, 85 West Division Street #15, Chicago, IL, U.S.A. I dropped onto the couch and simply gazed at the writing for several more seconds before teasing open the flap.

The letter inside was dated December 28, 1975. One month before the fateful telephone conversation in which I first acknowledged my intention to stay on in India. One and a half months before I next heard from her when she wrote suggesting we file for divorce. How could I have missed it? I used to rifle through this box two, often three, times a day. Nothing could possibly have escaped my attention. I turned the empty envelope over in my hand and examined the postmark: September 14, 1976. There could only be one explanation. It must have been lost in the post office here in Delhi for several months—or held up by the censors—then eventually processed and delivered sometime after I had gone. And ever since then the envelope had been lying here in this box. Waiting. I slumped back into the couch, unfolded the translucent stationary and began to read.

Dearest Stanley,

So, Christmas is over. Our first Christmas apart. I know how much you hate all the commercial hype, but it's still a time when families are supposed to get together and I've missed you.

Will it really be four more months before we see each other again?

I am chez parents—since a few days before Christmas. I don't know how much longer I can stand it. The place is insane as ever. Mom insists that Dad is putting on weight and she rides him about it constantly. Of course he ignores her. Since I've been here (for the last week) he's spent most of his time sitting in front of the TV with a bowl of Cheetos watching football. Matt came home for Christmas, but he's leaving tomorrow to go back to school early to meet some new girlfriend—the second one in the past six months.

It's been okay, I guess, but it does seem pretty strange not to have you here.

Thanks so much for the gifts. You must have mailed them months ago! I love the perfume. Really. Even the bottles are exotic. Sealed with wax, no less. I hated to open them. But the silver necklace you sent—I don't know what to say. It's absolutely beautiful. Thank you, Stanley. Mom is so happy with the silk scarf, and the wallet is perfect for Dad. You know how he is. He immediately emptied out his old one and put everything into the one you sent. He couldn't get over the idea that it's made out of water-buffalo leather. I heard him telling one of his friends on the phone. And the shirt was ideal for Matt. It's loose enough that it fits great. A "kurta," right? (I'm sure you're happy to see that I've picked up a few Hindi words from your letters.) Anyway, thanks for being so kind. Now I feel more guilty than ever for not sending you a Christmas present. But remember—you told me not to!

Mom and Dad haven't said much, but it's obvious they want to know what's going on. I've been thinking a lot about us lately, and the only thing I know for sure is that I still love you. In spite of everything, this love I have for you is still there. You're my husband and I can't seem to get beyond that fact. We agreed to spend the rest of our lives together, and it does mean something. "The bondage of holy matrimony," as you used to say. You are the most perverse man on earth. How many times did you refuse even to give me a hug or a kiss when I asked? It had to be "spontaneous" (whatever that means) or you couldn't do it.

So here we go again . . . I'm so tired of raking back over all the horrible stuff we've been through. I wish I could just forget all those times you turned away from me, and how angry it still makes me. Sometimes I think you never really wanted to be married. Or at least that you regretted it within a week.

Look, I'm sorry, but it's true. It seems like you did everything you could to deny we ever got married. I'll never forget your toast the night of the rehearsal dinner: "In sixty years everyone at this table will be dead." I know it was supposed to be a joke, but it was still a horrible thing to say the night before our wedding. And you weren't even pretending to joke when you told me that as far as you were concerned marriage was just a word. A "legal fiction," you said. "And who could commit their life to a fiction?" Your obsession with some kind of capital "T" Truth was like a big steamroller crushing every scrap of romance out of our marriage. The whole thing makes me feel so helpless.

Stop, Judith. Just stop it.

I start thinking about this stuff, and I get very angry all over again. And I don't want to get angry. There's no point. First of all, it's over and done with. I mean the past. The past is over. Even more important, though, I need to remind myself constantly that the shit we went through was not entirely your fault. For one thing, I could have told you how much the things you said and did really hurt me. Maybe I didn't even know myself how old fashioned I am in some ways. I know now that it was a big mistake to keep my feelings to myself, but I was so afraid that you would get claustrophobic if I was completely open about how much getting married meant to me. That's why I didn't argue when you refused to get rings, even though I wanted them. And that's why I went along with it when, later on, you threw away all our wedding pictures—so we could "start over," you said. I guess I thought that I had to go along with it. I don't know what I thought. I guess I loved you too much. I probably still do.

Honestly, when I look back at what I've just written, I don't even know how much of it is true. I mean how much of it is true for you. I've never had your side of the story, really. Maybe sometime we can actually talk about all of this.

Speaking of capital "T" Truth—Bruce and I got into a

terrible argument a few weeks ago. He found one of your letters—the last one, where you talked about coming back in the
spring. It's not like I've lied to him or anything—he knows very
well that I haven't given up on us. I've been totally honest with
him about my feelings. It was a beautiful letter, though. All your
writing has given me such hope for us. I tell myself that I'm a
fool to open up to you again. But this time you really do seem
to have changed, and in spite of myself I'm beginning to believe
all over again that you love me.

I can hardly wait for you to see my new place. It's tiny, but
it's a real home. A room of my own (ha ha)—something I've
needed for a long time. So when you come back we'll have dinner here together. I'm still no fabulous cook, but after a bottle
of wine it won't matter. Maybe we really can start over.

Oh Stanley, as the months pass I find myself remembering
mostly all the wonderful, magical adventures we've shared.
Like the time we were hitchhiking in Tennessee and got picked
up by that guy driving the refrigerated truck, and he had us sell
cold watermelons at all the rest stops. Remember? He took us
out to dinner with the money! I'm almost scared to say it, but
lately I've been feeling more and more that we will work this
out. Somehow we'll make it.

Well, I'm tired and it's time for bed. I love you dearly, husband of mine. It's true. And I miss you. I miss your hair on the
pillow "like a sleeping golden storm." I miss the undeodorized
smell of your body. I miss your touch. God help me, but I even
miss those horrible conversations about suffering and death.
I know this time apart is good for us—another adventure, I
guess—but I do wish you could be here with me tonight. Is
that okay?

The letter was signed in that same scratchy, schoolgirl handwriting.
Underneath the signature she had written, "p.s. Merry Christmas and all
that."

I read the postscript over and over. I just sat there on the couch, holding
her letter in both hands, reading and rereading that last line. Her mention
of Tennessee and the watermelons reminded me of another time we were
hitchhiking—standing by the road just east of Barstow, California, wait-

ing for a ride. We had driven from Chicago to Los Angeles in a brand new Cadillac Seville; its owner had flown out, arranging beforehand for the car to be delivered to him through a drive-away service. Gas for the trip was paid for, so for us it was free transportation, a way to visit friends in Venice Beach. The only problem was that now we had to get back to Chicago—some 2,500 miles away—and it had taken all day just to hitch this far. It was early evening and the desert air was baking hot, the sun shimmering orange just above the horizon. Judith was singing the title song from the musical *Oklahoma*. We hitchhiked a lot in those days, and she would often sing while we waited for our next ride. She seemed to know the lyrics to every corny Broadway song ever written. The memory was flawless in its detail—the acrid smell of diesel exhaust from the eighteen-wheelers, air rippling over the hot asphalt, the skin on the back of my sunburned neck tight and warm, the sound of Judith's voice holding us there together, safe. One moment we had shared.

Merry Christmas and all that.

My Judith. My dear one. My precious wife. How could our life together be at once so excruciatingly real and so completely, irrevocably lost? How could we have let this happen?

> I am time, almighty destroyer of worlds,
> appearing here for their annihilation.
> With or without your consent,
> these warriors ranged for battle
> shall cease to exist.

I finally understood: We are made to be broken. To love is to be shattered beyond repair by the realization of an infinite, unending loss. And we all do it, in one way or another, wisely or not. Love is our common offering, a spontaneous giving over of the self to the sweet, sad perfection of this world that slips so easily into memory, this dying world.

I folded the letter carefully, slid it into the envelope, and walked through the door, wiping my eyes with my sleeve. I hadn't cried since those early days in Agra—not even when Penny left and I knew she had taken everyone with her and she wasn't coming back. But now the tears came again, and this time they were for all of us.

38

My ALARM WENT OFF just before sunrise. Today I would meet Nortul. If I were going to arrive at Delhi University by midmorning, I needed to get an early start. I knew the trip through the old city would take at least an hour by auto rickshaw—especially since traffic would be worse than usual because of the recent election. I cleared a place in one corner of the room where I could meditate and settled in.

There was an open window above the door to my room—which could not be closed—and before long I could hear people outside going to and from the communal bathrooms. They were shouting to each other, singing, whistling, and yelling at their kids. The sounds reverberated up and down the hallway as if it were a gymnasium. Every now and again someone would slam the door with such force that the walls shook. I was already in a dismal mood, and the racket outside my room made it worse. My attention jumped from one sound to the next, and every sound was the catalyst for a frenzy of self-righteous indignation. *How could people be such totally thoughtless assholes?* Looking at my mind was like standing knee deep in the middle of a stinking, polluted swamp that extended out to the horizon in every direction. Anger and irritation, guilt and regret and fear, all of it smothered in an endless toxic babble of thought. Me, me, and more me, as far as the eye could see. I sat there with my eyes closed for about two hours, watching things come and go, until finally I'd had enough. By that time it was around seven; I opened the drapes and sunlight exploded into the room.

I took my towel and headed down the hall for a shower. After that I went downstairs for breakfast. Over a pot of coffee, I took stock.

Nortul Rinpoche was sorting through a collection of old texts that had been brought, in the early sixties, from impoverished monasteries in the hinterlands of eastern Ladakh, a region that is politically Indian but culturally and linguistically a part of Tibet. For the first time, it occurred to me that this was the very same region where Colonel Singh from Corbett

Park had commanded a regiment during the Sino-Indian War. He had actually talked with Penny and me about the artifacts in these monasteries. How is it that I had never before made this connection? Singh himself could have been involved in shipping these very texts to Delhi.

In any event, it was possible that the material in these crates had not been studied—or even looked at—for several generations. The tiny monasteries in eastern Ladakh were provincial, to say the least. The texts now being stored at Delhi University's library came from monasteries that had been isolated from the political and scholarly centers of Tibet for hundreds of years. It was at least conceivable that some of them may have been safely locked away from the outside world since the ninth century or earlier, when this area played a critical role in the transmission of Buddhism to Tibet.

It was just as Penny had said that evening in Corbett—Ladakh had been a crossroads of the Buddhist world. Beginning in early Christian times, and perhaps even before, there was a steady stream of traffic passing back and forth between Mediterranean Europe and Beijing. Merchants moved along trade routes passing near this area on their way to and from Kashgar, on the edge of the Taklamakan desert. And in the third century, when Buddhism was just beginning to enter China, this was where Indian Buddhist monks and Chinese scholars met. Kumarajiva—one of the most famous Chinese translators—journeyed to Ladakh and studied Sanskrit there with Indian pundits, who sent him back to An Jing with bundles of texts, including scriptures on the perfection of wisdom and commentaries by Nagarjuna and other early Indian masters. Several hundred years later, Buddhist teachings began to filter into Tibet via this same route. And now, another thousand years down the road, several crates of texts from the region had been transported to the library of Delhi University, where they were at this very moment being pried open by the lama I had been sent to meet.

I had trouble finding an auto rickshaw willing to make the trip all the way up to the university—and once I did, the driver refused to go by the meter. My driver unwisely decided to take the shorter route—going by way of Chelmsford Road through Azad Market—and the traffic was a nightmare. It was almost noon when I found myself climbing the front steps of the library.

A uniformed guard asked me for identification at the door. I knew the drill from past experience; Western scholars frequently conduct research at the university, so all I needed to do was show him my card. On the advice of the Fulbright office, I had arranged to have a box of absurdly pretentious business cards printed up shortly after my arrival in India for situations precisely like this. Unfortunately, the chaukidar appeared to be new at his job. Unsure of what to do, and obviously uneasy about this foreigner who was neither student nor faculty, he summoned a tired old man clothed in rumpled khaki shirt and pants—standard issue for every Indian peon. He took my card and disappeared. Several minutes later he returned and motioned for me to follow him up the stairs to a second-floor office. The doorway was hung with a dingy curtain, and a sign on the wall read "Subdirector of Acquisitions." The peon pulled back the curtain, and I stepped through.

Inside a ceiling fan propelled a steady blast across the vast arid plain of the subdirector's desk. The surface area that opened out between us testified to this man's position in the library hierarchy. Disorderly stacks of parched requisition slips, withered forms, and mummified interoffice memos rattled in the breeze. Several rubber stamps dangled from a little wooden rack shaped like a tree; one or two had dropped to the desk and lay scattered about under the branches like over-ripe fruit.

The subdirector had been scrutinizing my business card, which he held before him in both hands. When we entered he looked up at me through a pair of very large, very thick lenses. Somewhere back there I could make out two filmy, jaundiced eyes engaged in calculating my dependence on his authority. I knew instinctively that this man was not the least bit interested in why I had come. On the other hand, I was a diversion, an unexpected distraction from the routine of rubber stamps and endless forms, and to this extent I must not be permitted to escape before he had extracted some pleasure from my need.

"Please sit down, my dear sir. Take your chair, please." He extended one arm toward the center chair. "From what place you are coming?"

"Banaras," I answered, realizing immediately that I should have brought a briefcase. Any real scholar would be carrying a briefcase.

"No, no. My dear sir," he offered a cramped chuckle and rapped the edge of my card against the desktop once or twice. "I mean your country. Surely you must be having a country?"

"The US."

"America." Again the tapping of the card. "New York?"

"Chicago," I replied. "I'm from the University of Chicago. It says that on my card." I nodded in the direction of where it now lay, on his desk, just under his folded hands.

"Ah, yes. So it does." He picked up the card and read it out loud. "*Stanley Harrington, B.A, M.A, A.B.D. Fulbright Scholar. University of Chicago.* Very good. Very, very good." He eyed me in silence for a moment. "How long you have been in India, my dear sir?" I told him that a little less than two years had passed since my arrival. This seemed to make a positive impression. "Two years. And you are receiving salary from government side, isn't it?"

"Fulbright is a federally funded agency, so yes, from the government, you could say." My Fulbright had expired almost a year before, but as I was still living off the original stipend, the lie seemed justified.

"You must be receiving dollars. No?"

"No," I corrected him. "Not dollars. The Fulbright is paid in rupees."

"And, may I ask, how much they give to you each month?" He arched one brow over the black ridge of his plastic frames.

I offered the stock reply. "The fellowship pays my living expenses— room and food, travel costs. A stipend for books." I had discovered early on to deflect these queries about salary. If I were to reveal how many thousand rupees a fellowship actually doled out, no working-class Indian would ever have believed it. And if they believed it, I'm not sure what the reaction might have been. During my first year in India I had probably saved at least ten times more than this man could ever dream of earning in the same period.

"I see. And you are happily married man, sir?"

I hesitated. "No, I'm not." This response was greeted with another brief silence.

"I see. And your father, what he is doing?"

"My father is a businessman."

He nodded in approval.

This sort of thing went on for several minutes until he grew tired of probing into my personal life and got around to inquiring about my business at the library. I told him I had come to meet with a Tibetan lama—Nortul Rinpoche—who was presently engaged in research here. The name drew a total blank. I reminded him of Dorje Sherap's visit. He had never heard of any such person. I mentioned the texts from Ladakh. He assured me that I must be mistaken; there were no such texts. I insisted that there most definitely were. Not a chance. Certainly as subdirector of acquisitions he would know, wouldn't he?

We went back and forth on this for a while until I suggested that we consult the records for the early sixties. We batted this around for five or ten minutes before he decided that might be a good idea, after all. The subdirector stuck a hand under one corner of his big desk and pressed a hidden button. A buzzer sounded in the room just outside his door. The peon emerged from behind the curtain, bowed, and was summarily dispatched. He reappeared some ten or fifteen minutes later with his charge—a small, harried man decked out in a snugly tailored, baby-blue leisure suit with permanent sweat stains under each armpit. The little man crept past me, lugging a dog-eared tome that he dumped onto the subdirector's desk with a thud. Several dozen slips of white paper had been stuck between the pages. When he pulled open the cover, they were immediately sucked out into the breeze from the fan and erupted in a miniature white blizzard, dancing and fluttering around the office while the four of us—myself, the reference librarian, the subdirector, and his peon—rushed madly here and there, tramping them with our feet or snatching them from midair, until we managed to retrieve most, if not all of the scraps.

After considerable searching, the librarian located an entry made on November 28, 1962, which indicated that three crates of materials had been received from Ladakh and placed in storage. This seemed to jog the subdirector's memory, for suddenly he acknowledged that there was, in fact, an old Tibetan monk who came now and again to the library. Indeed, he had seen this monk fairly recently, now that he thought about it. As it turned out, he had himself signed the authorization form. Where was it . . . ?

Once again the peon was sent forth, returning after a blessedly short time with yet another record book that was deposited on the desk. The subdirector leafed through its pages for a minute or two, then stopped and read carefully, nodding. "Yes, yes. Here it is: *Nyingpo Toobpa. Authorized by the Ministry of Home Affairs.*" He poked at the page in front of him. "The form is signed by one of the ministry's agents."

"But that's not the person I'm looking for," I objected. "I'm here to meet someone named Nortul."

"Nortul?" He seemed puzzled. "But that is not the name on the form. Look here—see for yourself."

He pushed aside a stack of papers and slid the book across his desk. It was just as he said: Nyingpo Toobpa. I was about to object again when it occurred to me that if I insisted this was not my man, the whole deal would fall apart, and I'd never get beyond this office. "Well then," I suggested, "perhaps I could just go meet with Mr. Toobpa. If you'd be so kind as to point the way . . ." I was halfway up from the chair when he smiled indulgently and swung his arm up like a traffic cop, motioning for me to remain seated.

"No, no, my dear sir." He shook his head profusely. "You are jumping off so quickly." Again the patronizing smile. "Please, please. Do try to relax. You Americans are so very jumpy people."

"Yes, but our business is finished so I . . ."

"No hurry, no vurry." He smiled at me and tipped his head. "Isn't it so?"

I remained where I was, poised in midair.

"Please be calm, sir. Be calm. *Please.*" Still smiling, he waited, unwilling to continue until he was sure I had regained my self-control. I settled back down into the chair and he spoke. "I am afraid to say, no one can be permitted to enter i-storage facilities. It is regulation. You know?"

I started upright. "But . . ."

Again he silenced me with a wave of his arm. "Patience, my dear sir. Patience. *Matlab ki*, no one may enter without receiving proper authorization."

"Proper authorization," I echoed his words. I was hot and itchy and thirsty. My patience—already in short supply—was rapidly wearing thin. This endless delay was starting to really piss me off. I'd already been sitting here for over an hour. But to show any sign of temper was out of the question. To lose your cool in a situation like this is simply to lose. This man sitting behind the desk held all the cards. He could easily turn me away, and that would be it. Game over.

He grinned, flashing a set of uniformly spaced, paan-stained teeth. "Even important scholar like yourself must collect proper form."

It turned out that the proper form could be issued in this very office, and to do so would require only a few minutes. Meanwhile I must have a cup of chai. He reached under his desk again and punched the buzzer several times before it dawned on him that the electricity was no longer functioning, something he should have noticed already since the ceiling fan had coasted to a stop several minutes earlier and we were both sweating copiously. No problem. He commenced violently pounding a bell on his desk as if we had already been kept waiting for hours. The same peon shuffled through the curtain, joined his palms and bowed, as before. He was again sent forth.

We waited, smiling and nodding at each other. Five minutes. Ten minutes. Fifteen. Eventually a ragged, barefoot urchin popped through the curtain with a wire rack containing six glasses of chai. The subdirector and I were joined by two assistant subdirectors, an accountant, and the head reference librarian, and I was compelled to endure the same pointless interrogation about where I was from, what was my business in India, how much money I made, and so forth. At some point we shifted into Hindi, and everyone, even my host, was favorably impressed. Finally, the peon returned from somewhere bearing the requisite permit, in quadruplicate. The subdirector extracted a sheaf of small pink stamps from his drawer and carefully pasted one to each of the four copies. He meticulously signed all of them over the pink stamp and passed each one along to an assistant, who also signed. I added my signature in the appropriate place on each form. After that the forms went back to the subdirector and were summarily pounded with one of the rubber stamps from the miniature tree. I received my copy, the subdirector retained his, and the remaining two copies were entrusted to the peon who would take them to be filed among the library's permanent records.

The guardians of the inner gate let me pass.

39

I FOLLOWED THE DIRECTIONS I had been given, back through the stacks to a heavy metal doorway, then down a flight of stairs that led to the basement storage facilities. Silverfish crawled over the walls and the air was tinged with mildew. At the foot of the stairs a single dimly lit passageway led through a jumble of packing crates and piles of musty books. A rat stuck its head out of the shadows, darted across the aisle and back in among the boxes, his tail slithering after him. I threaded my way along the path for fifty feet or so, to where it drew up in front of two narrow wooden panels standing slightly ajar. From inside came a rough bark, like the sound of a dog, and I instinctively recoiled. After a moment, the mysterious sound came again, and I realized it was someone coughing. This was followed by an indistinct mumbling and the rustle of stiff paper. I pushed the panels open and stepped through.

The periphery of the room was jammed to the ceiling with more boxes and crates, with bundles of books wrapped in dusty cloth, every seam stitched tightly and dotted with hard red puddles of congealed sealing wax. Directly in front of me, under a single overhead bulb, a table seemed to float among the packing debris. Behind the table sat a round, middle-aged Tibetan lama carelessly wrapped in thin summer robes bleached to the color of Portuguese rosé. He was bent forward, forearms resting on the edge of the table, the cat's cradle of a rosary slung between his hands—totally absorbed in the unbound leaves of a Tibetan text that lay open before him. His chin was fringed with long whiskers, and two gray tufts sprouted from the corners of his mouth. An array of red and yellow strings hung around his neck. One of them had been threaded through a chunk of smooth, honeyed amber. His long hair was coiled on top of his head and held in place with a silver stylized dragon studded with turquoise scales; a single coral flame trailed from the dragon's jaws. The lama's head was tilted forward so that both eyes were enclosed in shadow, and he was reading aloud to himself in a low murmur. The only other sound was the soft click of the beads as they passed between the stubs of his fingers.

I was debating how best to attract his attention when he brought his face up out of the pages. His eyes were closed, and he appeared to be reflecting on whatever it was he had just read. Before I could speak, both lids opened, and he found himself looking right at me. I was standing only a few yards away, and my presence obviously caught him by surprise. He jerked back in his chair, knocking over a crowbar that had been propped against the table. It clanged against the concrete floor.

I winced and smiled weakly. "*Maaf Kijiyay.*" Dorje Sherap and I had spoken Hindi together, and the language emerged from my mouth now without a second thought. "I startled you. I'm sorry."

He stared at me wide eyed, like one of the little monkeys outside my window in Banaras. I was about to apologize again when he cut me off with a series of choppy, heavily accented English syllables.

"Why you make no sound?"

"I . . . I was . . ."

"Creeping, creeping! Like *chuha!*" He hunched his shoulders, raised both hands in the air over the table, palms downward, and began to wiggle his fingers, presumably mimicking the tiny paws of a rat.

"You were reading," I said defensively, still in Hindi. "You didn't hear me."

"You speak English?" He looked at me hopefully. The fingers hovered, motionless now, just above the surface of the table.

I nodded. "*Ji* . . . I mean, *yes.* Sure. I thought you might feel more comfortable in Hindi."

This seemed to strike him as quite amusing. "*A-lay!* I look like Indian man?" His hands dropped flat on the desk. He puffed up his chest and put on a haughty, supercilious expression. "Maybe big sardarji, eh? What you think?"

"I, uh . . ."

"My English bad. I know. But Hindi . . ." He hauled up his right hand and held it aloft, palm up, in the space between us. While I watched he touched the tip of his thumb to the base of his little finger, then to the first and second joints, then to the tip, moving in this fashion from one finger to the next, all the while counting out loud in Tibetan. ". . . *chu-sum, chu-zhi, chu-nga, chu-duk* . . ." His thumb reached the tip of his pointer finger and he paused for a moment. "*Mindu!*" He raised his left hand and began the same process all over again, placing the tip of his left thumb at the base of his little finger. "*Chu-dun* . . ." He stopped, considering, then looked up and announced his discovery in emphatic English. "Seven-ten!" He stared at me in disbelief. "Seven-ten years now I am in India. But Hindi not so good." He shook his head sadly, as if mourning a lost opportunity. "Why you come here?"

The blunt question caught me off guard. "I'm looking for Nyingpo Toobpa."

He sat up straight and started in again running the beads of the rosary through his fingers. "What you say?"

"I'm looking for Nyingpo Toobpa. I was told that he was here."

"Who want meet this man?"

"Who wants to?" I adjusted my posture, straightening my back ever so slightly. "I do. Me." I placed one hand on my chest. "I want to meet Nyingpo Toobpa." It came out like a declaration of faith.

"Where you hear this name, Nyingpo Toobpa? Who tell you?"

I explained about the assistant subdirector and the authorization he had showed me, the one signed by an agent at the Ministry of Home Affairs. "It said there that Nyingpo Toobpa was sent to the library as a representative of the Dalai Lama."

"Nyingpo Toobpa. Very nice. Very important man." The beads clicked decisively. "But Nyingpo Toobpa not here."

"Well then," I cleared my throat. "Perhaps you can tell me where I might find him."

"Dead."

"Dead? What?"

"Nyingpo Toobpa dead man."

"But, when? When did he die?"

"Oh, not so long," he replied casually, shuffling the beads through his fingers. One of the silver tufts, the left one, twitched.

This man, whoever he might be, was most definitely bullshitting me.

"Maybe two, three year now." He shrugged and let his head tilt toward one shoulder—an Indian mannerism he had obviously picked up, even if he hadn't learned much Hindi.

I gathered my nerve. "Two or three years?"

"Four, maybe."

"Four." I looked him in the eye now, making a real effort to suppress my skepticism. "Maybe."

He nodded and leaned back in his chair.

I dipped into my pocket and pulled out the letter of introduction, unfolded it and spread it out on the desk near the text he had been studying. "Please read this. It should explain why I'm here."

He picked up the note and raised it a little closer to the light. I could make out the florid loops and swirls of cursive Tibetan script. His lips shaped the words as he read. The further he went, the more his expression softened. By the time he finished, the two silver flags were flying aloft at either end of what I took to be a genuinely warmhearted smile. He looked up and waved the paper in my direction, then let it fall to the desktop. "You know this Gelukpa lama? Dorje Sherap?"

I nodded vigorously.

"Your name . . ." He picked up the paper and studied it. "Tsan-lee Harring-tune. Is it?"

"Yes."

"Okay, then," he said, in a matter-of-fact tone. "I am Nortul."

"But what about Nyingpo?"

He silenced me with a wave of his hand. "Nyingpo Toobpa dead man. Is finish."

So the name was obviously an alias of some kind, which means that the authorization from the ministry must have been either forged or stolen. This was not a comforting thought.

"Nyingpo dead, but Nortul still here. Not so bad, eh?" He smiled. "What you say?"

I returned the smile; it was impossible not to. "Nortul Rinpoche," I repeated his name, joined my palms and offered a modest bow. "I'm honored to meet you."

Nortul mimicked my gesture, his rosary swinging from one hand. "Honor meet you, Mr. Tsan-lee. So what Dorje Sherap tell about me, eh?"

"He speaks highly of you. He tells me that you are an outstanding scholar."

"*Out-stand-ing.*" He pronounced the word carefully. "Means 'good,' eh?"

"More than good. Outstanding means that you're a *very* good scholar."

"Hmmmmm . . . good for *Nyingmapa* lama, no? Maybe not so good compare to Gelukpa." He laughed. "What else he say?"

"He's extremely busy these days at the institute, putting together the library. We didn't talk all that much." I immediately sensed that Nortul knew I was lying.

He picked up the note again and scrutinized it. "He say here you read *pecha* . . . He say you read *sherchin*—in Sanskrit."

"Well, yes. My Sanskrit's okay. And I've been reading the Prajna-paramita—uh, *sherchin*—in Sanskrit and in Tibetan. On my own, mostly." I smiled. "Well, the truth is I'm doing it completely alone. And I read Tibetan very slowly, and only with the dictionary. But that's why I'm here. I think Geshe Sherap wrote that I want to learn more. I'm looking for a teacher." It suddenly struck me as totally inappropriate that I should be asking this man to be my teacher. What right did I have to think he would be interested in teaching me? I eyed the note lying between us on the table.

"Yes," he nodded. "He say you want haggle."

"Well, I, uh . . . haggle?"

"What is it?" He squinted, studying my face.

"I don't understand."

"Is my English, no?" He dove into the junk on his desk and began rummaging around among the papers and books, shuffling things this way and that, rearranging the piles until he eventually fished out a dog-eared Tibetan-English dictionary and held it up for me to see, accompanying the gesture with a portentous gaze. He thumbed through the pages and finally stopped, running one finger down the column of entries until finding the right word. "*Je-gyap*. Haggle." He glanced up at me, then went on reading the other entries. "Also mean 'barter, trade, give or take in exchange.' Dorje Sherap say you want haggle English in exchange Tibetan. Eh?" He sat there with the dictionary in his hands, looking extremely satisfied with himself, as if he had just proven his point beyond dispute. It was the same look Mick had given me more times than I wished to remember.

"Yes, of course," I exclaimed, contritely. "That's right. I want to trade English lessons for Tibetan lessons."

At this he positively vibrated with delight. Maniacal glee radiated from his body like a gravitational force, pulling me into his orbit. I could think of nothing else to say, so I simply stood there with an idiotic grin on my face.

"Nice," he wagged his head up and down, "very nice! When we begin?" His eyes glittered with shameless exuberance. "Now?"

I explained that I had come from Banaras and that I would have to go back for another month or so, but perhaps we could start in May? This too was "nice." *Very nice*! He wanted to know if I would be willing to spend the summer in Dharamsala, near the residence of the Dalai Lama. "No

Indian people, you know? Only Tibeti." He gave me another meaningful look, one foreigner to another. "Good place for practice speak Tibeti language." He had a close friend who would help me find a place to stay. In fact everything would be fixed up when I arrived. How did that sound? I assured him that it all sounded very nice, and with that the deal was settled. We would meet sometime in late May. He gave me his uncle's name and told me to ask for him at the post office in McLeod Ganj; someone there would contact him for me. Part of me wanted nothing more than to sit right down and begin. No time to waste! *Let's haggle!*

The rosary hummed through his fingers. I watched the beads fly past and thought of how quickly the months had disappeared since coming to India. I noticed for the first time that he was wearing another fabulous ornament on the middle finger of his right hand. A chunk of ivory, or maybe some kind of bone, polished smooth and yellowed with age, the surface fractured by an intricate web of hairline cracks, like tiny veins in a dry leaf. It had been carved into a ghoulish carnival mask with two bulging eyes and a broad, hooked nose, nostrils flared over a row of crooked teeth that rose and fell hypnotically as the beads clicked by underneath.

"Well then," I said, pulling my eyes away from the ring, "I guess it's all set."

Again his hands groped out over the desk, stirring up the mess, shuffling and restacking, all the while importuning me to remain for just a few minutes more. He had something very important that he simply had to show me before I left. At last he produced a copybook of the sort that Indian schoolchildren use for their lessons. Several loose threads dangled from its frayed binding. *Delux Sarasvati Register* was printed on the cover in bold red letters.

"Come." He gestured in the direction of an unopened crate that rested on the floor in front of the table. "Sit." I obeyed his command; there was just enough room to tuck my knees under the desk. "My work," he exclaimed, patting the book with one hand. "Is *translation*." He spoke the word proudly and then seemed to reconsider. "Please, I must request you not laugh on my English. I work alone, you know? Like you!" This realization obviously restored his enthusiasm. "I have wait too long for meeting right person. Foreigner, you know. For help improve English. But now you come! From today we work together! No problem!"

He opened the notebook, turned it around, and pushed it toward me. "What you think?"

At first I assumed that I was looking at an idiosyncratic style of *umey*, the cursive Tibetan calligraphy that Dorje Sherap had used to write his letter of introduction, a script I had never learned. Closer inspection belied this initial impression. It was English. But if Nortul Rinpoche's spoken English was idiosyncratic, then his handwriting—and his prose style—was genuinely original. It passed through my mind that this might be a weird joke of some kind, but I took one glance at the face rising over my shoulder like an impatient moon and dismissed the joke hypothesis as improbable. His expression was far too ingenuous. Painfully so. There could be no question that he was anxious to solicit my reaction to his work. I swam through a quagmire of tortured syntax and highly inventive spelling, then stopped short when halfway down the page a single line of perfect English caught my eye:

> Those who do not tremble on encountering the perfection of wisdom called nonclinging, those who are neither terrified nor overcome by dread, they will be filled with wonder.

I read it a second time, then a third, for good measure, before turning to Rinpoche. "What is this?"

He was obviously taken aback. "Is English translation."

"No. I mean, sure. Right. From a Prajnaparamita text. I can make out that much. But which one?"

Now he flashed me a broad, knowing grin. "Mr. Tsan-lee never see this *sherchin*. Before today only one man see."

"You?"

"Yes. Is true. I am only one man."

I looked around me at the jumble of boxes and crates, and in that moment, somewhere deep inside the labyrinthine tunnels and chambers of my brain, neglected synapses crackled and sparked for the first time in months. Massive, dusty wheels began to revolve, decrepit machinery shuddered and groaned, setting in motion cranks and levers that dislodged the lid on a bubbling cauldron of ambition. I was growing ever more excited just imagining what a dissertation this would make. For the better part of a year I had barely thought about academics, and yet—in a matter of seconds—here I was, lost in a vision of my brilliant future as an internationally acclaimed Indologist. I saw myself walking into Abe Sellars's office with an edition, annotated translation, and text-critical study of Rinpoche's sutra. *So you think I've been fucking around over in South Asia, drinking chai and smoking ganja? Or, worse yet, playing out some juvenile fantasy of a spiritual quest? Is that it? Well take a look-see at this!* Tattered old Banarsi briefcase springs open and out it comes, five hundred pages of meticulous philological scholarship that lands on his desk like a mortar shell. And the journal articles it would generate, the papers ... I envisioned myself as the honored respondent to a panel at the national conference for the Association for Asian Studies, six top-drawer North American and European scholars presenting papers on a previously unknown Indian Prajnaparamita sutra rescued by yours truly. Edward Conze banging on my door. Lamotte might even drop me a card from Brussels. Suddenly I wished Margaret Billings were still in town so I could look her up.

"You found it here?" I asked.

"Oh no, no!" He flapped his hands in the air. The rosary was wrapped around his left wrist. "No, Mr. Tsan-lee." His voice roused me from the glory of my heraldic vision.

"No? No what?"

"No find in this library."

"Then where did it come from? Tibet?" I began to get excited all over again.

"Come from India. Is old sherchin sutra from India."

"But how did you find it?"

"Someone give me."

"Someone? Who?"

"Someone in here," he exclaimed with a broad grin, pointing a finger at his head. But his smile waned when he saw the unguarded look of utter disappointment that swept over my face as the big fantasy of academic fame and fortune evaporated. This old lama had not the slightest idea of why I might be so profoundly disappointed. How could he? "Come from mind," he repeated, as if perhaps I hadn't understood him the first time. "*Gong-ter.*" He smiled again, a bit meekly this time. "Very mystery, you know?"

"Are you saying," I cleared my throat, trying my best to appear as though it made no difference to me one way or the other, "that you, uh, made it up?"

His eyebrows rose uncomprehendingly. "Made up?"

"Made it up. It means, well, that you wrote the sutra. You know, all by yourself."

His fist thumped down on the open copybook. "No, I am not made it up. Is word of Buddha. Very old sutra. And now you help me translate to English." He smiled mischievously, and I felt for a moment as though I were being drawn into some outlandish conspiracy.

"Tell me," he demanded, "how you translate *sherchin yigey mepa*?"

I pushed the copybook over toward him. "Can you write it down? In *uchen*, please." He picked up a fluorescent pink ballpoint pen, wiped a blob of ink off the tip by smearing it onto the corner of the page, and began carefully printing the characters in a single line of surprisingly legible classical Tibetan script. When he finished, I studied it for a minute and then ventured a translation. "'The perfection of wisdom with no letters . . .' No, wait. How about, 'the *unwritten* perfection of wisdom'?"

"Yes," he said, nodding his head earnestly. "'Unwritten perfection of wisdom.' Yes, yes. Very nice." He gazed at the letters a moment longer and then looked up. "You hear before?"

I shook my head.

His question came back to me, though, on a late, gray winter afternoon several years later. I was ensconced in a library carrel in the Harvard-Yenching when I chanced to come across mention of the "'unwritten' Prajnaparamita" while perusing Roerich's translation of the *Blue Annals*. I found the insignificant reference tucked away in a history of the Shije lineage, where this "unwritten perfection of wisdom" is reported to have been taught by an Indian ascetic named Dampa. According to the *Blue Annals*, Dampa on his third visit to Tibet met Machik Lapdron, the woman who went on to found the influential practice known as Chö. The story is that they got together at the home of a wealthy merchant named Rokpa, where Dampa passed along to her "three words of friendly advice." This is the so-called "pith instruction"—*nying tam*—reported, once again, in the *Blue Annals* and other Tibetan chronicles. Rinpoche's lineage believes that the three words referred to in these texts are *see, relinquish, rest*, and that the whole thing is an esoteric reference to a particular "unwritten perfection of wisdom" that was passed along by Dampa that day.

As I say, I only put all this together much later, after returning from India, and even then it was many more years before I made any conscientious effort to document the claims made by Nortul Rinpoche. In India I pretty much swallowed whatever he said. For instance, according to what he went on to tell me that afternoon in Delhi, the "unwritten perfection of wisdom" was not a single sutra but an entire genre of Prajnaparamita teachings that circulated throughout India during the same centuries when most of the other famous Perfection of Wisdom scriptures—like the *Heart Sutra* and the *Diamond-Cutter*—were being recorded for posterity on the pages of hand-lettered palm-leaf xylographs. If what Nortul Rinpoche told me is true, however, then the particular sutra referred to in this passage from the *Blue Annals* is the very one that lay open before us—a sutra that had been passed along orally for generations but never before committed to writing. A sutra he was now translating into English.

"This sutra," he glanced at the copybook, then quickly back up at me so as to judge the effect of his words, "we call 'mantra healing all kind sickness.'"

I had been listening quietly until then, but with that remark I stopped him. "The perfection of wisdom is the medicine for suffering."

"Yes, is medicine for every kind suffering."

"Then why all this talk of 'terror' and 'dread'? It's supposed to be a *cure* for suffering, right? Not a *cause*."

He looked at me pointedly. "You want jump too far in front." He said this and continued to scrutinize me, as if he were slightly perplexed. As if he were sizing me up. Gradually his expression became quiet, thoughtful. "When I was young man in Tibet, many year before, I once know old lama, Tsering. Tsering say that most person always look for magic. No interest philosophy. You teach philosophy, they go for sleep. Very tedious." He actually used the word *tedious*. "Most people only want learn *mantra*—magic. So maybe you are same, eh?" He paused and searched my face for a sign of confirmation. And then in a flash his expression turned grave, his tone of voice uncompromising. "Mr. Tsan-lee, you want magic medicine for end suffering? You want make suffering finish? Right this moment?"

His eyes were locked on mine. My immediate impulse was to say, *Sure. Give me the magic pill.* But there was something about the intensity of his gaze that unnerved me. The beads clicked through his fingers. I quickly looked away—over his shoulder, then down at the copybook where it lay open on the table—and instead of answering, I deflected the question. "So what about the third noble truth of the Buddha? The end of suffering? Why should I *fear* nirvana?"

"A-*laaaay* . . ." He sighed.

I raised my eyes slowly and found him still watching me. Only now he appeared to be somehow disappointed.

"You read many Buddha sutra. Read in Sanskrit, no? But maybe you read too much quick. Miss important parts." He adjusted himself in the chair, arranging and smoothing his faded robes. "I give some advice, okay?" I nodded dumbly. "Forget third noble truth. You see? *Oos ko fenk doe!*" The Hindi phrase was amusing, arriving unexpectedly in his Tibetan accent. I started to object, but he waved it off and continued. "Now please you tell me. What is first noble truth of Buddha?"

"*Duhkha*," I replied confidently. "The first noble truth says that all life is suffering."

"Nice. All life suffering. First noble truth. Very nice." He looked at me and grinned. His mood seemed to have inexplicably improved. "Is true, eh? What you think?"

I shrugged. "I don't know."

"What?!" he cut me off. "You do not know? Then you must know some happy in this life?" He seemed to be incredulous at the suggestion that I might ever have actually experienced happiness. "You know what is happy?" Once again he looked as though he were actually expecting an answer.

"Happiness is . . ." I ventured, "it's what everyone wants. All people want to be happy."

"And nobody want suffer and pain. Is it not so? Everybody fear pain. Push away."

I nodded.

"I give more advice now. Okay?" He considered. "Look close at happy time. Happy time is always something welcome. You see? That is all. Very simple."

He examined my face and frowned.

"You not understand. Listen more close. Welcome is *enough* for happy. Reason not important. Whatever time is welcome, that is happy time. All other is suffer and pain. Suffer and pain is only that—what you *not* welcome."

"But of course," I shot back. "Pain is never 'welcome.' Nobody wants pain."

He studied me in silence, clearly evaluating my response. "You ever try?"

"Try what?"

"Try welcome pain."

"Rinpoche, why would I want to welcome pain?"

"Very simple answer: because pain is best teacher. That is why make pain welcome. Self never want welcome pain. Self always run from pain, run toward happy. Always make big difference pain from happy. Self always welcome happy, push away pain. *Fear* pain. You know?" He held up both hands between us, palms facing me, and turned his head back and forth, looking from one hand to the other. "Want happy. Not want pain. Want happy. Not want pain." He did this several times, looking from one hand to the other and repeating the same line, then he turned his eyes toward me again. "Self *made* from 'desire happy' and 'fear pain.' Self always judge. You know what means 'judge'?" He squinted at me, cocking his head to one side.

"Judge," I repeated the word. "It means to decide one thing is better or worse than another."

"Yes." He nodded vigorously. "That is meaning. First judge, then choose: Want or not want. Desire or fear. Self always must judge and choose. So everything very simple: No judge—no self. No self—no suffer! You see? Need only to stop judge and choose. Sit quiet, welcome pain and pleasure equal, like two stranger come for visit. No need for invite—guest come and guest go. Guest come, you be nice. Guest go, you be nice. Very simple."

He did a kind of Marcel Marceau routine, pretending to open a door between us, then bowing formally to his guest, welcoming his visitor: "Come in. Sit down. Drink chai. Good*bye!*" He delivered all this in a sing-song voice, tipping his head to one side and then the other, pronouncing the final syllable of "goodbye" with distinct irony while supplying a cute little wave with the fingers of one hand. "You see now? Self is finish." He caught my eye, his expression suddenly becoming grave. "*Tsa!*"

His hand chopped down through the air like the blade of an ax.

"Finish! Like tree cut off at root."

Back in the shadows something moved its teeth along the edge of a crate. Nortul studied my face, assessing my reaction.

"I . . ." My voice faltered.

"Yes?"

"I, uh, I still don't understand."

"What you not understand? Very simple."

"How am I supposed to just stop judging and choosing? It's not that easy, Rinpoche. People can't just make themselves stop wanting one thing and not wanting another. I can't just *do* that."

He shook his head. "Not do."

"But you said . . ."

He interrupted me. "Nothing you must *do*."

"Then, *what*?" I was losing patience.

Nortul was charming, no doubt, but this whole pantomime about "welcoming pain" struck me as somehow disingenuous. It was fine in theory—I understood the theory—but I didn't need more theory. I suddenly felt very much like I'd had more than enough theory to last a lifetime. Several lifetimes. All those classes and seminars at Chicago, reading the texts, arguing about grammar and syntax, writing papers so that Abraham Sellars could flood the margins with his vicious red scrawl, using his words to open wounds that would never heal because they weren't *supposed* to heal. That was the idea—right?—the arguments must never end, the words must never, ever be allowed to stop. All those massive intellects on parade, endlessly churning the soup of reason. *Words, words, words.* Words in Sanskrit. Words in Pali. And here I was trying to learn Tibetan when it should be blindingly obvious that all the words in all the languages on earth translate into nothing but more tears.

So why was I here? It seemed, at that moment, like a relevant question. A question worth asking. What exactly was I looking for?

"If there's nothing I can *do*," I said, "to make myself stop judging and choosing, then I . . . well, then I guess I'm lost. I don't see the point." I'm sure he heard the frustration in my voice, which I was no longer even trying to disguise.

"Not *do*," he said again emphatically. "*Do* mean *think*. No need for think. Only *see*."

"See? See what?"

"No, no!" He shook his head. "You not understand. Not see some *thing*. See mean *be*. See mean not come from any place, not go any place." He held his hands up, palms toward me, gently smoothing the air between us. "See mean *rest*."

After a moment he dropped his hands and wound the rosary around one wrist. He tugged on the wisp of straggly gray hair that hung from his chin like Spanish moss, all the while still studying my face. Then he began picking his nose. Once this task was complete he sat absolutely motionless, staring straight ahead into space. He appeared to have forgotten all about me. I thought for a second that he might actually have slid into some kind of trance. The corners of his lips were drawn up in an enigmatic smile that was collecting momentum as I watched. He reminded me of the Cheshire cat from *Alice in Wonderland*.

"Tibetan people have *muhavrah*," he announced from out of nowhere, using the Hindi word. "You know what is *muhavrah*?"

I nodded. I remembered learning the word in class, back in Chicago. A *muhavrah* is something like an English proverb, a saying.

"Tibetan people have famous muhavrah. We say 'better never begin.'" He looked at me expectantly. "You understand? Better *not ever begin* Buddha path. 'But if begin, better you finish!'" His head bobbed with unrestrained merriment. "Once begin," he repeated, "better you finish!" He started to giggle. "Better *never* begin. If begin, better you *finish*! *Hahahaha hee hee*! Big joke, no?"

I managed to crack a weak smile, but this time he really had lost me.

At first he seemed to assume that my uncomprehending expression was a bluff, but then his laughter faded into another silence and he frowned. "Why you not laugh? Very funny muhavrah. But maybe you know this joke from before. No? Someone tell you before?"

"I don't think so . . ."

He studied my expression for a moment, then leaned toward me. "When you begin Buddha path?"

In a flash, I recalled the conversation with Margaret, that afternoon in the Fulbright lounge when I'd wanted to tell her about my undergraduate years reading Herman Hesse and Alan Watts and Aldous Huxley. All that acid and mescaline. Throwing open the doors of perception. Judith and I sitting zazen with Kapleau's students. The whole long story of the spiritual quest that had brought me to graduate school and then to India. But I no sooner opened my mouth to spit it out than Nortul cut me off short, like some Zen master ringing the bell.

"Now."

He looked at me, thoroughly deadpan.

"You begin now."

I felt a prickly sensation all over my scalp, and I involuntarily shivered. He continued to hold my eyes. "And when are you finish? You know?"

I shook my head. Something about the way he spoke was not right. Something about the way he looked. In fact, something about the way *everything* looked was suddenly not quite right.

"I tell you."

He leaned forward across the desk, beckoning me closer, as if about to take me into confidence on a matter of extreme delicacy, something of considerable importance to the two of us, and the two of us alone. Once again I obeyed, drawing my head close to his.

He whispered in my ear, "You are finish . . . *now*."

The moment he spoke these words, I became intensely self-conscious, fiercely aware of how I appeared in his eyes. It was as if I were seated across from myself, looking at myself in a mirror, seeing myself as he saw me. It was as if I were looking into my own mind from some outside vantage point. All the pathetic games, the insecurity, the desperate need for validation, the fantastic panorama of yearning and fear. My whole life stripped naked under the brutal white glare of the incandescent bulb that hung over us like some unearthly fruit. Only now I had swallowed the fruit and it was inside me. It wasn't even him seeing me, or me seeing myself—there was only this immense *seeing*, this boundless light where thoughts, feelings, and sensations were unmoored and drifting like clouds in open sky. And in the midst of this Great Seeing the light coalesced and took form, crawling up over the horizon of consciousness like the fiery morning sun, absorbing my attention and focusing it on a single astonishing realization:

This is a dream.

This subterranean chamber stacked with books, this strange Tibetan man in robes with his creepy text. All of it suddenly felt exactly like the dream where I was driving the bus—not real, and yet at the same time impossibly, undeniably, vibrantly *present*. Or like the dream *after* the driving one—the dream where I dreamed I'd actually woken up. It felt like something I had once imagined, the dream of a memory, or the remembering of a dream I did not want to remember.

But now Nortul was laughing again, rocking back and forth in his seat, cackling like a hyena. His face was contorted with mirth, one hand slapping the table. I felt myself carried aloft by the frenzy of his rapture, a laughter so riotous, so insane and all-encompassing, it was impossible to resist. And when I, too, gave myself over and began to laugh, there was no turning back. Soon we were both laughing so hard, we began to weep. I saw myself lean backward, gripping the table with both hands. I saw myself wipe my eyes and struggle to breathe.

"Better never begin!" He pulled himself slowly up onto his elbows, as if his body were a slab of warm taffy, then wiped his eyes with the back of one pudgy hand. "Yes, yes! *Now* you see, Mr. Tsan-lee! *Now* you understand! Once begin, better you finish!" This cracked him up all over again. "*Hahahahaha hee hee!* Some funny muhavrah, eh?" Gradually his laughter subsided, and he mopped his eyes and nose, using the ragged hem of his robe as a handkerchief.

I took a deep breath and straightened up and said to myself: Now it is over. Now I will wake up. This is what I wanted. Or what, in that moment, I thought I wanted, for it immediately occurred to me, *What if the alarm actually sounds? What if I really do wake up and find myself lying in bed somewhere?* But there was no bell. We continued on, just as we were.

Just as we are, just as we shall be.

Sicut eramus in principio, et nunc, et semper, et in sæcula sæculorum.

And I thought, this is how it is: there are only the stories. Stories we tell to ourselves and to each other. Stories about ourselves in a world.

There is only this endless layering of memory and imagination.

Nortul finished swabbing his nose and grew calm. When at last he spoke, his voice was resolute. "Many things change after Chinese enter Tibet. Old ways dying. Old way of teaching no longer suitable. We live in . . ." He stumbled, searching for the right word. "We live in *eunuch* time."

Somewhere in my brain a switch flipped: where had I heard that word recently?

An image presented itself to me: the jungles of Assam, 1959. A refugee camp somewhere near the Tibetan border. Nortul Rinpoche and Dorje Sherap are sitting together in a missionary's tent, both of them learning English from the same old British Memsahab, both of them memorizing the same new vocabulary, testing and shaping each new sound in conversation with each other. Now this was funny. So why wasn't I laughing?

I want only warn you. Big yogi power.

"What did you say? What kind of time are we living in?"

He frowned. "*Eu*-nuch, eh? Means strange. Crazy. *Very danger.*"

"Un*ique*," I said, fighting to control the anxiety rising in my voice, for I abruptly sensed that I was in over my head, that the alarm clock might yet ring—that Nortul would somehow *make* it ring—that he was making it ring right now, and if I didn't very quickly find some way to shut it off, I really would wake up in Banaras—or somewhere else—Agra, *Chicago.* And if that happened, if I woke up, there would be no escape from the dream. No more dreaming of escape. And no way back into my old life with its habits of thought and reason, its perpetual conflict between the fear of loneliness and the fear of love, and all the other familiar certainties that make it possible to know who I am. I knew without the slightest doubt that to wake up in this dream—to truly see it for what it is—would leave me in ruins. It was the last thing on earth I wanted. It was altogether beyond wanting.

"The word is pronounced yoo-*neek*," I insisted, my heart pounding. "With the stress on the last syllable, not the first. And it doesn't mean crazy. Or dangerous." But he wasn't paying attention.

"Very danger time," he continued. "Old way of teaching too slow."

40

THE YOUNG MAN wore loose khakis and a white khadi shirt. He was obviously a foreigner—an American with shaggy, reddish blond hair and blue eyes. He climbed the stairs that led up and out of the storage facility and walked quickly through the stacks toward the front entrance, eyes down, as if he were making an effort not to attract attention. A guard sat at his post near the main door. He saw the pale foreigner coming from some distance off and stood up and saluted him effusively with joined palms as the man passed by and stepped through the door into the glare of the north Indian sun. The heat was ferocious, the air so dry it sucked the moisture from the young man's pores. Just outside the door he stopped dead, as if he had slammed into a barrier. He raised both hands to his forehead like a visor, shielding his eyes.

Across the lawn, a kiosk was tucked into a small grove of spindly trees that struggled to assert themselves against the parched landscape. A group of students gathered nearby in a patch of shade. The sounds of Bollywood music, conversation, and laughter drifted languidly through the air. The American felt his way carefully down the stairs, squinting and shuffling like a blind man. The soles of his sandals were worn into small pockets of warm rubber that cradled his calloused heels, the thongs nestling snugly between his toes. As he crossed the yard the packed earth momentarily stirred to life, and pink clouds of dust snapped at the cuffs of his pants.

At the kiosk an old man bent forward over the counter, resting on his elbows. He wore a Nehru cap and a short waiter's coat stained with perspiration and grease. Nearby a child squatted, washing cups under a trickle of water that spilled from a concrete cistern. Somewhere in the distance a dog was barking.

The young man ordered a Limca, paid with a two-rupee note, and retreated to a nearby bench where he could sit quietly and watch. The bottle was cold and wet against his palm. He tipped the neck away, running his tongue against the polished rim of the glass. An exquisite flurry of wet sparks showered up inside his nostrils.

The fear had withdrawn now, like the sea at low tide, leaving the world awash in a gentle sadness, an elusive, tender beauty that belonged to no one and to nothing. It was as if the present moment were itself only an especially vivid and compelling memory. Even these thoughts and feelings were beyond his grasp, things already lost in time. But hadn't it always been this way—everything secondhand? Always only the echo, never the cry itself. Only the tracks in the snow, the reflection of a face in the mirror,

A phantom's mask,
a shooting star, a guttering flame.
A sorcerer's trick, a bubble swept
on a swiftly moving stream.
A flash of lightning among dark clouds.
A drop of dew,
a dream.

Across from where he sat, the college boys strutted and crowed for girls who clutched their books tightly against their breasts, filmy dupattas fluttering like the flags of unconquerable nations. Several devotees were clustered around one of the co-eds. She was dressed in tight jeans, high heels, and a sheer kurta, her hair cut short and bobbed. She appeared to be genuinely amused by someone's clever remark. They were discussing, in a seamless blend of English and Hindi, the poetry of Thomas Hardy.

In the street nearby, an auto rickshaw was parked, a stunning yellow and black chariot, with red fringe trailing along the edge of the canopy. An elderly Sikh leaned heavily against the windshield, hands cupped over his mouth. A curl of smoke wound upward through his fingers. This time the young man was not fooled; he saw who it was. The driver spotted him, finished lighting the bidi, and took a long drag, simultaneously letting the match fall at his feet. He ambled over.

"Auto rickshaw, Sahab?"

The American nodded.

"*Kahaa jaanaa hai?*"

"Connaught Place. Jai Singh Road."

"*Aaiyay, Sahab.*" The driver tipped his head and turned, walking in the direction of the street.

The young man finished the last of his soda and set the empty bottle on the table, then followed his guide to the rickshaw and slid in back, skimming his fingertips over the glossy surface of the vinyl seat. A picture of Guru Nanak was fastened to the dashboard just in front of the handlebars. The saint in golden turban, luxuriant white beard spilling halfway down his chest, his right hand raised, bestowing a blessing. The ornate frame was wrapped in a garland of marigolds, remnants of a morning puja. Wilted orange petals lay slack against the glass.

In one graceful motion, the driver swiveled around and pushed the flag down on the meter and leaned over and yanked up on the starter handle. Beneath his seat the engine popped and whined, spewing a haze of burned oil into the air. His wrist cranked backward on the throttle and the vehicle threaded into traffic, heading for Ring Road and the maelstrom of Old Delhi, driver and passenger hurtling between iron monsters that bellowed and roared. Once again the young man was along for the ride in a crazed South Asian ritual of surrender to the road and its perils. He clung to the metal bar that held the meter; the canopy rattled in the wind.

Near Ramlila Maidan they were sucked into a tide pool of trucks and taxis, cycle rickshaws and bicycles. Two-wheeled carts stacked high with cargo were dragged along by oxen or pushed by sweating, emaciated spirits cloaked in rags. A camel towered above the chaos, gazing impassively out over the swarm that raged around his knobby knees. Strapped across his hump and suspended, one on each side, were two canvas saddlebags stitched together with hemp. A man perched just in front of the bags, his legs straddling the animal's neck. Everywhere horns screeched and two-stroke engines coughed up a poisonous smog. The maidan—a long meadow the size of a football field—was thronged with people. At one end a high platform had been erected, over which, in large red letters, a banner proclaimed the victory of the Janata Party. A group of politicians stood on the platform behind a table draped in orange, white, and green bunting. One of the politicians was speaking into a microphone, and his amplified voice boomed out over the crowd.

Inside the stalled auto rickshaw, the driver feverishly punched a button on the handgrip with his left thumb, which triggered an angry, insect-like buzzing. He persisted in this futile effort for a minute or two, then killed the engine and slumped back against the seat, wiping his brow with one sleeve. His face was visible in the rearview mirror above the windshield, his weary eyes gazed back at the American in apparent resignation to their shared fate. The two of them looked at each other through the reflecting surface of the glass. The old Sikh smiled and shrugged.

"*Araam karo, Sahab. Ham kahin nahin jaaengay.*"

"Relax. We are going nowhere."

A boy in shorts emerged out of the pandemonium and snaked his way barefoot through the dense tangle of traffic. He carried a dented aluminum kettle in one hand and with the other gripped a burlap sack slung over his shoulder. A frayed T-shirt clung to his ribs. The American leaned out and waved the boy over and purchased two cups of hot, milky chai: one for the Satguru—the True Teacher—and one for the pilgrim, come so far to learn.

About the Author

 C. W. HUNTINGTON, JR., translates and interprets classical Sanskrit and Tibetan Buddhist texts. He is on the Religious Studies faculty at Hartwick College and is the author of *The Emptiness of Emptiness: An Introduction to Early Indian Madhyamaka*. This is his first work of fiction.